THE GIRL IN THE ICE

LOTTE AND SØREN HAMMER

*Translated from the Danish
by Paul Norlen*

B L O O M S B U R Y

LONDON · OXFORD · NEW YORK · NEW DELHI · SYDNEY

Bloomsbury Paperbacks
An imprint of Bloomsbury Publishing Plc

50 Bedford Square   1385 Broadway
London   New York
WC1B 3DP   NY 10018
UK   USA

www.bloomsbury.com

BLOOMSBURY and the Diana logo are trademarks of Bloomsbury Publishing Plc

First published in 2010 in Denmark as *Alting har sin pris* by Gyldendal, Copenhagen
First published in Great Britain 2015
This paperback edition first published in 2016

British Library Cataloguing-in-Publication Data
A catalogue record for this book is available from the British Library.

ISBN: TPB: 978-1-4088-2109-1
        PB: 978-1-4088-4573-8
      ePub: 978-1-4088-4577-6

2 4 6 8 10 9 7 5 3 1

Typeset by Integra Software Services Pvt. Ltd.
Printed and bound in Great Britain by CPI Group (UK) Ltd, Croydon CR0 4YY

MIX
Paper from
responsible sources
FSC® C020471
www.fsc.org

To find out more about our authors and books visit www.bloomsbury.com.
Here you will find extracts, author interviews, details of forthcoming events and
the option to sign up for our newsletters.

THE GIRL
IN THE ICE

PROLOGUE

There is a price to be paid for everything.

And perhaps the price for centuries of ruthless exploitation of nature was being paid in Disko Bay in Greenland—or a small down payment anyway before the really big instalments fell due, thought the German Chancellor as she stared out over the fjord.

Denmark's Minister for the Environment involuntarily followed the direction of the chancellor's gaze. The journalist who was interviewing them did the same. The view was breathtaking. Ice floes of all sizes rocked sluggishly in the chill blue water. The glacier above formed a rugged white wall that reflected the summer sun and made the observers squint. Occasionally an iceberg calved, with a deep rumbling sound that carried through the clear air and echoed around the bay.

After a while the journalist cleared his throat. He wanted an answer to his last question and was discreetly trying to resume the conversation, but as the chancellor kept silent he addressed the Danish minister, this time in English.

"Why is it necessary to go all the way to Greenland to understand global warming? What can the world's decision-makers learn here that they can't just as well learn at home?"

The minister smiled obligingly while she polished her answer. It was clear that *the world's decision-makers* did not include her but rather her guest, which was reasonable but also made the topic sensitive. She was used to hearing this argument. After she'd given a guided tour to a handful of American senators a few months ago, the Danish opposition had accused her of climate-change tourism. In a way the journalist was right. The chancellor did not need to go almost four thousand kilometres from Berlin to Ilulissat in order to realise that the polar ice was melting. Anyone comparing satellite photos of the North Pole today and ten years ago would understand that immediately. The South Pole too for that matter. The important thing was what could be done to reverse the process—or, more realistically, limit the damage— and neither the glacier nor the satellite had an answer to that.

The chancellor turned her head and observed them with a teasing smile, apparently just as eager for the minister's reply as the journalist was. The minister indulged herself in a moment's paranoia, wondering if the two Germans were trying to stitch her up. Feeling hot and flustered, she unzipped her fleece-lined jacket. She hated being put on the spot like this. Besides leading a nation of eighty-three million people, her guest had a PhD in quantum chemistry.

The zipper stuck, which gave her a few extra seconds to consider her response. Then she said honestly, "Nothing."

"Then why are we here?"

She briefly considered telling the journalist about the roughly four thousand Greenlandic whalers whose ancient livelihood was now ruined by temperature rises twice as high as in the rest of the world. But that would be a mistake. Her climate conference was meant to be dealing with the problem on a global basis; she must steer clear of suggesting that she put Greenland's interests first. Instead she diverted the question, saying only, "Because politicians are people too, and no one forgets this scenery, right?"

The journalist seemed to agree with this and the chancellor smiled broadly, both of them apparently satisfied with the answer. The minister thought this lightening of the mood might be her way in. They were walking back towards the waiting helicopter. This would probably be her last chance to discuss the politics of climate change with the chancellor. If she could be persuaded to back them at next year's conference in Copenhagen it would be a major coup. But until now the German leader had concentrated purely on their experience of climate change and left politics off the agenda. The person she had talked with most was the glaciologist accompanying them.

The minister's hopes were dashed when in the helicopter too the chancellor sought out the scientist. She made sure that he sat next to her as they flew over the ice cap, and soon the two of them were deeply immersed in a scientific conversation, which the minister with her limited German had a hard time following. She felt her eyelids grow heavy and had to pinch her arm to stop herself from falling asleep. The scene glimpsed through the helicopter's windows was a uniform white, and the official by her side was already napping. From time to time he let out little grunts. She considered nudging him but fished a magazine out of her bag instead and started reading it listlessly, only to succumb to sleep herself after a short time.

The minister was jolted awake an hour later. The glaciologist was shouting and gesturing wildly. The chancellor had stood up in her seat and was gesturing out of the window, commanding the helicopter to fly back. After a while the pilot turned back.

CHAPTER 1

K onrad Simonsen, chief inspector in Copenhagen's Homicide Division, squinted up at the polar sun, hanging low over the long line of the horizon. Where sky met ice, clear pastel greens and blues hinted at more hospitable locations than this one, far, far away. What a place to be killed, it was plain wrong, he told himself, before dismissing the thought. As if it made any difference to the victim.

For a while he observed his own shadow in front of him, holding up one arm and letting its unnaturally extended counterpart reach impossible distances towards cracks in the ice. Eventually he grew tired of this game and glanced again towards the hazy sun, which seemed to radiate cold instead of heat. He found it disconcerting. The sun ought to rise and fall, not drag itself monotonously around the firmament, making day and night one and the same.

In a vain attempt to chase tiredness away, he closed his eyes and turned his face to the wind. He had not slept more than three hours in the past twenty-four, and it seemed unreal to him that a new day had begun. He rubbed his face with the palms of his hands and enjoyed the momentary darkness. He wondered if, in her last moments, the dead girl had thought about spring flowers, warm, sandy beaches or maybe a Midsummer bonfire? Probably not. All the same there was something terrible about the fact that she had had to die out here in this vast unfamiliar place where human beings did not belong. In a sense it was a double violation.

He glanced at his watch and noticed that the Danish time was seven-thirty. What that was in Greenland he could not immediately work out. He smothered a yawn, and realised he was more than usually exhausted. This morning he had forgotten to take his pills, or more correctly—there was no reason to lie to himself—he had forgotten *again* to take his pills, and now he was suffering the consequences. Desire for a forbidden cigarette gnawed at him cruelly. Just one or maybe even a half, a few restorative puffs to keep him on his feet a while longer. He tapped the chest of his padded jacket to reassure himself that his cigarettes were in the inside pocket. A year ago—or was it two?—he had been diagnosed with diabetes. The illness and the concern it had caused others had forced him to re-examine some of his bad habits. Or at least try to.

An unfamiliar feeling of anxiety made him consult his watch again. As before it meant nothing to him here. He turned to the man standing next to him and asked, "Do you know what time it is?"

The Greenlandic detective constable took a quick glance at the sun and answered curtly, "Almost three."

He was a man who said no more than was strictly necessary, which had not made the wait any easier. He was called Trond Egede, and that was about all Konrad Simonsen knew about him. He considered returning to the light aircraft that had brought them here and trying to get a little sleep while the crime-scene technicians finished up. The hard, uncomfortable seat that he had cursed on the trip over from Nuuk seemed tempting to him now. A little sleep was better than none at all and there was no sense in standing alongside a mute colleague staring at four people, who worked neither faster nor slower because they were being watched. But it might offend his taciturn partner if Simonsen abandoned him, and establishing good relations with the Nuuk police was essential if they were to crack this case together. Or he could always say to hell with procedure and join the technicians in their search. It was unlikely he could do much here to contaminate the scene of the crime. On the other hand he risked being turned away, which would be humiliating for him as well as making him appear unprofessional, so the conclusion he reached was as clear as it was depressing—he must remain where he was.

For want of anything better to do he tried to start a conversation.

"How can you know exactly what time it is just by looking at the sun? I mean, you don't have any landmark to work from here, just flat ice all around."

With difficulty the other man took off one glove and rolled back the sleeve of his polar jacket over his wristwatch. After he had laboriously put his glove back on, he said, "The time is thirteen minutes past three."

"So you were right."

"Yes."

"Based purely on the sun? Without any fixed reference point?"

"Yes."

Simonsen backed down and concentrated on setting his own watch correctly. It made the time pass anyway. Suddenly an unpleasant suspicion struck him, a nagging little doubt. This place had completely disoriented him. It was embarrassing to show it in front of the other detective.

"So…that's three in the afternoon?"

He aimed to make his voice as casual as possible but could hear that he had not succeeded. The Greenlander turned and looked at him appraisingly before he replied.

"Yes, in the afternoon. Are you sundowning?"

"I didn't know there was a word for that. But I guess you're right—I couldn't be sure for a moment."

"It can be pretty disconcerting."

Simonsen nodded and relaxed. With difficulty he fished out his cigarettes, ignoring all the health warnings, lit up and inhaled with pleasure. The silence didn't seem so oppressive with a cigarette in his hand. When he'd smoked it to the last shreds of tobacco, he bent down and meticulously stubbed it out on the ice, after which he stuck the butt in his pocket. The Greenlander observed him closely throughout. Simonsen tried to start a conversation again.

"Tell me, do you come here often?"

The other man's face reluctantly squeezed itself into a grin that made him resemble a mischievous troll. Simonsen could not help smiling back.

"Arne thought that too…your partner, I mean. I've forgotten his last name," said Egede.

He nodded his head towards the plane instead of pointing.

"Arne Pedersen. His name is Arne Pedersen," Simonsen told him.

"That's right. Well, he had this idea that I often go trekking about on the ice cap. Five hundred kilometres out, a quick walk around the old neighbourhood, then hike home again with healthy red cheeks."

The man's irony was more cheerful than sarcastic.

"Okay, I get it. You haven't been here before. Of course you haven't."

"That's not quite correct because I was here yesterday," said Egede, straight-faced, "but otherwise it's not somewhere I'd choose to visit. Why would I?"

They both nodded, and for a moment Konrad feared that they'd lapse back into silence. But the other man said, "Pedersen mentioned you don't like discussing a case before you've seen the victim. That it's a kind of principle you have."

"Principle is a bit of an overstatement, I'm not quite that rigid, but it is correct that I prefer to wait, if that's all right with you? There are a couple of things, however, that we might as well deal with now. It's probably no secret to you that I've been thrown headlong into this case."

The other man stopped smiling.

"Yes, I heard that. Pedersen said that you were about to leave on holiday. To somewhere more southerly and a whole lot warmer."

He gave his troll's grin again.

Konrad liked him more and more.

"Thanks for reminding me! Yes, I should be on my way to Punta Cana—it's in the Dominican Republic, by the way— where I was going to doze under a palm tree with my… my girlfriend, before being picked up by the good ship *Legend of the Seas* from the Royal Caribbean Cruise Line, and… Well, it hurts too much to think about the rest."

"You're welcome, it was nothing."

"Anyhow, there hasn't really been time to brief me about what happened yesterday, or maybe nobody I've talked to knows the full story. Was it really the German Chancellor who found the girl?"

"No, it wasn't, but almost. It was a glaciologist who discovered her first and pointed her out to the chancellor."

"Were you there when it happened?"

"No, but I got the story from someone who was. They were in a helicopter. In fact, there were three of Air Greenland's big Sikorsky S-61s. You know, the red ones they call Sea Kings."

Konrad had no idea what he was talking about, but courteously replied with a white lie.

"Yes, they're impressive."

"I think so too. Well, there was one machine for the chancellor and the Danish Minister for the Environment plus aides and hangers on, one for security people and subordinate German staff personnel, and the last one for journalists. The chancellor's helicopter led the way. The route was roughly circular, over the ice cap from Ilulissat at Disko Bay and down to Nuuk, from where they were scheduled to take commercial flights back to Copenhagen and Berlin respectively. She—the chancellor, that is—insisted on going all the way to the middle of the ice, possibly based on a misunderstanding that the melting is worst there. But that was what she said she wanted, and no one raised any objections."

"But what is there to see?"

"Nothing of any significance. Once you've seen the first puddle of meltwater, of which there are lots on the Ilulissat glacier within a ten-minute flight, there's no point in looking at the next hundred. Besides, they actually become less frequent the farther you go over the ice, and as you can see for yourself, there's not much else to look at out here."

Simonsen answered him diplomatically.

"It's fascinating, but perhaps a trifle monotonous."

"Yeah, you could put it like that. All the same, the chancellor found the tour extremely interesting, and the glaciologist thought the same. He was sitting beside her, lecturing away throughout the whole trip. To the Minister for the Environment's great irritation."

"Didn't she want to see the ice cap?"

"I'm pretty sure she'd rather have talked politics. There were two Greenlandic politicians along, one of whom I've spoken to, and she tells me they were laughing up their sleeves at the minister's disappointment. Who knew the chancellor would be such a keen student of glaciology? Not too long ago the Minister for the Environment hosted a bunch of US senators on a similar mission but they viewed the guided tour almost as a pleasure trip. One of them even asked if he might be able to shoot a reindeer—possibly in jest—but our local press was very indignant about it, and naturally none of the visitors was keen to see more of the ice cap than strictly necessary."

Simonsen brought him back on track.

"But the chancellor did?"

"Yes, like I said. The helicopter flew low and everyone was equipped with binoculars, which no one except the chancellor and the glaciologist used after the first half an hour. The Danes napped and the Germans worked on their computers, my source says."

He smiled and Simonsen interjected, "So far, so predictable. What happened then?"

"Nothing at all for a good hour...hour and a half. The chancellor got her climate lesson, and the others minded their own business. Until she and the scientist suddenly started calling out because they had seen the corpse on the ice. So after a little discussion the pilot got the helicopter turned around and they flew back and found it here."

"Did they land?"

"No, they just hovered in the air for a couple of minutes while the pilot reported the coordinates. Someone had the presence of mind to direct the journalists' helicopter away from the scene before the representatives of the world's press could slug it out for a photographic scoop. I mean, who's going to cover a climate-change conference when there's a juicy murder to write about instead? But they couldn't contain the story completely. Word got out, after the group reached Nuuk, and a couple of photos taken from the security helicopter are in circulation. It's front-page news all over Europe. *Chancellor Sherlock Holmes*—that's *Bild-Zeitung*. The London *Times*'s lead article is a much more staid *Chancellor Finds Murdered Girl*. The Danish newspapers are featuring it big-time, and CNN has had the story as 'breaking news' since last night. Do you need any more on this?"

"No, for God's sake, that's more than enough."

"Well, looks like … whoever he is … your colleague … was right. Now I've forgotten his name again, God help me—I have a thing about names, they get away from me. But he also said you probably wouldn't be too enthusiastic about the coverage. Don't you like the press?"

"If you mean in theory, then yes. I don't especially care for crime reporters, though."

"But the press made you famous, I understand."

"Famous? Nonsense. I'm not famous."

"Well known then."

"That's rubbish. I am neither well known nor famous."

Simonsen stamped lightly on the ice to emphasise his words and almost toppled backwards when his foot slid out from under him.

"If you say so, but somehow or other you must have made yourself really unpopular in Germany, since it's said the German Chancellor herself sentenced you to a spell in the freezer instead of letting you take your Caribbean holiday."

Strangely enough Simonsen found he didn't mind being teased by the Greenlander, maybe because the little man radiated so much friendliness once he had opened his mouth. And maybe because Simonsen secretly felt a little proud of the way his presence had been formally requested.

"All complete nonsense," he asserted, unconvincingly.

They stood there in a silence broken only by stifled laughter from Egede. Simonsen decided it was time to change the subject.

"I understand you've had the opportunity to see the victim?"

"Yes, yesterday, as I said. We had to make sure of what we were dealing with, but I haven't done anything out here other than look at her and then put up the barricade."

He nodded over towards a circle of iron spikes hammered into the ice around the body. Red and white striped crime-scene tape had been wound between them.

"It took us about half an hour to get those in. The ice is like stone, and they are clearly unnecessary out here, but I had strict orders to cordon her off."

"Is she a Greenlander?"

Egede's cheerfulness vanished abruptly. "Why do you ask that? Does it make any difference?" he asked sharply.

"It's a serious crime whatever her nationality. But that apart, it makes a world of difference when it comes to chains of command and jurisdiction. Besides, I have a hard time understanding how I can contribute to a case where a local woman from a community I don't know has been killed."

"She's not a Greenlander, she's Danish. And with respect to jurisdiction, that's not something you need worry about. You can consider yourself the leader of this investigation. All parties to it are in agreement on that."

"All parties? I didn't know there were more than two."

"Three. But as I said, there is no dissent as to leadership."

"You're saying the Americans are involved too?"

"I thought you wanted to wait for the details until you'd seen her."

"Yes, well, with a little luck that will be soon. It looks as if they've passed the first phase."

Simonsen took out his cigarettes again without really meaning to. Feeling guilty, he slid the pack back into his pocket unopened. Shortly afterwards a technician came over to them. She was Danish, and moved slowly and laboriously, taking infinite care over where she put her feet. Maybe she believed if she did not touch an old footprint in the snow she would win the lottery on Saturday. Simonsen did not recognise her.

"We're just about done. If you're going to wake up Arne Pedersen, it's time. And be careful over there, it's very slippery."

She pointed towards the crime scene. Trond Egede nodded amiably, he would no doubt walk carefully. Simonsen thought that it was slippery everywhere, and ignored her.

CHAPTER 2

The woman in the shallow grave in the ice was on her knees. She was half-naked, dressed only in panties and an undershirt that was torn in front and pulled down below her bare breasts. Her ankles were tied together with duct tape and her wrists attached to her thighs with further tape. Her long, black hair was hanging loose and reached to the middle of her back. A plastic bag was pulled over her head and tightened around her neck in a knot. Behind the plastic a grotesquely gaping lipstick-red mouth and her wild wide-open eyes revealed that death had not come easily. Konrad Simonsen felt nauseated by the sight. She had an athletic build and was no more than twenty-five or so. Around her meltwater trickled and pooled in the bottom of the depression in the ice to which her knees and feet were still attached. To the right of her body were her clothes: trousers, jacket, and a cap artfully knitted in shades of blue, violet and green.

The three men took their time. Arne Pedersen and Simonsen moved around slowly, peering down at the woman whose face was more or less on a level with their feet. The Greenlandic constable remained standing. It was as if none of them wanted to break the silence and disturb the others' concentration. The female technician had returned, leaving her three colleagues warming up in the plane. She stood a few steps away, shivering. At last she became impatient and asked, "Is there anything I can help with? Otherwise I'd really like to go back and have some coffee before we bring her up."

The question was mostly aimed at Simonsen, but he seemed distracted so it was Pedersen who answered.

"The grave she's lying in, is it naturally formed?"

"According to my Greenlandic colleague that's not the case."

"So it's been cut down into the ice by someone?"

"According to my Greenlandic colleague that's exactly the case."

"Why has the grave melted?"

The woman was unsure.

"That I don't know, I think it's global warming."

"But why here, where she is?"

The technician threw up her hands and shrugged; Trond Egede answered for her.

"There are a number of meltwater puddles in the area, although they're not common round here. The ice is actually building up hereabouts, while by the coastline it's decreasing. There is no obvious reason why she is kneeling in such a melt hole. It could just be chance. First she was buried, then the melt hole formed. If the technician says the grave is man-made, you can safely assume he's correct. He knows what he's talking about where ice is concerned."

The woman nodded in agreement and added, "Exactly."

Simonsen sent her back to the plane, ignoring Pedersen's look of surprise and subsequent question.

"Why did you snap at her like that, Simon? There was no reason for it, and besides I wasn't finished."

When Pedersen did not receive an answer from his boss, he sought the explanation elsewhere. He looked at the corpse and said, "This is pretty disgusting, and also inexplicable. We're several hundred kilometres from the nearest inhabited area. In the middle of nowhere, as they say. It's like a classic locked-room mystery turned on its head—the all too open room."

"I know who she was, and how she got out here," said the Greenlander.

Pedersen turned to Egede in surprise.

"And you're just telling us that now?"

"I didn't think you wanted to hear any information before you'd seen her."

"It's only my boss who has these purist notions. Personally I prefer all the facts as soon as possible, but you weren't to know that. Okay, let's hear it."

But Simonsen held up one hand and stopped them there.

"In a little while. First I need time to think."

Pedersen did not try to conceal his concern.

"Is something wrong, Simon?"

"I told you, I need a minute to myself. That can't be so hard to understand surely."

Most people would have backed off then, but not Pedersen. He ignored his boss's tone of voice and said firmly, "No, it's not hard to understand. Just like it shouldn't be difficult for you to comprehend why I asked if there's something the matter. Well, is there?"

Simonsen pulled his scattered thoughts together. No doubt about it, the Countess, or his daughter Anna Mia, or maybe both of them, had talked about his health condition behind his back. The Countess was one of his closest co-workers. Her name was actually Nathalie von Rosen, but everyone called her the Countess. Everyone except his daughter, who insisted on using her real name. The Countess was also quite possibly his girlfriend, though he couldn't as yet figure that out. In fact, neither of them could.

16

He supposed it was not so surprising that the two women in his life should discuss his state of health. There was cause for concern over it as the doctor had made clear the last few times Simonsen had consulted him.

"As a matter of fact, I'm not well," he admitted now. "But don't worry, my health won't affect the case."

He turned away from them but had barely taken a step before Pedersen blocked his way and looked him in the eye. They stood that way, toe to toe, for what seemed like an eternity, until Pedersen finally stepped aside and let him pass.

When Simonsen was ready to be briefed, the Greenlandic constable pulled a notepad from his inside pocket and removed one glove so he could browse through his notes.

"Her name is Maryann Nygaard. She was a trained nurse and worked at the now closed American base in Søndre Strømfjord, where she was employed through a Danish company, Greenland Contractors, which specialised in recruiting Danish civilian workers for the American bases in Greenland. I believe there was an undertaking from the US government to Denmark that all civilian personnel at the bases in Thule and Søndre Strømfjord should be Danish. But don't take my word for that. There may be exceptions I don't know about. In any event, Maryann Nygaard had a job there as a nurse from March 1982 until her disappearance the following year, on the thirteenth of September, 1983."

Simonsen, who seemed to have calmed down after his outburst, queried, "In 1983? So she's been lying here for twenty-five years?"

Only Pedersen, who knew him well, could hear that he was still not quite up to speed. There was something seriously wrong here. Their Greenlandic counterpart answered the question.

"Yes, she has, and if it hadn't been for climate change, she could easily have been lying here for thousands more, until one day she slid into the fjord inside an iceberg."

"Do you know her age?" Konrad pressed him.

"She was twenty-three years old when she was killed, but beyond that I don't know much about her. I've spoken with the colonel in command then at Thule Airbase—a man I know well, by the way, and have liaised with before—and he's promised to get more information to me as soon as possible. He's usually pretty quick, given the notorious bureaucracy of the American armed forces. Of course in the event of a case being opened by them it could take years to process, but there's nothing to suggest that will happen."

"You mean, so long as there were no American soldiers involved?"

"Exactly, and I don't believe there were."

Pedersen butted in, "How far away was this Søndre Strømfjord base?"

"Is, the base is intact, only the Americans are gone. In round numbers, three hundred kilometres to the south-west."

"Then why is she here?"

"There's a good explanation for that, but perhaps you'd like to see a couple of pictures of her first?"

Without waiting for an answer he unfolded a piece of A4 paper from the back of his notebook.

"The colonel sent these over last night. I don't know if they come from the US or his own personal files. They kept the pictures for identification purposes, in case she was ever found. It's standard procedure when someone goes missing."

Again it was Pedersen who interrupted.

"Does that happen often round here… people disappearing?"

"Yes, unfortunately it's not uncommon, especially in the winter. Greenland is a big country, and in certain conditions if you wander off course then it's far from a given you'll be found again."

They moved in closer and studied the photographs. The top one was a portrait that showed a smiling young woman who barely resembled the one in the hole below them, apart from her long, black hair. Below the portrait was an informal picture of the woman, taken in summer while holding a trout in front of her with both hands. The pose was meant to be humorous as the fish was small enough to be held easily in one hand. A lock of her dark hair was caught by the summer breeze and drifted behind her like smoke.

Simonsen studied the bottom picture thoroughly. When he was done, he grimaced and asked, "So what brought her out here?"

"It was her work. Have you ever heard of the DYE stations?"

Both men shook their heads.

"They were a kind of radar outpost from the base in Søndre Strømfjord. There were five such stations, simply designated DYE-1 to DYE-5, and three of them rank among the world's most isolated places, hundreds of kilometres from the nearest settlement. All five were built in the early 1960s as part of the American atomic early warning system, a chain of radar stations from Alaska across Canada to Iceland that were supposed to detect Russian bombers and later intercontinental missiles. The first four DYEs are spread along a line that roughly corresponds to the northern polar circle, starting with DYE-1 on the west coast at Sisimiut over the ice cap, and finally DYE-4 on the east coast at Ammassalik. DYE-5 is an exception, pretty far north of the other DYEs and, as I said, over three hundred kilometres from the base in Søndre Strømfjord. I have no idea why it was not built in a line with the others. Maybe there is a perfectly reasonable explanation if you're a radar engineer or maybe it's a military secret, who knows?"

Simonsen asked, "How big was it?"

"Not very big in circumference, but high. You can see a few pictures when we get back to Nuuk. It wasn't pretty."

"What does DYE stand for?"

"As far as I know, it comes from the Canadian town of Cape Dyer on the east coast of Baffin Island towards the Davis Strait. Cape Dyer was also part of the radar system, but I'm not sure about the linguistic connection. In any event, all five DYE stations were taken out of service in the late 1980s. The technology was antiquated by that point as Russian rockets could then be tracked better from satellites. The first to be shut down was DYE-5— that was here where we're standing—and unlike the other four it was removed completely. That was down to some desk decision or other in Copenhagen about not compromising Greenland's wilderness. The Americans were told to clean up after themselves so to speak, which they did quite effectively as you can see—or perhaps I should say, don't see. Later the Self-Government had to reverse the procedure so that the other DYEs were allowed to remain more or less as they were, and today two of them are used occasionally by climate researchers overnighting on the ice cap."

"Was it only Danes who were stationed on these outposts?"

"The agreement between Washington and Copenhagen allowed the station to be mixed. But the DYE commander and the radar operators were always Americans."

"Did the Danes have security clearance?"

"Yes, of course they did, though the process wasn't that thorough based on all the stories I've heard over the years about the DYE employees. There were, shall we say, some characters among them—not exactly the sort you'd encourage to wander around a top-secret installation today. In fact, though, the information they could have passed on was probably quite limited. The American Army can rightly be blamed for a lot of things, but being lax about national security is definitely not one of them. Especially not in the middle of the Cold War."

Simonsen nodded his agreement without completely understanding what the man was talking about. Then he asked, "How many employees were there at a radar station like this?"

"It varied from DYE to DYE. At DYE-5 there were twelve Danes on six-month periods of service. After that they were supposed to be relieved, but often they simply switched to serve a further six months at another DYE. That was one of the reasons many of them became noticeably strange. Some of them were out on the ice for years. At the same time they earned a very respectable salary without having any way to spend the money. When they finally got back to civilisation, things often went very wrong for them."

"And Maryann Nygaard was one of these workers?"

Pedersen sounded sceptical. It was hard to imagine a pretty young woman isolated for six months with eleven men.

"No, no, that wouldn't have worked at all. Out here there were only men, but in the American Army there are many crazy rules— and here I'm quoting direct from the colonel himself, who knows what he's talking about. One of these rules, which was strictly observed, was that once a year all medical equipment on a base should be inspected by a doctor or nurse. So on the thirteenth of September 1983 Maryann Nygaard came out here on such a medical inspection. The work itself was done in a couple of hours and required no contact but when it was time to leave no one could find her. She was missing and remained so, no matter where the men searched. Finally the helicopter had to fly back without her."

Simonsen interrupted. "Do you know the time of day? I mean, was it dark?"

"No, I don't know the time, but I expect there will be a comprehensive report available once we get back to Nuuk. I have people working on this there, and they are doing the same in Thule. The Americans have promised me a list of all the men who were at DYE-5 at the time of her disappearance."

"I would like a copy of that list."

"You'll get it. There's not much more to tell you now. The next day the base sent a large task force out to search the area, but in

21

vain. She could have been buried a hundred metres from the DYE without them having a chance of discovering her. I'm assuming that at some point she was officially declared dead, but I haven't been able to get that confirmed."

"Do you know exactly where she is lying in relation to the station?"

"No, unfortunately not. We searched for a couple of hours yesterday to see whether we could find traces of it, but were unsuccessful. The Americans can be amazingly efficient so it's not at all certain that we will find the exact location, but I intend to try again tomorrow with more people—if that's acceptable to you?"

The request was directed at Simonsen.

"Of course. And I should add that the Nuuk police have done good work here. I'm impressed by all you've found out in such a short time."

Trond Egede took the compliment with a smile. Then he peered down at the girl and said seriously, "I've seen a few murders in my time, but this one gives me the creeps and makes me afraid. I assume you feel the same way. That was probably why you stepped aside earlier?"

Simonsen answered heavily, "No, unfortunately it was something else that made me do that. But this is probably the right time to deal with the unpleasant part. Arne, you're the youngest, do you mind crawling down to her? I want you to investigate her nails and tell us how they're clipped."

The two others instinctively looked down at the woman's hands, but from where they were standing they could not make anything out. The Greenlander and Simonsen held Pedersen by the arms and took his weight so he could slide carefully down into the grave. He put his head alongside the dead woman's thigh—first one side, then the other—before he reported.

"She hasn't cut them herself…no woman would do it like that. It looks like it was done with shears, jerkily and fast. How could you know? Oh, no…"

The Greenlandic constable had understood too. He stared gloomily down at the sight before him as Simonsen answered: "Because, unfortunately, this is the second time I've seen a young woman treated in this barbarous way."

CHAPTER 3

The skies over Copenhagen were unsettled. Brief, torrential summer showers alternated with sunshine, which quickly dried the streets and enticed people outside—until the next shower drove them back again. The holiday season was ending, but there were still tourists in the city, easy to spot with their ambling gait and slightly too casual attire.

Simonsen was looking out of the window of his office in Police Headquarters, wondering whether he was clinically depressed. It was now forty-eight hours since he had stood on the Greenland ice cap observing the corpse of Maryann Nygaard, and ever since then he had not been himself. For the first time in his long career he was having difficulty concentrating on a case. Although he knew perfectly well that this state of mind resulted from the new case's connection to another equally disturbing homicide, the circumstances of which now had to be reassessed, this insight did not help him much. He told himself over and over that his reaction was a sign of good mental health, evidence that he was not emotionally burned out, but the fact was that he was barely able to suppress his mental pain and attend to his daily workload. On top of that there was his bad health, which he was finding harder and harder to ignore. For the last couple of days his feet had tingled and ached unbearably; he had given in to cigarettes again; somehow he'd stuck to his diet.

Last night he'd been unable to sleep. Thoughts were still churning in his head when the first birdsong of the day mocked his sleeplessness. His feet—and this was almost the worst thing—would not keep still, no matter how he arranged them. All morning he had solemnly promised himself to schedule an appointment with one of the police psychologists, but like so many of his good intentions nothing had come of it. Instead he made another appointment to confront his guilt later that day. Then he must sink or swim.

"Should I call downstairs and say you've been delayed?"

The Countess, who was sitting observing him with a worried expression on her face, sounded determinedly calm. She was fresh-faced, optimistic, healthy. He looked and felt like something you baited a line with to catch fish. When he did not reply, she continued speaking.

"We can postpone the meeting for half an hour, that won't do any harm. There's no rush at this point."

He snarled back, "Let them wait, damn it."

"Yes, we'll let them wait a little, serve them right."

"Why on earth has this become such an attraction? It's completely crazy. Originally it was simply intended to be an internal update. How can I work if anyone and everyone can just come running to my reviews?"

"Yes, it shouldn't be allowed."

"Stop agreeing with me! Can't you think for yourself?"

The silence that followed was fraught with tension. Other people's sweet concern... echoes of his own self-pity... what good was any of that to him? Anger bubbled inside him. He shut his eyes for a moment before collecting himself with an effort.

"Excuse me, Countess. I didn't really mean that."

"I know and it's all right, I'm not made of glass."

It was one of her good points that she didn't launch herself into any argument that came along. If she did their closeness would have ended long ago. Now their relationship was tender, cautious. They were like two thirteen year olds edging slowly towards one other. Small steps, cautious steps, the whole time.

Simonsen said sadly, "I don't know how many times I've said those words in the past four days. Excuse me, excuse me, excuse me—soon I'll be apologising to every other person I talk to. It must be unbearable for the rest of you."

"You mustn't worry about that, Konrad. Concentrate on yourself. Now I'm going to call and say you've been delayed."

He let her do that, it was reasonable and sensible. When she was done, he reverted to the subject of the uninvited guests who had intruded on his review.

"Who is it by the way who is coming from the Foreign Ministry?"

"Some bigwig… as far as I know a director. I don't know his name, or more exactly—I can't remember it. But the rumours are that the national chief of police's office is up in arms about it. They see his presence as ill-timed political involvement, but someone must have overruled them."

"That's also a little strange. What's the motivation? Is it that story about the chancellor again? I don't believe it, it just can't be true."

"The Germans, the Americans, the Greenlanders—all guesses, no one knows exactly."

"Could you take a look at this, Countess? I would really like to know what's going on in my own investigation."

"Sure, I can do that."

He broke into the first smile of the day then said almost cheerfully, "I asked you about that yesterday too, didn't I?"

"A good order can't be given too often."

Their laughter eased the atmosphere. He sat down heavily in his chair.

"You know perfectly well what the conclusion will be."

"All of us have read the case files for the Stevns homicide, and no one is in any doubt about how hideous it must have been for those of you who were there—especially for you."

"Yes, hideous."

"Mistakes happen. We're humans, not gods."

"A dog! She couldn't even make herself call me a cur…"

"I don't know what you mean, and now you're scaring me. Arne or I can take over if you can't manage it."

"No, I'll try on my own. That's probably best."

"Maybe."

"The truth is that I'm afraid of what will happen if I give up and throw in the towel."

"This isn't a boxing match, Simon, and you have to be careful. Some things you simply can't grapple with all on your own. You have to get help, professional help."

"I know that. Tell me, what are you doing this afternoon?"

"That depends on what you assign me to do."

"Do you want to take a drive with me? To visit a woman whose husband committed suicide in 1998."

The Countess did not reply, and he did not hurry her. After a while she said, "You want to tell her that you were wrong?"

"That *I* was wrong?"

"That you *and* a lot of others were wrong?"

"She believed in her husband the whole way through, never doubted his innocence for a moment, and she called me a dog. Just think, that was the strongest expression she would allow to cross her lips even though I'd destroyed her life, or more precisely the final remnants of her life, after her daughter had been assaulted and strangled."

"Do you think it's a good idea to visit her?"

"I've thought about it a lot, and yes, I really think it is. Besides it's the least I can do, after making her husband a judicial victim."

"He was never convicted."

"He would have been, the evidence was overwhelming."

"But he wasn't."

"Suicide was hardly a better option."

"I'll go and see her with you. Do you have an appointment?"

"Yes, we're supposed to be in Haslev at four o'clock."

"If things don't go as you expect, I'll drag you away, regardless of whether you whine or howl. Now you know. Believe me, I'll get you out of there if I have to."

He shrugged slightly and asked, "Will you do one more thing for me? I have an appointment in Høje Taastrup later today with ... a woman. Can I ask you to call and cancel it? Then I'll just have time to go and freshen up a little."

She nodded sympathetically. He wrote a telephone number on a slip of paper and gave it to her.

"Thanks, let's go down in five minutes."

He left, and the Countess phoned. She knew exactly who she was calling. Simonsen's propensity for occasionally discussing his cases with a psychic from Høje Taastrup was the Homicide Division's worst-kept secret, although in front of the boss all the officers had the good manners to act like they knew nothing. The Countess had no particular feelings about clairvoyance herself, so the form the call took frightened her.

Hold on to Steen Hansen, Baroness, don't let him go, no matter what. Stick to him like a burr, nothing must shake you off. This is a matter of life and death. No matter what ... no matter what, Baroness, there is nothing more important than that.

She had been given no explanation, nor any context for these remarks—only the insistent request. Like a call for help, twice, three times, five times, she did not remember how many, only that dry, rasping voice even after she'd promised to do as she was asked. And then the form of address—*Baroness*—was close, unpleasantly close. She stared meditatively into space for a while and decided two things. First, that she would say nothing to Simonsen about the call, he had enough to deal with; and second, she would go and freshen up a little too.

There was so much they hadn't had time to talk about that once the opportunity finally presented itself, en route to the lecture hall, Simonsen abruptly came clean. He said carefully, "I'm afraid of starting to cry when I talk about her. A blubbering homicide chief—*that* would really be weird."

"What if you take the first half of the review and then leave the rest to Arne? You need to rest, I can see that."

"Okay, that's what we'll do."

The answer was so surprising coming from him that she had to clear her throat to hold back all the arguments she'd held in reserve.

They passed one of the cleaning staff. With a colourful feather duster attached to a long bamboo pole she was capturing spider's webs from the ceiling. As if by mutual agreement they fell silent as they went past. The woman smiled at them fleetingly while with sparing movements she continued her work. When they were out of earshot, the Countess continued.

"And then you should consider coming home with me and staying for a week. I think that will be good for you."

The proposal was surprising. They had not yet reached this point. Or so they thought. But Simonsen did not even hesitate. "I'd like that," he said.

Sometimes life was no more complicated than you made it. She held him back with a gentle touch on his arm. Normally they never kissed at work and seldom even in private. Now it happened: chastely, at a proper distance, with pursed lips, like characters in a vaudeville act.

CHAPTER 4

The first combined review of the investigation was held in one of the large lecture halls at Police Headquarters. This was not due to the number of participants but to the availability there of an enormous screen that could display two images at once, extremely useful for photographic comparison. And parallel images of two different female murder victims made up the weight of this morning's message. How the Homicide Division would re-open the old case would have to await discussion in a closed forum, though today's meeting was originally intended to clarify the procedure. But that had been before the Foreign Ministry announced its interest in attending, and since then the office of the national chief of police as well. The rest of the attendees were Homicide Division people, of whom Pauline Berg and Arne Pedersen were among Konrad Simonsen's closest associates. In addition the department's student employee and resident computer genius Malte Borup controlled the images from an operator booth set at second-storey level behind the rows of seats. He was also in charge of the technical aspects of the presentation.

Simonsen arrived twenty minutes after the scheduled start time and nodded curtly at his audience. Mostly they occupied the first or second row of seats, Berg and Pedersen with a bit of space around them out to one side. The Countess took a vacant seat alongside Pedersen, but got up again when the man from the Foreign Ministry went after her boss before he had even started.

"Let me say right now, Chief Inspector Simonsen, that this is absolutely the last time you arrive late to an appointment with me. I hope you understand that."

The man was relatively short, middle-aged, and appeared harmless enough at first glance, dressed in a scruffy suit and with his hair badly in need of a comb. Strange, considering his place of employment. But something understated and ominous in his tone suggested that normally he was obeyed without any objection being raised. Not even his peculiar high-pitched voice, which sounded almost like a child's, detracted from the impression that this was someone you did not want to pick a fight with. Perhaps it was the calm way in which he spoke, the conviction with which he made the subtle threat.

The Countess tried to take the blame for the delay. You didn't need to be a fortune teller to predict that an unstable homicide chief and a conceited bureaucrat were not a good mix. Rescue came, however, from an unexpected quarter in the form of a secretary from the front office of the national chief of police, who was usually known for her friendly manner. With a completely unaccustomed show of aggression she spoke up, and there was no doubt as to whom she was addressing, even if she pointedly remained seated.

"The national chief of police asked me to say that you are a guest here, and if you can't behave properly, you can shove off. The last is a direct quote, which he specifically asked me to use, and afterwards to apologise for the fact that unfortunately he has not been schooled in diplomacy."

The Foreign Ministry representative got to his feet and left the room in dignified silence, ignoring the slide of Albert

Einstein sticking out his tongue, which Malte Borup had conjured up on the big screen like lightning. Immediately afterwards the secretary also left, saying her presence was no longer rquired.

As the door slammed behind her, Pedersen spoke for them all.

"Well, that was edifying. Without our visitors' presence we might even get something done…and then we'll have to face the music later, because there will be trouble. That gnome isn't to be trifled with. Malte, you could get five years' deportation."

Simonsen, who had not said anything throughout, suddenly took control.

"Then we'd better make good use of the time we have. Malte, give me the first images. The floor is open if anyone has anything sensible to contribute. No need to stand on ceremony."

Images of the two dead women quickly dampened the group's high spirits. The photographs had been carefully selected from the hundreds taken at each crime-scene, so that camera angle and distance were near-identical, further underscoring the similarities between them. Simonsen expanded on this.

"The woman to the left is Maryann Nygaard. She was killed on the thirteenth of September, 1983 at the DYE-5 station on Greenland's ice cap, and found just over a week ago in circumstances I'm sure you have heard about. The woman to the right is Catherine Thomsen. She was killed on the fifth of April, 1997 at Nordstranden outside Stevns's Klint. Her body was discovered some eight months later by two amateur archaeologists, who picked up her bracelet with their metal detectors. There is a long list of similarities between the two murders, which means, I believe, that we are dealing with the same perpetrator. I still want you to listen with an open mind and maintain your usual healthy scepticism, though. You all know how fatal to an investigation it can be to jump to the wrong conclusions early on."

There were nods of agreement. Simonsen continued.

"Both women's hands were secured with duct tape to their thighs, just above the knees. The ankles likewise were tied together with duct tape. This was done before death. Both women were dressed only in panties and undershirt. Both had their breasts exposed or partly exposed, their clothing torn in front. We know that Catherine Thomsen wore a bra, so that was removed. We do not have corresponding information on Maryann Nygaard. Both women's nails had been clipped, in all probability by the perpetrator. Both were buried immediately after their death—Maryann Nygaard in ice and Catherine Thomsen in gravel, close enough to the sea that her body was regularly covered with chalky water and thereby to some degree kept partially intact. Bright red lipstick has been applied to the mouths of both women before their death. In their mouths and throats textile fibres have been found—the result of a rag having been stuffed into their mouth. Specifically in the case of Catherine Thomsen some of these fibres contained microscopic traces of lipstick, while others did not, from which the technicians conclude that the perpetrator put the lipstick on while she had the rag in her mouth. We won't know if the same approach was used on Maryann Nygaard until we get the final autopsy report, and that won't be ready for a couple of days. Last but not least, both women were suffocated by pulling a transparent plastic bag over their heads and fastening it around their neck. The rag in their mouth was removed prior to that."

Simonsen paused briefly. None of his listeners said anything, and the mood was heavy. Malte Borup, who had illustrated his boss's points with corresponding close-ups, returned to the original two photographs.

"In addition to this, there are a number of features common to both homicides which may or may not be coincidences. Judge for yourself. Maryann Nygaard was twenty-three years old at her death, Catherine Thomsen twenty-two. Both women were

32

medium height and slender, almost athletic in build. Both had black, wavy hair down to the middle of their back, and in both cases their hair was let down when they were found. If you look at their faces, there are quite a few similarities. Both must be considered pretty, with fine features, high cheekbones and brown eyes. Naturally there are differences, especially around the nose, but without being able to support it objectively I would say there was a close resemblance between them."

Pedersen took Pauline Berg by the hand. She misunderstood and pushed him away, annoyed at first, only to freeze the next moment when she stared at the screen and, shaken, grab hold of his hand again. Simonsen went on speaking.

"For further parallels it should be mentioned that the women were not raped, and we must assume there had not been any other form of sexual molestation, apart from the exposed breasts. Maryann Nygaard's vagina contained an intact tampon, and Catherine Thomsen was a virgin—she was an active member of the Jehovah's Witnesses, who as you know do not sanction pre-marital sex. And besides, no semen residue was found at either of the crime scenes."

He paused here, waiting for a reaction which quickly came. They were all in agreement that the person who had murdered Maryann Nygaard in 1983 most likely also killed Catherine Thomsen almost fourteen years later. He took a deep breath. He'd reached the part of the briefing he'd been dreading. His words were chosen with care.

"What I have to tell you next isn't easy for me. Some of you who were also involved in the Thomsen murder case will know why, but for the benefit of those who weren't, I want to give you a brief overview and also talk about my personal role in it, to dispel any rumours you might have heard."

People shuffled in their seats. Heads were nodded. No one looked directly at Simonsen. An older officer fished a pair of mirrored sunglasses out of his pocket and took refuge behind them.

"Carl Henning Thomsen, a trucker, now deceased, was our chief suspect for the murder of his daughter Catherine. We know for a certainty, however, that he was not in Greenland in September 1983 as at that time he was serving a sentence in Vridsløselille State Prison for narcotics smuggling. Thus he did not kill Maryann Nygaard, and if we believe that one perpetrator was responsible for both murders then he was not guilty of killing Catherine either. The apparently damning evidence gathered against him in 1998 was therefore faked—a possibility that was considered back then, but unfortunately not followed up on."

Tears had started to trickle down Konrad Simonsen's face, but he kept his voice steady and accepted the handkerchief that Pauline Berg handed him, without ceasing to speak. He turned his head away, however, when the screen showed the photograph of a middle-aged man, tired and beaten-looking.

"Carl Henning and Ingrid Thomsen lived in Haslev, where together they ran a small removals company. They were Jehovah's Witnesses, and the same applied to their only daughter Catherine, who had moved to Østerbro here in Copenhagen where she was studying to be a physical therapist. In their free time the parents as well as Catherine went door to door evangelising. Often the parents drove in to the city to meet up with their daughter and all three of them spread the word together. On Saturday the fifth of April, 1997 Catherine disappeared; in the morning she took the train from Copenhagen towards Haslev and was last seen with certainty at Roskilde Station. Her mother was in Jutland at that time, visiting her sister, and the father maintained that Catherine never arrived at the family house. Eight months later her body was found at Stevns."

Simonsen returned the handkerchief with a little nod of gratitude to Pauline. The tears had dried now he had put the worst of it behind him.

"The investigation was exhaustive, of course, and a number of strongly incriminating circumstances soon pointed to Catherine's father. First and foremost fingerprints from both his hands were found on the plastic bag used to smother his daughter, in positions that indicated he must have held her around the head after the bag was pulled over it. In addition it could be proved that the plastic bag came from a roll discovered in the Thomsen family's garage. Furthermore he was seen on the beach at Stevns in March 1997, not far from where the body of Catherine was later found. He maintained he had been summoned by phone to give an estimate for a move, which turned out to be bogus. He'd been given directions to the address that involved walking along the shore. He was unable to account for the other evidence against him."

Here the Countess interrupted her boss.

"What about that phone call? Could it be confirmed or ruled out?"

"It was confirmed, but it was made from an unknown cell phone towards the cell-phone tower covering Carl Henning Thomsen's residence. We assumed he called himself, but could never connect the telephone or the call directly to him. Okay?"

"Yes, but what you have just told us seems to be incriminating enough."

"But unfortunately there were various discrepancies, which at the time were noted but dismissed. First and foremost, we could not understand why we found the father's fingerprints on the plastic bag while there were no fingerprints on the duct tape. Furthermore his truck's tachograph from the day of Catherine Thomsen's death showed that it had not been at Stevns, and we were never able to establish what vehicle had been used to transport her body. The family's other car was in Jutland. Then the nails being cut… we didn't understand that either. The girl's nails were not that long, and according to his wife he had never commented negatively on them. There were other small details that didn't fit either, but you can read those for yourself in the case notes."

A detective in the front row interrupted.

"You mentioned before that he was in prison for narcotics smuggling in 1983."

"Correct. Amphetamines and cocaine, if I remember correctly."

"Did he have a criminal career, and if so how does that fit with his being a Jehovah's Witness? It sounds like a strange combination."

"When he was younger he was sentenced twice, both times for importing narcotics, which was easy for him as a long-distance driver. Then he met his wife and by his own account was saved. Nothing suggests that his criminal activity continued after they were married in 1986."

"But Catherine Thomsen's age… I can't really get that to fit."

"Catherine was his daughter, later adopted by Ingrid when he married her. The girl's biological mother died in a traffic accident when Catherine was little. But remember, this isn't meant to be a detailed review. You can read up on all this for yourselves."

"Okay, I was just curious."

Simonsen gave a wry smile.

"It comes in useful in our line of work. Well, back to Carl Henning Thomsen. Troublingly, our murder inquiry never established any cast-iron motive for Catherine's death. We did know, however, that she had been keeping something secret from her parents. She had initiated what can best be described as a cautious or dawning lesbian relationship with a woman we know existed, but never located. The assumption was that the daughter must have informed her father about what was going on, after which, in an outburst of righteous fury, he killed her. But this was all highly speculative on our part, and there were timing issues there also. Another theory was that their daughter continuing her studies had offended the parents—Jehovah's Witnesses do not believe much in education—but that didn't carry water.

"Carl Henning Thomsen continued to maintain his innocence, again and again. I don't know how many hours he was questioned for altogether, but not for the briefest moment did he waver. My boss, Kasper Planck, thought for a long time that we had made a mistake over the prints, which unfortunately I finally talked him out of. He had all the proper doubts, I had all the good arguments, and sadly for Thomsen my view prevailed. In the past few days I've realised that I am going to have to live with this mistake for the rest of my life."

To Simonsen's own surprise he'd got through the admission he'd been dreading. Or maybe even thinking that way was symptomatic of his own self-importance—he was an egocentric fool, who could not tolerate being wrong, and now felt sorrier for himself than for those who had suffered as a result of his shortcomings.

Pedersen asked, "Should we take a break?"

Simonsen glanced at him in confusion.

"Excuse me, what was that you asked?"

"Whether we should take a break."

"Yes, in a little bit, I'm just about done. The investigation ended when we brought charges against Carl Henning Thomsen for the murder of his daughter. During the trial he had a mental breakdown and was admitted to Rigshospitalet, where despite close monitoring he managed to throw himself out of a ninth-floor window. That was in October 1998. The case was then archived. Two years later, however, there was an addendum to the notes when sophisticated listening devices were found in Catherine Thomsen's old apartment during its renovation, but no one knew whether these had anything to do with her murder, and no one made more than a half-hearted attempt to find out. Any questions or comments?"

His gaze was met with a general head-shaking; no one had any questions.

"Now let's take a break, and then Arne Pedersen will take over."

He took a step towards his colleague and added in a low voice, "I hope that's all right? The Countess did mention to you that it was a possibility, I hope."

"It's quite all right. I can easily continue, especially now it's just us present."

"I'm tired," admitted Simonsen, "and the last few weeks have taught me to listen to my body."

"You don't need to explain."

"Did that seem too self-important to you? The part about… about the father and my own role in his death?"

"It seemed very honest, and if you think you're the only one who was affected by that case you'd better think again. I don't know if you noticed, but there should be nineteen of us here today and there are only sixteen. Three colleagues who like you were involved in the investigation of the Stevns murder had to go home. They couldn't take the stress. And Troulsen went out for a walk, he wasn't feeling too good either."

"Well, it's out there and that's a relief. For now I know a secret couch that I want to visit for an hour or so."

Pedersen smiled.

"I know where that secret couch is too. I think a lot of people do, so I hope it's vacant. Shall I come up and wake you?"

"I'll set my cell phone, but thanks for the offer. I assume you'll review what DYE-5 looks like now, and then allocate our resources to individual DYE employees based on the list from the Americans."

"Yes, I'll do that."

"I would like to have an overview when arrangements are in place, and you should make sure that visits to any DYE employee are made by pairs of officers, one of whom must be male. Agreed?"

"Completely."

"A plan will have to be thought out soon for how we inform the general public. There will be an outcry."

"There already is. Go up now and rest."

Pedersen almost pushed his boss towards the door, which suggested goodwill combined with worry for his well-being, but Simonsen knew his colleague too well to believe that. "Tell me, what's going on here? Why are you suddenly so eager to get rid of me?"

Then he caught sight of a message from Malte Borup, in big letters on the screen: *Distinguished visitor en route to the boss*.

Pedersen did not give up. "It can wait. Come on, Simon."

But it was too late. An impeccably dressed man came into the room. Both Simonsen and Pedersen knew him from a previous case. His name was Helmer Hammer and he was employed in the Prime Minister's office—a charming person, who consistently downplayed his influence, and as a rule got things done the way he wanted them. Both detectives liked him, which did not however prevent Pedersen from receiving him with a bad-tempered torrent of words.

"We weren't the ones who embarrassed the little worm from the Foreign Ministry, and if you want to speak to Simon, you'll have to wait a couple of hours until he's rested."

As usual Helmer Hammer was one step ahead.

"Well, I don't mind waiting. It's no skin off my nose. But I thought you'd like to know that the little worm from the Foreign Ministry is in the process of arranging a videoconference for this evening, and he has asked if Simon has time to participate."

"Is it Berlin calling?"

It was Pedersen again.

"No, now it's a ship in the Caribbean… Though naturally it's wrong of me to come rushing in and then expect you to drop everything else. Even though my errand will only take ten minutes, I apologise…"

But a bell was already ringing in Simonsen's head. When he and the Countess had been obliged to cancel their Caribbean trip, she had suggested that his daughter Anna Mia should go instead. Completely free, with a friend if she liked. She did. The agreement was that Anna Mia would phone home occasionally, but so far he had not heard from her. He'd assumed it was due to poor signal.

"Just a moment. What kind of conference is this?" he asked.

"They are calling it a trust-building initiative. The kind they're really good at in the Ministry of Foreign Affairs."

"And what do I have to do in return?"

"Nothing, that's the whole point. Consider it his apology for flying off the handle at you earlier."

"Sounds like a trick to me."

"But it's not, you have my word on that. He made an ass of himself, and now he's trying to make up for it."

"Then I'd be happy to agree. Will you tell him for me?

"Yes, no problem. And while I'm here, tell me, is there a place we can talk undisturbed? I meant what I said, it will only take ten minutes."

Simonsen threw out his arms.

"No one will interrupt us here."

The two men walked down the corridor together while Helmer Hammer explained.

"I'm here because I want some advice from you, and at the same time I want to ask for a favour. First the advice: some people have become aware that there is a handful of young constables who have passed a number of examinations in legal studies before dropping out of university and attending the police

40

academy instead. Now, the idea is to help them complete their degree in law while they are training as constables. It's good economics: we gain extremely capable police employees for a relatively modest outlay. I would like to hear what you think about that plan, as a chief inspector."

Simonsen shook his head in disbelief at such a virtuoso display of manipulation, marvellously downplayed so that it was impossible to be genuinely annoyed by it. Helmer Hammer knew perfectly well that Simonsen's daughter had skipped two years of legal studies and would soon be finished at the police academy. He also knew that the loosely sketched education project was bait that her father could not refuse.

"You're simply too much. So how can I help you?"

"I'll take that as confirmation that you like the concept. With respect to the favour I want to ask for, I've run into a problem. The man from the Foreign Ministry who visited your lecture is named Bertil Hampel-Koch, and his title is actually not *worm*, but general director. God knows he can be a sourpuss sometimes and even a little arrogant. He's also constantly getting mixed up in every possible territorial pissing contest, which unfortunately he's not alone in, definitely not. Now and then the central administration at Slotsholmen is a real kindergarten, but Bertil is also a very competent person, who can be a good and faithful supporter if you get to know him. Besides, you can rely on him, he always keeps his agreements."

"And how do I get to know this gentleman?"

"By sending him a brief email, preferably just a couple of lines, every evening about how the investigation is proceeding. If there's nothing new, tell him that. If an important development happens, email as soon as you have time."

"Is that all?"

"No, not quite. You will also get to know him by visiting him every now and then, if he wants that."

"According to my calendar, not his."

"I have emphasised that detail."

"And he went along with it?"

"He is always guided by expediency. Otherwise he wouldn't be in the exalted position he now occupies."

"If I receive a written instruction from the police commissioner that I have to … get to know your friend, then we can reach an agreement. That is, not from the national chief of police, it has to be from my direct boss, Gurli—"

"The instruction is waiting on your desk alongside a business card with the telephone number you should call concerning this evening's arrangements. There is also his email address."

The agreement was in the bag, and like a couple of old horse traders they shook hands on it. Simonsen had another question, however, now that he had the chance.

"Tell me one thing: who actually decided I should lead this investigation? I mean, all the stories about the chancellor, they're not for real, are they?"

Helmer Hammer shook his head, smiling.

"No, I can promise you that they're not. It's always amazing what garbage the media can get people to believe."

"So who was it?"

"It was me."

"You! Why in the world …?"

"Because you're capable."

"Nonsense. Others are too. Did you know I was about to go on holiday?"

"Yes, unfortunately. But I was not aware that you were in poor health, I'm sorry to hear that."

"Hmm, it's no worse. But you haven't answered my question. Why me, and why are you involved in this at all?"

"I'm doing my job, and it wasn't nonsense when I said you were chosen for your competence."

"But there are other things behind this too?"

"If there are, it's not something that involves you or your investigation. You can count on that."

Helmer Hammer consulted his watch.

"See, what did I say? That took only eight and a half minutes. Now I just need to find my way out."

He looked around in confusion. The building's maze of curved corridors, which all looked identical to the untrained eye, had him temporarily at a loss.

"That's only possible when you've worked here a dozen years. I'll accompany you... no, wait a minute, damned if I will. You're not going to win on every point, that's not healthy for anyone. It will probably be more beneficial to your mental health for you to wander around in confusion for at least fifteen minutes."

"Everyone a winner... therein lies the politician's art! Very well, I'll try and find my own way out. Greetings to your daughter. I hope we meet again soon. And sleep well, Simon."

CHAPTER 5

While the boss slept, the break in the Homicide Division's review of the Nygaard and Thomsen murders dragged on. People had a lot to talk about, and besides, Arne Pedersen, who would be continuing the review solo, could use a few extra minutes of preparation. He had stepped aside and was studying the PowerPoint slides in conjunction with Konrad Simonsen's notes. Pauline Berg went up to him. He glanced up quickly and waved her away.

"Whatever it is, Pauline, it will have to wait."

She snatched his ballpoint pen.

"Damn it, do you always have to push the boundaries with me? Can't you understand that I need to run through this? Or maybe you'd like to take over. You do the review while I sit and listen."

Pauline gave him her sweetest smile. Not without effect.

"You'll manage," she told him.

"I'm pleased you have so much confidence in me. Of course I'll manage…if you'd just let me get on with it! Oh, all right then," he sighed. "What is it? Are you spooked because you resemble the two murdered girls? There's nothing I can do about that, although I understand perfectly well why you reacted as you did once you'd noticed it."

"It's creepy all right, but I'm blue-eyed not brown-, and my hair colour doesn't match either. I just felt a little uncomfortable when it occurred to me. Everyone was looking at me, without saying anything."

"No one was looking at you. What is it you want?"

"That thing on the screen, what is it?"

Pedersen looked up and saw that Malte Borup had the starting image ready: a photograph of a peculiar building that resembled a drilling platform about to swallow a giant egg. He suppressed his irritation.

"That's DYE-5, as you can read below."

"But it wasn't that big surely."

"Not that big? I'd say it was! The building stood on eight gigantic pillars and was six storeys high. The dome on top was the radar installation, covered in plastic, that's why it's white. If you look at the woman you can see in front of the far-left pillar, you get an impression of how big it was in reality. It was a tough job to build out there, when you think that every piece of kit had to be transported by air. 'Eyes of Freedom' is what the Americans called their radar stations."

Pauline waved away the information, as if swatting a fly. Pedersen continued undaunted.

"The whole building can be raised if there is more snow and ice. That makes the design many times more—"

She interrupted him, irritated.

"I don't care about pillars and storeys, where's the rest of it?"

"If you wait another two minutes, I'll go through everything in detail. You will also have the opportunity to see a lot of pictures taken inside the building."

"But is it just that one, Arne? I mean, what about other radar stations?"

"That one was out on its own on the ice cap, though there were four other DYE stations."

"But they were far away, weren't they?"

"Yes, they were, that was the whole idea, they were supposed to form a chain, although DYE-5 wasn't quite…"

"Damn! Then it doesn't fit."

"What can't you get to fit?" he asked patiently.

Pauline hoped one day to be the one to solve a major case. Once she had found an important hard drive that no one else could locate, and still enjoyed thinking about that, but otherwise she did not have much to brag about. She knew that she was naive and romanticised things, so she kept her daydreams to herself, apart from a single occasion when she happened to say too much to Pedersen in particular… and maybe another time to the Countess… and possibly on a few other occasions too, but those were surely forgotten, and if her latest hypothesis was correct… well, she almost didn't dare complete the thought. She was bubbling with enthusiasm and did not let herself be deterred by Pedersen's admonition, when he sensed what she was thinking.

"Always bear in mind that investigation is teamwork."

"Obviously it's teamwork, but there is something I have to check out, so you'll have to manage without me for an hour or two."

45

Pedersen grabbed her by the wrist as she turned to go.

"Ouch, that hurts!"

"Nonsense, it doesn't hurt at all."

"The rest of you occasionally follow up an idea that's too exciting to leave alone. For once I'm going to do the same thing. I've been here a while, after all."

"We don't keep information to ourselves. That's a cardinal sin in any investigation."

"Can't you give me a little leeway, just today? I promise to call you no later than eight o'clock unless…You can come over too if you have time. So you can see my new house and maybe help me put my curtain rails up."

"Your boyfriend can do that."

"He can't because he's history."

Pedersen was sincerely amazed. Mostly because Pauline hadn't said anything about a break-up, although on the other hand she did not need to report on her personal life to him.

"But didn't you just buy a house together?"

"He was a little too close to one of his fellow students. So close that he's going to be a father soon, the jerk."

"What about finances? Can you afford to stay there yourself?"

"The Countess is helping me get a loan, and I'll have to teach a couple of dance classes at night school, but then it should all work out. Okay, will I see you or what?"

Pedersen let go of her wrist without answering. Instead he stood up and called out to his restless colleagues, "Sorry, but it will be another five minutes."

Then he commanded Pauline, "Sit down."

She obeyed him reluctantly. He too sat down.

"You saw those girls up there yourself, and under no circumstances do you have permission to go snooping around on your own without letting anyone know what you're doing. This is not

46

open to discussion, so either you tell me what you're up to or you stay here where I can see you."

"Okay, but remember now, this is my idea."

"What is?"

"Try looking at the coordinates under the picture."

"I'm looking, what about them?"

"They don't fit the scene of the crime. If it's not an identical error that is repeated in three places, then that DYE building was simply not located where Maryann Nygaard was found."

Pedersen observed Pauline with equal parts distrust and excitement.

"Do continue."

"I noticed it because the coordinates where Maryann Nygaard was buried correspond to my cell phone number... apart from the seconds obviously. So listen, DYE-5 was located at 68°47'02" North and 45°14'03" West, as you can see, but Maryann Nygaard was buried at 68°37'02" North and 45°41'03" West—that's shown by the very first report from the chancellor's helicopter to the control tower at Ilulissat Airport and corresponds to the technicians' GPS measurements. So at first I thought such a DYE installation was pretty big, that is in terms of area, but that's evidently not the case, and I think... well, I'm no expert in spherical geometry, but I've gone to school, and a north-south minute is equal to two kilometres, and an east-west minute is one kilometre in Denmark. So don't you see, Arne?"

"No, don't see a thing, you've lost me completely."

"Well, despite the fact that the east-west distance decreases the farther away from the equator you get, Disco Bay is not so far north that you can make it fit at all, if you calculate using Pythagoras, even though it is curved and may fudge a little..."

Pauline was getting carried away. A couple of colleagues turned round to look at her, which immediately made her settle down.

"There is at least fifteen kilometres' difference between the scene where the body was found and the location of DYE-5, probably a bit more. Even you must realise that?"

Pedersen did not calculate, he had given up on that; instead he looked Pauline in the eyes.

"Are you certain?"

"Yes, I am. Where would it be wrong?"

He turned his head and stared up at the screen for a long time while he recalled standing out on the ice cap. Pauline Berg stayed silent in the meantime.

"Fifteen kilometres, you say?"

"At least."

"The helicopter pilot?"

"Exactly."

It was a piece of information that had to be digested. Most likely her mathematical calculations were off somewhere, and that would be the end of that. On the other hand it would explain why the Greenlanders had not found any trace of DYE-5. Even if the American Army according to Trond Egede could be particularly efficient, it hardly seemed probable that such a large building could be removed without trace. Besides, it was not unheard of for an investigation to founder on a simple confusion like this. He said cautiously, "What do you want to do now?"

"Jump up on my perch and work with the coordinates. There must be a distance formula somewhere on the Internet, or maybe Google Earth can help me. And if that all goes haywire, I know someone who can do such a calculation, though I don't have any desire to contact him."

"Start by going into my office and finding the card from Nuuk police on my bulletin board; then call the number on the back, get hold of Trond Egede, and tell him what you've explained to me. But be a bit careful how you phrase the coordinates error... if it is an error, that is. Ask him to call back when he has clarified whether your hypothesis holds water. You don't need to underscore its potential importance, he'll see that for himself. While you're waiting, you can make your own calculations."

"If it turns out to be correct, I would really like to go out and speak with the nurse that Simon has on his list of witnesses," Pauline said eagerly.

Pedersen considered that.

"Okay, but stick your head in and inform me first. And take the Countess along, and tell her what you've figured out."

"Fine, but I would also like to speak with one of those who worked at—"

Pedersen's interruption was sharp.

"Absolutely not alone! You are forbidden to do that. Period. Or... wait a moment."

He leafed through his papers and found what he was looking for.

"Give me my pen."

She obeyed.

"Look at this. You can talk to him, and only him, none of the others. He is in a wheelchair and has been since 1992. You can figure out for yourself what that means. You're capable, Pauline. The day you also become a profession—"

She put her hand over his mouth.

"If I find out the killer's name, I want to be able to announce it myself. That is, only to the inner circle."

"That's okay with me."

"Do you think I'm vain?"

"Yes."

"The Countess says so too, but she laughs at it. I'm sure you think I'm a terrible person."

"You know perfectly well that I don't, Pauline."

"So are you going to come and help me with my curtain rails?"

She hurried out of the room without waiting for an answer.

Less than twenty minutes later she was back and giving him the thumbs up before closing the door to the lecture room. At that point Pedersen was in the middle of his review, major portions of which seemed suddenly irrelevant. The Countess got up from her seat and left the room. Pedersen was thinking about what he should say to his wife to explain his absence tonight.

The two women went over to the Countess's office. Pauline Berg started talking immediately they came in, but not about the coordinates error. She said, "Simon managed that really nicely."

The Countess answered a little abruptly, "Well, what else did you expect?"

"Nothing, except that it would work out, but there was a lot of talk that it might be difficult for him. I mean, with the father and all that."

"What have you discovered, Pauline? Arne said that maybe it was important. I'm a little annoyed about not hearing his review. Tell me now, why are we sitting here?"

Pauline told her. This time she was better prepared, and the Countess understood her immediately. The reaction came promptly and echoed Pedersen's.

"The helicopter pilot?"

"That's a good suggestion."

The Countess also sat a while and processed the new information in her mind. Then she asked carefully, "And the Greenlandic police have confirmed that the location of the radar station is wrong?"

"Yes, they have. Trond Egede is the name of our contact. He was the one who was with Arne and Simon on the ice. He called five minutes ago and confirmed it. He also apologised. It annoyed him no end that he hadn't discovered the error himself. Yes, he said that, it's a direct quote."

The Countess nodded, as if she echoed Trond Egede's annoyance. Then her face lit up in a big smile and she said, "Nice work, Pauline. We could have wasted days on that. You've earned your pay today."

Pauline was blushing with pride.

"Thanks. Arne promised me that I can go out and talk to a witness who knew those DYEs. Although he wasn't too excited about it."

"Phooey, just get going. But that witness list of DYE employees—it's not a good idea for you to visit any of the men alone. Or... no, I really want to be clear about this. Helicopter pilot or not, you stay away from them. Is that agreed?"

"It's agreed, I'll stay away from them. Arne said that too."

"Good, because it's only sensible. You can take my car if you want."

The Countess watched Pauline leave, feeling a stab of envy. Not because her colleague had discovered something that no one else had, the Countess did not begrudge her that, but at her bubbling enthusiasm and the pride she took in standing out. This was part of being young and would fade in time, even for Pauline Berg. Sooner or later you admitted to yourself that the current, crucial case was not so crucial after all. A new one was always waiting around the corner, and another one, and the next. That insight gradually made investigation a job more than a lifestyle. In the long run you became more efficient but decidedly less enthusiastic. The excitement of the job, which could only be experienced by those who were still green, was gone for good. The Countess thought it was probably the same in many other occupations.

Then suddenly she had an unpleasant recollection of someone rather like Pauline. The Countess's ex-husband's new secretary had also been ambitious in her time. Erna with the Elbows, that's what they'd called her in the beginning, the two of them, both the Countess and her husband. She corrected herself: ex-husband.

And noted at the same time the hateful vacuum in the pit of her stomach, which she had felt every single day for over a year after the divorce, and which still yawned inside her from time to time. With undiminished force, too.

Now Erna had just had her second child with the Countess's husband… her ex-husband. They'd kept the first one secret for months, until the Countess had her suspicions and hired a private detective to follow him. The break-up was irreconcilable and hard on her. *So now I'm free to wake up every morning with a woman whose only goal for the day is to be perfect.* Those were his parting words, before he betrayed the Countess totally and disappeared from her life. To his new family.

She sighed and tried to dismiss the negative thoughts, knowing full well that they would last for at least a couple of days and in her paranoia she would live in fear of running into the pair of them by chance on the street. It was usually like that. On the other hand it helped a little to think that she still received photographs every month or so from the private detective. Just to help her keep up a little and at the same time feel in control. He had orders to take his photos openly, so as to cause maximum embarrassment to them. It helped to think about that too.

CHAPTER 6

On a street in central Roskilde Pauline Berg tracked down the nurse, who was sitting in a small red car belonging to the municipal home health care service, filling out a form.

The woman was only in her fifties, but despite her attractive, blue-grey uniform and well-cared-for appearance, she looked used up. Her face was tired and her movements seemed grudging, as if she was irritated with herself. After briefly hearing about Pauline Berg's inquiry and suspiciously inspecting her ID, she allowed the young woman to get in on the passenger side. The nurse continued her paperwork without seeming to notice that she had company. When she was finished and had carefully put the results in two different folders, she glanced at her watch tensely and said, "I'm already eight minutes behind schedule. My next citizen is two streets away, but the one after that is in Viby so there we'll have some time. If you don't mind waiting, that is."

"I don't mind waiting."

The woman started the car and expertly pulled out into the afternoon traffic. Then she said, for no reason, "Citizen, yes. That's what we call them, and we use that term so much it's completely natural to us, but I'm very aware that in other people's ears it sounds like something from the French Revolution. And you can stay in the car. It's against the rules, but you have to be able to trust the police."

Soon they had arrived at her citizen, and the nurse leaped out of the car.

"This one will take fifteen minutes at most. If I'm lucky I can make up a minute or two. I'm only going to change a dressing."

When seventeen minutes had passed, Pauline Berg began feeling stressed.

On the drive to Viby they had time to talk. Pauline asked, "Were you a colleague of Maryann Nygaard in 1983, at the American base in Søndre Strømfjord?"

According to the woman's schedule they now had twenty minutes of driving ahead of them, so there was no reason to force the conversation. For that reason Pauline started with the fundamentals.

53

"Yes, we were both nurses there. The base rules were that there should be double staffing, even if there wasn't enough work for a part-time position. The US Air Force is a strange mixture of admirable efficiency and exceptional waste."

"How long were you employed in Greenland?"

"From 1980 to 1984."

"Was it difficult working there?"

"Not particularly, not if you were a nurse. You had to speak a reasonable amount of English and be sociable. There were rumours that you must not be politically suspect—a communist, that is—but I don't know if that was correct."

"Do you know what happened to Maryann Nygaard?"

"Of course I do. She was the one the chancellor found out on the ice. I try not to think about it too much. It's not that hard. It was a long time ago, almost another life."

"How did you get along with each other?"

"Not very well, we were constant competitors."

"To be the best nurse?"

"To score the best men. And she won by a landslide there."

"Did she have a lot of them?"

"Maryann basically had the men she wanted, but if you mean did she hop into bed with just anyone, the answer is no. All things considered we were no different from many girls in that age group. Though in our cases you need to factor in a lot of free time and parties with endless quantities of cheap alcohol, not to mention the ratio between men and women being extremely favourable, if you know what I mean."

"Hmm, I think I get your point. Can you remember whether Maryann had any female friends? Or friends of either sex for that matter. I mean, someone she would confide in."

The woman answered without a pause.

"Yes, she did. There was a girlfriend who was half Greenlandic and half Danish. She was if possible even prettier than Maryann, a tall, good-looking girl. She was studying at Aarhus University and had taken a year off, but I can't remember her name, only her nickname. Almost everyone had nicknames. It might seem a little strange, not to mention stilted, but today that's often what you remember."

"And her nickname was?"

"Six Feet of Love."

"And you don't know where I can find Six Feet ... I mean, the girlfriend now?"

"No, not at all. I remember that she was always reading, so it's a given that she did something with books. Librarian, book dealer, translator, editor—"

Pauline Berg interrupted.

"Thanks, I get it, something with books. Tell me, what did you think when Maryann Nygaard disappeared?"

"That it was terrible and also hard to understand. Most people thought she had deliberately gone out on the ice. That is, committed suicide. It happened, and fairly often too. Sometimes people were never found again, but no one had suspected Maryann of harbouring such suicidal thoughts, so in her case it was a shock. That was actually why I went home when my contract ran out."

"Her disappearance happened in connection with a visit to a place called DYE-5, a radar station on the ice cap as I've understood it. Have you been there yourself?"

"Twice. I've been to all five DYE stations, but only once to DYE-4. It was all the way over on the east coast. Unfortunately I have a hard time differentiating the various visits from each other twenty-five years later, so I can't remember my trips to DYE-5 in particular. All the stations more or less resembled each other."

"Try to tell me about a typical trip. How did you get out there?"

"We were flown, either in a plane or a helicopter. To DYE-4 always by plane, it was too far away for a helicopter."

"Was the flight just for your sake, or were there others along on the trip?"

"Just for us. A few times there were packages too and always letters, but otherwise it was just us."

"So you were alone with the pilot?"

"Yes, that's how it was."

"Were the pilots Americans or Danes?"

"It varied a little. As a rule they were Danish. According to military regulations I suppose it should have been Americans doing the flying, but all rules were systematically broken, except the unwritten ones. Some of the Danes got their pilot's licence up there, for helicopters too. I think that was in their contracts, but I'm not sure. You have to recall that most of us had a lot of free time, and the Americans were helpful if you wanted some form of training. For the most part they were very accommodating, capable people, but crazy when it came to wasting resources. They didn't give a fig if their government threw a lot of money out of the window."

"Did it take a long time to learn to fly a helicopter?"

"Eight weeks, and it cost a hundred and fifty thousand kroner, I recall. And then of course you only got a PPL licence. Private, that is, not commercial."

"You say that as a rule it was Danes who flew you to the DYE stations. How can that be?"

"Not just to the DYE stations, but everywhere. The reason was that the professional pilots didn't care, and the Danes thought it was fun. The Americans simply signed in with their own names and let the Danes fly for them. But obviously only when they were quite sure that the newly trained pilots could manage the job. A helicopter like that costs an arm and a leg, and if something went wrong with an uncertified pilot behind the wheel, or the joystick or whatever it's called, well, then Washington kicked up a fuss. It happened once up in Thule, and after that the flying rules were strictly observed for a few months, until the matter was forgotten."

"Will you tell me how a visit to a DYE station was structured?"

"Well, there wasn't much to it. I would count the stock of medicines and inspect the first-aid kits, and there was nothing to that. It could be done in an hour, if you hurried, and in two hours if you took it easy. What I remember best from the counting was that malaria pills were included in the inventory, because American bases all over the world had the same supplies no matter where they were. Once we made an urgent order for a shipment of new malaria pills and said the old ones had expired. You know, just for fun, to see what would happen."

"And what did happen?"

"Nothing. Or to be more exact, we received a shipment from the US without protest. Four excellent lawnmowers also arrived once a year. They were much sought after and quickly distributed to good Danish homes."

"Okay, but did you do anything on the DYE trips other than inspect the medicines? What about the men, were they checked?"

"No, only the medicines. The men you didn't see, apart from the DYE leader. It was always an odd experience because everyone knew when we were coming, and I've been told it was a big day on the base. It broke the monotony, and remember it was the only woman they would see for months. All the men would take baths before we arrived, and then you felt them watching you from every conceivable hiding place as you were walking around; a head popping up here, a pair of eyes behind a crack there. The whole time you were observed and monitored, but never approached. Yes, it was really odd. If ever I happen to see a chipmunk on TV, I think about those men … their heads popping up all around and then disappearing again."

"But you didn't feel unsafe?"

"Not at all, there was no reason to."

The car lurched briefly towards the hard shoulder as the nurse involuntarily tightened her grip on the wheel. She immediately corrected it.

"That is, I didn't think there was any reason to. Ugh, this is unpleasant to think about! Will you tell me how Maryann died? They write so many horrible things in the newspapers, are they correct?"

"Yes, unfortunately, she was suffocated in a plastic bag."

"That's disgusting. And it could have been me."

"It couldn't have been. The killer supposedly went after a very distinct type of woman, and you don't fit the profile. Can you recall who flew Maryann out to DYE-5, the day she disappeared?"

"Yes, I recall that very well because obviously that day stands out in my memory. We were all terribly upset when we heard that she was missing, because we knew full well what that could mean. As I said, it had happened before. And the helicopter pilot had to tell the story again and again, even if there wasn't that much to tell. I mean, what was there to say? She was there and then she wasn't. They searched for her in every direction and couldn't find her. But he was all we had, and we went over that search again and again."

"Was it just him and Maryann Nygaard who flew out there?"

"It must have been, yes, just those two. As I said, that was normal too."

"Was he a Dane?"

"Yes, he was Danish."

"What was his name?"

"Good Lord, is he the one who killed her?"

"We don't know that, but I would really like to have his name. Can you remember what it was?"

"No, that's difficult. I can remember his face, and also that he was an engineer and very handy with electronics, but his name…well, wait a minute. His real name I can't remember, but he had a nickname like everyone else—Bundy or Blondie or something like that—no, no, now I have it: Pronto. It was Pronto. Maryann had a nickname too, I remember. We called her Polly because she had an irritating habit of repeating everything like a parrot, if you understand."

"Sure. Can you tell me anything else about this Pronto?"

"I remember that he was unbelievably naive. It almost didn't matter what you told him, he believed it, and sometimes he got teased. It was just too easy."

"Do you remember any examples?"

The woman thought, but not for long.

"There was one time in the chow hall—that is what we called the mess—when in the fast-food line you could get one of those breaded, formed pieces of ham. It was three-cornered like the ears on a hog and rubbery besides, so we called them flap ears. They tasted very good, though. Well, there was also a soft ice cream machine, and someone told Pronto that flap ears with soft ice cream was an amazing dish that many people in America ate at Christmastime. He ate that steadily for a while. Even once during the evening meal, when he usually sat by himself, I saw him with a plate of ham and soft ice cream."

"Was he unintelligent?"

"Not at all, just childish. He was actually fairly bright, as I recall. As I said he was a trained engineer, but he was simply the type that takes everything too literally and can't imagine that others talk nonsense or perhaps flat out lie."

"What was Pronto's function at the base?"

The woman shook her head, she couldn't remember.

Pauline Berg concluded, "So the helicopter pilot who flew Maryann Nygaard from the Søndre Strømfjord base to

59

DYE-5 on September the thirteenth, 1983… that is, the day she disappeared… was known by the nickname Pronto?"

"Yes, that's the way it was."

"When was the last time you saw Pronto?"

"He went home a short time before me. It must have been in early 1984 because I went home in the middle of March. And I haven't seen him since."

"Where can I find someone who knows his real name?"

"That won't be hard. Many of those who were at the base back then still see each other, it's almost a kind of cult. I haven't been involved for several years but there is a website, *modnord.dk*— and there you can see his real name because his nickname is in parentheses, I recall. There's also a picture, if you're interested. Oh, no, not again!"

She struck the steering wheel and slowed down the car. Ahead of them a handful of vehicles were lined up, and a motorcycle cop was waving them to the side of the road.

"It's another random car check, and this is the second time this month."

"Don't stop, drive up alongside him."

The woman obeyed. Pauline Berg got out and showed her badge while she put in a good word. After arranging a lift for herself, she went back to the nurse, who had rolled down the car window.

"Thanks a lot, you've been a big help. You can drive around."

"I should thank you. I hope you find Maryann's murderer. She did not deserve that fate."

Pauline watched the car for a long time as it drove away. She should have said, No one deserved a fate like Maryann Nygaard's.

Eight hours later Pauline Berg was in her bathtub, playing contentedly with the foam around her while the hot water washed away the hardships of the day. She had left the door standing open, and a smile broadened across her pretty face when she heard the front door to the house open and then close again. Without hurrying she let herself glide down in a carefully conceived tableau, her hair floating in a golden wreath around her and one arm dangling over the edge of the tub in a refined swoon. Millions of small bubbles covered her nakedness—like a coverlet of coquettish virtue, where only one well-formed knee suggested what was hidden below.

"Hi, Arne. Good thing you read the note. I'm not out of the bath yet. You'll have to excuse me, there's been a lot going on."

She heard no answer and called again.

"Arne, what are you doing?"

Still silence. She straightened up and in the process destroyed her pose.

"Stop teasing me, it's not funny. I don't like it!" she called at top volume.

At the same time the light changed slightly in the corridor outside the bathroom. Then she heard the front door slam again. She started to feel anxious, until she heard his voice.

"Pauline, where are you? Is there something wrong?"

Suddenly he was standing in the doorway, and anger replaced panic.

"What are you doing? Why didn't you answer? I was scared to death."

"I forgot I'd left my toolbox in the car. Are you in the bath?"

The seductive prelude was spoiled, and Pauline made no attempt to revert to it.

"What does it look like?"

"I got your message. You did an amazing job today, and this is such a nice house. May I look around while you get ready?"

"Wait a little. Are those flowers for me?"

"That was the idea, as a housewarming gift."

"They're really beautiful, thank you. Would you mind setting them in the sink and putting a little water in the bottom? I'll try to find a vase later in all the moving mess."

He did as she asked. Then she told him to sit on the chair beside the bathtub. The house he could see later. She related her talk with the home care nurse in Roskilde and described the website where she had found the helicopter pilot.

"I've also cross-checked that he was the one who flew Maryann."

"How could you do that?"

"The DYE-5 employee in the wheelchair, I found him at Østerbro. Strange man, almost impossible to get away from, but he was quite sure about it. At Roskilde Library I printed out twelve random faces and put the helicopter pilot in the middle, and the man in the wheelchair recognised him right away."

"Brilliant, Pauline. They'll be surprised tomorrow. I'm really happy for you. But you're going to call Simon this evening, if you haven't already done so."

"Why is that?"

"Because that's what you do when you've found out something important."

"Okay."

"By the way, I spoke with Greenland. They've found the remains of DYE-5 and you were completely right about the coordinates."

"I'm good, aren't I?"

He grinned.

"Do you happen to know how far it is between the two places?"

"I made it thirty-one kilometres," Pauline told him.

"Thirty-one point three is what they got."

"Greenland is welcome to those three hundred metres."

She blew a puff of foam at him and slyly released the plug with one foot.

CHAPTER 7

Ingrid Thomsen did not say a word when she answered the door to Konrad Simonsen and the Countess. For a brief moment she silently assessed them both from head to toe, then turned on her heel and went inside, leaving the door standing open as a sign for them to follow her.

The living room was as Simonsen remembered it from ten years before. Minor details he had forgotten in the meantime were now brought back to life before him. They made him feel sad. The light red imitation marble of the windowsills that clashed with the flowered curtains. The bric-a-brac shelf with the polished conch shells, neatly arranged by size and shape. A picture of Jesus over the sofa posing in a jewel-studded purple tunic, an abundant halo around his head. And then her hands. They were bony like she was, red and strong, hands that were used to hard physical work. She twisted them around in a slow, methodical movement, as if all the pain in the world could be kneaded away between them. That's how it was then, and that's how it was today. He tried to ignore the movement, holding her gaze while he explained rather clumsily why he had come. She listened without comment.

He sat down on the couch alongside her. The Countess had chosen a chair by the dining table at the other end of the room. She did not get involved in the conversation. From time to time he sneaked a glance at her and every time felt a sting of irritation at her presence. She should have stayed in the car. This situation was hard enough for him and superfluous listeners did not make it any easier. He explained about Greenland and then compared the killings of Maryann Nygaard and Catherine Thomsen. Twice he confused the victims' names without noticing it himself. Ingrid Thomsen listened, condemning him while saying nothing. His legs were tingling worse than ever, which for once he welcomed. It was as if he deserved the pain. Suddenly Ingrid Thomsen interrupted him.

"That's just the way it is."

Those were the first words she had spoken since they arrived. Her voice was dark and melodic, and suited her poorly. He had also forgotten that. She repeated the statement in slightly varied form.

"Things can't be done over again. That's the way it is."

He did not know if he should continue his monologue, but chose to remain silent, while still looking her in the eyes. The pause was long and awkward, and finally she continued speaking.

"What is it you really want? My forgiveness for what you did to my husband? Is that why you've come? Or do you expect sympathy perhaps?"

Simonsen had asked himself several times what the purpose of his visit really was, without finding a reasonable answer. Suddenly it felt imperative that he should tell her that the police, and he in particular, had made mistaken accusations against her husband. But would that be enough? Perhaps, just as she had said, it was her forgiveness he wanted, whatever that meant. He avoided answering. Suddenly she stopped her hand-wringing and struck the palm of one hand on the tabletop in front of her. Although the sound was not loud, it made him jump.

"Carl Henning and Catherine are in Ulse Cemetery, under the chestnut tree out towards the parking lot. Why don't you go there and talk to them?"

Simonsen got to his feet and answered her quietly.

"I did not fabricate false evidence against your husband, while in all likelihood Catherine's murderer did. And I did not kill your husband, he did that himself."

"You were just doing your job."

The sarcasm did not affect him. He maintained his calm.

"Yes, exactly. I was doing my job. Regrettably for you I was mistaken, which was very unfortunate. But yes, I was just doing my job."

They let themselves out.

He sat in the back seat of the car, where he took off his shoes and put his feet up on the seat. That helped the restlessness in his legs. The Countess drove out of town. As the buildings began to thin out, she asked carefully, "Do you want to go out to that cemetery?"

"No, we'll skip the church, but stop if you see a pub. I want a beer and a cigarette."

She turned her head and smiled quickly at him.

"That sounds like a splendid idea."

"And then I want another beer and cigarette."

He smiled defiantly, almost childishly. She gave him another quick smile. Then she started looking for a pub.

CHAPTER 8

"Andreas Falkenborg!"

Konrad Simonsen's deep voice commanded the attention of the listeners packed into his office. Pauline Berg thought that only now were her efforts of the day before validated. Arne

Pedersen and the Countess were content to nod, Poul Troulsen did not react.

"Helicopter pilot, electrical engineer, presumed double murderer. That's what we know about him at the moment, so the task for today is simple: we have to fill in his CV. Arne and Poul, you take his life here in Denmark, form groups and let them do the work. I'm especially interested in any links to Catherine Thomsen. Where did he meet her? What relationship did they have? Including the false evidence against her father, how and when he fabricated that. Also try to get a current photograph of him, and if you don't find one, take one without him knowing. Tomorrow I'm putting a full surveillance team on him, maybe they can take a picture. If you leave HS, I want to know where you are."

HS stands for Head square, and Konrad Simonsen normally avoided the abbreviation, which he found stilted and redundant, but right now he was too tired to care much for his language.

Pedersen nodded bleary-eyed. Troulsen raised a thumb in the air and asked at the same time, "So we have him under surveillance already?"

"Yes, more or less. We're discreetly following what he's doing, but not intensively."

"Why isn't he under intensive surveillance? He's not a man who should be going around without supervision."

"We're in the process of freeing up resources. That will happen in the course of the day."

With Troulsen satisfied, Simonsen continued.

"Countess, you get Greenland. Your primary focus is to delve into whether we can nail him to the murder of Maryann Nygaard in a way that will hold up in court. I also want to know whether he had contact with her in Denmark, or if they first met in Greenland. Use Trond Egede up there, he's competent, but you are not allowed to ask the Americans officially. Not Thule Air

Base or anywhere else, unless I specifically give instructions. And just like Arne and Poul, don't go anywhere without my knowledge. Are you with me?"

The Countess agreed, and Simonsen turned towards Pauline Berg.

"What you accomplished yesterday was an outstanding piece of investigative work. Today you get the easier, but also the most important, assignments. First and foremost you will find out whether any witness in the Stevns case knew Andreas Falkenborg. There are a lot of them, but you will take all the people you need to help you. I would specifically like to know whether he was known by the Jehovah's Witnesses. That would be a good way for him to approach Catherine Thomsen. Then I want you to review all the missing person cases in Denmark since 1968 that involve women in the age group fifteen to thirty-five. Get pictures and compare their appearance with Maryann Nygaard and Catherine Thomsen. If there is one that matches, compare that to the CV we are constructing on Falkenborg. Are you with me?"

Pauline Berg was happy. The most important assignments. She liked hearing that.

"It will be done."

"The fact that the two women resembled each other may be a coincidence, but the similarity is so striking I believe it has significance. In any event, it's our working hypothesis."

"Agreed."

"Good, and then one more thing—a press conference has been called at two o'clock. What do you say about going along with Arne?"

"But I've never done that."

"It's easy, you just avoid saying anything."

Simonsen got up and went over to the window.

"All of you take note: you must not contact Falkenborg directly. At the moment I do not wish him to know that we have him in our sights. There is one last thing—Malte and the Countess have convinced me of the benefits of exchanging the bulletin board for the computer while we research our suspect's life. Malte will make a website, password-protected obviously, and the idea is that we will gradually fill it out as information comes in. He has sent you all an email about how to participate, and you can log in and continuously monitor progress for yourselves, see how far we've come. As you know, I'm a bit of a diehard when it comes to the blessings of information technology, but in this case I want to give it a try."

"It's also the only correct way to do it."

Pedersen's comment earned him a bad-tempered glance from Simonsen, which his colleague simply sneered at. Simonsen concluded.

"Malte should be here now, so he'll probably arrive in fifteen minutes. You should get going unless you have any questions?"

He paused and looked around the team.

"Which does not seem to be the case. Okay, great, have a good day. Pauline, you stay here, I have a couple of things I want to discuss with you."

The men got up and left the office. Pauline Berg remained seated, unsure whether being asked to stay behind should be interpreted positively or negatively—an uncertainty that was quickly eliminated.

"How long was it between you learning the name Andreas Falkenborg and letting me in on it?"

She tried to wriggle out of answering the question.

"Well, it's hard to say exactly."

"Measured in hours and minutes, and without any evasions, please. I don't have time for that."

"Nine hours and a few minutes."

"Yes, that fits very well with what I came up with myself."

He stepped behind her and placed one hand on her shoulder.

"I really ought to lecture you, Pauline. Tell you about twenty colleagues of yours wasting time visiting old DYE-5 employees yesterday afternoon—which they didn't do, however, because Arne is more responsible than you are. But I have neither the time nor the desire to hang you out to dry. I also spoke with the Countess yesterday, and she very rightly pointed out that personnel management and development interviews and that sort of thing are not my strong suit, so as an alternative I have chosen to give you a very quick introduction to—"

Just then Malte Borup came crashing into the office, out of breath and sweaty, with a laptop computer in one hand and a six-pack of Coke in the other. Konrad Simonsen sent him out again and continued his lecture, though a good deal faster and less forcefully than he had originally intended.

"Have you ever wondered why you were hired here in Homicide, and in particular why almost from the first day you were included among the few I consult the most? You don't really think it was down to your intelligence and good looks, do you?"

Pauline Berg turned painfully red.

"I don't know what to say."

"It's because you are young and ambitious. Your age gives you a perspective on things that the rest of us don't always have, and ambition is a necessity in any career—otherwise you learn too slowly. When I was twenty-seven myself, I dreamed of solving a great mystery all alone. I thought I was unique in those thoughts, so I kept them to myself. Later I discovered that all my colleagues that age shared the same fantasy."

"I'm that way too," she admitted.

"Really? Well, things clearly haven't changed much. Later I learned that it was acceptable to take personal initiatives if I was the only one who paid the price, and also if I reported back important results promptly—which is to say about two minutes after I achieved them. In the interests of truth I must regretfully admit that I learned that lesson the hard way. Once I sat on the name of a perpetrator for two days before my boss exposed me. And do you know what happened then?"

She shook her head.

"I got bawled out so badly the hair was almost blown off my head, so luckily for you it seems some things have changed. Pauline, look at me."

She obeyed.

"Next time… and I am in no doubt that there will be a next time, because this talk does not change the fact that you were completely outstanding yesterday… *next time* inform me promptly. Are we in agreement?"

"Yes, we're in agreement. And sorry."

"Hmm, I thought I had copyright in that word. Go and do your work. Start by typing up the two witness interviews you did yesterday, if you haven't already done so."

She got up and left, aware that she had been let off easily. In the doorway she turned around.

"Thanks."

"When an employee thanks me after I've told her what's what, I know I must be getting old. Get going."

No sooner had Pauline Berg left the office than the Countess appeared. Ironically, given what he had just told Pauline, she was asking him to break his own rule. The Countess got right to the point.

"You're going to have to cut me some slack in this case, Simon. I have a line of inquiry I have to pursue but it may take some time."

"And what line is this?"

She shook her head at him, refusing to be drawn. "No more than the rest of the week. It won't take any longer than that. And you have to trust me when I say that I will inform you if necessary."

"Which is not now, I take it?"

"No, preferably not."

She smiled and added with a note of appeal in her voice, "This is not something I usually ask for. When I think about it, I believe this is the first time."

He muttered to himself and then unwillingly gave his consent. After which he quickly added, "This is a decision that can be reversed at any time if I can't do without you. I also want you here today while we research Andreas Falkenborg. Besides, ten minutes ago I gave Pauline a lecture for working a bit too independently."

The Countess's expression turned sceptical.

"She didn't look very upset by it."

"No, I'm too nice. When we're through with the helicopter pilot, then see about getting started on what you're going to do, whatever that is. And you'll have to explain yourself to the others. Goodbye."

"Are you throwing me out?"

"That's exactly what I'm doing. Get out of my office. One of us needs to do some proper work."

CHAPTER 9

The day was productive, and for the first time since Greenland Konrad Simonsen felt as if the inquiry was on course. Even if the visit to Ingrid Thomsen had not gone terribly well, it felt as though a burden had been lifted from him once it was over. He had also talked to his daughter via video streaming for almost half an hour, and that too had put a charge in his run-down batteries. This evening he would pack his clothes and move in with the Countess for a while, which to his own surprise he was looking forward to. He threw himself into his work.

Bit by bit the mosaic of Andreas Falkenborg's life was being pieced together and developed by Malte Borup as a website. The collaboration between the student and the homicide chief was going splendidly. Simonsen had feared he would be left out and not be the one in the middle gathering the threads spider-like, as with the old whiteboard method, but that worry quickly proved to be unfounded. The fact that Malte was never quite sure what was important and should be entered, and what should be filed as background material, possibly cross-referenced, meant that Simonsen had constantly to make decisions about the material, which kept him just as updated as he usually was in these situations. He was also freed from a number of practical tasks and could concentrate on more essential things, mainly prioritising their resources through Pedersen and Troulsen on a regular basis, and deciding which people were assigned which tasks.

Malte Borup briefed him on the timeline they had already established for Andreas Falkenborg.

"Born in 1955 in Hillerød, grew up in Holte north of Copenhagen, primary school with secondary school examination, graduated from Holte High School in 1972, the same year starts at Denmark's Technical College, parentheses nowadays DTU. Graduated as an engineer in 1979 with a good degree and a specialty in audio. Is that okay? There are a lot of fancy words about his final project, do you want those included?"

"No, make a reference, and delete the parentheses about DTU."

"Should I put the particular subject he graduated in into the timeline—that is, in his combined chronology?"

"Yes, excellent, but can you make the details less bold?"

"I'll make them grey."

Malte typed, Simonsen thought, and shortly thereafter their division of labour produced the day's first bonus.

"Malte, there's a gap in his student years in 1977," said Simonsen, staring at the screen. "Is that an error?"

"No, he doesn't pass any examinations then."

"Email or text Arne, I want to know what Falkenborg was doing that year. All of his other exams sit regularly placed like pearls on a string, with excellent results, so something must have happened to him then."

The student typed away.

"I've emailed and texted, and now the overview of his addresses is done."

"Let me hear, but not the addresses, only the cities."

"That would be Holte, that is, at home, until 1973, student residence in Lyngby until 1979, and then four different places in the Copenhagen area until today: Frederiksberg, Østerbro, Dragør, and finally Frederiksberg again. Do you want the years?"

"No, thanks, but write that down in the chronology, and make links to the actual addresses."

"What about summer houses?"

"List those too. Houses, you say… did he have more than one?"

"One down at Præstø that he's had for many years. It's rented out. And then one in Liseleje and one in Sweden, but they were sold again."

"Write down when he buys and sells them and then a note that refers to the addresses."

"Yes, sir. And what about Greenland? Then he still has his apartment in Frederiksberg, the first one that is."

"Make a special page on Greenland, note the date he leaves, and cross-reference."

"I don't know the date, nothing at all has come in from the Countess, but there is a strange thing about one house."

"What's that?"

"In 1986… no, sorry, 1996… in December 1996 he buys the second storey of a house in Rødovre and sells it again in January 1997, which costs him over forty thousand kroner. There are a lot of papers about it already scanned in."

"Hmm, that's interesting. Write *house purchase* and *house sale* on the line, refer to the papers, and then can you make a special page for unanswered questions? At the moment it should read *interruption in studies 1977*? and *house in Rødovre 1996/97*?"

"I'll do that."

"Is there anything about workplaces besides Greenland? I mean, he must have earned money somehow."

"He has his own company, and I have his tax information from 1973, that just came in, so I can tell you what he earned."

"I would really like to know that. Later, when you're not as busy, put the details in a spreadsheet and send me a bar chart for the whole time period."

"I'll make a note of that. Last year he had an income of just under nine hundred thousand kroner."

Simonsen whistled.

"Is that standard or a one-off?"

"It varies a lot. Some years he's above that, other years he earns almost nothing at all."

"Can you see anywhere what kind of company he has?"

"In a little while I should be able to, but there's something else… Poul Troulsen is on his way with a witness. And there's news from Greenland."

Before Simonsen could respond, Troulsen came in escorting a tall, thin man.

"I have something you should hear, Simon. It's quick, but important. Please sit down there."

The latter was directed at the thin man, who bashfully scuttled over and sat down at the little conference table at the back of the office. Simonsen followed suit without raising any objection, although his stomach was starting to tell him that it was time for lunch. Troulsen wasted no time.

"Will you please tell the head of homicide, Chief Inspector Konrad Simonsen, what you told me before?"

Simonsen's long title clearly made the impression Troulsen had hoped. The man looked deferentially at the Chief Inspector and opened his mouth to speak. Then his shoulders slumped a little.

"Yes, but this is a bit personal," he objected. "It's not exactly something I'm proud of."

Simonsen followed the man's gaze towards Malte Borup, lost in his tapping at the keyboard.

"Malte, you can take a break. Go out and charm some of the young constables."

Malte left willingly. He was used to being thrown out according to his boss's whims. Troulsen helped the man along.

"You shouldn't be embarrassed, not at all. You haven't done anything illegal. Besides, we've heard a lot of things in here, and we don't judge people."

The man found his tongue, and this time was pleasingly precise.

"Two years ago I had a suspicion that my wife at the time was having a relationship with another man while I was away travelling. I'm a project manager all over the world and often away from home for months on end. For example, at the moment I'm working on the construction of a new domestic terminal at Dubai Airport. I'm only back in Denmark for three days. Well, I turned to Andreas Falkenborg, someone I knew was an expert in dealing with that type of problem. We had a meeting and agreed on the conditions, which primarily meant that he would conduct surveillance on my wife while I was abroad. His price was sixty thousand kroner per week, with three weeks payable in advance, and it was not open to negotiation. The money was to be paid in cash without receipts or papers of any kind."

Simonsen interjected, "That was a stiff price."

"He's regarded as one of the very best, extremely discreet and very reliable. That type is always expensive. Besides, I had the means. I'm very well paid too."

"You say that Falkenborg is regarded as an expert. How did you find that out?"

The man raised his hands limply and let out a small, sorrowful sigh.

"There are plenty of others with the same problem as I had. I've never been good at attracting women, but just because you're ugly doesn't mean you're stupid."

"There may be something to that, of course, if you think that's the way it is, but how did you come into contact with Andreas Falkenborg? Could you explain that in more detail?"

"I'm part of a group on the Internet, an exclusive group you might say, and I wrote around and enquired. Then I was given his name and telephone number."

"What kind of group is this?"

"People with prestigious positions and major responsibility in their jobs. It's mostly men, and you have to be recommended by two members to be able to join."

"What is the group's purpose?"

"To help each other when we can. It's a kind of virtual lodge."

"Okay, I see. Where did you and Falkenborg meet?"

"At a restaurant in Lyngby Centre."

"How many times?"

"Three in all. An introductory meeting, one where I paid his advance, and a concluding one, where he submitted his results and we settled up."

"Same place all three times?"

"Yes, same place."

"What impression did he make on you?"

"A very pleasant impression, perhaps a trifle…childish is the word, I guess, but very pleasant. As I'm sure you can imagine I was not particularly pleased about the situation I found myself in, and especially during our first meeting I was somewhat nervous, but he was quickly able to get me to relax. That is, he kept the whole thing very subdued, and while I told him about my wife, it was almost as if we were sitting making small talk. I mean, he didn't take any notes or anything. He also explained to me that in the majority of cases where a man has suspicions like mine, they are later proved to be correct, and unfortunately he was right about that. Also during our last meeting, which was not fun for me, he was very honest. The assignment only took sixteen days and he wanted to pay me back a good fourteen thousand kroner, but I wouldn't take it. All in all I was very satisfied with his efforts, and if I were ever to get into a similar situation—heaven forbid—then I would definitely use him again."

Simonsen thought that he wouldn't, unless he wanted his wife ending her days in a plastic bag. He briefly considered delving a little into the childish element in Falkenborg's character, but decided to leave that to Troulsen. He lumbered heavily to his feet and said in farewell, "I'm sincerely happy that you—"

He got no further, as Troulsen said, "There's something else, Simon, that's why we came in right away. I think you should sit down again."

Simonsen did so. The man asked a trifle uncertainly, "It's that thing about the access card, isn't it?"

Troulsen nodded.

"Exactly. It would be helpful if you would also talk about that again."

"Well, at home I had a security system installed, and according to experts it's supposed to be one of the best on the market. It was very expensive too. Sirens, sensors, video monitoring, super-secure access control and central connection to the security company. It was guaranteed to be as safe as a bank. It's not that I'm more afraid of burglaries than other people are, but I have a handful of paintings that are worth a bit of money and if I don't take proper care of them I can't get them insured. So you mustn't believe that I'm paranoid or anything."

"It's not paranoid to protect your valuables."

"No, I don't think so either. Well, at the same time that the security company installed all that hardware, they also changed the locks to my outside doors, so instead of an ordinary key I use a card. You're familiar with the system, of course."

Both of his listeners nodded to show that they were so he continued speaking.

"At our first meeting Andreas Falkenborg asked about getting a card, and I brought it to him the next time."

Simonsen asked, "You barely knew him, but you felt secure giving him free access to your home?"

"Yes. Perhaps that seems naive to you. But bear in mind he would destroy his own business if he helped himself to my things. I mean, you don't easily get people to vouch for you like they did for Falkenborg. It must have taken him years to build up his reputation, and reliability is a necessary prerequisite."

"Did he say what he was going to do at your place?"

"I didn't ask, but it wasn't too hard to guess."

"No, of course. So you gave him an access card?"

"Yes, or I thought I did, but later I found out that it didn't work. I happened to give him a card that was cancelled. I only discovered that when the whole thing was over, and he had returned the card besides."

"Well, that was unfortunate. What did he say about it?"

"Nothing, he didn't comment on it at all, but I'm quite sure that it didn't work because I tried it when I got home."

Simonsen had a hard time seeing the point of this piece of information. He looked at Troulsen, who simply said, "We're almost there."

The witness continued talking.

"The surprising thing was that he gained access without a card. Normally that should be impossible, or so I had been promised. At our last meeting he showed me some film clips and played a couple of conversations concerning my wife…"

He looked imploringly at Simonsen.

"I would rather not relate them in detail."

"There's no reason to."

"No, but then I realised that he must have set up cameras and microphones in at least five different rooms in my house. That is, the living room, the dining room, the kitchen, the bathroom and, well, our bedroom too. But everything had been removed again, I've assured myself of that with two separate inspections."

"How did he show you this material?"

"On a laptop computer, and he only played the beginning. The other parts he was content just to refer to. It was very thoughtful of him to spare me like that."

"Didn't you get the recordings delivered to you?"

"I got the whole thing on a flash drive, and I think it was the only copy. He made a big fuss about the fact that there was no way for me to get an extra one."

"Do you still have the flash drive?"

"I have the drive, but I deleted the contents. I didn't see the point of keeping them."

His listeners agreed and had no other questions.

When Troulsen had shown the witness out he returned to Simonsen's office, where his boss was in the process of methodically munching through a large plate of vegetables. Malte Borup had returned and resumed work. Simonsen complained between mouthfuls, "I've grown used to the taste and basically I don't miss my old diet, but I never get used to the time it takes to eat. You really have to work to feel full and healthy. Interesting witness by the way. It's disturbing to imagine Andreas Falkenborg with a job that primarily consists of eavesdropping on women, but it fits hand in glove with the listening devices found in Catherine Thomsen's apartment. On the other hand it seems strange to me that he didn't remove those. We'll have to look into that in the next few days. Another thing I can't get to add up either is that his annual income, or what he has declared, is quite significant, compared with his requirement for cash payment. That reeks a long way off of under-the-table work. Do you know anything about that?"

"His father was a manufacturer of microphones. Had a factory in Valby. In the early 1970s the operation was restructured from production to importing and distribution, still of microphones. Then his father died in a shooting accident in 1983. That is, while Andreas Falkenborg was in Greenland. Mother and son continued the operation, but little by little the product range was changed to what can best be described as amateur spy equipment. They served as wholesalers and sold to mail order companies, later on the Internet. It's a more or less suspect enterprise where you can buy everything you need to spy on your neighbour or perhaps have a long look through his daughter's bedroom window.

"The business was not very big; in that period there were from three to ten employees, all of whom were fired in 1992 when Falkenborg's mother died and he became sole owner. Currently he doesn't have anything other than a VAT number and presumably a customer database. At the present time I don't know more than that, but I have a couple of men on the case, and hopefully they will produce a more detailed account before the day is through."

Troulsen looked at Simonsen, who was diligently chewing his cud and thereby limited to non-verbal communication.

"Unfortunately, I also have an unpleasant announcement to make," continued Troulsen.

His boss twirled a finger in the air, which Troulsen had no difficulty interpreting.

"The listening devices that were found at Catherine Thomsen's are gone, or more exactly at the moment no one can find them, and the only thing we have in writing is a meaningless note that mentions *finding of listening devices*. That is, no details whatsoever. They are searching high and low in the archive, but no one knows whether they'll find it."

"Damn it!"

"Yes, it's the pits. If we can't get him solidly connected to the other murder, then it's even more doubtful we can put together something that will hold up in court. Greenland is a long time ago, and I seriously doubt we'll arrive at anything there that will carry an indictment. I also have to admit that I would like to confirm that Falkenborg at least knew Catherine Thomsen, mainly for my own peace of mind. Even though I'm quite convinced we are only searching for one killer, I still am not quite certain Falkenborg is our man, despite his business and the listening devices in the apartment. This time we really have to get it right. I feel bad when I think about Carl Henning Thomsen, but I don't need to tell you that."

Simonsen continued chewing without showing any desire to corroborate this. His relationship to Troulsen was mainly professional, a fact he did not wish to change, and as Troulsen had nothing more to say, he went on his way.

During the course of the afternoon one small breakthrough followed another, while the gaps in the Homicide Division's knowledge of Andreas Falkenborg's life became smaller and smaller. Simonsen commandeered Malte Borup as if the student were an extended version of the computer he controlled so easily.

"Malte, you entered his applications to Greenland a couple of hours ago. Look those up and tell me when they were sent."

A couple of clicks later came the answer.

"You mean his applications to Greenland Contractors?"

"Yes."

"Okay, I have them here. Do you want all the dates? There are seven applications. Apparently he applied for any available position."

"No, just give me the first one."

"It's dated the eleventh of March, 1982, and it was for a position as a receptionist."

"Good. And when did Maryann Nygaard go to Greenland? Do you have that date anywhere?"

"She is employed as of the fourth of March, 1982. I don't know when exactly she goes up there."

"Direct from her position at the nursing home?"

"Yes, if you mean that she didn't have another job in the meantime, but not all the case files on her have been digitised."

"I'm aware of that. Get Pauline to find out more about Falkenborg's helicopter course. It seems like a very short time to get his pilot's licence. Has anything arrived yet from the Jehovah's Witnesses?"

"No, but there's another thing. Do you want to hear it?"

"Definitely."

"It seems that Carl Henning Thomsen—you know who I mean?"

Simonsen sighed and forced himself to answer calmly.

"Absolutely. What about him?"

"Carl Henning Thomsen apparently did some moving for Andreas Falkenborg."

"Apparently?"

"I can't really figure out what they mean. Well, wait a moment…now I see. Carl Henning Thomsen had a transfer from a warehouse in Herlev to Bækkevang 19 in Rødovre, but Bækkevang 19 doesn't even exist, the road only goes to 17. The next house in the row, which should have been number 19, is a corner house with an address on Bakkehøjvej 45, which Bækkevang runs into."

"The half of the duplex that Andreas Falkenborg bought and sold again right away?"

"Yes."

"Give me the date of the purchase and also the date Catherine Thomsen disappeared."

"His share of the house was bought on the fourth of December, 1996; Catherine Thomsen disappeared on the fifth of April, 1997."

"Get Arne and the Countess in here."

Simonsen took advantage of the wait to study the picture of Andreas Falkenborg he had received half an hour ago and immediately put up on his bulletin board. An amiable man in his early fifties smiled back at him. There was something anonymous about his face, and Simonsen thought that it could serve as representative of the general Danish public in any advertisement.

Pedersen was the first to arrive; he brought positive news with him and was in a good mood besides.

"We've found a witness who makes a link between Falkenborg and Catherine Thomsen more than probable, actually a double witness, namely a Jehovah's Witness witness."

The witticism was lost on Simonsen, and the Countess, who had just come in, did not seem inclined to joke either. Pedersen hurried on.

"There is a man who possibly partnered Catherine Thomsen in the movement's door-to-door campaign, and he is quite sure that he has spoken with Andreas Falkenborg. Not because he remembers his face but the officers spoke to him in the stairwell of the apartment block where Falkenborg lived at that time, and he clearly recalls seeing a picture hanging on the wall outside the main door—a picture he looked at for a long time while his partner spoke with the inhabitants of the apartment. Unfortunately he is not equally certain who his partner was that day. It was probably Catherine Thomsen, but he is not completely sure."

The Countess asked in wonder, "Who hangs pictures in stairwells?"

"It's not really a picture but a kind of decoration. Its purpose was to cover a window into a bathroom, and don't bother asking me why such a window was even made because I don't know. The picture depicts a horse, by the way. One of the men took a photo of it. He's the meticulous sort."

"Is it possible that the other potential Jehovah's Witness partners can confirm that they haven't visited the place? I mean, so that Catherine Thomsen is the only possibility?"

"That's being worked on, but bear in mind that when you do outreach you visit a good number of addresses every day. And the episode is over ten years ago."

"What about a date?"

"Not exact, but it would have been within the first three weeks of June, 1996, and he is sure of that."

"That is, over nine months before she was killed?"

"Yes, that must be right."

The Countess shuddered.

"But tell me something," Simonsen continued. "We've had nothing so far on domestic partners, lovers, men, women, in-between, anything at all?"

Pedersen shook his head.

"I haven't run into anything along those lines, and he's always lived alone. Officially in any event."

The Countess was on the same track.

"Nothing from me either. At the base he was well liked, helpful but not particularly social, and had no lovers that we know of. Some perceived him as slightly eccentric, but he wasn't the only one, and no one I've talked to had anything against him. All in all I can't contribute much about Andreas Falkenborg, but there were around nine hundred people at the base, and they were constantly being replaced, so I'm not even close to having exhausted witness possibilities. With respect to Maryann Nygaard it's a little easier because she was a woman. There were so few of them that most remember her, mostly thanks to her appearance. But is it relevant to follow that trail further? Your call, Simon."

Simonsen hummed absent-mindedly, which after a brief hesitation the Countess interpreted as encouragement for her to continue speaking. To give them an overview she started describing life at the Søndre Strømfjord base during the early eighties. Simonsen tuned out her words and observed her blouse. He thought that it was definitely bought at an ultra-expensive designer boutique, the sort that offered "collections" and "diffusion lines". It was made of silk, patterned in light green and brown, and reminded him of autumn beech trees. His lapse in concentration was vaguely worrying. He pinched himself on the arm and recovered in time to answer her, though he had only heard half of her report.

The Countess asked, "What do you think? Shall we continue with them tomorrow? And should it be both him and her? That is, Falkenborg as well as Maryann Nygaard?"

"No, we'll drop the base for the time being. There's not much there, and we can always go back to it if things change."

"Okay, that's what we'll do."

Perhaps there was a slight hesitation in her voice, perhaps it was because he had so many years' practice in reading other people, or perhaps it was because she had gained his permission to operate for a couple of days on her own. In any event, he thought it over and changed his mind.

"Do I understand correctly that you would like to dig a little deeper?"

If she was surprised by his intuition, she did not show it.

"It's not something I can make an argument for, but one witness says that Maryann Nygaard's behaviour changed the two or three weeks before she was murdered. Among other things she stayed away from parties and gatherings and that sort of thing, which she definitely had not done before. It's aroused my curiosity, though as I said it's probably not something we can use."

"How will you investigate this more closely? Do you have a source?"

"I may have a line on a friend of hers, I'll know tomorrow."

"Okay, take a couple more days and see what emerges. Meanwhile let's concentrate on some key dates. We have reason to assume that Andreas Falkenborg met Maryann Nygaard for the first time in a nursing home where his grandmother lived. This may have been in January or February 1982. Not until September the thirteenth, 1983, that is more than a year and a half later, does he murder her after having pursued her all the way to Greenland. The pattern is just as sinister in relation to Catherine Thomsen. They met by chance in June of 1996, and her murder happened about nine months later. Presumably after his having made enormous efforts to get her father's fingerprints on a plastic bag, which—"

Simonsen got no further than that. He was interrupted by a pale-faced Pauline Berg, who came rushing into his office without knocking. In her hand she held a photograph of a young woman—a young woman who resembled Maryann Nygaard. Or Catherine Thomsen. But was neither of them.

CHAPTER 10

When the work day was over, Konrad Simonsen sometimes treated them to beer—which did not happen often, so was greatly appreciated when it did.

This took place by established custom at Copenhagen's Bodega, an unpretentious bar opposite Glyptoteket that was mostly patronised by police officers. The Countess, Arne Pedersen and Poul Troulsen sat down at the same table as their boss. Their remaining colleagues found other places and did not disturb them, except for occasionally raising glasses towards their table. The establishment was half full, the mood upbeat without excessive hilarity, with muted pop classics playing and a quick-witted bartender who charmed everyone with his contagious smile. Shortly after they'd sat down Pauline Berg joined them. She had been out on an unexplained errand and had returned with a bag from Illum, which despite the Countess's inquisitive gaze she shoved under her chair. Everyone made toasts in draft beer, and Simonsen said a few predictable things about good work that no one heard. Then the conversation flowed. "God knows how many people he's killed! Maybe we've only seen the tip of the iceberg," said Pauline Berg, disregarding the convention of not mixing details of an investigation with a social gathering.

Troulsen immediately picked up on this remark.

"There may be a lot, worse luck. It's not enough to review our own lists of missing persons. There may be tourists who never returned home or he may have murdered on his own holidays, not to mention that young women with black hair are perhaps only one of his preferences. Maybe he also has an eye for red-haired boys—who the hell knows? I hope you've got him nicely contained, boss, until we're ready to put him in the hole."

Simonsen answered gruffly, "I'm taking good care of him with the resources I have."

"Maybe those can be extended a little in this case. Or else use our pension fund. Just so long as he isn't running around loose."

"The most unpleasant thing is that he looks so ordinary. And then of course the faces of those girls in the bags…What a way to die! There should be the death penalty for such a psychopath."

It was Pauline speaking again.

Troulsen nodded agreement. The Countess shook her head, clear about where this was headed. "And summary trial, I assume? And royal permission for painful interrogation, like in the old days? I understand that sort of thing is popular with our major ally at the moment."

It was like pushing a button, and she knew it. Pedersen shook his head, and Troulsen replied sharply, "We didn't have three thousand of our countrymen murdered at a stroke. To be honest, I can well understand why many Americans aren't too concerned about the legal niceties where those behind the massacre are concerned."

"Except what you call legal niceties, I call human rights."

Pauline appealed to the Countess.

"I don't follow you. What are you talking about?"

"We're talking about torture, my friend. Or more specifically the US rendition programme, where in the best management style the torments are outsourced to executioners all around the world. Mistreatment by proxy, please. And don't believe that Denmark isn't involved. Kastrup Airport has been visited many times by the torture jet, but it's poor political form to point that out. For your information, torture affects alleged, but never convicted, terrorists."

Troulsen shrugged his shoulders provocatively.

"If it saves innocent lives, I'm not one to lose sleep over it."

Simonsen entered the fray.

"I know how many witches were burned in Denmark in the sixteenth and seventeenth centuries—there were about a thousand—and the interesting thing is that almost all of them were guilty, because by far the majority confessed their crimes after being on the rack for a while. The truth is that torture, besides being deeply repulsive, is also counterproductive. You simply can't rely on the results of such interrogation."

Pedersen was the first to finish his beer. The discussion was about to become a trifle too heated for his taste. To be conciliatory he said to the Countess and Simonsen, "You always make it sound so easy, and sometimes I wish I had your sense of ethics or whatever it's called. But I also know that if someone threatened my family, I would damn well not shrink from anything."

He glanced at his watch and added, "I'll buy the next round and then I'm heading home."

CHAPTER 11

It was difficult to trace the woman who went by the nickname "Six Feet of Love" twenty-five years before at the American military base at Søndre Strømfjord in Greenland. And when, ironically, after many twists and turns, the Countess finally did find the woman's real name, it turned out that she had emailed the Homicide Division two days earlier, because she thought she had information about Maryann Nygaard that might interest the police. The email included the data it had taken the Countess hours to find out a different way. The woman's name was Allinna Holmsgaard, and the nurse Pauline Berg had interviewed in the car between Roskilde and Viby was not far off in her prediction that the woman's career probably had something to do with books. Allinna Holmsgaard was Professor of Rhetoric at the University of Copenhagen.

The Countess responded to the email and tried the listed cell phone number a few times, but without success. A call to the Institute for Media, Perception and Communication, which she did not expect much from as the autumn term had not yet started, produced unexpected dividends. A friendly secretary said that the professor was at work, but she did not know exactly where. The building was on Njalsgade at the Iceland Wharf, which as the crow flies was less than a kilometre from Police Headquarters and thus within acceptable walking distance—a good excuse for the Countess to enjoy the summer weather, and a suitable way to prove to herself that she could walk where she wanted, regardless of whoever she risked running into.

The city smiled at her, and she smiled back. Until a woman walking towards her with a pushchair made her turn her back to the street and inspect a random shop window until the danger had passed. One wheel squeaked, which irritated her. How hard was it just to put a few drops of oil in the hub, so other people were not disturbed? She saw her reflection in the shop window and felt ugly. Thickset, wrinkled, fifty in a few years. Soon it would be almost two years since she'd last slept with a man. She'd been invited to a confirmation ceremony and could not decline, although her ex-husband and his live-in were also coming. She had hired an escort; the thought of going to the party alone had been unbearable. Later she paid him to take a week-long vacation with her, which she was not exactly proud of afterwards. It had been divine at night and catastrophic during the day. The man proved to be as self-centred as he was untalented at anything but sex, which was saying a lot. Now she had a man again—in her house in any event. The rest would come eventually, little by little. She turned, looked around carefully and walked on.

Allinna Holmsgaard had aged gracefully; she was in her midforties and still lovely. A tall woman with a lightly lined face and graceful movements, standing by the board while she alternately wrote and gestured. The Countess had quietly slipped into the classroom where the witness was teaching, and received a few minutes of free coaching plus time to observe the professor as well as her students. There were only five of them in the class, all young women, sitting in the front row taking notes on their laptops. One woman was recognisable as a TV host and another as a politician. When Allinna Holmsgaard caught sight of the visitor she interrupted her teaching and went up to the Countess, who briefly introduced herself. The professor looked her over from head to toe and said, "Do you have any ID?"

The Countess found her identification card and showed it to her. Allinna Holmsgaard studied it carefully, after which she said apologetically, "Sorry, but for a moment I suspected you were from the press. A couple of journalists have called. It was almost impossible to get rid of them."

"It's quite all right. Actually I ought to show my ID routinely."

The other woman nodded her acceptance of this.

"I assume that it is about Maryann?"

"Yes, it is. Do you have time to speak?"

"I will very soon. What about you, are you in a hurry?"

"Not particularly."

"Do you know Kulturhuset down on Bryggen?"

"Yes, very well."

"Why don't we meet down there when I'm through here? As I said, it won't be very long. There's no reason to stay inside on a day like this."

Half an hour later the two women were sitting on a bench at Gaswerkshavnen with a view over Kalvebod Brygge. The distorted reflection of a glass facade caught the sun at an unfortunate angle and momentarily blinded them. From time to time one of the broad canal excursion barges passed; then they had to smile and wave, while tourists from far and near photographed them for their scrapbooks, and the tour guide's school English interrupted their conversation. The two women hit it off from the start. For instance, even when they were ordering something to drink, they both agreed that it was too early in the day for white wine, after which they each ordered a glass anyway. They talked about architecture; it was a difficult subject to avoid when they were sitting where they were, and they could have talked for a long time about everything under the sun if the situation had been different. They both felt that way. The Countess took hold of herself first; she was in the midst of a murder investigation after all.

"Were you and Maryann Nygaard friends in Greenland?"

"We were, yes. Very close. It hit me hard when she died, or disappeared rather, but we knew perfectly well what that meant. For a long time I hoped against all the odds that she would be found alive, even though deep down I knew that wouldn't happen."

"But you didn't suspect she was the victim of a crime?"

"Absolutely not. It came as a shock when I read that, and I'm still pretty upset. It's disgusting to think about, but hard not to."

"Yes, unfortunately it is disgusting. In your email you said you have information that you think might interest us. Would you like to tell me about it?"

Allinna Holmsgaard drummed her fingers on the table. Her nails were cut short, but nevertheless the sound irritated the Countess.

"When I sent the email, I meant it. But after thinking things through I'm not so sure how important it is."

"Let me decide."

"So, you do know that Maryann was pregnant when she…disappeared."

Just this morning the Countess had read about the pregnancy in the autopsy report. It had surprised her and raised a few questions. She said, "We know that, and it makes us wonder a little."

"Why is it so strange?"

The Countess could have bitten out her own tongue. Allinna Holmsgaard did not need to know anything about the tampon, but now the revelation was hard to avoid. The Countess vainly tried an evasive manoeuvre.

"Things don't work that way between us. I ask, you answer. Not the other way around. Tell me about…"

The sentence faded out, the professor had guessed the reason for the Countess's surprise. The finger drumming stopped, and she said in distress, "Maryann's pregnancy was not proceeding normally. She was bleeding, although she shouldn't have been, and was flown to Holsteinsborg for a closer examination but there was nothing wrong. She was menstruating when she died, is that it?"

"Yes, that's how it was. Do you know the child's father?"

"No, I don't. That is what I thought might interest you. You see, the whole thing was very mysterious, almost cloak and dagger, and Maryann did not want to come out with it when she finally found out. His name, that is."

"Maybe you should start from the beginning."

"Yes, of course. Maryann got pregnant about ten weeks before she died. It was by a geologist who was staying at the base for a few days while he waited for good weather, so he could continue on to Thule. They fell in love, just like that, like you read about in romance novels. Or in any event, Maryann did. I have my doubts about what it was like in reality for him. His name was Steen Hansen, he maintained, but that was a lie—"

The name struck the Countess like a blow from a hammer. Her jaw dropped and then her glass too. The stem broke, and wine spilled over the table. Allinna Holmsgaard asked worriedly, "What's the matter? Are you all right?"

The Countess pulled herself together. With all her strength she tried to repress the dry female voice that was suddenly echoing in her head. *Hold on to Steen Hansen, Baroness. Hold on to Steen Hansen, Baroness.* The psychic's words, and even on the phone they had been unnerving. Now it was much worse.

"No, it's nothing, just go on."

"So, I did not find out that the name was false until later, but there were other strange things about him…things that didn't seem right. I remember that we women said that we had never seen such a well-dressed geologist. They usually resemble something they dug up. It was unusual besides that the Americans provided an aircraft for him alone when the weather cleared up. We speculated like that without really getting into it very deeply. There were always all sorts of stories in circulation, it was a way to pass the time."

She poured a little water in her empty wine glass and drank it.

"But then Maryann found out that she was pregnant, three or four weeks after he had left, and abortion was ruled out. She'd had an abortion once before, and mentally she couldn't take it. So she wrote a letter to the father. She did not have his address, only his name, she thought, so she addressed the letter to GGS, where he said he came from."

"GGS?"

"Greenland's Geological Surveys, it was under the Greenland Ministry at the time. The department was housed on Øster

94

Voldgade along with the other geological institutions. Today GGS has merged with its Danish sister organisation. Well, the letter was returned, no one knew any Steen Hansen apparently. Maryann was down in the dumps for a couple of days, but then she thought of writing to the base commander at Thule. That was not normally something you did, but on the other hand, what else could she do? She explained the situation and asked that he forward her letter to Steen Hansen, if he could. She also sent a picture of him. It was just a snapshot, but all in all her persistence paid off because two weeks later Steen called her. Yes, he was married and had a child, the jerk, but he had backbone enough to contact her."

"Why didn't she want to tell you his real name?"

"I don't know, she didn't want to say. I recall that it irritated me. We also nagged her about that, but there was no getting her to budge. And then she disappeared, of course, and after that I had a really bad conscience because maybe she had gone away by choice, if you understand."

The Countess understood only too well.

"Still, for a long time I hoped as I said that she would come back. Things did not really add up because she was simply not that depressed. She withdrew into herself, but two days before her trip to the ice cap we talked about baby clothes and that sort of thing. But that's really all I wanted to tell you, and I can't see how it will help you very much."

"Maybe it will, maybe not. This fake Steen Hansen, what did he look like?"

"Very ordinary. Light hair, crew-cut, not that tall, in his early thirties. The truth is, I don't really remember him. I only spoke to him a few times."

"Any distinguishing features?"

"Not that I remember, apart from his hair that is. I mean, he was probably the only Danish man who had such short hair. All the others at that time had long hair, at least below the ears. Oh, yes, and… there was actually one other thing about him, now I remember it. He talked in an unnaturally high voice like a girl's, a falsetto it's called. Someone called him the Castrato… well, as a nickname, that is. Everyone got a nickname, even after a few days, and…"

The Countess tuned out the professor's words for a moment. She had never before known a witness, twice within a minute, give her information that almost made her fall off her chair. This time, however, she subdued her reaction and admonished herself that the lead about a voice was subject to interpretation and had to be backed up, and that could be damned hard to do. She concentrated again on the conversation.

"Is there anything else you know about him?"

"Well, he gave her his cap, but that probably doesn't have any great significance."

"Just tell me."

Allinna squinted briefly and then said serenely, "Well, he had one of those knitted caps with interlaced fleur-de-lis in different colours. His mother had made it for him, he said, but that was definitely not true because there was a manufacturer's tag inside. Well, whatever, Maryann loved that cap, and so he gave it to her."

"As a memento?"

"Yes, maybe. She was very happy about it anyway. Personally I thought it was hideous, too many colours in it. I recall that once she was standing in front of a mirror with it on, and I must have commented on it. And then she said something along the lines of it probably could attract a few males if ever she was short of money for rent. Well, that was only in jest, but she wore it a lot, and I know that she had it on when she disappeared because I brooded about that for days afterwards. For me it made her disappearance even sadder, though that doesn't make any real sense."

The Countess nodded; she had seen the cap herself. It was lying beside Maryann Nygaard's corpse, and quite involuntarily she thought that Allinna Holmsgaard had been right—it really wasn't very pretty. She dropped the subject and asked instead, "And you have no idea why he used a false name?"

"No, unfortunately. Maryann maintained that he really *was* a geologist, and he was there to negotiate some sensitive concession agreements with the Americans on extraction of underground minerals. At first that didn't sound completely off the wall. There were a number of disagreements between Danish and Greenlandic atomic power opponents on the one hand and GGS and Risø on the other. This visit allegedly concerned extraction of uranium and perhaps thorium from the Kvane field in Narsaq, and the subject was sensitive to say the least, but…well, it wasn't logical. I mean, what was he doing in Thule in that case? The American Air Force was not involved in mining operations, and Thule Airbase is almost two thousand kilometres from Narsaq."

"So you didn't believe that?"

"Not really, but I didn't say anything about it. In 1983 the Cold War was still being conducted, so it wasn't so strange if there were things going on that the public shouldn't know about."

"You may be right about that. Tell me, the picture of the man you mentioned, what should I do if I really want to see it?"

Allinna Holmsgaard thought about it, then she threw out her arms regretfully.

"It won't be easy. I can't even remember who Maryann got it from."

The Countess waited, there was more to come.

"You do understand that he had left for home a long time before Maryann died?"

"Completely, but I would still like to see his picture."

"Maybe there is a chance, although it's slight. Do you know Knud Rasmussen's House?"

"No, unfortunately not."

"It's a museum in North Zealand, Gribskov Municipality, I think. The former museum director collected personal photos from both bases. It was a kind of hobby for him. I have also sent him copies of my own pictures."

"This sounds like a real uphill climb, especially since I don't know what Hansen looks like. Can I convince you to assist me a little?"

The Countess waited patiently while Allinna Holmsgaard considered. Finally she said, "Tomorrow my husband and I are leaving for Zurich. This trip has been planned for a long time, and I would be loath to cancel or postpone it. On the other hand I owe Maryann, and society for that matter. Only you can decide if it it's important enough for me to cancel."

It was tempting, but the Countess controlled herself.

"No, go on holiday, it's not that important."

"I'm happy to hear that, but I can easily assist you over the Internet. If I send you an email this evening about the exact period of time when our friend was at Søndre Strømfjord then there won't be very many pictures to investigate, if there even are any…"

Together they went over the details. When it was decided, the Countess had only one thing left to do. From her bag she took a picture of Andreas Falkenborg in 1983, and set it in front of the professor.

"Do you recognise him?"

"Yes, it's Pronto, of course, that childish soul. What do you want to know about… oh, no…"

The Countess questioned her closely but Allinna Holmsgaard could not contribute anything groundbreaking.

CHAPTER 12

While the Countess was enjoying her white wine at Islands Brygge, her immediate associates in Homicide were en route in two cars to South Zealand. Konrad Simonsen and Poul Troulsen took the lead, with the older man at the wheel. Following right behind them were Arne Pedersen and Pauline Berg. Troulsen squinted out and looked distrustfully at the summer weather, which already by late morning was hot and sunny, then glanced at his boss in the passenger seat, reading a memorandum.

"I don't understand how you can stand it, Simon. The sweat is running off me even though I only have a T-shirt on, and you're sitting there in a jacket as if the heat doesn't bother you in the least. Have you heard the weather forecast?"

Simonsen looked up briefly and observed his colleague, not without envy. Despite his age there was not much surplus fat on Troulsen's well-trained body, and the muscles of his upper arms bulged nicely out of the sleeves of his T-shirt. A faded pin-up girl, from the days when Nyhavn was raunchy, preened on his forearm. Simonsen's own temperature regulation varied more than it should. Sometimes he sweated when there was no reason to; other times, like now, he almost didn't sweat at all. Both situations were a consequence of his diabetes. He said teasingly, "Yes, it's going to be hot."

Troulsen dropped the subject with a sigh and said instead, "Yesterday the wife and I babysat the grandchildren and I didn't have a minute to spare, so unfortunately I don't really have a good grasp of what we're doing right now. I was wondering if you would care to give me a run-through."

Simonsen consented; the alternative was that they change roles so that he drove while Troulsen read, and he had no desire for that. Besides, he could hardly reproach the man for having a personal life. Normally he was well prepared, and rarely complained about his hours.

"Where should I start?"

"Preferably from the beginning."

"Okay. Annie Lindberg Hansson, age twenty-four, from Jungshoved on Præstø, disappeared on the fifth of October, 1990. She worked at an office in Vordingborg, from where she took the bus in the evening towards Præstø and got off at her usual stop four kilometres from home. Her bicycle was waiting for her on the hard shoulder. Since then no one has seen her. The reason that she is interesting to us now is her appearance. Have you seen her picture?"

"Yes, I got that far. She resembles Maryann Nygaard and Catherine Thomsen."

"She does, yes. Same black hair, same brown eyes, body build and pretty face with fine features and high cheekbones."

"And Andreas Falkenborg lived in the area at the time she disappeared?"

"In August 1990 he bought a summer house in Tjørnehoved, which is less than five kilometres from Annie Lindberg Hansson's home, and you must allow for the fact that this is a sparsely populated area, so five kilometres is not that much, if you see what I mean. Besides, the area is not a typical place at all for a summer house."

"How did she disappear?"

"Basically as I told you. There's not much more to say. She got off the bus at eight o'clock in the evening, and since then she's been missing."

"What about her bicycle?"

"Never found, but if you stop interrogating me, I'll tell you about the circumstances at my own pace. I do believe I'm capable of covering all the essentials."

"Sorry, it's in my genes, as you know. And then the heat—it's almost unbearable."

Simonsen's sympathy was lukewarm, he had his own concerns. A couple of sores on his ankles were itching like hell, small, bright red blotches that would not heal, and made him feel ridiculous, almost embarrassed. In contrast the morning's usual round of sweating had not materialised, probably due to the nutritious breakfast the Countess had served him. All in all moving to Søllerød had worked out beyond his expectations. He had most of the second storey in the big house to himself. The Countess helped him unpack, showed him around, insisted on taking care of the practicalities, and not least—the awkward episodes he had feared in advance would arise between them had quickly faded into quiet cosiness, yes, even laughter. He enjoyed it, not least being fussed over a little. It had been a long time since he'd really laughed, and it had also been a long time since he'd slept so well. Not until now in the car did regret for his past mistakes around the murder of Catherine Thomsen gnaw its way in again and with that the longing for a cigarette. He leaned over to scratch his sores, thought better of it, and concentrated on updating Poul Troulsen.

"Annie Lindberg Hansson lived with her father, who is a bit of a social case, reading between the lines, but we'll soon find that out. Their house is isolated, out by Jungshoved Church, a place where there's not much besides sheep, water, and then the church and Lindberg Hansson's little homestead. This meant that Annie had to bike alone most of the way home from where she got off the bus, and you can hardly imagine a more perfect route on which to assault a young girl: dark, deserted, and a bicycle light you can see from far off."

"I'm liking this case less and less."

"We don't get paid to enjoy ourselves. Well, where was I? Yes, that evening the father reported his daughter missing and again the next morning. A search was put out for her, but the police efforts were pretty half-hearted, and I think I'm being kind saying that."

"Why? Didn't they believe him?"

"Keep quiet now, damn it, you're being a pain! So, everyone expected that the daughter would soon show up again, presumably in Copenhagen. She and her father had had some heated discussions before she disappeared, because she wanted to move to the city and get ahead—or perhaps more precisely get started—with her life. He on the other hand thought that she had a duty to remain living there and more or less take care of him, since his wife had died a year before. For a long time therefore the authorities assumed that she had settled the disagreement in her own way by abandoning him, and that she would later make herself known again when she was established and her father had grown used to the idea. Even though the father regularly visited the police in both Næstved and in Præstø, for a long time he was more or less ignored and the case was correspondingly downplayed."

"That really makes me angry, but probably only because I know what I do. By far the majority of young people who disappear turn up again at some stage or another."

"Yes, and that's a good thing, but Annie Lindberg Hansson never showed up. Still no one really believed there'd been a crime, but were more inclined to think she had cut the bonds to her childhood home and was maybe living in the city or else abroad somewhere."

"Then we can only hope that's what she's doing."

"Do you believe that yourself?"

"No, unfortunately not. Not since I've seen her and know that Andreas Falkenborg was in the area. God knows whether he bought that summer house in Tjørnehoved before or after he met her."

"That's one of the things we'll try to find out today, but if I had to guess, I'd say *after*. That would fall neatly in line with the other murders, where he is obviously prepared to reorganise his entire existence to position himself for his misdeeds. He displays a strange combination of extremely goal-oriented activity once he has met his victims, while he does nothing actively to find—how shall I put it?—appropriate candidates. We'll have to bring in a psychologist to analyse this."

Poul Troulsen thought a while then said tentatively, "If women don't have exactly the right appearance and the right age, he's harmless. If on the other hand they are black-haired, slender and pretty in a very specific way, then he kills them?"

"It undeniably looks that way, but as I said, we'll have to call in a psychologist."

"It will make me very happy to turn him over to the correctional system."

"You'll have to get past a judge and presumably a jury first. And it will probably be Nykøbing Zealand secure prison, when we get to that point."

"He's cost us two resignations from the force over the Thomsen affair—and don't misunderstand me, I know full well that the murders, whether there are two or three of them, are much, much worse—but I can't help being angry with him about that too. As far as I'm concerned I wasn't doing too well either when I realised the truth, and I was only peripherally involved in the Stevns case. Even so I couldn't attend your review on Monday."

"I was very close to being the third to resign, you know that, don't you?"

"Yes, I knew, and this was just my clumsy way of asking how you're doing now?"

"If he has killed someone after Catherine Thomsen, then I don't know…I almost don't dare think about it, but otherwise I guess it is what it is."

Troulsen looked at his boss with disapproval. The reply did not invite further discussion, so he concentrated on his driving. Simonsen immersed himself in his papers again.

An hour later they were nearly at their destination. Poul Troulsen honked briefly at Arne Pedersen and Pauline Berg, as he turned left and drove toward Jungshoved while his colleagues' car continued on the highway. A gentle rural landscape unfolded before them with a view over Bøgestrømmen, the crooked stream between Zealand and Møn. Five minutes later they stopped in front of a small homestead close to Jungshoved Church, all the way out on the promontory.

At the top of the driveway the two men stopped and looked around. The house consisted of two low, white-plastered wings, which created a contrast to the black-tarred concrete tiles of the roof. The small garden was overgrown, with a couple of beautiful old fruit trees and a weed-infested terrace stretching from the farmhouse out to the lawn, while a high beech hedge behind hid the view to the church. Simonsen recalled the boys' books of his childhood, where Svend Poulsen Gønge's guerillas had numerous encounters with the Swedes at this very Jungshoved, without his really knowing whether this was fiction or Danish history. Troulsen commented soberly, "It was probably sold off by the church at one time."

At the house they were met by a man in his sixties, who opened his door without a word and waved his arm to invite them in. His appearance was neglected; his face looked older than it should, his eyes shiny, almost runny, and his clothing in a state that a second-hand shop could not even give away. The room they were led into was low-ceilinged and dark despite the radiant sunshine, and it took a little time before the eyes of the two officers grew accustomed to the dim light. The furniture was sparse and worn, but not casually arranged and had originally been expensive.

The man gestured to them to sit on a couch with a sturdy, low oak table before them while he sat down in an armchair opposite. He had made tea for them and poured without asking. They thanked him and drank. Simonsen thought that the tea tasted surprisingly good. At one end of the table were two photographs, which evidently had been placed there for the occasion. The first showed a picture of a healthy little troll in a snowsuit, sitting on a swing being pushed by her father while she showed off for the camera like a prima donna. The second showed a lanky, thirteen-year-old girl in a white skirt, balancing awkwardly in high-heeled shoes in front of a church that was not the neighbouring building. The frames were gilded and hideous. The man followed the direction of Simonsen's gaze, and said, "Every morning when I wake up I think about her, and every night I cry myself to sleep. I miss her indescribably. She was the only real blessing in my life. Yes, I have brought her out because I think she has a right to be here."

"It's appropriate."

"Yes, very appropriate. It's my home, after all, and I decide which pictures will be displayed in it."

Simonsen said quietly, "We have come to find out what happened to your daughter."

The man took out a dingy handkerchief and dabbed his eyes.

"You believe that she was killed like the two girls in the papers, right?"

"Why do you think that?"

"Because she resembled them, obviously. I have eyes in my head."

"Yes, we are afraid that she was killed, although we don't know anything specific at the present time."

"I've known all along that she was dead, but I hope she didn't end up like them."

"We don't either, and you mustn't believe everything you read in the newspapers."

A small ray of hope was ignited in the man, they could hear it in his voice.

"So it's not really true. I mean, all those horrible things about adhesive tape and plastic bags over their heads?"

Both detectives cursed the tabloids for wallowing in macabre details on page after page, but unfortunately depicting the murders quite correctly. Annie Lindberg Hansson's father was now paying the price for the previous day's sales figures. He and others like him.

"Well, sadly, those things are not wrong, but bear in mind that we know nothing about what happened to your daughter."

The words bounced off him disregarded. The man crumpled a little.

"What do you want from me?"

"First and foremost, to tell us about the day your daughter didn't come home."

He did that, painfully and weighed down with grief, so his two listeners almost felt embarrassed to admit that he had not told them anything they did not already know. When he was done, Troulsen asked as carefully as he could, "You and your daughter argued a bit in the months before she disappeared."

"Yes, I was the one who was unreasonable. I simply could not cope with her leaving me. It was selfish, I can see that now, but not then."

"Did she plan to move to Copenhagen?"

"Yes, she really wanted an education, and I also believe she wanted to be with others her own age. There wasn't much of that out here."

"She was a pretty girl, what about boyfriends or that sort of thing?"

"Not many, I think, but that was not something she shared with me."

"Because you were jealous?"

"I'm sure I would have been."

"Did she want to move to Copenhagen together with a boyfriend?"

"I don't believe so. No, she wasn't planning that."

"Did she have any connections with Copenhagen?"

"She had an aunt there."

"Whom she visited?"

"Occasionally, not that often."

"Where did the aunt live?"

"Well, in Copenhagen. That's what we're talking about."

"I was thinking more about where in Copenhagen. Do you have her address?"

"Platanvej, I can't remember the number, but I can find it if it's important."

Troulsen looked at Simonsen, who shook his head. He let the thread fall.

"You say that she wanted to get an education. What kind of education?"

"Cosmetologist, but she was going to earn money first to pay for school, so she was applying for jobs there."

"What kind of jobs?"

"Anything at all. She went for two interviews, but didn't get either of them. I hoped every time that they wouldn't hire her. It's unbearable to think about today."

"Do you know the companies where she got an interview?"

"One was at Irma's headquarters. The other I can't remember…it was a smaller place, exactly where I've forgotten. But I've saved her papers, and I think it's there. Is it significant?"

"Maybe. In any event we would be pleased if you'd look."

He got up without further encouragement and left the room. Soon after that they could hear him in the attic. He had left the handkerchief lying on the chair. Simonsen looked at the grandfather clock against the wall and the garden beyond. It had stopped, in the same way as the man himself had. Yes, the whole place appeared to have frozen in time after that evening in October eighteen years ago when Annie Lindberg Hansson did not come home. Troulsen looked at the pictures and sweated.

After a while the man came back with a letter, which he silently set in front of them. It was an invitation to an employment interview dated Friday, 14 April, 1990. The letter was brief and consisted only of two lines and Andreas Falkenborg's signature in neat handwriting. Konrad Simonsen folded it up and placed it in his inside pocket without worrying about possible fingerprints; there was no doubt about the sender.

"We would like to examine this letter more closely, if that's all right with you?"

The man clenched his fists and hissed, "Is he the one who killed her?"

"We don't know."

"But you think so. I can see it on your face. You think it's him."

Simonsen made an effort with his explanation.

"When you're talking about something as final as killing another person, it's not enough to think so. There has to be more than that, much more."

CHAPTER 13

Arne Pedersen and Pauline Berg took a walk in the summer forest after conducting two interviews, which combined lasted less than five minutes and produced nothing. Andreas

Falkenborg's summer house proved to be a modest country place, one side bordering the forest they were now walking in, and the other side a farm whose fields were in front of and behind the house. Since the summer of 1991 the place had been rented out to a childless couple, both of whom were teachers. They met the woman at home, but she had nothing to say about her landlord, whom she had never met, and assured them her husband had not either. They paid the rent, which incidentally was extremely reasonable and had not been raised since they signed the lease, to a law firm in Præstø. She had nothing else to contribute, and the two officers had to leave empty-handed.

They achieved roughly the same negative result with the neighbour they encountered in the midst of repairing his tractor. He had no knowledge of Falkenborg either but was sure his parents did, without elaborating as to why. Unfortunately his father had just lain down for a nap while his mother was in town. A resolute attempt on the part of Pauline Berg to get him to waken his father had no effect, but on the other hand he said they were welcome to come back in an hour. And so it was.

Pedersen kicked at a stone on the forest path. It sailed between the beech trees in a lovely arc. He followed his success with another stone, but this time missed badly. Pauline Berg, who was posing a few steps ahead of him while she imagined his gaze running up and down her body, was abruptly torn out of her fantasy. She said, "Would you mind stopping that? It irritates me."

In response he stepped over to her side and they strolled slowly back towards the farm with—as if by mutual agreement—enough distance between them not to risk physical contact. Even so she asked, "What about us?"

And sensed at once how he stiffened. She chose to forestall him.

"Okay, I know what you're going to say, if you even dare. Your kids count more than me."

"Yes."

"I'm really very clear about that, and the strange thing is that I don't even know if I want you, but it offends me to be rejected. Do you understand?"

"Yes, I do."

"But that's how it is? Like last time."

"That's how it is."

She felt exposed and quickly hid behind a more teasing facade.

"Now I've got a house where there's plenty of room for both of us."

"Yes, and a lovely house, I must say. Although there is one thing I've thought about, Pauline. Maybe you should consider getting a dog."

"As a substitute for you? That's worth a thought."

"Go ahead and joke, but you live in a very isolated spot and so close to the forest. Any Peeping Tom can sneak up and look in at you without being seen."

"Does it bother you to think that others can look at me too?"

"It's not about me, it's about you."

"I have a cat, that must be good enough."

"Take this a little seriously. It's meant seriously."

She considered it briefly and then rejected the thought.

"No, Gorm will never allow it."

"Who is Gorm?"

"That's my cat."

They laughed, and for the rest of the way they held hands, until they were out of the forest.

When Pedersen and Berg came back to the farmyard, the retired couple were sitting on the terrace waiting for them. The man was a round, short fellow with a bald head that seemed to sit right on his body, as if his neck had been cut away. The woman looked stern. They were sitting at a garden table, set with a pitcher of water and two cut-crystal wine glasses. The woman was working on a large dish of strawberries, which she expertly trimmed and let fall into a bowl below her chair. She barely greeted them when they arrived. The man on the other hand was more lively, and extended a short, fat arm towards two vacant chairs.

"Sit down. Mother has put out iced water, if you want a little against the heat."

They poured and drank, while they let the man talk.

"My son tells me that you've come from Copenhagen to question Director Falkenborg, who once lived in the neighbouring house, and we know all about him. He was a very unsympathetic type, isn't that right?"

The question was aimed at the woman beside him, whose mouth tightened though she did not respond.

"One of those types who will do anything to bother other people, not at all the sort we like down here," the man continued.

Pedersen sensed that the conversation could easily veer off track, so he tried to guide it in the right direction.

"When did Andreas Falkenborg live in the neighbouring house?"

"Well, that I can't remember, but in truth I recall that he poisoned our existence for an entire autumn break and most of the winter too."

The woman surprised the officers then by pressing her husband to answer the question as fully as possible.

"Listen to what the officer is asking you. He wants to know when Falkenborg lived there."

The man nodded his head tolerantly.

"When was it? Well, it must have been in the mid-1980s or thereabouts…1987, I think. Yes, 1987 it was—now I remember."

The woman cut him off.

"Nonsense, it was late summer of 1990, and in July less than a year later the teachers moved in."

He tried sheepishly to save face.

"Yes, that's even more correct."

"Did he live there year-round?" Pedersen put in.

"Yes, he was always here."

The woman intervened again.

"In the beginning he was in Copenhagen twice a week, from Monday to Tuesday and Thursday to Friday; later he almost never came here."

"How did he acquire the house?"

"Well, he bought it."

The woman confirmed the response with a little grunt, throwing a bad strawberry into the flowers for emphasis.

" I mean, was it up for sale or did he approach the owners and make them an offer?"

Pedersen directed the question at the woman, but it didn't work. She ignored his gaze and waited for her husband to answer, obviously satisfied to correct him when he made a mistake.

"It was up for sale, I remember that. I went to school with the man who lived there before, but he moved to Lolland to live closer to his son. Well, he's dead now."

Again the woman agreed. This time with an indifferent nasal sound that clearly indicated what was to be expected if you moved outside the parish.

"I see that you did not get along with Andreas Falkenborg. Why was that? Was there a specific episode that began the difficulties between you?"

"He was bad-tempered from the first day he moved in. By the day after he'd come over and complained to us."

The man stopped talking and waited for a comment from his wife. Pauline Berg urged him on.

"About what?"

"At that time we drove slurry out over the fields, and he objected to that. But we had a right to do it, if it wasn't at weekends or holidays. And if he had problems with the odour, he could always have stayed in the city. We weren't the ones who forced him to buy his summer house."

"And you told him that?"

"You better believe it! Even though he shouted and fussed like nobody's business. Swore that we would pay, and poured a whole shit bucket of abuse over us."

"So since that day you were enemies?"

"Yes, and after that there was the business with the pig. A few weeks later he got hold of a sow. It wasn't even a dead one, because later on we found out that he'd bought it from a farmer in Allerslev and had it slaughtered for the occasion. And just imagine, he nailed it up on the old poplar that stands almost on the boundary with our land. That is, he didn't do the work himself. He hired four men, and they went to work with pulleys and everything until they got the animal hung up. I don't know if you're aware how big a pig's carcass is?"

"What kind of tree did you say?"

"That one, right over there."

The man pointed to an old, slightly crooked poplar that badly needed pollarding and had seen its best years besides.

"If you go over there you'll see the iron plates are still attached."

"I can see them fine from here, but why do you think he did that?"

"Don't you understand? It was revenge. That giant sow was hanging rotting on the tree until there was almost nothing but the skeleton left. It stank worse than you can possibly imagine. We couldn't even be out here on our terrace, and when it was at its worst it was almost unbearable if you so much as opened a window. We had to dry laundry in the attic. Otherwise the rottenness clung."

"But wouldn't the smell also have affected him?"

"Yes, just as badly as us, but he seemed indifferent to it. Just strutted around, grinning arrogantly, and went up and patted the carcass occasionally."

"Didn't you report him to the authorities? That sort of thing isn't allowed. Not even out here in … in this place close to nature."

The woman's mouth pursed like a hen's behind, but the man did not notice Pauline Berg's slip and answered proudly, "No, we don't do that here. But after a couple of weeks I'd had enough and went in and gave him a good thrashing."

"Nonsense! He played you like a fiddle."

Both Pedersen and Berg turned expectantly towards the woman, and this time she spoke for herself.

"Falkenborg let himself get beaten up, that's the truth of it, and somehow managed to record the whole thing on videotape. He called emergency services and was driven away in an ambulance, while he moaned and groaned and made it sound much worse than it was. Then two days later he came in and showed us the video on some kind of little portable machine and said he was going to set both the police and a lawyer on us if we didn't let the pig hang and suffer the punishment we deserved. That's what he said, think about it, *the punishment we deserved*."

The two officers dug deeper into the neighbours' feud for fifteen minutes, but there was not much more to be learned. In conclusion Pedersen set a photograph of Annie Lindberg Hansson on the table between them.

"Do you recognise her?"

The man did not recognise the girl and said so. The woman on the other hand cast an acid glance at the picture and said, "That's Annie, the drunk's girl, from out at Jungshoved Church."

"She disappeared in 1990."

"Disappeared? Don't give me that nonsense. She ran off to Copenhagen. There's no doubt about it."

CHAPTER 14

The day after their excursion to South Zealand Arne Pedersen was on the move again, this time to the opposite end of Zealand. Konrad Simonsen had sent him to Hundested, where he was going to meet a man who might possibly be able to help explain the gap in Andreas Falkenborg's studies. Well in advance of the meeting they'd arranged, Pedersen turned up at the restaurant where he sat enjoying the view of Hundested Harbour, a charming spot that merged busy late-summer tourism with the local fishing industry and ferry service to Rørvig on the other side of the fjord. The day promised to be almost as hot as yesterday. Above him the sky was filled with slow-moving fleecy clouds, and the coffee he had just been served was strong and good, so all in all life seemed quite pleasant, although he was extremely tired.

The man he was going to meet arrived late and apologised half-heartedly, saying it had been difficult to find the detective in the mass of tourists, although Pedersen had seen him steer his clogs directly from his car over to this table. Simonsen had not said much about this witness, other than that he was a former police commissioner in the town and concisely described him as *colourful*, whatever that might mean. The ex-police commissioner was a big man in his early sixties and quickly proved jovial and winning in his manner. Pedersen took an immediate liking to him. He was also apparently popular with the locals, as many of them greeted him as they passed the table. The man's name was Hans Svendsen, and he began, "What has Simon told you about this meeting?"

"Not much, I'm afraid, he's pretty busy. We all are."

"Simon is always busy, he was born busy, don't give in to that."

Pedersen protested that the boss's workload was considerable at the moment. His own too for that matter. Or more correctly it felt that way because he had not really slept much the past few nights. The thought made him yawn. Then he said, "You met a man named Andreas Falkenborg in 1977, and we are strongly interested in what he was doing that year. I haven't been told much more than that, apart from the fact that you were a police commissioner in this town."

"Yes, though I started out as a common or garden constable. You usually do."

Hans Svendsen had an engaging laugh, and Pedersen laughed with him.

"I should begin by saying that I know something about the murder they called the Stevns case, but this story goes back much further. Were you around under old Planck, when he investigated Stevns?" asked Svendsen.

Pedersen shook his head.

"Well, during that case I was contacted by a woman who lives here in town. She told me that when she was young she was involved in an episode that in many ways resembled what happened down at Stevns. What was that poor girl's name now... I've forgotten?"

"Her name was Catherine Thomsen."

"Amazing it slipped my mind, but it wasn't my case. In any event, this local woman contacted me one day. I actually knew her rather well from old times, so we sat and had a nice chat in my office. That was in 1997."

"Were you police commissioner then?"

"Tell me, do you have a thing about police commissioners? No, I wasn't. Then I had an office at city hall, but that's by the by. The woman's name was Rikke Barbara Hvidt, and she told about an assault she had been subjected to all the way back in 1977.

It happened in Kikhavn, a small historic town a couple of kilometres along the coast. I could easily remember the case myself from back then, I was involved in it a little on the sidelines, but she had apparently forgotten that. Fortunately she got away from her attacker."

"How was she assaulted?"

"One evening, when she was alone in her parents' house—yes, she was living at home at that time—a man broke in and forced her to go with him down to the shore after stuffing a rag in her mouth and tying her hands behind her. Or that's what she said afterwards."

"You make it sound like you didn't believe her."

"There were many others who didn't. As far as I recall, I was one of the moderate doubters, but possibly that's a later rationalisation. But I'm talking about in 1977, because twenty years later, in 1997, I believed every word she said."

"Why did you doubt her originally? Was there some reason for that?"

"It concerned her parents. Neither of them was what you'd call an upstanding citizen. It's no exaggeration to say they were hard-core criminals. Their home was almost a distribution centre for smuggled or stolen goods, mostly cigarettes, jewellery and hi-fi systems, but also hash and other drugs. Rikke had had a child at a young age too, and... Well, not everyone was tolerant about that sort of thing back then."

He waved his hand to apologise for the viewpoint and continued speaking.

"The majority thought that the attack was a way of putting pressure on her parents. A score being settled between criminals, something law-abiding citizens didn't need to get mixed up in. A few even believed that the whole thing was a lie Rikke made up to get attention."

"How old was she when she was attacked?"

"Mid-twenties, I think."

"Was she a criminal too?"

"No, not in the least. But tainted by association in the eyes of some people because she had stayed living in that robbers' den. But she had a child, and financially it was probably easier for her to stay put. The old crook her dad was actually good to his kids, I have to give him that."

"And so she got away? That is, when she was attacked."

"I think she saw her chance to run and took it, but she was completely convinced that the man who attacked her wanted to kill her. He had dug a grave for her, and he behaved crazily. That is, over and above the insanity of just breaking in and dragging her down to the shore."

"And she didn't know him?"

"Well, that's what makes the whole thing even more peculiar. It's one of the reasons many people didn't really believe her story. She maintained that he had a mask on."

"A mask?"

"Yes, that's what she said. And today I firmly believe her, because since then she has built up a lot of credibility. She became a book dealer and member of the church council—an ordinary, respectable citizen—but she has always stuck firmly to her story from back then. She described it as a kind of ghost mask with black cloth down the sides of the head, a bit like an Egyptian headdress. But you can ask about that later.

"First let's finish talking about 1977. There was an epilogue. A couple of weeks after the assault—by then Rikke had collected herself—a strange man began sneaking around after her. It was a small town even then, and people kept an eye on each other, so rumours about it quickly spread, and the man was real enough. Soon he could barely step outside his door without someone keeping an eye on what he was doing. Nevertheless he continued to live at the inn for over six months, wherever he got the money for that. A few times he avoided surveillance, and on several occasions was spotted out in Kikhavn, either in the countryside or on the shore. Rikke was convinced that he was the one who had attacked her, but she could not give a facial description because of the mask he'd worn so we had no way to intervene. But the same rules did not apply to her father, and at one point the Peeping Tom got a beating that sent him to the Emergency Room."

"Did that put him off?"

"Not in the least. Within a short time he was sneaking around again. Not that he was doing anything illegal, but no one thought it was particularly funny. And besides, we feared that next time her father would really let him have it and then we would have an assault case to deal with.

"I saw what it was like for her myself, close up. One day Rikke decided to get her hair cut short, and the guy who was pestering her just couldn't handle that. He ran completely amok in the salon and made a scene, begging and pleading and crying. Naturally the salon owner called us, and I was the one who was sent out."

"So you overpowered him?"

"I didn't have to use force exactly. He was more like an out of control child, but I dragged him away and along to the station. He reacted hysterically, howling and calling Rikke terrible things. It was obvious that he was out of his mind, so we locked him up overnight and served him an injunction against approaching the salon or Rikke again, but then we had to let him go."

"Was he questioned about the attack on the shore?"

"Not so far as I recall."

"And all of this was about Rikke Barbara Hvidt having her hair cut short?"

"Yes, and all right, she did have beautiful hair, but it was none of his business whether she kept it long or not."

"Do you think she had her hair cut on purpose?"

Hans Svendsen furrowed his brow and shook his head good-naturedly.

"What kind of question is that? People always get their hair cut on purpose."

"Yes, obviously. I mean, did she get her hair cut because she had been attacked by him? Was there any connection?"

"Not to my knowledge, but you'll have to ask her about that yourself."

"I will. What about afterwards, when you released him?"

"Yes, it was strange, because the same day he checked out of his room and went home, or more exactly left Hundested— where he went, I don't know."

"So he was no longer interested in the girl, once she was short-haired?"

"It seemed that way."

Arne Pedersen summarised.

"Rikke Barbara Hvidt pointed out much later, more exactly in 1997, that in her opinion there were similarities between the attack she herself had been subjected to on the shore at Kikkehavn and the murder of Catherine Thomsen in Stevns?"

"Correct, apart from the fact that it's called Kikhavn. Yes, the Stevns case was played up in the newspapers in the same way as today, and what she read about Catherine Thomsen's fate made her remember what she had gone through herself. I contacted Planck, but a couple of days later Catherine's father was arrested and charged, and I never heard anything from the inquiry team. But someone must have made a note because otherwise you would not have contacted me today."

Pedersen was surprised.

"I thought it was you who contacted Simon."

"No, it was one of your students who got in touch with me originally. Apparently they found a cross-reference. Tell me, don't you talk to each other in Copenhagen? Or perhaps that's out of style in the capital?"

The man had a point, thought Pedersen.

"As a rule we do, but I must have misunderstood something in this case. So didn't it surprise you that the woman was never questioned?"

"No, because by that time everyone thought the perpetrator was the Stevns girl's father, mainly because his fingerprints were on the plastic bag. It seemed pretty obvious. How do you explain that, by the way? The fingerprints, I mean."

"We think that the perpetrator tricked Catherine's father into carrying something around with a protective plastic bag around it during a move. A fragile vase, for example. Or maybe one of those busts on plinths that people sometimes have. But that's still just speculation. Tell me, do you have anything against looking at a couple of pictures and telling me whether you think they resemble Rikke Barbara Hvidt, as she looked in 1977?"

"Not in the least, but I wonder if she herself has a picture from back then, so you can just compare your photographs with that. It will probably be easier because there's been a lot of water under the bridge since then."

"I would really like your assessment to start with, if—"

Pedersen was interrupted by a hollow, howling sound that resounded twice over the harbour. Everyone stopped what they were doing and looked tensely out over the basin, where the ferry from Rørvig was about to make close contact with a pleasure boat. Hans Svendsen got up.

"Look at those idiots, what are they thinking? A ferry like that can't just change course in an instant. So much for getting out of the way, mate … no, it looks like he'll manage it. Sometimes people are just too stupid. He has children on board too."

He sat down heavily.

"Out with the pictures then, I'll take a look."

Pedersen placed the photographs on the table before him. Maryann Nygaard, Catherine Thomsen and Annie Lindberg Hansson, three smiling, pretty women with a remarkable resemblance to one another. Hans Svendsen took a quick glance at them and said, "Yes, they look very like Rikke did back then."

"You remember her so clearly?"

"Rikke has a grandchild. The girl is not quite the age of these women yet, but she resembles them very strongly."

"And the granddaughter looks like her grandmother did at that age?"

"That's what people say, and also what I recall. She's a very pretty girl anyway. They often take walks together, Rikke and she, so you will probably meet her later."

Pedersen took the opportunity to show him a picture of Andreas Falkenborg also. Without saying anything. This time too Hans Svendsen answered without reservation, although after taking a slightly longer time to consider it.

"Yes, that's the culprit. Even after all these years, I have no doubt that's the man I removed from the hair salon. Is that the type he goes after? That is, pretty young women with black, wavy hair?"

"We assume so, but his taste is a bit more rarefied than that and the victims have to meet it in every respect. In addition there is reason to believe he does not *go after* his victims, as you put it. He does not actively seek them out. They have to come to him. But when that happens, he strikes. At least that's how we see the cases at the moment, but there are still a lot of unknowns."

Hans Svendsen nodded seriously.

"I assume that this time you have the right man in your sights."

"We do. The problem will be proving it. But tell me one thing: how much of what we have talked about now did you explain to Konrad Simonsen on the phone?"

Pedersen raised his hand to forestall any objection from Svendsen. "And I'm well aware that I ought to know that myself, but I really don't."

"Okay, okay, no offence taken. I can easily imagine that you have an awful lot on your plate, but the answer is, almost nothing. We talked together for about one minute, and the rest he left to this meeting."

"I don't think he's aware of how significant our meeting Rikke Barbara Hvidt could be. I intend to call him at once and get him up here to take part. I think he should prioritise that over everything else."

To Pedersen's surprise Hans Svendsen did not seem too keen on the idea. He scratched his beard thoughtfully and said, "I don't really know…maybe that's not so smart."

"Why? What harm can it do??"

"Because two strangers may be one too many. Rikke is a very nervous sort. About two years ago she was the victim of a horrible accident, in which her daughter was killed and she herself became blind. A car drove right through the front window of her bookshop when she and her daughter were setting out a new display. The driver was drunk and unable even to brake before he ran into them. He was killed too. Since that day she has been very nervous and withdrawn, even with people who know her well. I don't know how she will react if two strangers suddenly turn up to question her. It's possible she won't manage to talk with you."

"I understand."

"Why don't I see if I can get hold of her granddaughter? It will depend on how she is doing, of course. You know, some days are better than others."

Svendsen got up and disappeared into the restaurant. It was twenty minutes before he reappeared.

"It's okay to try, but you should be prepared for the questioning to take time. It will be best if only one of you asks questions.

The granddaughter is taking a walk with her at the harbour in an hour, and Simon is en route."

"You called him?"

"I thought I might just as well, since I was on the phone anyway. Do you play billiards?"

"You mean that game with long sticks and balls on a table?"

"Exactly. It sounds like I've found myself a good mark. Let's go in and see if it's available."

"Okay, post and play, you can set up."

"Now you're sounding more like a shark than a mark, but let's see what you're good for."

CHAPTER 15

"What was the dyke angle, Simon?"

The door to Konrad Simonsen's office stood open and Pauline Berg marched straight in. She could see that her boss and the Countess were on their way out. She had no idea where to. Shortly before this she had been informed that the scheduled psychological review of Falkenborg had been cancelled. Why she did not know. She felt irritated and left out. Hence her question, spoken without any introduction and in an aggressive tone. Which to her own surprise she did not regret.

Simonsen observed her curiously. He had never seen Pauline this way before. She was standing with her arms folded, actually blocking the doorway. He had to hold back a smile. The last thing he wanted was to puncture her self-confidence, and especially not her persistence. The expression "dyke angle" he remembered well; he had simply forgotten ever using it himself. As far as he remembered, it was Kasper Planck, his old boss, who had come up with the phrase. Simonsen answered Pauline while with exaggerated obviousness he glanced at his watch.

"I'm not sure I know what you're talking about. Shouldn't you be leaving?"

The last was addressed to the Countess, who had sat down. She smiled a little too sweetly.

"No, I'll wait another five minutes. This I really want to hear."

Pauline Berg pointed accusingly at her boss and challenged him straight out.

"You know the Stevns case like the back of your hand, and in your handwriting in the margin of one of the interview reports on Carl Henning Thomsen it says: *Use the dyke angle*. Also in your review on Monday you talked about *a dawning lesbian relationship*. But now I've trawled through the case twice, and I cannot find any other reference to Catherine Thomsen having a girlfriend. It's a mystery to me how you even know she was a lesbian. It doesn't say that anywhere. Or dawning lesbian, whatever that means."

Pauline could hear for herself that this had come out in a jumble, but Simonsen said soothingly, "Maybe you should sit down and start from the beginning."

So she did that. Andreas Falkenborg's name and picture had been presented to all the witnesses in the Stevns case. It had been a big job that was finished in record time. But the result was negative. Not a single person among the many involved in the case had identified him positively. During the process Pauline had discovered that Catherine Thomsen's alleged lover was so to speak missing from the case. Her name appeared nowhere, which irked Pauline as the girlfriend had to be an important witness. The more she read the case notes, the more she wondered. The girlfriend was a complete blank apart from that fleeting reference in Simonsen's disrespectful margin note. And it didn't make sense. Catherine Thomsen could not be a lesbian, dawning or otherwise, without the presence of a girlfriend somewhere or other.

Simonsen listened to Pauline's objections without interrupting. When she was finished, he explained what had happened.

"We got the information very late in the process. Two to three weeks before Carl Henning Thomsen committed suicide. Who the girlfriend was we never managed to find out, but that she existed is certain. Probably we should have made more of an effort to trace and interview her. But by then, as you know, we were convinced that we had the right murderer."

"How did you find out about her?"

"Have you ever heard of a church called Lilies of the Field?"

"No."

"We received a letter from a minister there. Catherine Thomsen had sought her out in complete confidence, torn between her religion and her sexuality. Lilies of the Field specialises in counselling people undergoing crises of faith. I recall that we went through our photo material from Catherine Thomsen's burial, this time with a focus on younger female participants, and there was actually one woman we never managed to identify. We prepared a report—"

"There is no such report."

Pauline Berg had dared to interrupt her boss.

"Shut your mouth, Pauline, and listen. We prepared a report, but when Carl Henning Thomsen died, and the case was closed, I believe my predecessor moved it over into the Petersen file because the minister had breached her promise of secrecy. Which she felt very bad about, even though Catherine Thomsen was dead."

"The Petersen file?"

He looked encouragingly at the Countess, who however shook her head slightly. There wasn't time.

"I'll tell you about it if you call me in fifteen minutes. I have to go now, but I think you should continue to follow the track you're on," Simonsen told Pauline.

CHAPTER 16

The man must be close to retirement age. The Countess observed him without making any secret of her interest. He was on the chubby side, with warm-looking eyes and a friendly manner. He wore an old-fashioned charcoal grey three-piece suit, and had trimmed his moustache and exuberant sideburns so that they were neatly restrained. He could probably best be described as sober-looking. Calm and considered would also apply.

For over ten years he had been chief administrative officer in the Ministry of Finance with a brilliant career behind him and in all likelihood an even more spectacular one to look forward to. Then suddenly, from one day to the next, the stress of the job broke him. It was all very unpleasant, mainly for him but also for his colleagues. If someone like him could be so badly affected, one day they might be the ones who went down. After his convalescence it was clear that reinstatement at the Ministry was out of the question, after which a job was found—or rather, created—for him in the National Bank.

Here he sat now in the coin department, officially called the Royal Mint, with an address in Brøndby. His workplace was on Købmagergade, however, at Marskalgården, an eighteenth-century Baroque palace, and if you wanted to you could visit the

Post & Tele Museum on your way up. His coin-related duties were manageable to say the least, so for most of his working day he did as he pleased, which was mainly to advise any colleagues or associates in need of a little insider guidance to the highways and byways of Slotsholmen. His knowledge was considerable, and his good advice to anyone and everyone who passed by his little garret office correspondingly insightful. He was called the Oracle from Købmagergade in bureaucratese, and there were more than a few who in the course of time had discreetly consulted him. High and low, student assistants, department heads, they all came here. Even cabinet members occasionally.

The Countess had been interrupted in her introduction by her cell phone, which she had forgotten to turn off. She quickly ended the call and apologised.

"You'll have to excuse me, but that was my boss."

"Your boss, your lodger, your lover…a dear child has many names."

His voice was slow and characterised by an oddly displaced phrasing, as if his words and sentences were not coordinated. She concealed her surprise with a brief laugh and said, "As usual you are exceptionally well informed. Well, where was I?"

"Telling me that Helmer Hammer visited your lodger at Police Headquarters, half an hour after Bertil Hampel-Koch left you in anger."

The Countess reported further on how Konrad Simonsen now summarised the murder case in daily emails to the general director of the Foreign Ministry. When she was done, she paused; her host noticed her hesitation and said quietly, "These are very influential people you're talking about. If I'm going to help you, it's a good idea to tell me the whole story."

His argument was irrefutable; she pressed on.

"I believe that Bertil Hampel-Koch was in Greenland in 1983 and impregnated the girl who was later murdered on the ice cap."

He gave himself time to digest the statement then said neutrally, "That is a theory of a quality I don't hear every day. Now you've made me curious. But if you think he killed that girl, you're mistaken."

"No, he hasn't killed anyone, I know that perfectly well. Besides I'm still not sure about the other thing. As I said, it's just something I believe."

"Do tell."

The Countess told him about the conversation with Allinna Holmsgaard and then about her theory.

"When the professor told about Steen Hansen's voice, or more exactly Maryann Nygaard's unknown lover's voice, it struck me that I had heard a voice like that recently, namely Hampel-Koch's. Obviously it's all speculative, but the connection between the director and Chief Administrative Officer Helmer Hammer made me think, not to mention Hammer's peculiar interest recently in Homicide Division cases… Yes, it makes more and more sense, the longer I think about it."

The man asked curtly, "You don't think their involvement makes sense otherwise?"

"First Bertil Hampel-Koch almost forces his way into our investigation, by citing international complications between the Americans, Greenlanders and even the Germans. Then he stalks out of the first meeting he attends, after which Helmer Hammer shows up faster than you can say *agreed in advance*. I refuse to believe that the realm has a top executive in the Foreign Ministry who behaves so impulsively, not to say foolishly."

The man smiled briefly.

"That's what I like about you police people. It's harder to pull the wool over your eyes than it is with most people. But the rest of us can also put two and two together, and Bertil's voice is simply not enough to go on. You must have something more or you wouldn't be sitting here. Have you taken a close look at him?"

The Countess winced. The man was right, she did have something else, which she would have preferred to keep to herself.

"Bertil Hampel-Koch gave Maryann Nygaard his cap. Or I think he did anyway. He maintained that it was knitted by his mother, but the label inside referred to a little shop in Holte called *Witch Knitting*. The store was only in existence for a year and a half, from 1982 to 1983, and was run by three friends. Bertil Hampel-Koch's wife was one of them."

Her interlocutor's eyes narrowed, but he did not comment on this statement. Instead he said, "It's obvious that there are no foreign affairs implications in this case. Not in the slightest, and definitely not at Hampel-Koch's level."

"If I'm right, that opens up a whole range of interesting questions."

"Well, maybe it does. One of them is what you yourself will achieve by turning over too many stones. This obviously has nothing to do with your murder investigation. Have you discussed your theory with Simon?"

She reacted to the name. He had called him by his nickname, which only his friends used.

"Do you know him personally? I didn't know that."

"Yes, a little, but you're not answering me."

"I haven't told him anything, I only want to do that when I'm certain that Bertil Hampel-Koch really is the unknown Steen Hansen."

"That's probably where your theory falls down. If I recall correctly, in the early eighties Bertil was in the Ministry of Defence, and that actually fits very well with a trip to Thule, but he would never, ever use a false identity. You don't do that in Slotsholmen, not twenty-five years ago and not today. Although ..."

He drew out the word, and even if it was unnecessary, the Countess could not help pressing him.

"Although?"

"Although, at that time, Bertil was a bit of a fop, even an ass... a brilliantly talented ass. Since they polished off the rough edges, now he's only brilliantly talented. It could be a personal initiative, with a bold line under *could be*. But that's clearly what you are in the process of finding out for yourself, which brings me back to the question—what do you want to achieve? And what do you want me to help you with?"

The Countess felt put on the spot but forced herself to answer calmly.

"I don't like it when powerful people like Bertil Hampel-Koch and Helmer Hammer play games and no one else really knows what's going on. I'm afraid that the Homicide Division is getting caught up in some political game or other that we have no influence over."

"Do you fear the implications for Simonsen?"

"Yes."

"I think that the risk for him is far greater if you start muddying the waters and perhaps stir up things that don't concern you. So the best advice I can give you is: drop it, and forget it."

"Well, when you put it that way... But I'm not the only one interested in whether Hampel-Koch was in Greenland in 1983. When I called to make an appointment at Knud Rasmussen's House to look through the Greenland pictures, it turned out that two journalists had tried the same thing yesterday."

The Oracle's eyes flashed, and his voice suddenly became sharp.

"From where?"

"That I don't know."

"I hope these journalists aren't just figments of your imagination."

She shook her head, but did not comment. The Oracle said hesitantly, "Perhaps you ought to know a little more about the State Department."

"Please."

"It ought really to be called the Ministry of Lost Causes. This is where all matters that can't be resolved elsewhere end up, and there is no higher place to pass them on to. *The buck stops here ...* that was a sign President Truman had on his desk, but it could just as well be written over the entrance to the State Department. The Ministry itself is small, with barely more than a hundred employees, but the majority are hand-picked from other ministries, and no one refuses a posting there if they are asked to join. It is considered something of a public duty. There are four divisions, namely foreign, administrative, economic, and climate. Helmer Hammer is head of the administrative division. He was appointed three months ago, after campaigning for the position for a long time. Which by the way makes him an under secretary and not, as you said before, chief administrative officer. He negotiates at the highest level in Slotsholmen. There are four under secretaries in all and they either receive their assignments direct from the Prime Minister or have certain knowledge that he wants a matter resolved in a particular way, but simply does *not* wish to be involved in it himself. Perhaps not even to hear about it. You should also know that Helmer Hammer's daily work hours are unreasonably long, and for him weekends are a rarity. To put it briefly, he is unbelievably busy."

The Countess tried to sum up their meeting.

"So the newly appointed under secretary does not show up at Police Headquarters simply because it is pleasant to meet Simonsen, or because a director in the Foreign Ministry had an old personal relationship? The latter naturally under the assumption that my supposition is correct."

The Oracle did not answer directly but said, "There are two things that supercede any others in our bureaucracy. One is issues of security. The other is any threat to the prestige of the office of prime minister. And by that I mean not only the present prime minister's prestige but that of all his predecessors, regardless of party."

"That sort of thing could definitely get Helmer Hammer out of his chair?"

"I can promise you that."

"And which of the two possibilities do you imagine—"

He interrupted her.

"I cannot know at the present time, but what I do know is that you should be extremely cautious in your handling of this case. I hope you're clear about that. If you find the picture you're looking for, then you will invite me to a discreet lunch one of these days and show it to me. If on the other hand you cannot prove that Bertil was in Greenland then the journalists presumably can't either, and in that case you would do best to drop the matter."

The Countess reacted almost instinctively to this warning.

"And why should I be so eager to protect Helmer Hammer?"

He held her gaze as he said, "Because otherwise you stand to lose more than you gain."

She maintained eye contact as she told him, "There is another way to decide whether my theory is correct."

"Which is?"

"Whoever the anonymous Steen Hansen was, he left behind an excellent DNA trace on the ice cap."

The sentence hung in the air. It took a moment for it to sink in. When that finally happened, the man leaned across his desk and took hold of the Countess's wrist. She winced at the touch, but did not withdraw her arm.

He said slowly, "Do not even think about that."

CHAPTER 17

At first glance Konrad Simonsen seemed relaxed when he arrived at Hundested Harbour a good hour after he had spoken with Hans Svendsen. Arne Pedersen knew that it must have taken a major reorganisation of his workload for him to arrive so quickly. It was not difficult to imagine whose head would be on the line if the conversation with Rikke Barbara Hvidt did not bring any solid chunks of gold home to Copenhagen. Simonsen started by confirming Pedersen's thoughts.

"Hi, Arne. Yes, I cancelled the psychologist again."

Hans Svendsen lightened the mood. True to form, he took control in his own cheerful manner.

"Welcome, Simon, my old friend. It's very nice to see you again. The jungle telegraph says that you're about to hit the bull's eye or win the lottery, or however you put it."

Simonsen's cheeks grew red, but he said nothing.

"Hell, I think you've lost weight too. More of a middleweight than a heavyweight these days."

"Unfortunately I'm not even close to what I should be, but good to see you too, Hans."

The two men shook hands and patted each other's back.

"Come on, let's go over to the other side of the harbour, I've reserved a table for us."

Svendsen smiled and took Simonsen with him. Pedersen trotted behind, crossing his fingers for luck.

Their reserved place proved to be a combined table-and-bench set, placed so that a picnic could be eaten undisturbed while enjoying the view of the fjord. Two women were sitting waiting for them there, and the investigators from Copenhagen nodded briefly to each other when they saw Rikke Barbara

Hvidt's granddaughter. The men sat down, and Hans Svendsen spoke.

"Hi, Rikke, it was nice of you to come."

At the same time he reached across the table and gave the young woman a pat on the arm. He was acknowledged with a smile from both women. The older one turned her blind eyes towards him and said, "Good afternoon, Mayor. We were almost family, remember?"

The young woman blushed.

"That we were, that we were. And who wouldn't want to be part of your family? But that Mayor business, that was many years ago now. We've had a municipal merger, remember?"

He sat down next to her, and they talked for a while about old times, without worrying about the others in the party. Hans Svendsen gave Rikke plenty of time, and Pedersen felt anxious on his boss's behalf. After all, he had not been dragged to this out of the way place in Zealand, however beautiful and idyllic it might appear in the summer haze, to listen to small talk. Simonsen himself did not seem to be bothered by the long-winded preamble. He sat observing the sunlight, which through the staggered planks of the table surface struck the asphalt in distorted parallelograms. Finally Svendsen returned to the present. Carefully he said, "I've brought two friends with me. They are from the police in Copenhagen, and one of them would like to ask you a few questions."

"Two of them, Hans? Am I that interesting?"

"You've always been a popular girl, Rikke. Is it all right if he talks to you now? He is a bit busy, you know, they always are in the big city."

"That's fine, Jeanette explained to me what they want. But I would prefer not to talk about … that other thing, you know."

"We all understand, Rikke. And he is only interested in the assault."

He nodded to Simonsen, who echoed Svendsen's tone and approach exactly.

"My name is Konrad, but my friends all call me Simon. That's because my last name is Simonsen. May I call you Rikke?"

Simonsen could be very intuitive. Without at any point forcing the conversation, he spoke quietly and calmly to the nervous blind woman, whose voice soon returned to its normal range. Only once did he make a mistake, when he happened to call her granddaughter Pauline instead of Jeanette, but that misunderstanding was quickly smoothed over and forgotten. Only after Pedersen had looked at his watch numerous times, and even Hans Svendsen showed signs of impatience, did he tackle the subject he had come to broach.

"Rikke, will you tell me about back in 1977, when you were attacked?"

"Yes, I'll be happy to, Simon. I was living out in Kikhavn with my parents along with... Jeanette's mother, who was little at that time, and then one evening I was home alone. It was a Tuesday in May, I recall, and the others were at the movies. Suddenly there was a man standing behind me in the kitchen, and before I had time to do anything, he shoved me down across the table with my arms behind my back. I don't know if I screamed, I must have, but it was a long way to the nearest neighbour's so no one could hear me. He tied my hands together with that wide, shiny tape... What's it called again?"

"Duct tape?"

"Yes, exactly. Then he stuffed a rag in my mouth so I couldn't call out. The whole thing happened very quickly, and I was paralysed with fright. It was so terrible, I peed my pants in fear. He had a mask on."

"Yes, I've heard that, and I am very interested in that mask. Can you remember what it looked like?"

"Dreadful... like a ghost. But it was homemade: black and made out of cardboard, I think with holes for the eyes."

"Did you recognise the mask? I mean, did it look like any definite character?"

"I didn't recognise it, but there was more. Around his head and over his hair he had a kind of greyish-black cloth that went with the mask."

"So you didn't see his face?"

"No, not at all. Only his ears and a little of his head between the fabric and the mask."

"Did he have gloves on?"

"Yes, and they were black too."

"Did he say anything to you?"

"No, not in the house, not until we got down to the shore."

"He took you down there?"

"Yes, he grabbed my clothes and shoved me ahead of him. We went quite fast, and a couple of times I fell, and then he pulled me up."

"Did he pull you by the hair?"

"No, only by the clothes, and not brutally, more like firmly."

"What about light? It must have been dark since you were living somewhere isolated?"

"He brought along a flashlight, and he took me pretty far down by the shore before he stopped. It was there I knew that I would die. I mean, that he was going to kill me."

"You thought he would kill you?"

"No, I didn't think so, I was sure of it, and I still am today. Yes, he wanted to kill me. He had dug my grave. A deep hole down in the sand, a place where the beach was narrow and the water reached almost to the dunes. There was a shovel to one side, ready for him to cover me with sand."

"Did he use the flashlight to show you the grave?"

"No, the searchlight from the lighthouse at Spodsbjerg swept regularly across the beach, and then I could see it."

"What happened to you there?"

"First I was supposed to take my jeans off, but not my panties. Then he forced me down on my stomach and tied my ankles together, after which he tore up my blouse in front and removed my bra. I can't remember how, but I do recall that he looked away, as if he respected my modesty, and I also recall that I thought at least he wouldn't rape me… That is, because he tied my ankles together first. Then I had to sit up, and he released my hands. Is this too disturbing, Jeanette? You can take a walk if you don't want to hear this. Hans and Simon are with me."

The girl answered in a voice filled with hatred.

"It's not that I feel sick, Grandma, I just get so damned mad."

"That's the best reaction to have. Well, there on the shore, when I was sitting up, he took out a pair of scissors and sat down alongside me."

Simonsen asked carefully, "Where did he get the scissors from? His pocket?"

"No, he had a knapsack on, a small one, that was where he got the scissors from while he was talking to me for the first time. It was in such a strange way. He was saying 'she' the whole time instead of 'you', and behaved as if the whole thing was an act. And then that disgusting mask he was wearing. When he looked at me, it was as if he was spewing out all the evil in the world."

"What did he say?"

"*She's going to have her long claws clipped now, she's going to have her long claws clipped now.* That's how he said it at first, and then in a completely different voice to instruct me, *Then she shows her nails.* But he did not speak harshly, more like we were playing a game or something like that. I didn't understand at first, but then he simply repeated it. *Then she will show her nails, then she will show her nails.* At last I held my fingers up to him, and although my nails were quite short, he pretended that he was cutting them. That was with the first voice again. *Uha da da, they need to be clipped. Clip, clip. Uha clip, clip. Look now, that was good indeed that we got the scissors out. Clip, clip.* He spoke in that style, while he clipped in the air in front of each finger with his scissors."

Jeanette Hvidt hissed in English, "Fucking weirdo."

"What was that, dear? What did you say?"

"That he was crazy, Grandma."

"Yes, he was, and if I hadn't been so lucky, he would have killed me too. I don't doubt that for a moment. But while we were sitting there some mopeds came driving up towards the shore. It was the young hands from the farms, tearing around for fun. Out and in between the dunes and racing by the water's edge. Even though they were pretty far away, they scared him and he ran away. To top it off he asked me to wait. Can you believe that! I wriggled my legs free from the tape and ran for all I was worth in the opposite direction. I hid under an old rowing boat that was rotting on the shore. Then later, when the mopeds were gone, he searched for me. That's almost what I remember best: him calling and the flashlight shining around in all directions. *Where are you hiding? She has to come out for him. He wants her.* Again and again. Sometimes close by, other times farther away, so the sea distorted his words. But I stayed where I was."

Hans Svendsen said quietly, "I think it was good you did that, Rikke. I think it was really good."

CHAPTER 18

After the conversation with Rikke Barbara Hvidt, Konrad Simonsen and Arne Pedersen left Hundested Harbour together. By chance they had parked in the same car park, which gave them a few minutes to discuss the day's events with each other, an opportunity that Simonsen did not take, however. When he was summoned from Copenhagen on short notice he'd forgotten to bring along the lunch the Countess had made for him that morning, and now he was hungry. He steadfastly ignored a hot-dog cart whose enticing aroma of grilled sausages seemed to pursue him long after they had passed it. Crossly he said, "I think we both need to let this information settle a little. I do anyway. Will you write a report? Preferably before you go home, if you can manage it."

"No problem."

"Excellent. When you're finished, email a copy to our new psychologist. With one of those red exclamation points, if you know how to set them. I've never been able to work it out."

"I'll call and tell him that the information is important. That way he can't miss it."

Simonsen stopped by a bench and sat down. He pulled out his cigarettes and lit one. It was his third of the day, and it tasted like soap. Pedersen sat down beside him without commenting on his weakness. Shortly after he said, to make conversation, "How is Kasper Planck really doing?"

"Poorly."

"He's in a nursing home, I hear."

"That was several months ago. The man is dying, it's only a matter of time."

Simonsen inhaled with pleasure and noticed how, despite the taste, smoking helped his mood. He added, "I was out there last week. He barely recognised me, and for the few minutes when he was clear about it we mostly talked about whether anyone would remember him when he's gone."

"Hmm, doesn't sound much fun, but it's good that you visit him."

"I'm not sure it makes any difference to him, and the worst thing is the nurse told me he may be lying there like that for a while. Just how long she wouldn't say."

They sat in silence after that. Simonsen felt exhausted, and the drive home seemed an overwhelming obstacle. He lit another cigarette with the old one. The new one tasted better; the tiredness left him. Pedersen glanced worriedly at his boss, but turned his eyes away when he encountered a defiant look. Simonsen said a little tartly, "You don't look too good yourself. Are you stressed?"

"No, I just had a hard time sleeping last night. It happens sometimes. But there is one thing I've been thinking about, Simon, and of course you should say no if you don't agree. I've been thinking about…I mean, I'll understand completely if you don't—"

"Remember to walk carefully when it starts snowing?"

"Okay, I was wondering if you would like to play chess with me."

Simonsen did not answer right away. Conflicting feelings tore at him, but curiosity won out.

"How well do you play?"

"I don't know. Pretty well, I think. But it doesn't have to be now, we can wait until you're back home again. That is, if you go back home again. That is, what I'm saying is that I don't want to get mixed up in your—"

"Eight o'clock. Incidentally, the Countess won't be home. And you maintain that you play well?"

"I think I do. I'll be there at eight o'clock."

When Arne Pedersen smiled, he looked like an overgrown schoolboy.

A good six hours later Arne Pedersen resembled a little boy, a little boy who slowly but surely was being crushed at chess. The two men sat opposite each other at the dining table in the Countess's living room. The game went on for a long time, even though the outcome had long been ordained. Simonsen was on the verge of winning, yet thought for an unfeasibly long time over a rather obvious move. Pedersen could not understand why until suddenly it occurred to him that he had failed to mark on the chess clock between them the fact that he had moved. Annoyingly he stopped his own time for consideration and thereby activated his opponent's. Simonsen moved immediately and did not forget the clock. After another fifteen minutes of slow torture it was over. Pedersen gave up. Simonsen stretched and said, "Shall we play through the game again?"

"What good would it do? I won't gain anything from that."

Simonsen shrugged; it was obvious that chess protocol did not unduly concern his new partner. Nonetheless Pedersen had played well; considering that he had never been in a club or read theory, almost frighteningly well. Albeit mixed with amateurish errors, thank God, which had decided the game. "No, of course you won't," he said.

"Do you think I played badly?"

"Yes, you did."

"So you wouldn't care to play with me again?"

"Sure, now and then we can have a game."

They collapsed at either end of the Countess's sofa. Pedersen opened two mineral waters he had fetched, the one with the other, and then in reverse—in a quick pull, without spilling a drop. Simonsen followed the process with interest. He had seen it before and was equally impressed every time.

Both of them were tired. Pedersen actually looked even more worn out than his boss. He would have preferred to leave immediately after the chess match, but did not feel that was polite. They talked casually about this and that until the Countess came home a little later. By contrast to the two men she seemed energetic. She greeted them cheerily and sat on the armrest next to Simonsen. Then she pointed towards their bottles.

"Have you gentlemen ever heard of coasters?"

Both pretended not to have any idea what she meant. She dropped the subject, the damage was already done. Simonsen said, "How did it go?"

"Terrible, complete waste of time. She's a power-hungry bitch all right, and to top it off I have to fight with her again tomorrow evening."

Pedersen was not following this so he asked, "Who's this? And what have you been doing?"

"Waiting for a self-centred social services and cultural director to condescend to talk to me. I'm supposed to have access to some archives in a museum so I can check a small point about Maryann Nygaard's stay in Greenland. It's not even particularly interesting, but I'm digging my heels in about it. Even though it has proved so far to be unreasonably difficult to get her permission, not to mention a little help."

"Why in the world is that?"

"After the municipal mergers there was a lot of trouble about the old museum administration, so my simple request has now gone up to director level, and, ye gods, what a director. Helle Oldermand Hagensen, she and only she is the one who grants access for third parties to the museum's non-publicly accessible collections. The latter is unfortunately a quote. So I had to wait three solid hours until she was done with some public meeting or other—and that was after she'd cancelled our first meeting."

"Couldn't the museum appointment be made by phone?"

"Well, unfortunately not, the director wanted to see who she was dealing with in person."

"Did you say that this concerned a serious crime?"

"Yes, of course. But she was completely indifferent. The result was that I've been granted an hour tomorrow evening…"

The Countess stuck her nose in the air and said unctuously, "This must be done in an hour, Officer Rosen, I don't have more time than that, you must understand."

143

Pedersen observed her with curiosity and then said, "Your eyes look evil, that's unusual."

The Countess let out a curt, joyless laugh.

"Evil eye? Well, maybe I'm trying out a little good old-fashioned black magic. Abracadabra—Mrs Hagensen, may your milk never curdle."

She had spoken in a low voice, almost mumbling. Pedersen asked, "What did you say? I didn't catch that."

"Never mind, I'm just trying to distance myself from her a little."

Simonsen muttered in irritation. "It's completely indefensible that she is allowed to hinder a murder investigation. There must be someone she reports to. Should I exchange a few words with them tomorrow morning?"

"No thanks. I'll manage on my own, and maybe I'll find something that can put her in her place. I'm not completely new to this job after all. But the problem is that what I'm rooting around in is a trifle complicated. I don't want too much controversy about what I'm doing."

"No, I've noticed that."

The irony was clear. Pedersen wondered what was going on here. He had no idea what the Countess was working on, but that Simonsen was obviously not fully informed either seemed almost bizarre. The Countess guessed his thoughts and hurried to ask, "How did your chess games go?"

"Chess game. We only had time for one, and Simon won, obviously. Unfortunately I'm not as good as I thought I was."

Simonsen nodded his agreement. The Countess did not let herself be convinced. She slid down from the armrest and over behind Pedersen, where to both men's surprise she set one hand on his shoulder. In the past there had been problems between them, so the gesture was unexpected.

"I don't believe that for a moment. On the contrary, you are certainly a competent chess player or your game would never

144

have taken over three hours, but now you should head home so Simon can get his night's sleep. You look worn out yourself."

The two men said goodbye in the hall. Simonsen opened the front door. Pedersen pressed him about their next chess appointment.

"But we will play another time?"

"Absolutely."

"Is it true that I'm bad?"

"Yes, you mustn't listen to her, she has no appreciation of chess."

Simonsen's tune was a little different when fifteen minutes later the Countess kissed him goodnight and hustled him upstairs and into bed.

"If I had his talent, I could have reached IM level."

"And if I was sitting on a rack, I could have become a dress-maker's dummy. Goodnight, Simon."

"It's only a matter of time before he beats me."

"It's only a matter of time before you fall asleep. A short time."

"What are you going to do now?"

"Work."

"On what?"

"Goodnight and sleep well, Simon."

CHAPTER 19

He is a child, and he is lying in his bed at night. The room is illuminated by a weak bulb set directly in the socket, which gives off a subdued green light that has a soothing effect on children. He is afraid of the night light, but even more afraid of the dark.

In the room there is a window that faces the forest. It is made up of two parts, each with six small panes divided by peeling white bars. All four hasps are securely fastened, and the curtain is drawn completely. If the hollyhocks get too high, his father nails a tack to the sill and ties up the stalks, so they don't knock against the panes in the wind. He is afraid of the window, but even more afraid of the unknown outside.

When fatigue overcomes his anxiety he falls asleep, but is wakened by a soft sound coming from the window behind the curtain. A small, metallic *clack*. It is the witch pulling the hasps up one by one. A witch can do that sort of thing, pull hasps off windows from outside.

At first her dark green silhouette is enlarged upon the wall. Then he sees her little body as she crawls in with difficulty. Her limbs are long and slender like spider's legs, her fingers crooked, her nails sharp. With a quick pull she tears the curtain away and looks greedily at him with her small, blinking eyes. Her dirty hair sticks out in tufts, but the worst thing is the mouth. It is missing.

He runs.

As fast as he can, he bolts down a hallway. At the end his mother is standing with her arms open, but the faster he runs, the farther away she is. The witch is right behind him. He hears her panting, smells her. Finally, finally he reaches his mother, throws himself against her and hides his face in her skirt, while he weeps with relief and notices how she holds him protectively.

That is how the nightmare begins.

He looks up, but it is not his mother's face he is looking into; it is the witch's.

As far back as Arne Pedersen can remember, he has suffered from nightmares. Always the same, and always with the same result, namely that he wakes up bathed in sweat from head to toe, with a fear inside that it takes the rest of the night to overcome. In his childhood this happened often, once or twice a week when it was at its worst. As an adult he experiences it much less often. Six months might pass in between episodes; plenty of time to repress the memory, until one night there it is again. Like the flu, only over more quickly. For this reason his recurring nightmare has no further effect on his life, and so far he's paid no particular attention to it. It is a congenital nuisance, there is nothing more to say about it. His mother called it *the bad dream*. His wife refers to it simply as *it*…"My God, did you have *it* again?"…and always sweetly gets up with him and makes him a cup of chamomile tea, before she goes back to bed again. He wishes she wouldn't.

Now for the third night in a row he'd been awakened by the nightmare, and he could not remember that ever happening before. Either as a child or as an adult. His wife was worried. She set down the mug of chamomile tea on the table beside him and asked cautiously, "Is there something wrong, Arne? Is something bothering you?"

He shook his head, nothing was wrong.

"If this keeps up, you'll have to see a doctor."

She was right. He had basically not slept and that could not go on, as she matter-of-factly pointed out a few times. As if she needed to tell him. He shrugged it off, and shortly afterwards she went to bed. He chucked the chamomile tea down the sink and poured himself a cognac, moderate, not too big—it wouldn't help anyway. With the palms of his hands he massaged his temples briefly, while he hissed to himself, "I want to kill him."

And shortly afterwards, "I swear, I fucking want to kill him."

Then he turned on the television, turned down the sound and prepared himself for a long, sleepless night.

It was ironic. When he was a child, he couldn't tell his mother about his nightmare. Not all of it anyway. Now the same thing applied to his wife.

Because the dream had taken a new development and in the green light he now saw other things, worse than the witch's face.

CHAPTER 20

Under normal circumstances Arne Pedersen was one of the few men on the Danish police force who could mentally multi-task, which he regularly resorted to during boring meetings. But today's at Police Headquarters did not follow the norm. It was beyond difficult for him even to single-task. He was dead tired; small flashes of light were constantly exploding in his peripheral vision, while it seemed to him that in an unpleasant and uncontrolled manner his brain was working faster than normal. Poul Troulsen was having his third cup of coffee and was equally bleary-eyed. Pauline Berg on the other hand looked like she had just stepped out of a sports catalogue. Konrad Simonsen also appeared vigorous, even though this was already his second meeting of the day. The Countess had chosen to get an update later in favour of keeping a dental appointment already postponed several times.

The psychologist, or profiler as he called himself, was new and obviously needed a solid bolster of self-promotion before he dared start in on his business. He sat at the end of the table flanked by sizeable bunkers of papers to either side and reviewed his scientific career, putting particular emphasis on what articles he had published where and together with whom. This was not boasting, but simply a desire to establish that he was prepared for the task. His introduction was therefore met with accommodating nods and more or less effective attempts to conceal growing impatience. At last it became a little too exhaustive for Simonsen, who cut him off.

"No one around this table is in any doubt about your expertise, and besides we haven't come here to assess your qualifications but to listen to what you can tell us about Andreas Falkenborg."

The man blushed a little and feverishly flipped through his papers, which made Simonsen elaborate on his words.

"I can see and hear that you're nervous. There is no reason to be. In no way do we expect a flawless lecture and definitely not for you to have an answer to everything. Besides I'm well aware of your expertise. That's why you're here."

It helped. The psychologist smiled shyly and said, "Yes, I admit I'm a bit excited to be invited here. But I think I've prepared myself well, and would like to start by briefly sketching Andreas Falkenborg's psychological profile in relation to a so-called standard profile for serial killers. There are some interesting correspondences, but also some essential points where he does not match the profile, which are at least as relevant."

"We would really like to hear about those."

"I've written them all down but I can't find… Is it all right if I… Oh, there it is, sorry."

He looked around, the ice broken, and Pauline Berg thought he had happy eyes.

"First and foremost I want to state that Falkenborg cannot be characterised as a serial killer, based on the definition I am working from, as he does not fulfil the most essential criterion, which is having at least three *documented* murders on his conscience. I emphasise *documented*. I am not stating any opinion on the *probability* that the third woman, Annie Lindberg Hansson, was murdered by Andreas Falkenborg. That is outside my area of expertise. But the fact that our man does not qualify as a serial killer under this criterion should not keep us from comparing him with the general profile we normally see among this type of offender."

He looked up and encountered nods of agreement. No one in his audience felt compelled to apply the designation "serial murderer" to their suspect.

"The first similarity with serial murder that jumps out is the very high level of orderliness displayed in connection with the two homicides. An order that has a ritual character. Serial murderers often kill their victims in the same way each time they strike. One example among many is John Wayne Gacy, who killed thirty-three boys in Chicago in the 1970s by garrotting them with a rope and a stick while he read aloud from the Bible. Both of Andreas Falkenborg's known murders proceeded in the same way down to the slightest detail, and I am almost certain that what the women were subjected to before their deaths happened in the same sequence.

"Supported by Rikke Barbara Hvidt's testimony, which I was able to read here this morning, this sequence consists of the fact that he isolates the women in a place where he won't be disturbed, he takes off their outer clothes but not their panties, and makes sure that their breasts can be seen by removing their bras and tearing their underclothes in front. He cuts, or acts as if he is cutting, their nails, he attaches their hands to their thighs, he puts red lipstick on them, and finally he suffocates them by pulling a clear plastic bag over their heads and tightening it around their necks. In addition their grave has been dug in advance, which he does not try to conceal from them. Here it is obvious that Andreas Falkenborg fulfils the serial killer criterion of killing victims in the same way. Even if the statistical material in his case—fortunately, I would add—is slender, I am convinced that if he has killed other women, it has happened in exactly the same way."

The profiler took a sip of water and continued speaking.

"It is also worth noting that he is white, male, that he tried to kill for the first time when he was in his twenties, and that he was not closely linked to his victims. It is also significant that both his victims were of his own race—all indicators for the classic serial killer. On the other hand, he does not commit his murders within a geographically limited area, which is otherwise the norm for serial killings. And he apparently does not kill to achieve excitement, sexual satisfaction, domination or a combination of the three. The fact is, I can't really ascribe any of these motives to him, although I must clearly emphasise that this concerns an assessment that I am not certain holds up. I was actually doubtful whether I should even mention it, and when I do, it is over-whelmingly due to the new angles about Falkenborg's behaviour that you collected in Hundested yesterday."

Simonsen asked soberly, "What are you basing your assessment on?"

"Excitement is the easiest element to rule out. Serial murderers who get a kick out of killing seldom plan the scene of the crime and almost always commit their murders quickly and not far from potential witnesses. That is a significant part of the excitement for them. If we take a serial killer such as Peter Sutcliffe, the so-called Yorkshire Ripper—"

Simonsen looked at Pedersen, who shook his head in annoyance, and then politely interrupted the psychologist.

"We recognise that this is your area of expertise. You don't need to give examples to back up your argument."

Pedersen put in, "It gets a little too much like answer key logic."

"Fine by me, I'll drop the examples. Where was I? Yes, excitement is easy to rule out in this case. Falkenborg isolates his victims, seems afraid of possible witnesses although they are far away, and takes as few chances as possible. One small exception to this perhaps is the way he presumably tied Maryann Nygaard's arms behind her back, gagged and concealed her in his helicopter, while everyone else was running around searching for her at the radar station. But that was done from necessity and was not particularly risky for him."

Simonsen agreed. "He does not kill for the sake of excitement."

"Then there is the sexual motive, which I also think can be ruled out in Falkenborg's case. In by far the majority of cases where serial murder is sexually motivated, the murderer's treatment of his victims is brutal or sadistic, often to a horribly painful degree, and that applies not only to actions, but almost always to the words used as well. But apart from the fact that Falkenborg suffocates the women with a plastic bag—"

Here Troulsen interrupted.

"You have to excuse me, but to be frank I have a hard time overlooking that."

"Let me put it differently: he suffocates the women, but what does he do in addition that underscores sadistic behavior? The answer is nothing. He uses neither torture nor rape. On the contrary—taking the full situation into consideration—he is relatively careful with his victims. He does not offend Rikke Barbara Hvidt's modesty more than is strictly necessary when he takes off her bra, he asks her to please wait until the moped riders are gone, and he gets her to hold her hands out not by threatening her, but by patiently asking her to. And these arguments can also be used to reject dominance as a motive. I have never heard of a dominance murderer who spoke in that way to the victim he was killing. It simply doesn't tally."

Simonsen said, "But he frightens them with his mask, if we assume that he was wearing one at the other murders he committed."

"I feel quite certain that he did."

"But isn't that a kind of torture? I mean, the women must have been terrified."

"The mask is extremely interesting. I think he used it to frighten them, but also to hide himself and conceal his own anxiety. But may I have permission to wait for now before I consider the mask?"

"Yes, absolutely."

"Another circumstance that puzzles me is that if he kills to achieve dominance, as I believed in the beginning, why does he choose to operate in darkness? The dominating effect and thereby his enjoyment of the killing would be much greater if he could observe the women's reaction clearly and in detail, which he cannot under artificial light on dark beaches or in the Greenlandic polar night. Many dominance murderers kill at a place other than where they leave the bodies purely so that they have better conditions in which to kill.

"Furthermore our killer goes to great lengths to put the blame on Carl Henning Thomsen for the murder of his daughter Catherine. This does not tally in any way with a dominance motive, where the murderers very often make claims on both the victims and the crime even after the murder. Like a hunter who is proud of the animals he has killed and hangs them on his wall as trophies. With Catherine Thomsen the opposite happens. But having said this, our man's very eagerness to lure Carl Henning Thomsen into a trap, and also his strange behaviour in 1990 with the pig that he nails on the tree to bother his neighbours, are two elements in his conduct that I simply don't understand."

The profiler stopped talking for a moment and looked around at the group.

"They don't fit with his other conduct, and here I am not only thinking about the murders but also about the other witness statements that describe him as quiet, capable, sociable, well liked, but also very naive and almost infantile. Do you have any observations about this?"

Pedersen said categorically, "The important thing for me is whether he was quiet and capable as a child."

The psychologist's eyes wandered uncertainly.

"Yes, well, that may be an interesting angle. Are there any other comments?"

His four listeners all shook their heads. Simonsen interjected, "This puzzled me too. The episode with the pig doesn't tie in with his other documented behaviour, and I was hoping you could help us get an insight into that—along the lines that perhaps he has two personalities."

"No, he's not schizophrenic, if that's what you mean. Absolutely not. But it may be necessary for us to let that be for the time being. Unless…"

He looked around, but no one had any further ideas.

"The last and most important reason that I am rejecting dominance as well as sexual satisfaction as motives, is that he does not take the initiative himself, and his cooling-off periods…that is, the period between his murders…is far too great. If he was dominance or sexually motivated, we would have experienced more—certainly a few more—murders. So my conclusion is that he derives no satisfaction from his misdeeds. Bear in mind, however, my initial reservation. I am doubtful that he derives enjoyment from frightening the women, but I cannot be sure he does not."

Simonsen had clearly hoped for a different interpretation.

"But what help is this? I mean, this leaves me no further forward."

"Exactly! The English, or to be more exact American, designations of the different classes of serial killers are *thrill killers*, *lust killers*, and *power seekers*. If we refuse to group Andreas Falkenborg in any of these categories, the obvious question of course is what groups remain. There are four, but none of these fit our man. If we look at them individually—"

Pedersen interrupted the survey.

"Okay, none of the remaining four groups can be applied. Maybe we should be more interested in what we don't know that we don't know, than in what we know we don't know."

Pauline Berg turned her head and gave him a friendly nudge.

"I didn't understand a word of that. What in the world do you mean? And can you stop drinking my coffee? You have your own."

Simonsen took out his cell phone, stood up and turned his back on the group. Shortly afterwards he said, "I'm sorry but I have just received instructions that can't wait. We'll have to take a ten-minute break. Arne, can you help me?"

CHAPTER 21

The room adjacent to the meeting room was used to store cleaning supplies. With a light hand between Pedersen's shoulder blades Konrad Simonsen pushed him inside, turned on the light and then closed the door behind them. At the far end of the room stood a solitary chair. Simonsen pointed towards it, and Pedersen sat down.

"Tell me what the problem is, Arne."

Pedersen avoided his eyes.

"Nothing important, I just haven't slept very much. Look, this Andreas Falkenborg guy, are you thinking of arresting him soon?"

Simonsen did not answer at first. That was not the topic he had taken his subordinate aside to discuss. Then he changed his mind.

"That's the plan, but first I want to hear all that the psychologist has to say. Later today I'll discuss the case with the district attorney, but she'll only tell me that at the moment we'll be lucky if the judge will let us keep him more than three weeks on remand. Will you please look at me when I'm talking to you?"

"But we will get a search warrant?"

"Certainly."

"So we have to hope we find out something more."

Pedersen's gaze wandered around the room, first here, then there, and his hands were restless.

"Yes, we have to hope so. Are you ready to tell me what's wrong?"

He was.

Simonsen waited patiently and did not interrupt his colleague as Pedersen related his nightmare in unnecessary detail, and explained about his resulting insomnia. He concluded despairingly, "Two days without sleep is okay. I even think it was an advantage to me yesterday, when we were playing chess. Strangely enough. But three…"

He shrugged his shoulders.

"Now you sound completely normal. What does Berit say?"

"That I should see a doctor if it continues."

Simonsen refrained from seconding that advice, however reasonable it was. He knew that Pedersen's marriage was not always harmonious, and Simonsen himself didn't care much for Berit, which he was always careful not to show. Instead he took a dishtowel from the shelf beside him, soaked it in cold water and wrung it out before handing it over. Pedersen took it and dabbed at his temples.

"I'll get someone to drive you home, Arne. And I don't want to see you here again until you've slept. Do you hear me?"

"I hear you, but there is one thing. That is, I know you need to get back to the meeting—"

"Out with it then, they will wait for me."

"It's Pauline. Well, I'm sure you've noticed that she resembles…them. She mustn't meet him."

Simonsen had noticed the resemblance and was well aware that it was the topic of lively discussion in the whole Homicide Division, without anyone seeming to comment that Pauline Berg was also light-haired and blue-eyed—not insignificant in connection to this case. The talk irritated him. He would never dream of playing roulette with a co-worker's safety, but it was obvious that if Andreas Falkenborg had not been quite so particular during his whole life over his choice of victims, they would have found two dozen and not two dead women in his wake. Or three, if they were counting Annie Lindberg Hansson, which they probably should. Jeanette, Rikke Barbara Hvidt's granddaughter, would of course be kept at least ten kilometres away from Andreas Falkenborg, but Pauline Berg…that was simply an over-reaction. On top of that, Simonsen was not the least bit interested in hearing about Pedersen and Berg's relationship, if they even had one at the moment. On the other hand he had not intended to use Pauline in an interrogation situation anyway, she was still far too inexperienced for that.

"You would prefer that I keep them separated when we confront Falkenborg, is that it?"

"I've been imagining all kinds of things, even during the day, and her house is very isolated. It's right next to the forest, so unless we can spare ten men—"

Simonsen interrupted.

"Stop this nonsense, Arne. If it makes you happy, of course I can keep Pauline away from him. Now let's get you home!"

But Pedersen did not stop. Suddenly it poured out of him. About Pauline, thrashing around when the oxygen in the bag was used up. About her clown-like red lips, stuck to the plastic. And about evil Pharaoh eyes that delighted in witnessing her death struggle.

When it finally dawned on Pedersen that his wish to separate her from Andreas Falkenborg was actually granted, he collapsed like a punctured balloon. Simonsen decided to drive him home himself.

In the car Pedersen fell asleep.

CHAPTER 22

Retired crane operator Olav Petersen killed his wife at the age of eighty-six by striking her repeatedly on the head with a pipe wrench. The murder happened in the winter of 1962 in Vesterbro in Copenhagen and was quickly cleared up. According to the killer, the victim had tormented him for most of his life, and he could not bear the thought of dying before her. At the time of the murder the old man was terminally ill, and he passed away peacefully two weeks later at Copenhagen Municipal Hospital. He was never brought to trial. In many ways Olav Petersen had committed the perfect murder.

The case folder concerning the murder was both comprehensive and thin. In any event, immediately after his death the case was closed. But as the years passed, the file grew, and in time became two. The name of whoever first had the idea of lodging sensitive or controversial documents from other closed cases inside the file dedicated to poor crane operator Petersen was lost in the mists of oblivion. Only the initiated knew about the procedure: the annotation with a number beside it in a case folder meant that there was further information to be had in "Petersen".

Pauline Berg felt proud to have the two Petersen case folders on her desk. She had slipped out of the meeting about Andreas Falkenborg's psychological profile, right after Simonsen and Pedersen left, as she knew from experience that when her boss said ten minutes that was usually a very relative concept. Poul Troulsen got to entertain the psychologist in the meantime, which was a little annoying, but work came before pleasure, especially when the work was as exciting as this. She looked up and found note 57, a plastic sleeve with a numbered, bottle-green label in the lower right-hand corner. It contained a picture of a young woman and a three-page report, dated 23 August, 1998. She did not look at the other papers. That was an unwritten rule that Konrad Simonsen had carefully impressed on her, and which she intended to observe. She read and formed an overview of the contents of the plastic sleeve only.

In the early 1980s Pastor Mie Andreasen established the Christian congregation Lilies of the Field as a branch in Copenhagen of the Universal Fellowship of Metropolitan Community Churches. The congregation was based on God's love for *all* people, including gays and lesbians. This tolerance was in glaring contrast to what Catherine Thomsen had been brought up to believe, namely that homosexuality was a serious sin against God. Nothing less. Twice Catherine had visited Mie Andreasen to seek consolation. The first time was in November 1996, the second time a month later. In July of 1998 Mie Andreasen came home from a long-term stay in Holland. When she heard about Catherine Thomsen's fate, she contacted the Homicide Division.

The dialogue between the young woman and the minister had in the nature of things been of a religious character and was therefore of no real value to the investigation. But through the conversations Mie Andreasen learned that Catherine Thomsen was in a secret relationship with a woman her age, with whom she was in love, and that the love was reciprocated. Sexually, however, Catherine Thomsen did not dare move beyond the kissing stage. She was afraid of her God.

Without hurrying, Pauline Berg read through the report again to see whether she had taken in everything. Disappointingly enough that was the case. She had expected something more, something sensational even. A little disappointed, she concentrated on the picture. It showed the face of a woman in her early twenties with plump cheeks, layered, short blonde hair, and a small but obvious scar on her forehead above the right eye. There was no text with the portrait, but it was not hard to figure out who it depicted. So Pauline wrote a note to Malte Borup about electronically enhancing the photograph to make the woman ten years older, and emailing her the result. Before the weekend.

CHAPTER 23

The meeting with the profiler resumed when, a good hour later than promised, Konrad Simonsen again took his seat at the conference table. The episode with Arne Pedersen had lowered his spirits. Not so much the incident itself—Pedersen would get a good night's sleep now, there was little doubt about that—but more as a result of his reflections on his colleagues and himself. The truth was that the male part of his inner circle,

Simonsen included, was a sorry collection of wimps. Poul Troulsen was on the verge of retirement, Pedersen was bedevilled by compulsive thoughts due to a relationship he couldn't handle, and Simonsen himself—well, what was there to say really? Perhaps he should be thinking about applying for a pre-retirement position, somewhere he could wind down gradually while letting the younger men take over the big investigations. One thing was certain: if he were to remain in the saddle, he needed a colleague among his small circle of assistants with some strength in him, one who could kick down a few doors without getting out of breath.

Simonsen concentrated on the meeting and summarised the previous findings as he turned to the psychologist.

"You rejected grouping Andreas Falkenborg among the thrill killer, lust killer and power seeker groups of serial murderers. When I left, you were going to review other possible groups."

The psychologist continued his review, as if the interruption had lasted only a few moments and not over an hour. Berg and Troulsen also acted as if this type of break in their meetings was normal. No one asked about Pedersen.

"A possible grouping is *gain killers*—that is, serial murderers who achieve material goods or financial gain by their murders. But we can rule this out. Then there are two relatively synonymous groups, namely *visionaries* and *missionaries*. The first group is guided by voices or thinks that in some other way they are directed from outside, for example through a spirit who has possessed the neighbour's dog, to take a specific example. The second group sees it as their mission in life to free the world from a particular type of person, whom they consider to be a danger. Here there are actually some slight points of resemblance with Andreas Falkenborg. The ghost's mask could fit into that pattern, and also his victims' marked external similarity, but serial killers in both these groups are almost always psychotic or schizophrenic, and that does not apply in his case. In addition they are seldom organised to such an extreme degree as he is, and—this is the most significant point—as a rule they are of low intelligence, with an IQ between ninety and one hundred. Falkenborg's intelligence quotient is significantly higher."

Simonsen interjected, "So there is only one group left, as far as I can see."

"Yes, that's correct. The final group is *hedonist killers*, that is, serial murderers who simply find enjoyment in killing other people. This group is very uncommon in its purest form—that is, where there is not also an element of dominance or sadism. I don't consider the lipstick, the nail clipping and the similarity between victims to fit with this profile either. And definitely not the fact that on the one hand he is uncommonly persistent with respect to Rikke Barbara Hvidt, even after his first attempt fails, but then gives up the minute she cuts her hair. To witness her death, with her hair cut short, would obviously give him no satisfaction. I have never heard of such an exclusive hedonist before, nor anyone as tireless in pursuit of his victims once he has chosen them."

Troulsen asked, "But you would not completely rule it out? That the motive is pure enjoyment of killing?"

The psychologist considered for a moment. "This is not an exact science, but … No, it simply can't be correct."

He looked at Simonsen, who said, "So what could be correct?"

"Tell me, how interested have you been in his childhood? I have read almost nothing about that period."

It was Pauline Berg who responded.

"That's because there is almost nothing documented. But obviously that's a mistake?"

"Yes, that is a mistake. Almost all serial murderers have had a dysfunctional childhood, which often involves sexual abuse, the parents' abuse of drugs or alcohol combined with exaggeratedly harsh punishment for insignificant offences. One of the classic reaction modes for the child is to resort to daydreams, which later in life may develop into a fantasy universe. This may very well be lived out in parallel with the person's regular life and concealed from those around him."

Troulsen raised an objection.

"We have nothing that points in that direction, his childhood home seems normal enough."

"Then dig deeper, because his childhood home was not normal. Something or other in his childhood or early adolescence has left its mark on him and led him to kill two women. Or three, if you will. Maybe there is a single, overriding circumstance you need to find, typically one that involves a death, or else there is a general failure of care combined with abnormality between his parents. Possibly both at once."

Simonsen asked, "Is this where the mask comes into the picture?"

"Yes, though that's not necessarily to say that you are looking for an episode in his childhood specifically involving a mask, whereas I am guessing that red lipstick and long fingernails do figure somewhere in his background. His mask, on the other hand, he more likely uses to conceal himself from the real world while he lives out his fantasy. The covered face is his protection and at the same time a way to activate his fantasy. Not as dominance in the usual sense, more as a means of being taken seriously, and possibly also in his own self-understanding avenges a childhood injustice."

"What about the type of woman he pursues? Does this also derive from his childhood?"

"That's my guess, and I think he is afraid of that type of woman. That is why he does not seek them out himself. But once they intrude on him, he is forced to react. For him they are a life-threatening danger, and therefore he has to conquer them and

163

ultimately eradicate them, whatever the cost. Perhaps the action of killing itself involves some form of regression—that is, a return to childhood—but on the other hand he knows full well that he is doing something wrong, both before, during and after his murders."

"What is the probability that he will confess when we confront him with the evidence we have against him—as slender as that might be at the moment?"

"That I don't know. He is intelligent and can presumably assess for himself how seriously he is implicated, in legal terms, and what is only speculation on our part. On the other hand it will be painful for him to realise that other people have seen through his deepest secrets. He is unusually naive besides, and this particular character trait may very well prove to be decisive."

Simonsen attempted a conclusion.

"But will it be doubly painful for him if we can directly refer to motives stemming from his childhood?"

"Painful times ten. I'm guessing he couldn't handle that. But as I said, I don't know. Bear in mind that he has been living a double life for many years."

Troulsen had a question.

"Does he take trophies? Say, something he stores at home?"

"Hardly. He has no desire to be reminded of the women, more likely he prefers to forget them entirely. Or that's my guess."

"What about his business as a professional spy and eavesdropper?"

"Perhaps that too has its background in his upbringing, business often does, but I don't want to speculate further."

Troulsen consulted the notepad he had in front of him and said, "I would like to hear more about his childishness. It keeps coming up. Is he really childish or has he mentally gone off the tracks? I mean, has he developed abnormally?"

"If you are thinking about a personality disorder such as Asperger's, Tourette's, autism, ADHD, any of these diagnoses, the answer is clearly no. These disorders are burdensome for those affected and their surroundings, but they definitely do not create serial killers, although I will grant that sometimes they incorporate a certain element of childishness. Perhaps it is better to think of him as a person who easily lets himself be dominated. Uncommonly easily, I would say, based on what I've read about him so far."

Simonsen looked around. No one had any more questions. He gathered together his papers and concluded, as he let his eyes run over his two remaining associates, "Falkenborg's childhood. Keep working on that and get some groups organised. Playmates, hobbies, studies, teachers, and above all his parents, the whole kit and caboodle, everything we can find. If he scraped his knee at an end-of-season dance or stumbled on the first verse of a hymn, I want to know it. And as quickly as humanly possible."

CHAPTER 24

After the meeting Pauline Berg caught up with the psychologist in the corridor and favoured him with her most charming smile.

"Excuse me, but I have another question, if you have a moment?"

"Fire away."

She glanced over her shoulder at the door to the briefing room.

"Maybe I can follow you out?"

"Please do. Is this something the others shouldn't hear?"

She gently placed her hand on his upper arm and led him along.

"You're good at reading a situation."

"Thanks. So is this something the others shouldn't hear?" he repeated.

He was no pushover. She hauled in the big guns; this conversation was important to her.

"Are you married or do you have a girlfriend?"

If he was surprised by the question, he did not show it.

"Why do you ask?"

"I was thinking that maybe we could have coffee sometime."

They walked along the corridor and were now out of range of possible long looks from her colleagues, so Pauline relaxed and added, "If you want to go out with me, that is?"

"Are you always so direct?"

"No, not always, but who knows when I will see you again?"

"You know that yourself—within the next few days, when Andreas Falkenborg is brought in for questioning."

Pauline Berg thought that this conversation was about to be derailed before it had really started; this was not a man to be effortlessly manoeuvred.

"Okay, what I want to ask you about I would prefer to keep to myself, because the others will definitely be against it. I mean, the question alone will set them rolling their eyes, so that's why I ran after you to get you one-on-one. And as far as coffee goes, I was toying with the idea while you made your presentation, but forced the issue a little because what I want to know is important to me."

"Reasonable enough. Tell me, do you have any idea where we're headed?"

"Yes, I do, but now it's your turn to come clean."

166

"Then let me start by saying that this is the best offer I've had all morning," he said, laughing.

Pauline Berg smiled, then said seriously, "I don't want to date you if you have a girlfriend or are already married. I've had enough of that."

"Then I'm afraid we'll have to have our coffee separately. You see, I'm married."

She was more annoyed than she would admit, and for a moment considered stretching her principles a bit. Again.

"But next month, when my divorce has been finalised, perhaps we can return to the subject. Unless you dare go out with me in anticipation?"

"I've taken bigger chances than that."

"Should we have a bite to eat before that cup of coffee?"

Pauline Berg agreed.

"Is there somewhere I can pick you up, so I can find a restaurant and reserve a table?"

She thought about it.

"At eight o'clock on Dantes Plads. Do you know where that is?"

"Yes, across from Glyptotek. It's a deal."

"Do you have a cell-phone number, in case I have to cancel? If there are any breakthroughs in the case, I can't go off duty. This is too high-profile."

"And you like that?"

"Could you please stop? I don't like having my every word and action weighed up like that. It was what you were doing for Falkenborg. Do you get that way from being a profiler?"

"No, you get that way from having heard hundreds of slightly too intimate excuses from female students who have missed the deadline for their assigned papers."

"That just about hit the mark. I'm blushing! Is it okay if we wait with my questions until this evening?"

"Hmm, you slipped in a plural form there. Do you think I work for free?"

"Yes, I do."

"Then you should also show me that famous row of columns you have. I've seen it on TV many times, but never in reality. Is it far from here?"

"No, it's not far, but you'll have to take a rain check. The others are probably wondering where I am. And one more thing—we'll split the bill this evening, so please find a place that's not too expensive. I recently bought a house and I'm feeling the pinch."

"So I won't be after you for the money?"

"Time will tell, but whatever happens, you won't get any further tonight."

On her way back Pauline Berg ran into Malte Borup, who was curious.

"Who was that, Pauline?"

"A man."

"Yes, I could see that, but is it someone you know… well?"

She ignored the question.

"I'm very happy to see you," she told him. "I put an assignment on your desk earlier. Please try and get to it today. It would take you less than ten minutes."

The student confirmed he could spare ten minutes. Then he said, "See, I shouldn't even be at work today. It was a coincidence that I was in the area when Simon called. Anita and I were out looking at clothes… that is, Anita was doing most of the looking, I was just there, but she got really upset when I left. Can you imagine? She took hold of the cell phone and chewed out Simon."

Pauline Berg did not respond. This did not sound like something she should get mixed up in.

Konrad Simonsen turned eagerly towards Malte and Pauline as they came into the room. The tirade from Malte's girlfriend had not been without effect, as he remembered the girl from a previous case and knew that she was neither hysterical nor unreasonable. From time to time he needed to draw heavily on Malte's labour. Best to keep his girlfriend happy too.

"Thanks, Malte, for taking the time to drop by. You and Anita can go out for lunch at government expense. Do you mind being reimbursed later?"

Malte Borup looked like someone who had won the lottery. A free lunch would surely appease his girlfriend, and shorten the shopping trip considerably besides.

"Thanks a lot. No, Anita won't mind being paid back later."

"Great, so should we think about getting started? I asked you to come in because your database system or cross-reference program is simply more efficient and reliable than our memories. We'll start by uncovering Andreas Falkenborg's childhood and possibly his early adolescence. I want to see what you can conjure up out of the computer before the rest of us start running in every conceivable direction."

Simonsen was referring to a computer that had been brought out so everyone could follow along on the screen. Malte Borup sat down.

"No offence, but why don't you use the system yourself? I've written a whole interface where you can search in free text and issue SQL orders, if that's what you want. Is it my manual that's not very good?"

Poul Troulsen patted him on the shoulder.

"No, we're the ones who aren't very good—and too lazy besides. But we'll take that up another time."

Simonsen did have something to add.

"Because there are searches, and there are searches."

Malte's neck changed colour; this was a delicate subject with him. Despite that Simonsen expanded.

"The searches we are making, or rather are not making, are not quite as—shall we say, exhaustive?—as the ones you are responsible for."

The student tried to defend himself.

"The Countess says that we will save the judges a lot of time by not asking for court orders, if we are sure that we don't—"

"I don't want to hear any more about that! Just concentrate on this. What can you find for us about Andreas Falkenborg's childhood? I'm well aware that we don't have too much at this point, but can you conjure up some reasonable witnesses for us to start with, even though it's a long time ago?"

"You mean besides the maids?"

Malte Borup misunderstood when he didn't receive a response.

"Is it wrong to say *maids*? There are two of them calling themselves that. Is it called *domestic help* nowadays?"

When he still did not receive a response, he turned to face them. The three detectives were astonished. None of them had heard anything about maids before this. Malte was a genius with a computer but seldom presented the information he gained from any angle related to solving a case. Simonsen spoke first.

"We didn't know there were maids in his childhood home. How did you get that information?"

"Completely legally. Some municipalities are digitising their census record archives. It's a research project in cooperation with the CPR registry and Copenhagen University. Rudersdal Municipality is part of the collaboration, and they have reached all the way back to the 1920s, long before the period you're interested in."

"So we can see who is registered as living at the address in Holte where the Falkenborg family lived when Andreas was a child?"

"Exactly, and I've also made a list of the maids. It's in the system."

"I don't doubt that you have. Can you call up that list?"

Malte typed a command. Shortly after that a list of female names came up on his screen.

"There were eleven of them in the period from 1956 to 1967. Most of them were employed for one or two years, some for only a month. Should I see how many of them are still living?"

"Yes, please."

"You'll have to wait for the result, it may take a long time."

A long time in Malte Borup's universe was three minutes. The computer said that two of the maids were dead.

"Can you find out how old they were when they were employed by the Falkenborg family?"

"Yes, but you'll have to wait again. If you'd said that before, I could have done it in one swoop."

"We don't mind waiting."

This time however the student was cheated; the data appeared at once.

"That's strange, they must have stored my records in a buffer. Maybe they've improved the system."

Simonsen's focus was elsewhere. "All aged nineteen to twenty-three…this looks promising. Malte, can you get us the current addresses and possibly telephone numbers too?"

"If they live in Denmark, that's no problem. Otherwise it's hard."

"And then there is the very big question: what about pictures of them?"

Malte looked down at the corner of the screen, towards his computer's clock, and answered hesitantly, "Pictures are not that easy."

"But?"

"If they have a passport or driver's licence or, well, something else, then there will be a picture, but normally it's not digital, and then…it's not that easy."

"So what do you do in that case?"

The student squirmed, but buckled under the pressure of a meaningful pause left by Simonsen.

"Well, we have a service and return system."

"Who is we?"

"A lot of us who work with computers on a daily basis. If we help each other out, we earn points. Or the other way around. Well, we call them *Guilt* or simply G. The system's very efficient, and I have a lot of G."

Simonsen could not conceal his dismay.

"You're not telling me that you trade information from the police for G?"

"No, the Countess says that—"

"I don't care what the Countess says. I say that under no circumstances do you sell data from our registries, regardless of whether you settle up in G or any other currency."

"I don't do that, I'm well aware that it's strictly forbidden. I've earned every G I have by helping other people with computer problems and never by anything else."

Simonsen cooled down.

"I'm very happy to hear that. What about the pictures?"

"Maybe I can get someone to scan the girls' pictures and send them to me, and then we can run them through the LifeCycle program if you want an impression of how they looked when they were employed with the Falkenborg family. But that will only be an indication, remember, because the source will certainly not have much information."

"What are we talking about in terms of time, Malte?"

"Half an hour to an hour. Anita will skin me alive."

"I'll talk to her, you get started in the meantime."

"Okay, I'll call you when I'm ready. I mean, maybe you could use the time better…"

They understood what he meant, and left him alone.

Twenty minutes later Malte called his audience back. The G system had again proved effective. The detectives had used the waiting time to chat together. Simonsen had started in on a large portion of salad after turning over the job of calling Malte Borup's girlfriend to Pauline Berg. The two women were still talking, but by now it was about clothes and good, inexpensive stores, so everyone assumed the student would be let off the hook when he saw Anita. Meanwhile on the computer screen seven of the nine maids had been given a face, even if their digital rejuvenation had in several cases given them a bizarrely animated appearance. Nonetheless it was obvious which of the seven manipulated images was the most interesting. Poul Troulsen said the name.

"Agnete Bahn."

Konrad Simonsen agreed.

"It's a bit grainy and strange, but it's close enough, even though the three murdered girls and Jeanette Hvidt resemble each other more than they resemble her."

Malte explained, "Her real appearance may deviate quite a bit from what you see here. The driver's licence photo is small and does not contain much information."

Simonsen asked, "How old was Andreas when she was employed?"

"Ten when she was first hired, and then eleven."

"Where does Agnete Bahn live now?"

"Copenhagen. In Østerbro it appears."

"Let's go out and visit her."

Pauline Berg's reaction was quite different when shortly afterwards she saw the picture and the name of the Falkenborg family's old housemaid.

"Oh, no—this can't be right. Does she have anything to do with this case? I mean, was she in the house back then?"

Simonsen sensed problems.

"Do you know her?"

"Do I know her? The whole of Vice Squad does. This is Brothel Bahn."

"Let me take a guess as to her occupation."

"A madam on a large scale, treats her girls awfully, is more money-grubbing than Scrooge McDuck, and she despises the police. She has a lawyer in attendance at all times and consistently refuses to say anything at all to anyone at all. On top of that she is uncommonly unsympathetic unless she can see any advantage to herself in behaving better. In that case she can be quite pleasant, but I've only experienced it once."

"You make it sound like she wears horns."

"Maybe not, but she's going to meet someone who does, and the sooner the better."

"We'd like the opportunity to question her first."

"You can forget that. She won't say anything to the police, if for no other reason than to annoy us. And don't think that you can appeal to her conscience, because she has none."

"But I assume that she has a brothel. Is she still active? She must be over sixty."

Malte interjected, "Sixty-four. Should I see if she has a criminal record?"

Pauline Berg answered, "She has a catalogue of crimes longer than your arm. Her establishment is on Gudhjemgade, a side street off Nordre Frihavnsgade, she lives on the second floor— and, I promise you, she is active. She won't let go of the reins until the day the devil calls her down."

"It sounds like we have a good way in here. A madam's business rarely withstands close scrutiny from the police, and she loses nothing by helping us, if she can."

"She calls her business a massage centre, of course, and forget about pressuring her—that's been tried many times. She keeps everything in meticulous order: accounts, so-called employment,

VAT, you name it—even the fire department couldn't find anything when we set them on her once."

"And you've met her personally?"

"Several times. The hag usually offers me employment. On the other hand that's the only thing she likes to talk about."

The slightly dirty grin this received from the men did not go unobserved by Pauline. She snapped, "And she's like that with everyone. It's one of the many ways in which she harasses people."

"Will it help if you talk to her, do you think? Or would a strange face be better?"

"I don't think it matters, but I would really prefer not to."

Simonsen sent his troops out. Malte was released for further clothes-shopping with his girlfriend, Troulsen got the interview with Agnete Bahn, and Pauline Berg covered the remaining maids. To start with they would be contacted by phone in order to get a general picture of life in Andreas Falkenborg's childhood home. Simonsen himself went to the Foreign Ministry, and what he had to do there he did not say.

By later that afternoon a picture had started to form of the environment in which Andreas Falkenborg had grown up. The summary took place in Simonsen's office, though he was the last to arrive. He turned up ten minutes after the scheduled time, drenched after a summer shower but in a sunny mood.

"It seems that the American Army has gotten a move on, as they say. My friend at Slotsholmen has pulled a few strings, and the Americans have promised to expedite the investigation into the helicopter trip to DYE-5. It's far from certain that this will result in anything, but we'll get an official letter detailing the usual procedure with helicopter overflights at that date. That should be helpful in court."

While he was speaking, he found a package of hand towels in a cupboard and started drying his trousers by pressing the towels against his thighs one after another, and then tossing them in the wastebasket when they could absorb no more water.

"Now, Poul, I'm anxious to hear how things went with you."

Troulsen shook his head phlegmatically.

"Pauline was right, she was completely impossible. Spotted right away that I was from the police, and before I even introduced myself had fired a whole arsenal of swear words at my head. I finally had to shout to have any chance at all of telling her why I was there, but it made no impression on her. She is truly not a person with a well-developed sense of civic duty."

"What did she say specifically?"

"That I could run and shit and fart back home to my sod house in Jutland. I've been living here over thirty years, so her ear for dialect must be good."

"That was all?"

"Well, then I gave her my card, in case she changed her mind."

Pauline Berg broke in.

"Give me one guess…she tore it to pieces and then gave you hers and offered you employment?"

"Yes, exactly as you say. She was very impudent."

Simonsen asked, "So you received no impression of whether she had anything to tell us about her time with the Falkenborg family?"

"Yes, I did actually, because right before she slammed the door in my face, she made us an offer. If the tax authorities repay her the thirty-six thousand kroner they unfairly robbed her of four years ago, she had salacious things to tell about Andreas Falkenborg and his pestilential family. Something along those lines—it's not word for word, but almost."

Simonsen thought about it. The towels were used up, and he had folded the plastic packaging into a roll that now resembled a conductor's baton, as if orchestrating his thoughts. The tempo was *andante*. After a while he asked, "Did you see whether or not she was open for business?"

"I saw a few scattered customers, but it wasn't rush hour. She lives on the second floor besides, with a separate entrance, so I didn't have the opportunity to inspect the establishment."

Simonsen turned to Pauline Berg.

"And you say she's very money-driven?"

"Greedy is an understatement."

"Okay, we'll probably crack down on her, but that will have to wait until Monday."

Berg remained doubtful.

"I'm ready to bet a bottle of good red wine that you can't."

Her boss gestured towards the photographs of the three dead women displayed on his bulletin board.

"I don't think they would like it if we took things easy."

Pauline felt humiliated and instantly apologised. She missed the guiding presence of the Countess, who should have arrived long ago.

Simonsen gave up the topic of the brothel owner then and asked, "What about the other housemaids? I assume they weren't quite as impossible as Agnete Bahn."

Pauline Berg answered tonelessly, "No, they weren't. The majority remember their time with the Falkenborg family well, and paint quite a uniform picture of the household. Alf Falkenborg, Andreas's father, was a domestic tyrant, in a big way. He and he alone ruled the home, and the mother was completely cowed. He didn't hesitate to give her a good thrashing occasionally, whereas he never laid a hand on his son. He also degraded his wife by openly having relationships with other women, even in their home, including with at least three of the maids we contacted, but I'll return to that later. Elisabeth Falkenborg was hardly a lovable person either. Her husband's infidelity, and perhaps simple jealousy too, resulted in her taking out her anger

177

on whichever maid was employed at the time. Nothing they did was good enough. She'd peck around after them, just to find something to complain about."

Troulsen asked, "Why didn't they leave? It must have been unbearable."

"There were a few who did. But for many of them it was not that easy. Two, for example, came from Funen and had no desire to go home any time before they had to. Besides, the Falkenborgs paid well, at least fifteen per cent above the norm for those days, and beyond that several of the maids were duped."

She took a sip of water from a bottle, glanced through her notes and continued.

"Andreas Falkenborg feared his father but at the same time looked up to him. He was what the boy aspired to be, but also a potential threat—first and foremost to Andreas's mother. At school Andreas got by reasonably well, but no more than that. He often brought friends home to play but the maids describe him as prissy, soft and childish for his age. In other respects the boy's treatment of the maids was arrogant and snooty, a reflection of his parents', and he told tales on the women to his mother at the slightest excuse. In general he was most attached to Elisabeth and slept in her bed until he was almost eight years old. The parents had separate bedrooms, by the way, I forgot to mention that."

Troulsen said, "Yes, it sounds like a recipe for a psychopath."

"And it gets worse. If Andreas did not live up to the demands his father placed on him, especially when it came to doing well at school, Alf took it out on his wife. He considered their son's schoolwork to be her responsibility, so she had to pay when Andreas did badly. On at least two occasions the boy had to witness his mother being punished after he came home with mediocre marks in a couple of subjects."

Pauline Berg stopped speaking briefly and took another sip of water.

"Yes, there are certainly goodies here for the psychologist. But I have another little gem too—Elisabeth Falkenborg was obsessed with the household staff having short nails, and if they couldn't keep them in check themselves, then she did it for them. One of Andreas Falkenborg's favourite tricks, which he learned as a little boy, was to maintain that they'd scratched him, and then his mother was right there with the scissors, to his great delight."

Simonsen looked at his watch, a sure sign for them to speed things up. "A picture is beginning to form, you might say. How were the maids duped?"

Pauline Berg closed her notebook. She knew that part by heart.

"Into having sex with their boss. Well, that applies to three of them, and possibly more. None of them was specific about it over the phone so we'll go out and visit them to get the whole story. Maybe Agnete Bahn was also taken in."

"We'll have to find that out on Monday," said Simonsen, disappearing from his office without so much as a goodbye.

CHAPTER 25

Pauline Berg was enjoying her dinner with the psychologist. His surname was Madsen, but for some reason he would not reveal his first name. She got no further with him than *E. Madsen*, and as the evening progressed was running out of Christian names starting with E. During dessert she thought of two more.

"Ebert or Esben?"

"Why don't you just enjoy your ice cream while you tell me a little more about yourself?"

"But is that correct?"

"No."

"Neither of them?"

"Neither of them."

"Hey, what about Emmerik?"

"Good Lord, you can't be called that unless you're a canary."

"I promise not to laugh."

"People always say that, and then they laugh anyway."

"Not me. I won't laugh, no matter what it is. I swear by all that's sacred."

"Forget it, I don't think you're particularly religious. What was it you wanted to ask me about?"

Pauline Berg set down her spoon.

"Listen now, you're really sweet, but I can't date a man I can only call Madsen. It sounds like something out of a nineteenth-century play. Tell me now, then I'll tell you what my question is."

"That's an unreasonable trade, you'll have to think of something better."

"Okay, you get to decide on the first movie we go to see."

"I didn't know we were going to see a movie."

"You know now. I love going to movies. We'll find an evening next week, or maybe on Sunday, we'll arrange the details later. Okay now—out with the name."

"So, my parents were hippies, I was actually born in a collective, and I was named after one of their great role models. Do you know Che Guevara?"

"The guy on the T-shirts?"

"Hah, they should hear that. Yes, exactly, the one on the T-shirts."

"What about him?"

"He and I have the same first name. Ernesto."

Pauline Berg stared at him in disbelief.

"Your name is Ernesto? Ernesto Madsen?"

"Yes, unfortunately."

Tears were forming in her eyes.

"That's not so bad."

She almost sounded sincere, then a snort of mirth slipped out and betrayed her. The next moment she was howling with laughter. She reached her hands across the table and held his, as if she wanted to beg forgiveness even as she laughed. Fortunately her mirth was contagious, and he laughed too. Even the couple at the next table started smiling, without knowing why.

"Ernesto Madsen! That's just God-awful. I really feel sorry for you."

"Thanks for your honesty, I don't like Pauline as a name either."

Not until coffee did she have enough control of herself to ask her original question.

"What I was thinking about in connection with Andreas Falkenborg… you may recall that Simon asked whether you thought he would confess, when we questioned him?"

"Of course I remember that, how forgetful do you think I am? And I also remember that I didn't have a serviceable answer."

"No, I can see that, but… what if one of those questioning him had the same appearance as his victims? I mean, if the one questioning him resembled the women he killed. That is, was the same type, if you know what I mean?"

"Where would you get someone like that?"

Pauline Berg thought that obviously he was better at seeing into people than he was at observing them from the outside. In this situation that was a clear advantage, however.

"Well, this is just theoretical, but can you imagine his reaction?"

Madsen thought for a while and then answered hesitantly, "I think that he would be frightened out of his wits and presumably also confess, if he was in any condition to—basically do anything to get away from the situation. From his viewpoint, this would be a form of torture. But I would absolutely not recommend putting him on the spot like that, not even as a last resort, because if he ever got out again, you don't need to be particularly imaginative to work out what could happen."

"But he would confess?"

"I believe so, unless he completely broke down first."

"Thanks, I just love you."

"Is there anything else?"

"No, I'm a woman who doesn't demand too much, Ernesto."

CHAPTER 26

The director of social services in Gribskov Municipality, Helle Oldermand Hagensen, was a powerful person who demanded a lot from her fellow human beings when she could get away with it, which—given her exalted position—was often the case. Such as this evening, when the Countess was following a winding gravel path through Tisvilde Hegn, which ended at last in a deserted parking lot. There were only two cars here, an older model Renault and the director's black Audi, which the Countess recognised from the day before. No director of social services was in sight; it was obviously up to the Countess to find her own way to the museum. She got out of the car and cast an assessing glance up at the sky, then made sure her umbrella was in her bag; it looked like rain. She checked her watch and saw that she had a good ten minutes for her walk, which ought to be plenty.

The path from the parking lot meandered up through an irregular moraine landscape, where only small clumps of crooked pine trees occasionally interrupted the view over Kattegat, grey and rain-drenched below her, with more dark clouds quickly approaching. A few drops landed on her head and she picked up her pace for the last stretch of the path.

The museum proved to be a thatched building three storeys high, reminiscent of an outsize coastal villa and poorly suited to its setting. The director was waiting under the roof overhang along with a younger man. She was a tall, almost stately woman in her early forties, expensively dressed but with an uncertain style, which the Countess with her expert eye quickly noted. From a distance the woman was quite good-looking, with regular features and thick, reddish-brown hair that billowed down over her shoulders, but close up her face was marred by her badly pitted skin, where it seemed like cosmetic laser treatment had gone wrong.

The Countess nodded affably while trying to convince herself that this time they would hit it off. Anyone could have a bad day, and nothing good ever came of nursing yesterday's grudges. But Helle Oldermand Hagensen chased these positive thoughts far out into Kattegat with her very first sentence, when she said, "So there you are. You arrived just in time. You have an hour, starting now."

The Countess controlled herself.

"Thanks for your kindness."

She received a gracious nod, which was hard to interpret, whereas the director's little snap of the fingers and about turn towards the main door was indication enough. The employee took out a set of keys and let them in. With the Countess bringing up the rear, the young man led them down a stairway and into a basement room, whose walls were covered more or less floor to ceiling with cabinets, shelves and all kinds of cases of various sizes and shapes. The illumination was poor, as the room's only window was partly blocked by stacked trunks in serious need of cleaning. Alongside all this a narrow workspace had been squeezed in, with a desk, office chair, and a computer that had been obsolete since the nineties. Helle Oldermand Hagensen threw open her arms like a ring master and said, "Well, be my guest. You have fifty-five minutes, and of course must not remove any of the museum's artifacts. I truly hope you know what you're looking for because otherwise you are wasting my time."

"I know that, and thanks for agreeing to help."

"Did you bring a camera?"

"Yes. I'm searching for a picture I would really like a copy of, when I find it."

"That's out of the question. Give me your camera now, please."

The Countess had controlled herself for a long time, far beyond what she would normally put up with in terms of obstructive behaviour from a witness in a murder case. The reason for that was simple: the clue she was pursuing had its basis in a telephone call with a clairvoyant and as time went by the message she'd received then seemed more and more as if it had been meant for her, and her alone. Furthermore, her parallel investigation was controversial in itself. All in all, she preferred to keep a low profile, but enough was enough.

She walked slowly up to the director, only stopping when she was just a bit too close, after which she looked her straight in the eyes and said, "Now you have a choice. You can stop your pompous meddling and leave right now. I'll come and get you when I'm finished, whether that takes ten minutes or the whole evening. The other possibility is that you let out just one more negative word, in which case I'm putting handcuffs on you and locking you to a water pipe until I've done my work. Be kind enough to tell me which you prefer, before I choose for you."

Helle Oldermand Hagensen's face turned dark with anger and for a moment the Countess feared she might be having a stroke. She sucked in air, which saved her, however. The Countess wagged her finger again.

"Bear in mind now, a single derogatory comment and you're out."

The director turned on her heel and left the room with a red face. The Countess glanced at the young employee and discovered he was grinning from ear to ear. She asked, "Is she always so accommodating?"

"Yikes! You should see her when she really gets going. My wife works at one of the municipal nursing homes… well, obviously it's in the social services area, and there they really suffer. She just had twelve people fired in Home Health Care at the same time as she is recruiting to build up her own organisation at city hall. She and the two other assholes who are her assistants… those three truly understand how to tighten others' belts nice and snug. On the other hand, she is not particularly competent. I think basically that's the main reason for her behaviour. But almost the worst thing of all is how she toadies upward. That's simply unbearable to watch."

"Well, there are people like that in every walk of life. But we'd better get to work, although—"

The Countess looked around, disheartened.

"—this doesn't look easy. I hope you have a cataloguing system or I might just as well give up sooner rather than later."

"Cataloguing system? There's no such thing down here, but I have something I believe you'll think is better."

He fished a USB flash drive out of his pocket and gave it to her.

"What is it?"

"Thirty-eight pictures from the Søndre Strømfjord base, all taken in the first fourteen days of July 1983. The picture you are looking for is number four."

The Countess was overwhelmed.

"You must be joking? How about that!"

"Yes, but I hope you'll keep it quiet otherwise she'll fire me and probably my wife too, if she has a chance."

"I won't say a word. So you've spoken with the previous museum director?"

"Yes, he told me what you wanted, and where it was."

"And picture number four—I haven't told anyone about that."

"No, but two freelance journalists have been calling around a lot of the people who were on the base in that time, and they're looking for him so I assumed you were too."

He removed a photocopy from his wallet and unfolded it. A young, crew-cut man smiled out at them. The Countess asked, "Where did you get this picture from?"

"The journalists visited me at home two days ago. They gave me this, but didn't say who it is."

"Did you help them?"

"No, I didn't much like them, and I also don't think that murder is entertainment. Poor girl, imagine being killed that way."

"Well, I can hardly disagree with you about that. May I have that piece of paper?"

"Please, I have no use for it. But who is that really?"

"A man from the Foreign Ministry who has done nothing illegal. Do you know the names of the journalists?"

"No, but one of them left a card. I can call you about it when I get home."

"Please do. Did they say specifically why they were interested in the man in the picture?"

"No, just like you're not either."

A paranoid thought suddenly struck the Countess.

"The former museum director, why was he discharged?"

"Hmm, that's a very long story, and there are many truths in that matter, but it has nothing to do with these pictures, if that's what you're suggesting."

"Okay. I didn't really think it had."

"Basically it was bad luck for all of us. There was no one like him for telling tall tales from Greenland; all kinds of delightful stories, some of them even true. Now the whole thing has been made the responsibility of the Agency for Cultural Heritage and various museum politicians, but the majority of visitors here are regular people, and they would rather hear the tall tales."

"Do you know any of them?"

"Lots, but I'm no good at telling them. Not as good as my former boss anyway."

"But you practise?"

The man blushed.

"Yes, a little. For my own amusement."

The Countess glanced at the window, where the rain had started to drum against the glass. It was no weather to go out in. So she looked at her watch and said, "Why don't you tell me a story?"

CHAPTER 27

The weather changed on Saturday afternoon. The sultry heat that had settled over Copenhagen was released in thunderstorms and rain as the train approached Roskilde. Pauline Berg found the outburst liberating, although it made no difference in the coach where her clothes still clung to her body. She looked out of the window and saw the faraway cathedral with its twin towers lit by sharp flashes of lightning under the leaden sky. Shortly after that the rain hit the train and obscured the view.

For a while she observed the irregular tracks of the water down the window and wondered why some drops remained in place while others pelted across the glass at a furious speed. Then she turned towards her neighbour and fellow passenger. He was a soldier, and in Copenhagen she had just beaten him in the race to get to the window seat first. Since then he had tried to initiate a conversation the whole way, but she had rejected him with monosyllabic answers or else simply ignored him. Now he was one of the first passengers to stand up, obviously eager to get away. She smiled at him, which she had otherwise been careful not to do during the journey, and noticed how he considered sitting down again. It remained just a thought, however. He returned the smile and left.

Roskilde station was the oldest in the country. Opened in 1847, it was constructed to serve Denmark's first railway between Copenhagen and Roskilde. Pauline Berg had prepared herself on the Internet. On Saturday, 5 April, 1997 just after nine o'clock, Catherine Thomsen arrived on the regional train from Copenhagen. Several other passengers had seen her and could confirm that she was travelling alone. In Roskilde she got off at platform one, closest to the station, which was also confirmed by witnesses. From here she would take a short walk through a tunnel that led under the tracks and up on to platform six, where the train to Næstved by way of Haslev would arrive in seven minutes. No passengers had seen her on the Næstved train, and most likely she never got on. The weather that day had been rainy and windy with temperatures in the mid-forties. So it was unlikely that she left the station area, unless she had an errand to run.

Pauline Berg followed in Catherine Thomsen's footsteps five times. Slowly and systematically she wandered from one platform, down through the tunnel and up on to the other, as she tried to take in everything around her at the same time. The rain was splashing down, and the butterfly roofs of the platforms provided only partial protection. Her jeans were wet, but she was too preoccupied to notice.

In 1997 Andreas Falkenborg owned a silver-grey Saab 900. He might have parked either in front of or behind the station area. But what could persuade a twenty-two-year-old woman to interrupt her journey and follow a middle-aged man to his car? Seen from Falkenborg's point of view, this place was almost the worst imaginable if he was going to use violence or threats. There were far too many witnesses around. Pauline sat down in the station cafeteria with a cup of coffee and cemented the conclusion she had reached several days ago: Andreas Falkenborg and Catherine Thomsen already knew each other. But an acquaintanceship did not fully explain the circumstances either. The two platforms and tunnel were a strange setting in which to feign a coincidental meeting and offer a ride. The sequence of events only made sense if they had a prior agreement. If Catherine Thomsen of her own free will had gone to Falkenborg's car, where he sat waiting for her.

In the train back to Copenhagen Pauline Berg visualised the meeting. She imagined how the young girl, half-soaked and bent over against the wind, had jogged the final metres to Andreas Falkenborg's Saab. Did he reach out and open the passenger door himself, when he saw her coming? Yes, he probably did. *Nice to see you, can you believe this weather, there are tissues in the glove compartment*. Her path to the morgue was paved with friendliness. No, *constructed of friendliness* sounded better. And what was their drive like? Pauline Berg daydreamed further and shivered with joy. She loved her job.

At Copenhagen's Central Station she called Konrad Simonsen and informed him of her conclusions. Her boss was interested, if far from as enthusiastic as she was. But he agreed she should continue her research. That was enough for her. She had contacted Simonsen over the weekend as if it were the most natural thing in the world, just like Poul Troulsen, the Countess and Arne Pedersen did when they were on to something important. And she would just continue, as he had said. Just continue.

This led her two hours later to Gammel Torv in Copenhagen.

The day before she had contacted the National Association for Gays and Lesbians and asked for help in tracing Catherine Thomsen's unknown girlfriend. After being transferred a few times, she ended up with a woman who neither rejected nor agreed to her proposal, but however agreed to listen to her. They had arranged to meet at the Caritas Fountain, Christian IV's beautiful Renaissance mineral spring from the early seventeenth century.

The woman proved to be in her late forties, which surprised Pauline Berg. On the phone she'd sounded younger. In addition Pauline was almost sure she had met her before, without being able to recall where and in what connection. Only that, as far as she remembered, she didn't like her.

They introduced themselves. The other woman was tall and gangly with a self-aware gaze and red hair that was coloured a shade too harshly for Pauline Berg's taste. She did not want to see identification, and limited her introductory polite phrases to a minimum. With a curt "Come", she led them across the square to a bench, where they sat down. She also took the lead in their conversation.

"What do you know about the National Association?"

The question took Pauline Berg by surprise. What significance did that have? Besides it was asked with an air of authority, as if she were taking a test and the other woman was the examiner. Pauline briefly considered not answering, but thought better of it.

"Not much. You were founded in 1948 as one of the first organisations of its type in the world. You work with the public in an advisory capacity as well as lobbying for sexual equality. In general terms that's what I know."

The woman was obviously satisfied with the answer. In any event she abandoned the subject and commanded instead, "Show me the picture, and repeat your explanation from yesterday."

Pauline Berg complied with the request. Suddenly, while she was speaking, she recalled where she had met her witness before. In a courtroom—the woman was a judge. Years ago she had skewered the prosecution lawyer and released defendants on the spot in a case that had taken Pauline Berg and her colleagues of the time weeks to build up. Today she was probably sitting in the High Court.

The woman studied the picture of Catherine Thomsen's presumed girlfriend thoroughly in Malte Borup's age-progressed version, before she said, "You say she's a lesbian?"

"It's likely, but I'm not certain."

"Does she live here in Copenhagen?"

"I don't know that either. Only that she lived here ten years ago."

"Do you have a digital version of her picture?"

Pauline Berg handed over a flash drive and a card with her cell-phone number on it.

"We'll search for her on the Internet. Facebook, our email list and our website. That's probably the most efficient way. I'll contact you if we find her."

"What do you think the chances are?"

"How would I know? Is there anything else?"

There wasn't.

On her way up Strøget toward Rådhuspladsen Pauline Berg had a good feeling in her gut. The Falkenborg case was hers, she could sense it clearly.

CHAPTER 28

The parting on Monday morning between the Countess and Konrad Simonsen at Polititorvet in front of Police Headquarters was awkward. The Countess dropped her boss off before continuing on to her breakfast meeting. In the car she had explained to him in detail for the first time her parallel investigation around Bertil Hampel-Koch on which she had spent a good deal of time over the past week, including this morning, which meant that she was removed from the actual case. She still kept her peculiar phone conversation with Simonsen's clairvoyant friend to herself. Even though it was her actual motivation—which she had admitted to herself early on—it was impossible for her to justify her actions based on that kind of metaphysical warning. But she told him everything else. Everything except the most important thing.

Simonsen was not impressed, primarily because he had a hard time seeing the purpose of her exertions. She had fallen for one of the classic temptations in detective work: namely to pursue a false track and uncover a story that may very well be exciting, but which had nothing to do with the relevant crime. He had experienced that many times before, and it was his job as chief to allocate her time in a more productive direction; well, after hearing her explanation he might say in a *much* more productive direction. The problem was that he didn't, which—in all honesty—was because he was living with her now.

He opened the car door to get out, but had second thoughts and turned towards her. She anticipated him.

"I know what you're going to say, Simon, and you're right. What I'm doing is a little on the periphery of what we are otherwise occupied with. But I have a very strong intuition about it."

"Combined with a very strong curiosity about matters of state that don't concern us. That's also why you spent the whole weekend Googling Greenland and talking with anyone and everyone on the phone."

"The whole weekend is overstating it. I seem to recall that we were at the Louisiana museum and the theatre."

"Granted, but when we get home, we have to find a way to get you back on track."

"You promised me that I could have a week."

He ignored his own promise as well as her imploring tone.

"A way that holds up."

"Okay, I promise you, dear chief."

That combination of words went straight to the heart of his dilemma, and he knew her well enough to realise this was no coincidence. So he left her and went to work, with the pointed comment that someone had to.

The Countess had invited the Oracle from Købmagergade to breakfast. When he'd agreed, he requested a discreet location, a wish she did not accommodate however, for much could be said about the SAS hotel, Arne Jacobsen's functionalist mastodon of a skyscraper in the heart of Copenhagen, but discreet it was not. On the other hand she had arranged a quiet meeting room just off the lobby, where a sumptuous morning buffet awaited them. Her guest was already enjoying the delicacies when she arrived.

They greeted each other, and the Countess poured herself a cup of coffee. She was nervous, which surprised her. He asked in amazement, "Aren't you going to have anything else?"

"No, unfortunately. It does look delicious."

"It is delicious, but go ahead and start. I can listen and chew at the same time."

She showed him the photograph of Bertil Hampel-Koch in Greenland. In the foreground was a young, crew-cut man in the process of lighting a pipe, while a pretty woman with black, wavy hair smiled into the camera from the background.

"Bertil Hampel-Koch, alias the geologist Steen Hansen, and Maryann Nygaard—the woman who was later murdered—photographed at the Søndre Strømfjord base on Saturday, the ninth of July, 1983. The picture is verified by her female friend at the time."

Her guest finished chewing and said in his gravelly voice, "Well, it's confirmed then. Bertil Hampel-Koch was in Greenland in July of 1983."

He did not ask the question, but the subtext *and what about it?* was obvious. She resorted to her last card in a bid to get him to play along.

"The two freelance reporters in whose wake I've been sailing are political journalists, not crime correspondents."

"I hope that isn't a concealed threat that you would share your knowledge with the press."

"No, but if they are also trying to find out what Hampel-Koch was doing in Greenland—"

He interrupted her.

"Also?"

She would have preferred to wait before she revealed her own research, but…

"Yes, I've been curious, and I actually think I've tracked down the truth, but of course I've had a considerable head start on them."

"Do you mean the picture?"

"No, not at all. I mean my knowledge of Helmer Hammer's involvement combined with what you told me last time we met."

He poured himself a glass of apple juice, slowly and deliberately. Then he said, "You are right that our two eager journalists may cause problems for the under secretary, especially if their— shall we say focus?—spreads to the other media, which however there does not seem to be any danger of at the moment. But they have tried to get an interview with Bertil Hampel-Koch, which definitely does not please him. So yes, they constitute a problem and potentially a big one too, because Helmer Hammer can control many things but not the press. On the other hand that's his headache, not yours. Or not necessarily."

The Countess sensed an opening.

"Not necessarily?"

He ignored her and said instead, "Tell me what you have found about Hampel-Koch's Greenland trip. And also, please, your conclusions."

"I was hoping that you would explain to me—"

He interrupted.

"Maybe later, you first."

The meeting had barely started, and yet she felt cheated. He should be talking, not her. She was the one, after all, who had paid dearly for their arrangement, out of her own pocket besides. Normally that sort of thing meant nothing to her, but here and now it seemed unreasonable. But there was no alternative. She finished her coffee, took a notebook from her bag, cleared her throat a few times and began.

"So, what has made the biggest impression on me, and what has also been my starting point, is the revelation in 1995 from Prime Minister H. C. Hansen's well-known letter to the Americans in 1957. You must know the story better than anyone."

"I would like to hear your version."

"What can I say that you haven't heard before? But the story is that in 1957 the Danish Prime Minister received a highly unwelcome query from the American Ambassador about whether Denmark wished to be informed if the US stored atomic weapons in Greenland. Officially there was no doubt about the matter. Denmark and therefore Greenland was an atomic-free zone. Unofficially, on the other hand, matters were diametrically opposed. The Americans could do what they wanted, so long as they kept it to themselves. H. C. Hansen therefore wrote a reply, together with a senior official, which, reading between the lines, accepted the existence of atomic bombs in his country, but at the same time made it clear that no one in Copenhagen wanted to know anything about anything. Hear no evil, see no evil, speak no evil. The letter was only reproduced in two copies, one delivered to the American government and one stored in a safe in the Foreign Ministry. The Danish copy was found and published nearly forty years later in 1995. Is that more or less correct?"

The man confirmed this with a little grunt.

"The surprising thing was the reaction in the media. The discovery of the letter was described as a genuine revelation and evidence that H. C. Hansen had deceived his own government, Parliament, and not least the Danish people. By his own account the Foreign Minister of the time, that is 1995, had his summer holiday spoiled. Even though so much time had passed, and all the individuals involved were long dead, the case stood out as extremely embarrassing, not to mention harmful."

"Yes, the scale of the reaction was surprising."

"But that's nothing compared to how a corresponding revelation would have been received in 1983."

"You'll have to expand on that."

"Nineteen eighty-three marked the middle of the Cold War. The year that saw medium-range missiles set up on both sides of the Iron Curtain, multiple nuclear test explosions, major peace demonstrations all over Europe. It was the year in which President Ronald Reagan introduced his Star Wars project, to mention just a few of the security issues that characterised the time. In 1983 the revelation of the Hansen letter would have been a catastrophe, both foreign and domestic, for Poul Schlüter's coalition government. And for the opposition too. If it turned out that top Danish politicians verifiably knew about the Greenland atomic weapons, but lied to the Danish population about them, many members of Parliament would have been in hot water."

"*Would have been … if it turned out.* You're speculating."

"Somewhat but not entirely. Jens Otto Krag was familiar with the secret letter to the US, because a short time after it was sent, the American Secretary of State, John Foster Dulles, thanked H. C. Hansen for it at a NATO top meeting in Paris, after which the Prime Minister was compelled to inform his Foreign Trade Minister, that is, Jens Otto Krag, who was also at the top meeting. We know that today."

"This is certainly very interesting, if you're an historian."

He said this without exaggerated sarcasm, but the put down was unmistakable. The Countess threw out her arms.

"I readily admit that for a little while I seriously considered giving up. On the one hand I had no doubt that if in 1983 a case involving atomic weapons in Greenland had been hushed up behind the scenes, it could easily explain Helmer Hammer's current interest. Many ministers from 1983 are still active today, and perhaps a similarly explosive document is lurking somewhere in the archives. A document that journalists with the Freedom of Information Act in hand can demand to see, if they know it exists. On the other hand I could not find any such case in 1983, and Hampel-Koch's trip to Thule did not fit with that scenario."

"But you didn't give up, I understand?"

"Almost. I rummaged around in every conceivable American newspaper database without getting any further, and then suddenly it all fell into place due to a Danish radio broadcast."

"Let's hear it."

"It was a feature from this winter, where no fewer than three former Danish Foreign Ministers jointly commented on the H. C. Hansen letter in a very knowledgeable and informative manner. And then, almost in passing, one of them mentioned how in early 1968 Jens Otto Krag, as Prime Minister, visited the American Air Force headquarters in Colorado Springs, where he was shown a map of how the American B-52 atomic bombers patrolled Greenland. He even talked with one of the pilots."

Her guest almost imperceptibly changed his attitude. Years of experience in interrogation rooms told her that she now had his full attention.

"The story is correct, and the April 1968 issue of *Air Force Journal* includes a picture of the leader of the Danish government shaking the pilot's hand and thanking him for his efforts. That's what the caption says anyway, and it also gives the pilot's name: Clark Atkinson."

She looked at her guest. There was an attentiveness in him which he no longer tried to conceal. She enjoyed the moment, like an actor who for one magic minute enchants her audience.

"By 1983 Clark Atkinson had risen through the ranks, namely to the position of base commander at Thule Airbase, but he was on his way to early retirement from the American Air Force. He wanted to go home to Idaho, where he intended to try for a political career, and for that reason he wrote a book, you might say his memoirs, about life in Greenland. The book was entitled *On Guard in the North*, and it came out in 1984 from the publisher Magic Valley Silhouette. But before it was published, the Idaho *Times-Chronicle* newspaper published extracts from two chapters. The first was in the Sunday paper on the fifteenth of May, 1983 and is uninteresting. The second came out the week after, the twenty-second of May, that is, and must have created panic in Copenhagen when it became known. Because it did become known, I have not the slightest doubt about that. But fortunately for the powers that be not by the Danish press, who overlooked it. Otherwise all hell would have broken out here."

"Continue!" he almost snarled at her.

"Perhaps it is worth noting that what in 1983 was a secret in Denmark absolutely did not have to be in the United States. Commander Atkinson related in exhaustive detail his meeting with the Danish Prime Minister in 1968 and mentioned H. C. Hansen's letter of 1957, praising courageous Danish politicians who did not let themselves be cowed by left-oriented public referenda. I have a copy, shall I read you the relevant passage?"

"No. What about Bertil Hampel-Koch? You're not mentioning him."

"My guess is that to start with it was through general diplomacy that attempts were made to get Clark Atkinson to withdraw his book, but this did not succeed. When the articles came out, the book was already printed but not yet released. Finally a representative was sent from Copenhagen to Thule Airbase to speak personally with Atkinson. His name was Bertil Hampel-Koch, although he used a different name on his trip, and he was a man marked for greatness. In high school he was considered brilliant, so brilliant that in 1972 after graduation he was named by the teaching staff of Gammel Hellerup High School as the school's annual scholarship winner to the US, where he was accommodated for the first six months by a young American couple in Twin Falls, Idaho, namely Helen and Clark Atkinson."

"You maintain that they knew each other?"

"Yes, and that is of course why Hampel-Koch was sent. Otherwise he would have been considered too young for such a mission. But his personal acquaintance with Atkinson was the decisive factor, for Bertil Hampel-Koch met with success where others had failed, and it is a fact that when Clark Atkinson's book finally came out in August of 1984, the section about Jens Otto Krag was gone. I wonder whether the Danish taxpayers bought the whole first edition or whether a different solution was found."

If she had hoped for praise for her detective work, she had miscalculated. When he had heard the whole thing, her guest resumed his customary indolent expression and simply asked, "All this you think you have found out, is there anything you have worked out alone?"

"No, I've had help."

"From whom?"

"From good friends, on a somewhat unofficial basis."

"Good friends in Denmark?"

"A particular good friend with connection to Gammel Hellerup High School, but otherwise not Danish."

"American?"

"That almost speaks for itself."

"We're going to meet again tomorrow, I'll call and tell you where and when."

The Countess answered hesitantly, "I'll try to—"

"Trying is not good enough. Make sure you're available."

CHAPTER 29

The telephone call on Tuesday morning did not come as a surprise to Konrad Simonsen. He had expected it, but not until later in the day. To top it off it was from Agnete Bahn herself and not, as he had anticipated, from one of her many lawyers. The woman was sputtering with anger, obviously her default mood, and the dialogue was thus quite a one-sided performance, as she showered him with invectives in gutter language of the worst sort, some of which Simonsen had never heard before. He listened with interest for a while and hung up when she started to repeat herself. Arne Pedersen, who had just shown up for work and as usual started the day by stopping off at Simonsen's office, asked with curiosity, "Was that the Bahn woman? Yes, Pauline called yesterday and told me about her."

"At full throttle. Did you get any sleep?"

"Most of the weekend, so I'm completely rested. Thanks for your help, by the way."

Simonsen nodded. Pedersen asked, "What did she say?"

"She was scolding me. Couldn't you hear? Do you happen to know what a rumpledick is?"

"I have no idea. But what have you done to her, Simon?"

Simonsen said affably, "Nothing, nothing at all. Besides taking good care of her."

"Which means?"

"A couple of patrol cars, or is it three, in front of her garden gate."

"Since when?"

"As of Friday afternoon."

Pedersen grinned.

"And this has not improved business ?"

"Apparently not, which is actually surprising. I mean, there's nothing wrong with a good professional massage, but many customers obviously chose a different form of relaxation when they saw our cars. Actually all of her customers, from what I've been told."

"How long do you intend to maintain your siege?"

"Well, I had to ask higher up. This is a slightly alternative way to use our hard-pressed resources, but so far I've been given five days, and maybe I'll get five more, if I ask nicely. Although I don't really think it will be necessary."

"So why did you hang up on her?"

"Her tone was starting to bore me, and she'll call again when she finds out that not even the most expensive super-lawyer can stop us making our own decisions about where we want to park in a public space. I should really write some of those swear words down before I forget them."

Pedersen answered, "I know what you mean. I've been brooding the whole weekend, that is when I haven't been sleeping, because there's something important that I've forgotten."

"You're speaking in tongues."

"Yes, the wife and I were at a parents' meeting at the twins' school on Friday. As I had managed to sleep for a couple of hours, it went pretty well, but imagine scheduling that kind of thing for a Friday evening, I don't know what they're thinking. Well, the twins have a new teacher, and it's not going well with her and the class, so it was almost a crisis meeting. But there was something the teacher said, just some throwaway comment or other, and it made me think of something in our case... something significant... that I forgot about right away because a hotshot who is chairman of the board of governors, and also a conceited ass, drew attention to himself with his insufferable self-satisfaction. He really pisses me off."

"Yes, I hear that."

"And now I can't remember what it was. Either what the teacher said or what it was she made me think of. Only that it was important to us."

"The best thing you can do is stop thinking about it, and then as a rule it comes back of its own accord."

Pedersen nodded uncertainly but did not look like someone who could take that advice.

The phone rang. Simonsen glanced at the display.

"It's her again."

He picked up the receiver and said calmly, "Welcome back, Ms Bahn, and now listen—either we talk calmly and quietly together or else I'm hanging up. It's your choice. But I don't have time for another monologue on your part, and I also think I've had my quota of swear words here this morning, so if you will please try to observe a basic level of civility, I would be very grateful."

He listened and then said sharply, "Until you go bankrupt or until you tell me about your time in the house with the Falkenborg family back in 1965, and you will not get a krone, only the joy of conducting yourself like an upstanding citizen."

Shortly after that he hung up.

"Ms Bahn is ready to see me in private in half an hour."

"Should I go with you?"

"No, I'll deal with her alone. The more of us there are, the greater the possibility that she will revert to her default frame of mind. She's only just managing to control herself."

"That's too bad, I really wanted to meet her. So Pauline was right. With Bahn greed outweighs everything else."

"Yes, evidently. But can you gather people together for a meeting this afternoon? I'm seriously thinking about bringing Andreas Falkenborg in tomorrow or the day after. We have him under close surveillance, as you know, but of course I don't like the fact that he's on the loose. On the other hand we don't have much on him as yet, so I would like to discuss the situation with all of you before I make my final decision."

"How democratic."

"Go to your perch and do what I ask."

"Yes, sir, I'm gone already."

Ms Agnete Bahn's appearance surprised Konrad Simonsen. He had expected an old harpy in cheap, gaudy clothes and with the cold manner of a whore, but instead he was met by a presentable older woman dressed in a demure tailor-made suit. She had an attractive, middle-aged face only lightly enhanced with makeup and—if not absolutely accommodating—a business-like attitude. It was difficult to recognise the hetaira who less than an hour ago had gathered a thistle bouquet of the worst words in the language for him. She led him to a couch and fetched a can of cold juice, which she placed before him along with a glass. Then she got to the point.

"Do we have an agreement that you will remove the three cars parked in front of my home if I tell you about when I worked in the household of factory owner Alf Falkenborg?"

"Yes."

"Then let's get going. We're both interested in getting this conversation over with as quickly as possible."

Simonsen got his Dictaphone ready and placed it between them. Agnete Bahn looked distrustfully at the machine and said, "And we're only going to talk about back then?"

"Only about back then, yes, I am completely indifferent to what you've been doing otherwise, Ms Bahn."

"Fine, and just call me Agnete, it's simpler. What do you want to know?"

Simonsen told her about the murders and his suspicions about Andreas Falkenborg without elaborating on the concrete evidence he had. She was not unduly concerned to hear the accusations against the child she had cared for long ago. Apart from nodding occasionally as a sign that she understood, she showed no interest in the story. Simonsen continued.

"Do you have a picture of yourself when you were young that I can take with me?"

The woman's surprise was unfeigned.

"What the hell do you want that for?"

He had made up his mind that it was unlikely she would go to the press. He answered her honestly.

"I think that your appearance as a young woman has imprinted itself on Andreas Falkenborg's mind, and later he has chosen his victims based on the way he remembers you."

Simonsen thought that perhaps she would be angered by his supposition, so he spoke quietly, almost earnestly. Agnete Bahn remained unaffected.

"My looks then are the role model for the girls he's butchered. Is that what you're telling me?"

"Yes, it is, apart from the fact that he hasn't butchered anyone."

She thought briefly and then said, "It's going to take a little time. I have to go up in the attic and take one of my employees with me, I'm not that young any more. But if it's necessary..."

"It's necessary."

"All right, I'll call for one of them, they're just sitting around anyway. You can pass the time by going below and—"

Simonsen cut her off.

"No, thanks."

Her laughter was dry and joyless, almost scornful.

"That wasn't what I was going to say, although you would be surprised how many men there are in positions higher than yours who wouldn't refuse—"

She glanced at the Dictaphone again.

"—a turn on the couch, so long as they don't have to pay the bill for it afterwards."

"I believe that."

"You'd better. But what I meant was that you can go down and get a newspaper or two in reception, so you have something to do while I'm in the attic. And I forbid you to snoop around my home."

"Thank you, but that's not necessary. I have some papers I can read in the meantime."

She shrugged her padded shoulders and left.

The photograph she set before him a good half an hour later left no remaining doubt as to where Andreas Falkenborg had acquired his taste for a certain female type. Rikke Barbara Hvidt, Maryann Nygaard, Annie Lindberg Hansson and Catherine Thomsen were all a copy of the young Agnete Bahn. She said, "I was twenty-one, this was taken on my birthday."

"Brilliant, thanks very much."

"I was pretty, wasn't I?"

Her voice, previously crisp and businesslike, had taken on an insinuating tone which, combined with a misplaced hand that squeezed his arm, made Simonsen's flesh crawl.

"Yes, definitely, very pretty."

The compliment obviously was not enough. She sighed and said, "No matter where I went in those days, I was always the prettiest."

He could not make himself praise her appearance further, and besides she had managed her Norn-given talents poorly. He turned on the Dictaphone, which he had turned off when she went to the attic, and said dryly, "Well, the years catch up with all of us."

She released him and returned to her normal tone of voice.

"Shall we continue?"

"Yes, let's. Can you remember approximately when you were employed by Falkenborg?"

"It was in 1964 and 1965. I started right after school summer holidays, it must have been in August, and I stopped just over a year later, one happy day in October."

"What were you employed as?"

"*Young girl in the house*, I think it was called."

"You say a 'happy day', didn't you like being there?"

"No."

She made no attempt to expand on this, and Simonsen took the opportunity to outline their agreement again.

"It's not enough that we're talking. I also demand a certain degree of willingness to answer on your part, so I'll ask you again: didn't you like being there?"

He made a rolling gesture with his hand; she was expected to be more expansive. It helped.

"No, I definitely did not. It was an awful family, festering like the clap from one end to the other. Alf Falkenborg was an asshole, his wife…I can't even remember the old lady's name…"

"Elisabeth Falkenborg."

"Yes, that's right. She was a cowed old hag, constantly on my ass to find something to complain about in my work, and Andreas was an annoying little prick who should have had a good thrashing a few times a week."

"That sounds a lot to put up with."

"It was way too much, every word of this is true, and actually there was quite a bit that was worse than that—filthy petit-bourgeois, pissing on everything and everyone, including each other."

"Could you make your vocabulary a little less flowery?"

"What the hell do you mean by that?"

"Stop swearing so much."

"Why should I, are you getting queasy?"

Simonsen dropped the idea of explaining how exaggerated use of strong language could weaken a witness statement in certain circles, thus removing the focus from what was important, namely the truth. It was many court sessions ago that he had last believed in watertight compartments between form and content. Maybe Lady Justice was blind but she was not deaf, and at some point a transcript of this woman's questioning would end up in the hands of Andreas Falkenborg's defence counsel. Simonsen gave her the short version.

"Yes."

"I'll try."

"Thanks, that would be kind. Tell me, if you were so dissatisfied with the conditions there, why didn't you give notice? Or simply leave? I mean, what could they have done about that?"

"My mother was employed at Alf Falkenborg's factory, she might have been fired. That would be like him, the filthy pig... yes, excuse me, but he was one. It would have been just like him to take it out on her, if he couldn't get at me. Actually I have no doubt he would have done that, but it's not something I can prove."

"Was that the only reason you stayed?"

"Yes, and then the pay was good. Strangely enough, although—well, obviously they weren't short of money."

"There were no other reasons?"

"No."

Simonsen held her gaze.

"And you're quite sure of that?"

She hesitated and then asked despairingly, "You've spoken with the other maids, right?"

"Yes."

"I happened to run into someone who had also been employed with the family, my predecessor by the way, and she was subjected to exactly the same treatment as me. The thought had simply not occurred to me. For many years afterwards I dreamed of killing him... for example, coaxing him into a solid case of syphilis of the throat. That wouldn't have been impossible. And then hope, naturally, that he would pass it on to his wife, although that was unlikely. But though I'd have liked my revenge, I didn't kill him."

"I know that."

"Sometimes I regret that I didn't. Even so many years later. He would have deserved it, the old... libertine. Do you understand?"

"Yes, easily. But let's leave that story for a moment and come back to it later. Can you tell me how the Falkenborg family functioned on an everyday basis? You said that Elisabeth Falkenborg was cowed, and the family in general was awful. I would like you to expand on what you experienced."

Surprisingly enough Agnete Bahn ignored the encouragement and suddenly said, like lightning from a clear blue sky, "I know why that perverse animal has a mask on when he kills. I know exactly why, now that I know it was him... Andreas Falkenborg, that is."

Simonsen straightened up on the couch and said sharply, "Mask? I haven't told you about a mask."

"No, but it says so on the *Dagbladet* website, I just read it, and I'm sure they'll give it a lot of space in the newspaper tomorrow. The journalist spoke with a girl whose mother was once attacked by him. Or was it grandmother? And the thing about the mask fits brilliantly, although... maybe I'm the only one who knows that, besides Andreas Falkenborg himself."

This was both good and bad news for Simonsen. The phone call to Police Headquarters could not be postponed. He got hold of Poul Troulsen, told him about the situation and asked him to assess the risk of the leak and provide Jeanette Hvidt with any necessary protection. Finally he took the opportunity to call off the blockade of the brothel. Agnete Bahn, who had followed his calls with interest, revealed her overly white teeth in a broad smile when she heard that her business could look forward to a normal turnover for the rest of the day. He wiped the smile off her face as soon as he ended the call.

"Bear in mind that I can resume my surveillance of your house in the space of ten minutes."

She accepted this without visible annoyance.

"I'll keep my part of the agreement."

"That sounds sensible. Now the mask you mentioned...you can work out for yourself that this is not just something the newspapers made up, and I am very interested in what you can tell me about it, but I would prefer to take things in sequence."

"Okay, but tell me what you asked about last. I've forgotten."

"Tell me about conditions within the Falkenborg household, as you experienced them."

"So, first and foremost, Alf Falkenborg decided everything. He was totally high-handed when he chose to be. But often he was indifferent to the way things were going at home, although you could never really tell which way he'd jump. One day Andreas would have to stand there and talk about his scouting trips, what merit badges he had earned and which ones he still hadn't finished, how many kilometres he had walked without complaining, and so on in the same vein. The next day the kid might be completely neglected."

"That doesn't sound healthy for a boy."

"Definitely not. It was bad for him, though I couldn't see that then. The truth is that I was delighted when his father took things out on him. I couldn't stand the kid."

"Was he beaten or punished severely in any other way?"

"No, I wouldn't say that. His mother never hit him, he was almost her only consolation, and occasionally his father gave him a slap, but very seldom. He also got slapped around at school now and then, but you couldn't say he was beaten up exactly. No, it was much worse for the mother. Alf hit her so often she had to wear sunglasses all the time. I'm sure you know the type."

"Yes, I do. Was Andreas Falkenborg present when his father was violent towards his mother?"

"Yes, and I was too. The old man was not too particular, he always did as he pleased. He didn't hesitate to beat her if the son had been up to mischief. Andreas's conduct was her responsibility, and if he didn't live up to his father's expectations, she could expect to pay for it immediately."

"How did she react to that kind of payment?"

"Well, what do you think? She whined and pleaded."

"In front of the child?"

"Absolutely, and he would have to console her afterwards. It's not so strange that he became a monster."

"What other forms of abuse did you see? Did you have any impression that Andreas Falkenborg was sexually exploited? By either his father or his mother?"

"No, it wasn't like that. The only one who was sexually abused in that house was me."

"What about alcohol or drugs?"

"Nothing of that sort."

"So the situation was not that Alf Falkenborg came home drunk and beat his wife?"

"Not at all. I don't recall seeing either of them drunk. Maybe they were on some occasions, but it was definitely not something that characterised their home life. I remember that they always drank water with meals."

"Why was Elisabeth Falkenborg beaten?"

Agnete Bahn thought briefly before she answered. "Except when there was trouble with Andreas, I don't think there was any particular reason."

"Was there a lot of trouble with him?"

"No, I can't say that.

"But you said she was hit often."

"Yes, she really was. At least once a month, but why I don't know. Maybe he simply liked hitting her, who cares? I never thought that much about it, either then or later."

"Why didn't she leave him?"

"No idea. But where could she go?"

Simonsen shrugged and dropped the subject.

"You didn't like Elisabeth Falkenborg?"

"I didn't like any of them, not the husband, the wife or the son."

"Because?"

"She was so unbelievably arrogant, along with the fact that nothing I did was good enough. I had to pay the price for her beatings. Among other things. And Andreas was a quick learner. Sometimes he sneaked up behind me to see whether I was cutting corners on the cleaning, for example, and then he tattled to his mother. That was one of his favourite pastimes."

"What happened then?"

"She yelled at me. Yes, it doesn't sound that bad, but she would degrade me so that I almost cried. She was also after me constantly about my appearance. I was supposed to wear this maid's uniform with a silly little apron tied around my waist, and it was supposed to look laundered and ironed the whole day, even after I'd had it on for eight hours, and that was practically impossible. My hair was supposed to be set neatly, she checked that too."

"What about makeup?"

"Totally forbidden."

"And nail polish?"

"The same. That sort of thing was completely forbidden."

Simonsen tried pausing in the hope that he had put relevant associations in motion. Agnete Bahn continued speaking.

"She was completely hysterical about my nails. They had to be cut short and completely clean, I had to show them to her often. That's one of the things I remember best about the wife, how I stood in front of her looking down and showing my spread fingers for judgment. It was so humiliating."

"Did she cut your nails if she wasn't satisfied?"

"No, that wasn't necessary, but she probably would have if she'd thought of it."

"Did Andreas Falkenborg watch when you were being inspected?"

"He might have occasionally. It wasn't something she tried to hide, if that's what you mean."

"You mentioned that you were sexually abused. I assume that it was by Alf Falkenborg."

"Yes, that's correct. The wife was not active in that way, but she knew what was going on. To that extent she was also involved in deceiving me, but I only understood that when I was older. Although—well, she was probably forced to, otherwise he would have beaten her."

"How were you deceived?"

"I forged cheques, but not to steal. I didn't swipe so much as a krone for as long as I was there. That would have been impossible anyway, because every øre was accounted for when I was done shopping, the wife made sure of that."

She stopped talking then and Simonsen said, "You forged cheques?"

"Yes, eleven to be exact. On Fridays I was supposed to do the grocery shopping for the week, and the husband always wrote a cheque to me—for four hundred kroner, I recall, and that was a lot of money back then. The wife was gone that day. I don't remember why, but that's how it was. So one Friday he forgot to write the cheque, and he called from the factory and told me, but to avoid having to come all the way home, he asked me to write one myself. The first time he had to instruct me thoroughly, over the phone that is, about where the key to his desk drawer was, about the fountain pen and how to do it in general. But he took his time, the piece of shit."

"What about his handwriting?"

"It wasn't hard. He wrote in block letters, and his signature was neat cursive, probably for the same reason. Obviously I didn't think for a moment that what I was doing was illegal. I mean, when he was the one who asked me to do it."

"It wasn't either, not something you would be convicted of."

"Shut up! I was so naive. Well, I can't do it over now, and later I learned a few tricks myself."

"I believe that. Then I suppose at some point he accused you of forgery?"

"No, she did. The wife, that is."

"She was the one who accused you?"

"Yep. She was the instigator. She had lined up all eleven cheques on the dining-room table and carefully ordered them. Well, all in all it added up to almost five thousand kroner, and that was a real fortune, don't you follow me?"

"Yes, I follow you."

"I protested my innocence and explained the circumstances. To start with I wasn't worried, but when the husband came home and said he could not recall anything about any telephone calls— yes, he only called the first time, later it became a fixed routine—then I got really, really scared. But he said he couldn't be bothered to listen to me and left, after which the wife twisted the knife in the wound by telling me about the punishment for forgery. The end of it was that I had to go to my room. She said she would see if she could placate her husband, so that there would be no scandal. Or that's what she said."

Agnete Bahn poured herself a glass of juice and took a sip before continuing.

"So I sat there alone, shaking, and every time I heard a car on the road, I thought it was the police coming to get me. Not until a long time after that did Mrs Falkenborg ring for me, and then she told me that they would temper justice with mercy if in return I would sleep with her husband. No beating about the bush or anything, it was straight from the hip. Sunday evening, without any whining, which the factory owner didn't like, and then in return he would forget about the cheques and cover the loss. What do you make of that? Cover the loss! They had eaten every krone of that money."

"But you went along with the agreement?"

"What else could I do? It was terrible. I recall that I threw up afterwards, but prison would have been worse."

"Yes, I'm sure it would."

"Five years or spread your legs, that was the choice. Bear in mind I was no more than twenty-two, and the wife was very convincing. And the next Sunday evening he came to me, and it was revolting—he was affectionate, said sentimental things and even acted shy, while he drooled and sighed and unwrapped me like I was a Christmas present. Damn, how I hated that."

"When was that? More or less?"

"Sunday, the fifth of December, 1964, at eleven-thirty."

"And how long did this go on?"

"Until I left the family. I don't believe he skipped a single Sunday, except naturally when it couldn't be otherwise. But I couldn't cheat, because the wife kept close track of my periods. Gradually at least I got him out of the affectionate crap, and thank God for that, because that was the worst. And then the anxiety every month about being pregnant because he didn't use a rubber, the pig. I've often thought that he must have produced a few bastard children at the office. I mean, if there were many others like me. Well, finally it was all by schedule, so he came home on the hour and screwed me like I was a cylinder, then left again."

Simonsen speculated about whether her dubious career might have a connection to Alf Falkenborg's assaults. He did not ask, however, but said instead, "You mentioned that you knew something about a mask. What did you mean by that?"

"It was a Sunday evening and as usual he was there, but that evening it went completely wrong. Tell me, do you remember *Belphégor*?"

Simonsen felt a stab of anxiety when he heard that name. A long-forgotten feeling of disgust was suddenly brought back to life after lying dormant for years. Only a split second later he remembered what the name referred to.

"You mean the TV series?"

"Yes, it was broadcast in the summer of 1965 and emptied the streets, as they say. There were four episodes, and they were scheduled for Saturday evening. I got permission to watch them in the living room with the family."

"I remember the film well, it was French. I was a little afraid of that Belphégor spirit, when he wandered around at night in the Louvre and smothered his victims."

"*She*, the spirit was a woman, it turned out."

"I didn't remember that, but how does Belphégor come into the picture?"

"Andreas, the little idiot, loved to scare me. He did that often, and it had nothing to do with Belphégor. He hid some place or other and ran out and said 'Boo'. A few times I got so scared I was on the verge of hitting him."

She clenched her fist before she continued.

"After he had seen that film, he made a Belphégor mask of black cardboard and papier-mâché, with fabric along the sides of the head. Well, it's hard to explain, but maybe you remember what the spirit looked like?"

"Yes, it was Egyptian-looking, and I remember very well how scary everyone thought it was."

Agnete Bahn confirmed that, and let out a little sigh before she continued.

"Well, one Sunday evening, when Alf Falkenborg was there to get his usual, Andreas sneaked out with the mask on and peeked in my window while shining a flashlight at himself to scare the life out of me. He succeeded. I screamed like an animal when I saw him. That is, while I was riding his father. I tell you, he froze up against the window, or to be more exact the mask did, as if he couldn't think how to get away. And that was right when the father got going."

"Alf Falkenborg discovered his son with the mask on?"

"Of course he did. I was howling with anxiety and pointing at the window, until…well, it didn't take long before I figured out that it was Andreas. The father went raving mad, and in no time had pulled the mother out of her bedroom and dragged her outside, after which he beat her so hard that it echoed in the night, and this time with a stick. I had never before seen her take such a beating. He was so angry, called Andreas everything imaginable…Peeping Tom, pervert, deviant, that sort of thing."

"What did Andreas do in the meantime?"

"He sat huddled up by the window wearing his crazy mask."

"You said that you were riding Alf Falkenborg. Would you please elaborate on that?"

"Tell me, do you like hearing that sort of thing?"

"No, but it may have significance…"

"So I was riding him, how hard is that to understand? I was sitting on top of him and pumping up and down. What the hell more do you want me to say?"

"Can you remember whether you had any clothes on your upper body?"

"No, not at all, but I probably didn't. Or, wait a moment… not so long before I left them he was indifferent to what I had on, so long as he could come in. So maybe I had my nightdress on."

"And a bra? Can you remember that?"

"No bra—he tore one in two once, so I never had one on when he came in, because I had to buy a new one myself."

"What about panties? Were you naked below, when you had intercourse?"

"Yes, what the hell do you think?"

"I don't think anything, but I would really like *you* to think it over before you answer."

Surprisingly enough she followed his advice, and having thought about it, doubt arose.

"Now that you mention it, I may very well have had panties on. In the beginning he liked to take my clothing off, but towards the end he just wanted in without a lot of fuss. Maybe he pulled my panties to one side to make room, I won't deny it, but I can't remember that."

Simonsen asked, "Tell me, when you were sitting on him, did you get any enjoyment out of it yourself? And the reason I'm asking is that I would like to know in detail how Andreas Falkenborg saw you, when he was looking in at the window."

She consented, and answered him frankly.

"I hated every breath, but I made it sound as if he was divine because that made it go faster. I discovered that long before. So if you want it spelled out completely, I obviously sighed and moaned and threw myself back and forth in wild ecstasy, which I didn't feel so much as a trace of."

"Thanks, that's exactly what I wanted to hear. Yes—one more thing. You said before that makeup was forbidden, so you had no lipstick on?"

She thought about it.

"I don't know if I had any on that evening, but I may very well have had. Sunday was my day off, and often I'd been out, so that's clearly a possibility."

"Did you use any particular colour of lipstick?"

"Red, always red. As red as possible, if I may say so. Red suits me."

"Splendid, splendid."

"Thanks. Tell me, is there any chance that I can get a reward for this?"

"No. What did you do while this scene was going on?"

"Well, I'm not proud of this, but by then I hated all three of them so much that I enjoyed it. Hearing her yell and plead while he thrashed her hide, that was music to my ears. And Andreas, that little piece of shit... I thought every second of his torment served him right, standing frozen at the window, as if he wasn't there. I went up to him on the other side of it and pressed my face against the glass, while I laughed right into his stupid mask."

"Could you see how he reacted? I mean, because of the mask."

"Easily, he had made holes for his eyes."

"So how was he reacting?"

"He was crying."

CHAPTER 30

Twelve days after the German Chancellor's glaciologist discovered the body of Maryann Nygaard on the Greenland ice cap, Andreas Falkenborg was arrested in Copenhagen.

The task was assigned to assistant detectives Arne Pedersen and Poul Troulsen and was carried out early on Wednesday morning, when he was unlikely to be awake. Konrad Simonsen's hope was that the same applied to the Danish press corps, so the event could proceed without media attention—an argument that was not met with unconditional approval by his two subordinates, as they parked their car after an interrupted night's sleep in front of Falkenborg's residence in Frederiksberg.

Pedersen yawned widely as he got out of the vehicle. He opened his eyes toward the wind, letting the fresh air chase sleep from his head. Then he caught sight of one of the police surveillance vehicles on the other side of the street, and put a finger to his temple in greeting, without being able to see whether he personally knew any of the officers. He received a brief honk of the horn in response. The sound caught Troulsen's attention, and he too gestured in greeting, without however receiving a response.

On their way up the stairs Pedersen commented, "I really hope we either find something incriminating or you and Simon manage to force a confession out of him, because in strictly legal terms we don't have much to hang on him. Not in my view anyway."

"Nor in the district prosecutor's either. She reckons he'll be held on remand for a maximum of three weeks. If the murders hadn't hit the headlines already, I don't think we would have been granted a search warrant at all."

"So for once I'm hoping you get to soften him up properly."

Troulsen was known for using force a bit too freely from time to time, which was not generally to Pedersen's personal taste, but today was obviously an exception. That was the reason why Simonsen had chosen Troulsen in particular, to exploit the suspect's marked childishness and hopefully give the police a solid mental advantage, before he was delivered for questioning at Police Headquarters. In the meantime Pedersen would get an overview of the extent of the search and then summon reinforcements when Falkenborg was taken away. The division of labour between the two men was already clear.

The nameplate on Falkenborg's door was made of brass, and recently polished. Pedersen let a fingertip glide over it before he rang the bell. He rang twice in a row, after which he pounded hard on the door with his knuckles and rang the bell a third time.

A short time passed, then the door opened.

Andreas Falkenborg was revealed, barefoot in a bathrobe. It was obvious that they had woken him, his disoriented expression and dishevelled hair spoke for themselves. Pedersen began the procedure as he held up a piece of paper in front of the face of the half-asleep man and immediately stepped past him.

Falkenborg moved to one side, but then called to Troulsen in a formal voice, "I ask that you identify yourself as a police officer."

The request was presented without panic or aggression, but much louder than seemed necessary, like a scene from a bad comedy. Troulsen concluded that there might be a good reason for this behaviour. The combination of Falkenborg's occupation, the cornerstone of which was eavesdropping, and his choice of words as if lifted straight from the national chief of police's proclamation on identification of the police, reeked of their conversation being covertly recorded. He pulled the man outside onto the landing without a word and pressed him against the wall. Then he commanded authoritatively, "Stay there."

Falkenborg complied, but at the same time called towards the open doorway, "Ow, ow…ow, that hurts! Oh, no, why are you doing that? Ow…"

He was a miserable actor, and Troulsen answered calmly, "Shut your mouth, you're not hurt, but if you try that nonsense again, you'll get one on the head. Do you understand?"

"Yes, sorry."

"Andreas Falkenborg, the time is six-oh-eight a.m. and you are arrested, accused of the murder of nurse Maryann Nygaard in 1983, and physical therapist Catherine Thomsen in 1997."

Troulsen called out to Pedersen, "I'm pretty sure our friend here has set up microphones in his own apartment. I thought you should know that."

Pedersen's face brightened.

"You don't say? How ingenious. But I think I know some people who are good at tracing that sort of thing. Thanks, both of you."

Troulsen led Falkenborg in through the apartment door and on into the bathroom, which he located at once. The man went along willingly and let himself be pressed down on the toilet seat without protest. Here he sat quietly while Troulsen quickly and expertly opened cabinets and drawers to make sure that nothing surprising or unpleasant was inside.

During the search Troulsen decided to take a chance. The probability that Falkenborg had also wiretapped his bathroom was not great, and if it later proved to be the case anyway, the recording could be deleted by a regrettable "accident". Furthermore, the prisoner's submissiveness and cowed, almost imploring eyes told him that he could probably go a bit further than he had intended to start with. He turned toward the man and said harshly, "Don't you ever take a bath?"

"Yes, I do. Every single morning. Of course I do."

"I don't think you smell very good."

"I do."

"My nose is seldom wrong. And to be quite honest, with the sort of hygiene you practise, I wouldn't want to be you if the boss doesn't take to you."

"Your boss?"

"Tell me, are you deaf or dumb? Yes, my boss. He can be very bad-tempered. Vindictive and mean. I don't understand how but he gets away with it. So I hope for your sake that he likes you, although it's not very likely."

Falkenborg asked, terrified, "Why is that? What have I done to him?"

"Nothing... not yet."

"What do you mean? You're scaring me."

"That's really not the idea, partner. Look, forget it. Let's just wind things up here then I can get home and hit the sack."

"No, what do you mean? I really want to know."

Troulsen let him sweat while he pretended to think about it. Then he said casually, "So, you'll end up in prison for the rest of your life for double murder, that goes without saying, but I'm sure you're prepared for that, in one place or another?"

Falkenborg answered gloomily, "Yes, I suppose so."

"You'd better be. Your biggest problem now is where you end up. Tell me, do you know much about Danish prisons? I mean, have you been convicted before?"

"No, never, and I haven't killed anyone either."

"Stop right there! Of course you have, we both know that, but I don't care what you've done with those two bitches. That's not my business, especially not if they annoyed you, I know what a pain that type can be. Well, forget about that, I'm just the one who brings you in, and the only thing I'm interested in is that you get completely clean. Otherwise I risk the boss getting mad at me, and I have absolutely no desire for that to happen, so you're going to take a bath, do you follow me?"

"I would like to, but can't you tell me more about the prisons?"

Troulsen looked at his watch and pretended to consider the suggestion. Then he said, "Andreas, my friend, we can make a deal: you promise to be thorough in the bath, so I don't get into trouble for delivering you unwashed. Then I can tell you which prisons you should avoid, if the boss even gives you the option. What do you say about that? Something for something."

Falkenborg accepted, eager to avoid incurring the boss's anger, it seemed.

After his bath Andreas Falkenborg followed instructions like a lamb and let himself get dressed under expert guidance. Troulsen commented in detail on his choice of clothing and rejected three ties before finally forbidding him from putting one on at all, since it would only be taken away from him in prison. He also got involved in everything from the man's choice of underwear to his shoes. He gave only the vaguest information about Danish prisons, while stroke by stroke painting a terrifying picture of Konrad Simonsen—the cop any sensible prisoner had best not antagonise. Falkenborg said nervously, "You promised to tell me about the prisons."

"That will have to wait until we're in the car, I don't like being recorded."

"May I take my cell phone with me? I have the right to a telephone call at the police station."

"That's okay, so long as it's turned off."

"It is, see for yourself."

Falkenborg meekly held out his phone.

In the car Troulsen put handcuffs on his prisoner, but placed him in the front passenger seat, although that was not normal practice. He wanted to see the man's face during their conversation, which he started bluntly as soon as they drove off.

"There are two prisons you should avoid at all costs. You see, there's an iron-clad pecking order among the cons there, and you'll come in at the very bottom, partly because you have a tendency to smell, and partly because you've killed women. Both are looked down on by the tough nuts and…"

Troulsen continued in the same vein without mercy most of the way to Police Headquarters. Maliciously he told Andreas Falkenborg in detail about how he would be tormented and tortured in prison. That is, if the boss took against him and decided to recommend one of the harsher places. And the lies worked. His prisoner was intimidated.

Although he had an explicit prohibition from Simonsen about doing any definite questioning, Troulsen nevertheless tried, shortly before they arrived. The temptation was simply too great.

"And bear in mind now that the most important thing is not to start sweating with anxiety, because then you'll smell again and that makes the boss hopping mad. It's much better to put your cards on the table right away."

"I'll try not to sweat."

The man was already sweating like a pig, but was possibly not aware of it himself. Troulsen continued casually, "By the way, the girl down in Præstø, what was her name again? The one who disappeared?"

"Annie."

"Yes, exactly. Or was that her name... are you quite certain? Wasn't it Lone instead?"

"No, I'm sure, Annie Lindberg."

"Okay, you would know, so it's Annie now—where did you bury her?"

"But I haven't done that."

"Why drag this out?"

"But it's the truth, I haven't done that."

The man sounded sincere in his own childish, naive way. Troulsen dropped the subject without any real annoyance, knowing full well that Konrad Simonsen would soon be conducting a full-scale interrogation.

CHAPTER 31

The psychologist Ernesto Madsen's assessment was that Andreas Falkenborg would benefit from stewing behind bars for a few hours before questioning began. Simonsen followed the advice and therefore had plenty of time to accompany the Countess to a further meeting with the Oracle from Købmagergade. They walked there together, she half a step ahead of him on the pavement as if she wanted to lead the way now that she had convinced him to go along. A sultry high-pressure system hung over the city. Streets and people sweated, while the liberating thunderstorm that the weather prophets had promised still bided its time. Simonsen said, "I hope he doesn't think we're going into the greenhouse itself, because then we'll melt. This is bad enough."

The Countess had been asked to meet the Oracle in front of the Palm House in the Botanical Gardens. She had accepted without question; one place was as good as another.

"I doubt he does."

Simonsen's legs were tingling and itching; he felt clumsy. On top of that he was panting from the heat.

"We should have taken the car."

"And driven around half an hour looking for a parking place? It's good for you to walk a little. We can take a taxi back, if this drags on."

"It won't drag on. I have other things to get done, you know."

The reproach was subtle, but it was there. She said, "I'm glad you came along."

"I'll be glad to get this over with."

They went in at the gate to the Botanical Gardens; she held it open for him and closed it behind them. Soon the urban noise faded out to a background hum, and the Countess took Simonsen's arm as if the calm legitimised intimacy. She said, "It's pleasant in here, don't you think? All the lovely plants…it's almost semi-Mediterranean, and all so well tended."

"Yes, it's a nice place."

Simonsen's knowledge of field biology was limited to his ability to identify a dandelion with great certainty and a few other plants with a degree of difficulty. He stopped and scratched one ankle, then the other while he was at it.

"Tell me one thing, Simon. Your clairvoyant friend in Høje Taastrup, whom you consult now and then, how often is she actually right, if I may ask?"

"Why are you speculating about that now?"

"Oh, general interest."

"She gets it right occasionally, mostly she's not that useful. But don't ask how she does it, because I've given up trying to figure that out."

"But sometimes she helps?"

"As I said, yes."

"Can you give me an example?"

"Many years ago I had a case where a lunatic had stretched a thin wire across the street in a small provincial town. The purpose was to stop a handful of local moped drivers once and for all. They used to tear through the town on Saturday night, to the detriment of ordinary people's sleep. Fortunately the lead driver was leaning down over the steering wheel, so he hit the wire with his forehead. Obviously he fell over and got some nasty scrapes, but the driver behind him was less fortunate. The wire broke, and the recoil tore the boy's eye out."

"Nasty."

"Yes, not good, but the worst thing of all was that if the boys had been driving normally, they would probably have been decapitated, which was the intention. Well, in solving that case I was guided by my clairvoyant woman in Høje Taastrup, as you call her. She gave me a rather unusual name that proved to belong to the owner of a hardware store several hundred kilometres from the town. It was there the guilty party turned out to have bought his wire. He was a seventy-eight-year-old man, by the way, who had become sick and tired of the noise. Enough was enough, as he said. And now it's your turn, Countess. Why are you suddenly so interested in clairvoyance? Spit it out."

She told him about her brief but thought-provoking telephone conversation and noticed, when she was done, that she felt relieved. He walked for a bit in silence and then muttered, "Yes, she can be somewhat manic when it hits her. Well, we're just about here."

The Palm House towered before them, shining in all its glory in the hazy sunlight. The Countess searched in vain for her oracle, until a familiar voice made them both turn. Behind them, on the small patch of grass in the shadow of a "Water Lily" magnolia, sat Helmer Hammer.

The under secretary had shed jacket and tie, which lay neatly folded behind him, besides removing his shoes and socks. His white feet sticking out from under well-pressed Cerruti trousers gave a strange slant on informality. He smiled winningly as the Countess and Konrad Simonsen sat down opposite him, and then asked with a lively show of interest about their personal lives as well as about the investigation. Soon they were deep into a conversation that all three of them enjoyed.

This was one of Helmer Hammer's many strong points; he could get people to relax in his company, in part because he acted as if he had all the time in the world just for them. When he was in that mode, courteous and concerned, he did not seem like a man tormented by complex affairs of state, but rather someone who was naturally open and honest, the kind of person you would like to have as a friend. The Countess slid off her shoes too. Helmer Hammer passed around cold water, which he had brought along in his bag, and laughed good-naturedly at Simonsen's account of the photo search for the maids.

"So you thought that Malte Borup sold information from the police databases for G?"

"It sounded that way for a moment, and that made me furious. But the system was efficient enough: pictures of seven maids in less than half an hour is not bad going."

"Yes, you should never underestimate informal systems. That's one of the reasons I like this place so much. I have found many capable students for the ministries here ... that is, without all the usual employment rigmarole. When there isn't a university vacation, there are always a few promising young people here, reading or talking, so you get a proper impression of their potential."

The Countess asked, "Do you come here often?"

"Not as much as I'd like, not any more unfortunately. But isn't it lovely?"

Hammer threw out his arms as if he owned the garden, and continued.

"You should try coming here in early June when the magnolias are in full bloom. Then there's the Palm House, a true architectural gem. It was finished in 1874, one of the first Danish buildings where exposed steel was used for the load-bearing construction, as with the Eiffel Tower. The architects were not even architects but gardeners, and the whole thing was due to beer."

"Jacobsen the brewer was a patron, I believe?" queried Simonsen.

"He was, yes."

Helmer Hammer let the rest of his mineral water slop around in small, centrifugal swirls, while he silently observed the movement inside the bottle. Then he continued speaking.

"Well, Assistant Detective of the First Degree Nathalie von Rosen, I'm not the only one who is interested in Danish history."

The formal address was meant jokingly, but set things on a business footing. Surprisingly enough, it was Simonsen who responded.

"Both of us are interested, and it's easy to explain why but hard to understand."

"Okay then. Can I at least try?"

The power relationship between the homicide chief and the under secretary was as unequal as could be, and on top of that the police investigators' historical research was ill-timed, to put it mildly. Nonetheless Konrad Simonsen crumpled Helmer

Hammer like a piece of used sandwich paper: first he described the Countess's ominous Høje Taastrup telephone call without a trace of apology, then reviewed two specific examples of clairvoyance that had proved to be useful to the police, including the story about the moped drivers, this time narrated in spell-binding fashion. The Countess thoroughly enjoyed his performance, not least his lively descriptions and the way he refused to pour scorn on any of her actions. No one in his right mind would have done anything different if they had been warned in the same way, he implied. Obviously not, that would almost be dereliction of duty. Helmer Hammer was effectively up against the wall, a fact he quickly realised and humbly adapted to.

"I didn't see that coming. Yes, it is a little hard to discuss this with you when you have mediums in your back pocket. *Stick to him like a burr*, what a great sentence, and it must be admitted you have done just that, Countess. And to top it off, with great competence. You have my unreserved admiration."

The Countess nodded without saying anything. She felt more vindicated than ever about conducting her alternative investigation after Konrad Simonsen had described it in such glowing terms. He was right, it was simply something she *had* to do.

Helmer Hammer continued, still primarily addressing the Countess.

"Perhaps for a moment we could call what you think you've found out about Bertil Hampel-Koch's trip to Greenland in 1983, *truth number one*. I give it a number because I also have a truth in that connection, which we can suitably call *truth number two*.

"In the seventies and eighties it was established custom in the Defence Ministry to invite capable young officials to go along on the Sirius patrol for a few weeks—you know, the sled dog team that enforces Denmark's sovereignty in North and East Greenland during the winter. It was considered an honour to be invited and looked very good on a résumé besides, so almost everyone who received the offer accepted. In 1983 it was Bertil Hampel-Koch's turn, but here a problem arose. Bertil had very little desire to go to Greenland under his own surname, due to the fact that from 1978 to 1994 his uncle, Tyge Hampel-Koch, was defence chief. And that is easy enough to understand. It wouldn't have been the easiest starting point for him with the other men on the expedition. Completely without precedent, his chief administrative officer therefore gave Bertil permission to use the name Steen Hansen on his journey, or rather journeys, because there were two. How the job title geologist came into the picture, I don't really know."

Simonsen asked, "He made two trips, you say?"

"Yes, the first was in the summer of 1983, when he flew to Station North all the way up in Northeast Greenland in Crown Prince Christian Land. Here he met some of his future Sirius comrades and also helped set out stockpiles for the winter expeditions. It was on that trip that he made a stopover in Søndre Strømfjord, but you know that. The other time was for the sled trip itself in February 1984, and that is obviously not very interesting to us."

The Countess asked with surprise, "So he did not go to Thule—"

Helmer Hammer interrupted her amiably but firmly.

"Now, now. This is my truth, I am formulating it. It is undeniably correct that on his journey to Station North in 1983 Bertil Hampel-Koch made a stop at the military base in Søndre Strømfjord. And in that connection I have a problem, which I hope perhaps you will help me with."

Simonsen replied first.

"We're all ears."

"It's no secret that I prefer *truth number two* — that is, my own interpretation—which I promise you is reliable through and through. I should not conceal either that it is also preferable for my boss and his many predecessors. *Truth number one* on the other hand—seen from our perspective—still needs to be kept under wraps twenty, thirty years before it is carefully examined."

His use of the plural form was nicely judged. His two listeners were now painfully aware of what they were up against, if they did not play this Hammer's way, and both of them silently consented. He smiled winningly.

"My wife and my daughter always tell me that I should rely more on other people, and they're right of course. Will you help me in spreading *truth number two*? It would have the greatest effect, of course, coming from you. Besides, I never forget a favour."

Simonsen answered hesitantly, "What did you have in mind?"

He explained and again they accepted, the Countess however with a touch of resentment.

"In other words: no Thule, no book, and no letter?"

The under secretary shook his head apologetically.

"No Thule, no book, and no letter. That is unfortunately correct, but I well understand if you—in addition to doing what you have to do—have become a trifle fascinated by the story. That letter in particular is quite amazing. It is a real masterpiece and should be printed on the back of every single employment document in Slotsholmen, under the heading *Read and Learn*."

He looked at his watch and reached for his shoes, but then had second thoughts and carried on speaking.

"So, the US government asks Denmark about the country's attitude towards atomic weapons in Greenland. A simple, straightforward question. The response, on the other hand, is anything but simple. On the contrary, it is outstanding in its artfulness, and all down to one of Bertil's predecessors—Nils Svenningsen was his name. To start with, the reply establishes that the American Ambassador presented no specific plan for the introduction of atomic weapons in Greenland, which is completely true. Governments have generals for *specific* military plans. Also, *atomic bombs* are rewritten to *ammunition supplies of a particular type*. And then what is completely fabulous—director Svenningsen has his prime minister answer based on the absence of specific plans: *I do not think that your comments give reason for any comments on my part*."

He gestured eagerly.

"Translation: you may by all means introduce all the atomic bombs you want—although we officially forbid that—so long as we know nothing. *I do not think that your comments give reason for any comments on my part . . .* and this to the US government! That is damned ingenious."

This time it was Simonsen who looked at his watch. He had a double murderer to question, and besides, he had a hard time appreciating where evasiveness ended and ingenuity began.

CHAPTER 32

The questioning of Andreas Falkenborg began with silence. For a long time Konrad Simonsen stared down his prisoner, and watched the other man squirm under his gaze. It was evident that his discomfort at being observed made him restless and uncertain; he wrung his hands and stared down at the table like a guilty child. Simonsen let the other man stew and stonewalled the few times the prisoner looked at him, mutely imploring him to get the interview going.

Finally Simonsen recited the necessary preamble.

"Please state your name."

"Andreas Falkenborg."

"Birth date and place."

"July the eleventh, 1955, in Copenhagen."

"Where in Copenhagen?"

"The Municipal Hospital."

"And where did your parents live?"

"Bispebjerg, when I was born. I don't know the address, they moved shortly after."

"That doesn't matter. Andreas Falkenborg, you are accused of the murder of two women, namely the murder of Maryann Nygaard on September the thirteenth, 1983 near the radar station DYE-5 on the Greenland ice cap; and the murder of Catherine Thomsen on April the fifth, 1997 on Nordstrand outside Stevns Klint in Zealand. In addition you are a suspect in the murder of Annie Lindberg Hansson, who disappeared at Jungshoved near Præstø on October the fifth, 1990, and the kidnapping and attempted murder of Rikke Barbara Hvidt on May the sixth, 1977 in Kikhavn at Hundested. Do you understand these accusations?"

"Yes, but I haven't done anything."

"Do you also know that you have the right to a lawyer who can support you?"

"Yes, I know that."

"Would you like a lawyer?"

"No, thanks."

"I will make a note of that."

A brief shudder ran through Falkenborg then, almost like a slight epileptic fit. Simonsen wrinkled his brow; that reaction was not in his script, and the last thing he needed was a suspect who did not let himself be questioned. Falkenborg asked, "Can I change my mind later? And get a lawyer then if I want?"

"Yes, of course you can."

"And you won't be angry with me?"

"My reaction is unimportant. If you want legal representation, just say so, and I will interrupt questioning until the lawyer has arrived."

"Thanks."

"You should also know that you have no obligation to speak. If you choose to do so, anything you say can possibly be used against you in court. Do you understand that?"

"Yes, I understand."

"And even though you are not compelled to, you really want to talk to me?"

"Yes, I do."

Simonsen noted to himself that now not even the most meddlesome defence lawyer could reasonably maintain anything other than that the man was well acquainted with his rights. Simonsen's first actual question had been carefully chosen in consultation with Ernesto Madsen.

"You make a living by spying on other people. Do you like doing that?"

Surprisingly enough, the suspect answered honestly and without the slightest embarrassment.

"Yes, I think it's fun. I've always thought that, ever since I was a kid."

"Why is that?"

"I don't know, it's just the way I am."

"You like watching people without them knowing it?"

"Yes."

"Eavesdropping?"

"Yes."

"Preferably on women?"

"Sometimes it's men, it depends on who wants my help, and I also sell things… microphones, cameras, computer software and that kind of thing."

"Would you call that spying equipment?"

"Yes, that describes it well, but it's completely legal."

"No one is saying it isn't. Tell me, when you are spying on strangers, do you prefer them to be women or men?"

"Definitely women, I do best with them."

"Why is that?"

"It's easier. Women talk more than men, and I also think it's more fun."

"Why is it more fun?"

"I don't really know, I've never thought about it, but I guess it's because I'm normal."

"Normal?"

"Yes, that is, like other men. I'm not abnormal."

"It's not normal to kill three women. That's extremely abnormal."

This time Falkenborg seemed ashamed. He lowered his eyes and answered, "I know that."

"What you have done is very serious."

"Yes, when you put it that way."

"It almost sounds as if you're sorry."

"I am."

"Well, that's a start anyway. Tell me, why did you kill Maryann Nygaard?"

Andreas Falkenborg hesitated, trembled slightly and pulled back.

"I did not kill Maryann Nygaard. I didn't do that."

Simonsen noticed how he bent his neck and lifted one arm, as if he was going to sniff his own armpit.

"What are you doing?"

"Nothing … it's nothing."

"You're lying to me. Why did you kill Maryann Nygaard?"

"I don't know."

"You don't know? What do you mean?"

"I don't know why I killed her."

"What about Catherine Thomsen, don't you know why you killed her either?"

The man shook his head. Simonsen said, "The suspect Andreas Falkenborg is shaking his head. Please say that out loud."

"Excuse me, I forgot. I don't know why I killed Catherine… Catherine Thomsen."

"You waited for her in your car at Roskilde Station on April the fifth, 1997?"

"Yes, we had an agreement."

"What kind of agreement was that?"

"Catherine was abnormal, she liked other girls but that was a secret. She was also very Christian. Maybe I said that I could help her."

"With what?"

"She was made wrong… it's embarrassing… I don't want to talk about it."

"So tell me instead how you killed the women. First Maryann Nygaard, how did you kill her?"

And then suddenly they were back where they started. Falkenborg asked timidly, "But should I say that I killed them when I didn't do that?"

Simonsen was beginning to sense a pattern. To start with he refrained from answering, but he could hardly ignore it when Falkenborg added, "Will you be angry if I tell you that I didn't kill them?"

"Did you kill Maryann Nygaard and Catherine Thomsen or didn't you?"

"I didn't."

"You didn't?"

"No, if that's all right with you?"

Simonsen swore to himself; this could be far more difficult than he'd first expected. He decided to change focus. First however he leaned across the table, stared his prisoner in the eyes and said uncompromisingly, "When we're sitting here making small talk, you seem like a pleasant person, Andreas. But I also see something else: I see a young girl cast her head back and forth in a desperate attempt to suck in air while her eyes are about to pop out, and you just sit alongside and enjoy the view. And thinking about that makes me *so* angry."

Falkenborg's face twitched. Simonsen took a print from his folder and set it in front of the suspect, noticing how he pulled back in his seat, as if he wanted to put as much physical distance as possible between himself and the photograph.

"What's the matter? Are you scared of her?"

"Yes, a little—I don't like that type of woman."

"What type is that?"

"One like her."

"Can you expand on that?"

"It's hard. Just someone like that, they scare me. Won't you take her away?"

"No. Do you recognise her?"

"Yes, her name is Rikke, but back then she was young. She isn't any more. She can't be."

"Rikke Barbara Hvidt, and you're right, this picture is of her when she was young. It was taken in 1976, when she was twenty-three years old. When did you meet her?"

"A long time ago. It was in 1978, I think."

"Could it have been 1977?"

"Yes, that fits."

"Where did you see her for the first time?"

"On the ferry from Rørvig to Hundested."

"Tell me about it."

"Both of us were on bikes. That is, they were tied to a railing on the deck of the ferry. Then she came over to me and asked if I would help her fix the chain on hers. So I did that."

"You weren't afraid of her at that point?"

"Yes, very."

"Why didn't you leave or tell her she could get help from someone else?"

"I don't know, it's hard to explain."

"For the next six months you pursued her as often as you could. You interrupted your studies and moved into the Hundested Inn."

"Yes."

"Why is that?"

"I don't know. I was afraid of her, I guess."

"That doesn't make sense."

"No, I know that. But you mustn't be angry with me. I can't explain it."

"I won't be angry, but I would really like to understand. What did you want with her?"

"I don't know."

"I think you do know."

"Maybe I wanted to go out with her."

"Did you want to go out with her?"

"No."

"So stop saying that."

"Sorry."

Again Falkenborg sniffed himself, this time however without being tormented by spasms or other uncontrollable muscle movements. Simonsen continued.

"You made a scene when she cut her hair."

"Yes, I did."

"Why did you do that?"

"I don't know."

"You shouted and wept and carried on, isn't that right?"

"Yes, I shouted and wept and carried on."

"Where was that?"

"At her hair salon… the salon was on the main street in Hundested."

"Tell me about it."

"There's not much to tell, I followed her that day—"

"Which you had done on many other days?"

"Yes, that's why I was there, to follow her, and then I saw that she was going into the hair salon to get her hair cut short, and so I went in too and… shouted and screamed and carried on. They called the police. It wasn't pleasant."

"But after that day you stopped pursuing her, why is that?"

"Because she had cut her hair. But I didn't stop completely."

"What do you mean?"

"I was up watching her again after a few years. To see whether she still had short hair, but she did. It was maybe in 1980, and then she didn't notice me."

"You were only interested in her if she had long hair?"

"Yes, their hair should go down to their shoulders."

"Their hair? Who are *they*?"

"The women I'm afraid of, those types. They breed. They bring new ugly cuttings into the world. You have to deal with them at once."

Simonsen felt a cold shudder pass through him and asked sharply, "What do you mean by that? What do you mean, breed?"

"I'm sorry, I don't know why I said that."

"Who is an ugly cutting?"

"That I can't say. Maybe the ones I'm afraid of."

"Are you thinking about anyone in particular?"

"Rikke, I was afraid of her."

"No others?"

"Yes, others too, but mostly Rikke, since we're talking about her."

Simonsen observed him coldly. Falkenborg squirmed, but said nothing.

"How could you have been afraid?"

"I don't know, I was young then, maybe I didn't really know what I was doing."

"Stuff and nonsense, you knew exactly what you were doing."

"Sorry."

"But I think I know why you are afraid of women who resemble Rikke Barbara Hvidt."

Simonsen took out another photograph and set it in front of the suspect. Falkenborg looked and said, "Ugh."

"You say 'ugh', so you recognise the picture?"

"Yes, it's Belphégor."

"Explain."

"It's a demon from TV."

"*The Ghost from the Louvre* played by Juliette Gréco, broadcast in the summer of 1965?"

"Yes, that was it."

"Have you ever owned such a Belphégor mask?"

"No, never."

Again a shudder and the nose by the armpit. Finally Simonsen got the point.

"You shiver when you're lying."

"Yes, I've always done that. Or if I get nervous. I can't help it."

"You lied just now."

"Yes, I'm sorry about that."

"So you have owned such a demon mask?"

"Yes, when I was a kid. I made it myself, it took a long time."

"Where is the mask now?"

"I'd rather not tell you, it's a secret."

"Well, then, let's wait a little and see if we don't find it some place or other when we search your apartment. I would bet we do."

Simonsen reached across the table and moved the photograph of Rikke Barbara Hvidt over to the left of the man and the demon correspondingly to the right. Then he placed a picture of Agnete Bahn in the middle before him. Andreas Falkenborg started shaking.

"Who is she?"

"Her name was Agnete. She was our maid when I was a child. She was an evil person."

"One night you tried to scare her with your mask, didn't you?"

"Yes, it was a Sunday. I would prefer not to talk about it, if I can avoid it."

"You sneaked up outside her window with your demon mask on and shone a flashlight on your head so that she would be scared. What happened then?"

"Can I avoid saying anything about that?"

"No, you can't."

"I didn't kill Agnete."

"I know that, did she get too old?"

"She didn't look like that any more when I grew up."

"And she wasn't scared that night in the summer of 1965 when you were peeking in her window. The whole thing turned out quite different from the way you expected, right?"

"She screamed when she saw me."

"Tell me!"

"She was sitting on top of my dad, she shouldn't have been doing that, and I wasn't supposed to see that, definitely not. I don't want to talk about it."

"Your father got your mother and hit her, because you behaved as you did."

"My mother screamed, it was awful, I dream about it at night."

"While you were still pressed against the window with your mask on and all."

"I didn't know what I should do. You mustn't say anything else, my whole body is shaking and sweating. I can't help it that I sweat."

"What did Agnete Bahn do in the meantime?"

"It was terrible, I'll never forget it, it's stored inside me … deep, deep inside me. She pretended that she was kissing me, she thought the whole thing was very funny, her lipstick was on the windowpane for days. Should she have done that? I was just a kid."

"No, she shouldn't have done that."

"I hoped that she was dead, but you've spoken with her?"

"Yes, I have spoken with her."

"Can she go to jail for what she did?"

"No, she can't."

"What about me? Can I go to jail for what happened in Hundested? I mean, such a long time after?"

"No."

"Not for what I did on the shore either."

Simonsen shook his head insincerely.

"No, you can't, but we're covering the same ground without getting anywhere. Tell me, do they cry out from inside the bag, do they scream out their fear, or do they use their last bit of oxygen to beg for mercy? What does a dying woman's voice sound like, when her air passages are blocked by plastic? Resonant, shrill, distorted? I don't know, because I've never heard it. But you have, and I get hopping mad thinking about it."

Falkenborg asked in a whimper, "You want to hear about Rikke, right?"

"Yes, I would like that very much. Among other things."

"So it doesn't matter that I'm sweating?"

"No, it's all the same to me."

Falkenborg's story about his attack on Rikke Barbara was reasonably consistent with what the woman herself had told Simonsen last Thursday. Almost all the particulars fitted, which was good news, but nothing concrete connected him to the later murders, as the attack—even if brief—had been described on the *Dagbladet* website in Jeanette Hvidt's interpretation. Unfortunately also including the bizarre pretend nail clipping, a detail the police otherwise would have withheld. The same did not apply to his use of lipstick, but on the beach in Kikhavn he hadn't had time to use it before he was interrupted. In addition his strange way of talking had not been disclosed. The problem was that possibly he didn't know himself how he talked. Simonsen probed, but without much success.

"You dug a grave on the shore. When did you do that?"

"A few hours before I attacked her."

"And she was going to be buried there?"

"Exactly, but she got away from me."

"But you intended to kill her?"

"Yes, that was the idea, but it didn't happen."

"How did you want to do that?"

"I think in a plastic bag, like the two women that were murdered in Greenland and at Stevns."

"You think, you say, but wouldn't you have to know that?"

"So I know that."

"Did you have a plastic bag with you?"

"Yes, two bags."

"Where were they?"

"In my pocket, I think."

"In your pocket, are you sure of that?"

"No, I can't remember."

"Where could they have been otherwise?"

"In my other pocket, maybe."

"No other place?"

"It could be, I can't remember, it was a long time ago."

"Why did you have the mask on?"

"Because I like scaring them."

"Them…who do you mean by 'them'?"

"The ones I scare. I liked to scare Rikke."

"It's nice for you to see Rikke, and other women who resemble her, get scared?"

"Very nice, as scared as possible. Really, really scared, that's nice."

"You pretended you were clipping her nails, why is that?"

"My mother used to do that to them, I think that's where it comes from."

"Explain that to me."

"Yes, they just had to stand there and get their disgusting claws clipped. It served them right."

"Where did you have the scissors?"

"In my pocket."

"Also in your pocket?"

"I think so, couldn't they be in my pocket?"

"You decide that."

"Then it was there."

"Tell me, how did you get Rikke Barbara Hvidt to show you her nails?"

"*Out with the claws, stupid girl, he wants to see her nails.* I said something like that."

"Did it work, did she show her nails?"

"No, she didn't, she was contrary, she didn't want to obey."

"What did you do then?"

"Said it again."

"Said what again?"

"*Out with the claws, stupid girl, he wants to see her nails.* But she held her hands behind her back and drilled her nails down into the ice and was beside herself."

"You were patient, you just stood in front of her with the scissors and repeated your sentence?"

"Yes, that's how it was."

"But not with the flashlight, that wasn't necessary."

"No, no flashlight."

"Where did you get light from?"

"Maybe the lighthouse, there was a lighthouse."

"No, there wasn't, where did you get light from? A fine, sharp light."

"From the helicopter. The helicopter had lights in front."

"Exactly, but not all of them held their hands behind their backs, did they?"

"No, you're probably right. Not all of them."

"One of them was difficult for you."

"She didn't want to behave."

"In what way didn't she want to behave?"

"Maybe she clenched her fists, then it's impossible. And hit."

"I don't believe that. It wasn't impossible, just difficult. Why was it difficult?"

"Maybe she folded her hands."

"So you had to cut the way she was?"

"Yes."

"Why did she fold her hands?"

"She was praying to God."

"Yes, she did that, and what was her name?"

"Liz maybe."

"There is no Liz, stop lying."

"I'm not lying."

"You're sweating and shaking."

"I'm nervous."

"Well, what was her name then?"

"Her name was Catherine, she was very religious."

Simonsen considered taking a break. The man's accommodating and compliant language would not be convincing in court, if the testimony he'd just given were withdrawn. It was difficult to decide whether he cynically and consciously took refuge in naiveté, or whether he simply was like that. Conversely, Simonsen was afraid that his prisoner would demand a lawyer or refuse further questioning if he had a chance to think it over.

Falkenborg's next statement decided the dilemma.

"It was Liz who hit, you have to excuse that. But I would prefer not to talk about her."

The new name triggered a spontaneous outburst from Simonsen.

"Oh, no."

"I'm sorry about that, but you mustn't get angry with me."

The latest turn the interview had taken, combined with the casual way Andreas Falkenborg had leaped from the attack in Kikhavn in 1977 to the murder of Maryann Nygaard in 1983, meant that Simonsen did not feel he had control of this encounter, which as time passed was moving randomly in all directions. He wrote a message to Ernesto Madsen, who was following the interview through a one-way mirror in the adjacent room, and held up the paper to the mirror. Shortly afterwards the Countess came in and retrieved it. Then he pushed Agnete Bahn's photograph over next to Rikke Barbara Hvidt and placed a picture of Maryann Nygaard in front of Andreas Falkenborg.

"Her name is Maryann Nygaard, and she was murdered in 1983."

"I know her well. That's Maryann."

"Were you the one who killed her?"

"It almost must have been."

"Was it or wasn't it?"

"It was me, I'm sure of that. Who else could have done it?"

"Where did you know her from?"

"From Greenland."

"And where did you meet her the first time?"

"I can't remember."

"Stop these evasions. Tell me how you met her."

"She took care of my grandmother at the nursing home. Maryann was a nurse, but then she went to Greenland. It was at the American military base in Søndre Strømfjord. It's not there any more, they've closed it."

"And you followed her to Greenland?"

"All the way to Greenland, yes."

"You learned to fly a helicopter up there."

"Yes, I became a helicopter pilot, the Americans were very nice."

Simonsen struck his hand on the table and said slowly, "On September the thirteenth, 1983 you flew Maryann Nygaard to a radar station on the ice cap called DYE-5. There you attacked her, bound and gagged her, put her in your helicopter so no one could find her, and on your way back you landed on the ice, killed her and buried her. Is that correct?"

"I guess I did."

"I've been to Greenland to see the place where you killed her."

"It's an amazing country, isn't it?"

"Absolutely, but there is one thing that puzzles me. How you made her grave in the ice. It's very hard."

"You can hack down into it with a pneumatic drill, then it's easy."

"And you had such a pneumatic drill with you in the helicopter?"

"Otherwise it's impossible, the ice is hard as stone."

"Did you have a mask on when you hauled her out on the ice?"

"Yes, to scare her."

"Did she watch while you made her grave?"

"She was scared, you better believe she was. It was nice. That's the way it should be."

"What did you do with her, right before you pulled the plastic bag over her head?"

"Cut her nails."

"You did something else."

"Said that *he wanted to cut her nails*. That was just to scare her even more."

"Who is he?"

"Belphégor, the demon from TV."

"But you did one other thing. Tell me about it."

Falkenborg made a dismissive gesture, but did not answer.

"What else did you do? I want to know!"

"We're not going to talk about that."

"Yes, we are. Out with it."

"No, please, no. I don't want to."

Simonsen got a message in return, it was blessedly brief. *Pressure him about the breasts, and nail him with the lipstick. He's not play-acting, but knows full well what he shouldn't talk about specifically. N.B.: Arne Pedersen has found a bust of Mozart in his apartment.*"

Andreas Falkenborg asked, "What kind of notes are those? I don't like them, they make me uncertain."

"There won't be any more. See, now we'll put the picture of Maryann Nygaard over by your demon and let her wait a moment. I have another picture here, who is that?"

"Catherine, we've talked about her. She was the one we thought was praying."

Simonsen ignored the evasion.

"I am wondering about what you look at most when they are dying. Is it their half-naked breasts, or is it their lips, which are stuck to the plastic? Tell me where the bag came from, the one you used to smother Catherine Thomsen, and stop lying to me."

This time the intimidation did not work. Falkenborg's answer was almost dismissive.

"From my backpack."

"But where did you get the bag from?"

"I don't know, it was just a bag. I don't know what else to say."

"Her father was a removals man, and he moved once for you. A completely impossible move that you arranged purely to ensnare him."

"I can't remember, it's a long time ago."

"You stole a plastic bag from his garage and packed it around a bust of Mozart, why did you do that?"

"Where did you get that from? You can't know that."

"We know a lot about you, make no mistake about it."

"Yes, and you're very clever when you can think so clearly."

"Why did you do that?"

"I can't remember. Maybe because he was stupid."

"What had he done to you?"

"Some people maybe say vulgar things about other people to their daughters."

"Did he say vulgar things?"

"He might very well have. Because you're afraid when they visit someone for the second time and want someone to join the church."

"What did he say specifically?"

"I can't remember."

"You're shaking, and you're lying. Every time we get to something that only you know, and that you therefore can't retract later, you wriggle out of it."

"That's right, but it's not nice to hear you say it."

"Now we'll move Catherine Thomsen over to Maryann Nygaard and Belphégor. What about this one, you know her too, don't you?"

"I don't believe so."

"She lived less than five kilometres from your summer house in Præstø."

"So I almost must have known her."

"I'm tired of your 'almost' and 'maybe' and 'probably'."

250

"Yes, I knew her, her name was Annie."

"Annie Lindberg Hansson?"

"Yes, that's what it was."

"Where should we put her, do you think? With the living or the dead?"

"The dead, Annie is dead."

"You killed her, like you killed the others?"

"I probably didn't do that, she was never found."

"She resembled the other women to a T."

"So it must be me. Yes, I would think that."

"Where did you bury her?"

"I didn't."

Simonsen struck his hand on the table and raised his voice considerably.

"Then see about finding your tongue. Where did you bury Annie Lindberg Hansson?"

Falkenborg shrank back in fear and answered timidly, "Will you please stop yelling at me?"

"Where did you bury Annie Lindberg Hansson?"

"I didn't. I don't want to talk about it, see how I'm shaking?"

"We'll get to that. And Liz, did she die in the same way?"

"I think in the same way, that was why I bought my deserted farm. To get close to her. That was in 1992, the year Denmark won the European Championship in soccer. That was in Sweden too."

"What was Liz's surname?"

"Liz Suenson."

"How did you meet her the first time?"

"In a lift. It was stuck, it was only me and her and an old man. I couldn't get out, none of us could get out. It was on Vesterbrogade, right across from the small buildings that are in front of a museum. Copenhagen City Museum, I think it's called. I was going to the dentist."

"Where did you kill her?"

"In the forest, somewhere in the forest. We drove a long way."

"And you buried her there?"

"Yes, in the forest too. There are big forests in Sweden."

"What's the name of that forest?"

"I don't know, I don't think it has a name."

"Where is it?"

"In Sweden, I don't know exactly where."

Simonsen leaned across the table and snarled angrily, "Do they jerk back and forth when they can't get any air? Like Agnete Bahn, when she was whoring with your father?"

"You mustn't talk that way."

"What happened when you sat there by the window, Andreas? While your mother got a beating because of you, what was it you saw?"

"Her breasts. I looked down in Agnete's undershirt. There were her bare breasts…you could see down to her breasts."

"When should you be able to do that?"

"When they are dying; you should look down at their breasts when they're dying."

"Agnete Bahn kissed you on the other side of the window-pane, to mock you while your mother was screaming."

"This is not nice."

"What do you do with their mouths? Tell us that."

"I don't kiss them."

"No, but you do something else, something that only the two of us know. What is it?"

"I don't want to talk to you any more. This is disgusting."

"Tell me first, what it is you do."

"You mustn't tell it to anyone."

"I won't say a thing. Come on, out with it, what do you do?"

"Can I get into a regular prison then?"

"Yes. Say it then."

"I want to be in one of the regular prisons, I can't take the hard ones, I don't deserve that."

The woman who came into the interview room then interrupted them authoritatively.

"Let's see first if you're going to jail at all. It's not the chief inspector who decides that. Good day, Simon, I would like to speak to my client alone, and this interrogation has gone on long enough, hasn't it?"

Simonsen agreed reluctantly.

"Yes, it has. May I ask one final, simple thing?"

She gave permission with a nod, but added, "It has to be brief."

Simonsen asked Falkenborg, "Are there more than the ones we have talked about?"

"No, I swear. Only those three."

"Three, you say, what about Liz Suenson? Did you invent her?"

"No, but she wasn't Danish. So is she number four after all?"

Andreas Falkenborg looked as if he was honestly in doubt.

CHAPTER 33

After the questioning of Andreas Falkenborg the mood in the Homicide Division was guardedly optimistic. It would soon change, however. For the rest of the day misfortunes rained down on Police Headquarters in Copenhagen in general, and Konrad Simonsen's unit in particular, in one long, unbroken chain of news that seemed to go steadily from bad to worse.

With Ernesto Madsen's assistance, Simonsen and Arne Pedersen went over the questioning of Falkenborg, and in no way did the psychologist share the detectives' relative satisfaction with the results of the interview.

"This is not going to be easy for you. His childishness and spontaneous honesty, which he knows exactly when to use and when not to, provide him with effective protection. I am convinced that this is how he has managed his whole life when he's faced difficulties. We are talking about deeply embedded habits that he doesn't need to think about, not even in stressful situations. I assume you noticed how he glaringly avoided saying anything that he could not take back later."

The question was aimed at Simonsen, who was well aware of the problem, but did not care for the word "glaringly" and thought there were bright spots besides.

"This is only the start, he will be questioned again and again. Besides, I think he said things that were incriminating. He did confess his guilt several times."

"He almost confessed, but each time in a submissive manner, so the truth value depends to a high degree on whose eyes are looking at it."

"What do you mean?"

"You are his strict father, and he wants to please you in this situation. If I were called in for the defence, I would have some really good angles to exploit here."

"You almost sound as if you think that's how it was."

"I do think so. He's not play-acting, but just because he is infantile, he's not unintelligent. He concentrates on not telling you at any point in time those very few things that only he and perhaps you know. The rest he lets go simply by reacting, as he feels compelled to at the moment. An extremely effective strategy, which also gives him a certain advantage during the questioning, because he does not need to focus on anything other than concealing his knowledge of the lipstick and then naturally where he buried Annie Lindberg Hansson."

Simonsen looked downcast. Pedersen asked the profiler, "You sound like it's guaranteed that he will retract his statement. Are you sure of that?"

"I firmly believe that he has calculated that, or else his lawyer will advise him to do so when she has familiarised herself with the tape. But you know the drill better than I do."

Pedersen asked Simonsen, "I don't know her, is she any good, Simon?"

"Absolutely, but she is also very honest. Tell me, where did she really come from? She showed up almost out of a clear blue sky. He can't be the one who called her, because if so we would know that."

Pedersen answered, "He didn't, he didn't even use his phone call."

Simonsen asked, perplexed, "So it must be the press who informed her. They don't usually get involved in that sort of thing. But there's another thing I don't understand: it may well be that his defences in an interrogation situation are more effective than I was immediately aware of, but on the other hand it would be far more sensible for him simply not to talk to us. However we twist and turn it, we now have a taped statement that does not exactly put him in a positive light."

Madsen explained, "He doesn't think that way. In his world it is more a struggle between the police and him. I'm sure he thinks that he has won, because he got through it without confessing anything irrevocable, and then you must not forget that he was rather frightened. He had absolutely no desire to annoy you, as he clearly showed."

"What about the new girl he suddenly served up, Liz Suenson? Is she a lie or the truth?"

Pedersen was dead sure.

"She's a lie, we've already done searches on her, and the Swedes have too. No one knows that name in connection with anyone who has disappeared. Besides, we and the Swedes were both very thorough the first time we reviewed women who could be his victims. But I must say that it was rather effective to toss her into the interrogation. I think that was the only time when he was the one setting the agenda."

Ernesto Madsen was more concise in his assessment.

"Dig deeper, she's real."

Simonsen considered the contradictory assessments. Then he said, "We will all review the questioning a couple of times. We aren't pressed because, no matter what, we don't need to fear that he will be released in the near future."

Simonsen was allowed to remain under this illusion for exactly one hour. The call from the police commissioner to present himself to her immediately left no doubt of the seriousness of the summons. Nor could her stern expression be overlooked when shortly afterwards he obeyed orders and stepped into her office.

She was a tall woman with a cold radiance that was grounded in modesty and not, as most assumed, in arrogance. Everyone agreed that she had a burning desire to do her job well, whereas there was heated discussion about whether or not she succeeded. One of her strong suits was that she normally listened to her subordinates and often adapted to their expertise, which was a clear advantage, for her knowledge of practical police work was nearly non-existent. Like her fashion sense. She regularly outdid herself in her choice of hopeless outfits. The colour combinations were catastrophic, and often she squeezed into garments that were far too small, giving her a tasteless, little girl look. Once she showed up at a party with four inches of bare belly.

That was several years ago by now, but the story still flourished, especially among her female employees who told it with eyes rolling in contempt.

"Sit down, Simon, and listen. This is not good."

The not-so-good part would have to wait, however, because she immediately seemed to have second thoughts and instead took the time to assure Simonsen how much she valued him, his work and his department. He observed the framed photograph of Queen Margrethe hanging on the wall behind her. Her Majesty was in full regalia with hair put up and diamonds dangling from suitable places. The rumour was that if the police commissioner was on duty on Christmas Eve, she hung up a cardboard elf on the picture, but he had never personally observed this alleged frivolity. When she finally fell silent, he inelegantly but effectively warded off her torrent of kindness.

"I'm busy. What is it you want from me?"

She sighed a trifle theatrically, after which she activated an icon on her computer screen, and soon the voices of Andreas Falkenborg and Poul Troulsen were heard from her speakers.

"There are two prisons you should avoid at all costs. You see, there's an iron-clad pecking order among the cons there, and you'll come in at the very bottom, partly because you have a tendency to smell, and partly because you've killed women. Both are looked down on by the tough nuts…"

"Where's that from?"

The police commissioner put the dialogue on pause and answered, "From the car in which Poul Troulsen drove the suspect Andreas Falkenborg from his residence to HS."

"How could that be?"

"I don't know. I was hoping you could tell me."

"How do you know it's from the car?"

"By listening, it comes out clearly later. Besides, the file has been sent around under the name *Car ride with the police*."

"Sent around where?"

"YouTube and other Internet sites. But it gets even worse. I'll fast forward a little. Listen to this."

"Tell me, have you ever been thrashed really nastily, for example with a stick or a baton?"

"No, I never have."

"And you've never seen anyone who has? I mean, hear how they cry out and beg for their poor hide?"

"I've experienced that."

"Good enough, so you know how much it hurts. In the worst prisons it's much, much worse. You'll be beaten to a pulp every single day, simply because the others don't like you. Three hold you and two hit . . . that sort of thing is normal. I'm telling you, it's disgusting to see such a bloody back afterwards."

The police commissioner stopped the conversation and resumed her own with Simonsen.

"A little later Poul Troulsen frightens the prisoner with someone he calls the boss. That couldn't possibly be you, could it?"

"Yes, naturally."

"The connection is unambiguous. If the poor fool doesn't confess to you, then you'll put him in a place where he'll be beaten up. What are you thinking now?"

"That we're in the shit."

"We're in complete agreement."

"It seriously weakens our case against Andreas Falkenborg."

"Yes, I would think so, but fortunately that part is not my headache. My primary problem is that I can already read a transcript of the tape on the website of a number of newspapers and

TV channels, and I'm not just talking about the sensationalist ones, but also the serious, opinion-forming ones."

"The rotten Internet!"

"Yes, that's right, Simon—blame it all on the Internet. I'll shut it down tomorrow, if it bothers you."

Simonsen did not answer her, and she regained her normal controlled coolness.

"This is not the first time Poul Troulsen has got carried away. Actually this has happened often in his career. There must have been a dozen episodes, depending on how you count. And this time is one too many. What went on in the car with Andreas Falkenborg is completely over the line. Poul threatens him directly with a beating if he doesn't confess."

"Not too many months ago I had a car ride with a prisoner myself, and I was a good deal harder on him than Poul was with the suspect today."

"Maybe, but for one thing your car ride was not recorded on tape, and for another it's not about 'being hard on him', as you say, but about delivering specific threats to achieve a confession. Simon, I know he's going to retire in five months, but you are going to suspend Troulsen. I see no other way out."

"No!"

She set a memo in front of him.

"Then try reading the transcript yourself, it's completely shocking. The poor man did not have a chance."

"The idea was that he shouldn't have a chance. That's how we work sometimes, whatever you and the general public think. I was the one who asked Poul Troulsen to pressure him. And don't forget now, this 'poor man' has killed at least two and probably four women."

"So you say."

"Yes, and I guarantee you that he has."

"So you won't make the suspension yourself?"

"No."

"Then I'll do it."

"I can't prevent you."

Silence crept up on them. Neither of them wanted to pursue this to its logical conclusion. It was the police commissioner who reluctantly put it into words.

"What will you do with it?"

"You know full well."

Simonsen's voice was subdued, he had no intention to puff himself up, and nevertheless the response had an ominous quality that gave no possibility for compromise.

"I was afraid you would say that. Thanks, because you don't threaten me in the least."

"You are welcome."

"Simon, both of us know that you have particularly influential friends. Would you please…"

She had a hard time formulating her request. He did not help her out.

"…wait to inform the others about this… this conversation, that is, in relation to your own job, until… that is, there was some stupid nonsense… Damn it, Simon, what in the world do you want me to do?"

"I don't know."

"What would you do, if you were me? I would like to hear that."

"I don't know."

"You're not much help."

"I'm not a police commissioner."

She shook her head and sighed. Simonsen threw out his arms in a friendly gesture, the only backing he would give her. He liked her, but he had plenty of problems of his own without worrying about other people's. She sighed again and wiped her brow with the back of her hand in an exaggerated gesture that made him smile.

"You're smiling."

"I am smiling."

"If only I had your sense of humour, as strange as it seems to me. In any event I have to think this over for a while, and the last thing I need is Helmer Hammer or Bertil Hampel-Koch on the line with good advice. Or the Minister for the Environment, for that matter."

"The minister! Where in the world did you conjure her from? Don't you think you're overestimating the size of my fan club?"

"No, but I'm certain that you underestimate it."

"Let's not argue about that. But if you think I call around asking for back-up, you don't know me very well."

"I know perfectly well that's not what goes on. Well, off with you, you're not going to help me anyway. We'll talk later."

Simonsen left. Without feeling sorry for her.

Back at his desk he found Poul Troulsen's resignation on his chair. He caught his co-worker in his office, packing his few personal things in a plastic bag. Simonsen poured the contents back on the desktop and threw the bag in the waste basket.

"You can forget that, Poul. What in the world are you thinking?"

Troulsen's voice was bitter but steady.

"I don't want to be a burden on you and the department."

"Why are you behaving so foolishly? Can you see about getting started on identifying Liz Suenson instead of bothering yourself with things that don't involve you, and which are my job besides. Tell me, don't you trust me?"

"Yes, of course. But I don't want—"

His boss interrupted him rudely.

"Get on to Liz Suenson... now! I have a double murderer about to slip away from me, and I don't have time for your navel-gazing. Let's get a move on! I'm out of my office briefly. When I get back, I expect you to have some results for me."

Simonsen stalked out. On his way he crumpled up the resignation and threw it next to the plastic bag.

CHAPTER 34

After his trip to the magistrate and back again to Police Headquarters, Konrad Simonsen went to Arne Pedersen's office. His colleague was sitting behind his desk with an expression that proclaimed more bad news. Simonsen was not bringing good news either, so neither man seemed particularly eager to hear what the other had to say.

Nevertheless Pedersen asked, "You don't look like things went very well in court. Don't tell me he was released."

"No, in spite of everything. He withdrew his testimony, but we more or less expected that."

"Yes, that's not surprising. And otherwise?"

Pedersen was struggling against blinding sunlight reflecting through the window. Instead of moving, he held one hand to his forehead, with the result that Simonsen could not see his face clearly.

"Can't you sit somewhere else?" he growled. "Your hand is irritating me."

Pedersen obeyed.

"This heat is unbearable," he moaned. "My clothes stick to me and I'm sweating like a pig."

Simonsen ignored the complaint. He had his own sweating to attend to.

"It ended with the judge adjourning the hearing in order to compare my questioning with the recording of Poul Troulsen and Andreas Falkenborg's conversation in the car, at her leisure. There was a lot of legal nonsense about what was permissible and what wasn't, as if it ever could be permissible for prisoners to monitor conversations held in a police car! There is of course no precedent, so both the prosecutor and the defence got very absorbed in that."

"What about the judge?"

"She did not seem particularly interested in that aspect."

"When will there be a decision?"

"When she's finished reading, so no one has any idea. The court was full of media, and that doesn't make things any easier, as you know. But she'll probably end up at three weeks. She'll surely take a week off the normal procedure to show her dissatisfaction with our approach. Or that's my guess."

"We'll see. But how the hell did Falkenborg pull off that stunt with the recordings from the car? That's beyond my understanding."

"That's actually very simple to explain. The execution, on the other hand, requires an expert. He used his cell phone, which he politely asked Poul if he could take with him since it was turned off, and was allowed to. But it wasn't turned off at all, Falkenborg simply manipulated it so that it looked that way, and then he had phone connection to one of his own computers, where he also worked the same number—it looked inactive, while in fact it was running full blast. The last step was to digitise the conversation and make an automatic distribution to various forums on the Internet. Don't ask me how you do that, but one of the computer nerds who was involved in the search said that it wasn't difficult."

"Hmm, very crafty. When I hear all this, I have a hard time accepting E. Madsen's take that his naiveté isn't put on."

Pedersen's face lit up in a boyish grin.

"Do you know what the E stands for? In E. Madsen, that is."

"No, and I couldn't care less."

"Ernesto … the poor man's name is Ernesto Madsen. I heard it from Pauline, but you mustn't say I told you, because I promised not to."

"Well, then, why are you telling me? No, never mind—the essence of it is that Falkenborg is far more wily and calculating than I thought from our original picture of him. Or profile, if you will. But tell me about the search, although I can guess that you didn't find anything sensational."

"No, we didn't. They're not quite finished, by the way, but I doubt that anything else usable will be found today."

"Wasn't there anything at all to collect?"

"You heard about the bust of Mozart? He pulled a plastic bag over it before the move, which is how he got Carl Henning Thomsen's fingerprints. Later he used the same bag to suffocate the man's daughter. That's how we think it went anyway."

"Besides the bust and the fingerprints, Arne. That's pure speculation."

"There was one bad thing, really bad actually. We've been in touch with his Internet provider, and he managed to download the article *Dagbladet* had on their website last Monday, where they interviewed Jeanette Hvidt—there are also traces on his computer that show he has seen her picture."

"I'll be damned. More?"

"Nothing that stands out. We've found two keys whose purpose we can't identify, but one is possibly to a safe deposit box. The other is very special with a number of some kind on it. And then Falkenborg withdrew a large amount of cash from his bank last Friday, which we can't find either, more than eighty thousand kroner."

"No mask, I assume?"

"No, no mask."

"Microphones in his apartment?"

"Yes, and they are state of the art; little devils no bigger than an aspirin tablet with transmitter and all, and which can be hidden anywhere, voice-controlled and super-sensitive. They'll be the same ones he uses when he's at work…spying on people, that is."

"If you say so. But what about a receiver, or whatever it's called? I mean, there should be something that stores the conversations."

"In his apartment he used his computer, or more precisely one of his six computers. But we found a brochure, and those mini-microphones can communicate with a small battery-driven box that forwards the signal over the mobile network, and a box like that is not much bigger than a matchbox, so it's not difficult to hide. Four of his computers are password-protected, incidentally, and our technicians are working on those at the moment. One of them, the one with the picture of Jeanette Hvidt, they've got control of. There is a lot to suggest his expertise is not confined to audio and microphones. Advanced computer knowledge is also part of his repertoire."

"So it's not certain that the rest of his computers can be investigated, is that what you're saying?"

"Oh, no, it's only a matter of time… and hardly more than two or three days. I'm just saying, he's also skilful with a PC. And by the way, we've uncovered how he did his trick of breaking into the house of the witness who by bad luck had given him an old access card. Do you remember him?"

"Yes, I do. How did Falkenborg do it?"

"He had computer access to the security company, access he presumably stole in connection with their using him for a short time as a consultant. Is that something we should pursue further?"

"Have we informed the company?"

"Yes, and they've changed their systems."

"Excellent, so there's probably nothing more to do. What about a warehouse? Doesn't he have some place for the equipment he sells?"

"Yes, I'm sure he does, but we don't know where. The only thing we do know is that it doesn't need to be large. A garage would be sufficient."

Simonsen concluded gloomily, "We haven't got much out of this search. Do you have anything else?"

"We can't find his car. That is, one of them. He has two: a blue 2001 Mercedes E210 and a white 2004 VW Multivan, both registered as personal vehicles. The VW is a commercial vehicle with sliding doors, and that's the one we can't locate."

"Put a search out for it."

"I've done that."

"Anything else?"

"Not a scrap, but we're not finished. Should I head out again?"

"No, I would rather have you help Poul with Liz Suenson."

"The Swedish ghost girl, who exists only in the imagination of Andreas Falkenborg and Ernesto 'Che' Madsen?"

"Yes, the Swedish girl who perhaps is the breakthrough we so desperately need."

"Who, if she exists, has been shovelled into a grave in a forest in Sweden, and there are quite a few of them there. I have a hard time seeing that as a breakthrough."

"This isn't up for discussion, and don't insult her."

"Okay, no offence intended, I'll find Poul. How did he take the situation, by the way? I mean, with the media and all that shit."

"He's doing his job."

"Stop pretending you're indifferent because I know perfectly well you're not. I'm guessing you backed him against the sea witch on the top floor. By the way, have you seen that she's coming out with a statement this afternoon?"

Simonsen stood up. Surprisingly enough he didn't feel particularly tired, and even the itching on his ankles had stopped. On the other hand he was craving a cigarette.

"No, I'm not indifferent, but I prioritise double murders higher than things I can't do anything about. Yes, of course I backed him up, what else would you imagine I'd do? No, I haven't seen that the police commissioner intends to make a statement, and to get to your next question in advance—no, I don't know what she will say. Now I'm going into my office to review the interview with Falkenborg again. See if you can't produce some good news, I need it."

Simonsen got barely ten minutes alone before Pedersen had, if not good news, at least something new to tell. He slogged into his boss's office with a taciturn Poul Troulsen in tow. Simonsen took off his earphones and gestured to the two men to sit down. A superfluous gesture, as neither of them waited for permission.

"That was quick. Well, is she real or not?"

Pedersen looked at Troulsen and then answered as his elder colleague made no move to.

"There is still nothing official to be found, and this is the third time now that we've trawled through the registries. Even Malte is starting to get a little tired of us."

"But?"

"But we have looked at the entryways on Vesterbrogade across from the City Museum. 'Across from' can be interpreted with a lot of goodwill as nine entryways. Of those only three have an elevator, and only one housed a dentist in 1992. Now he has his practice in Ballerup, but he confirms that Andreas Falkenborg was one of his patients when he had a clinic in the city."

"I hope you have more than that."

"Maybe. Vesterbrogade number sixty-two—does that ring a bell?"

Simonsen smiled broadly for the first time that day.

"Snotfather? Alias Doctor Cold?"

Finally Troulsen joined in.

"Exactly, he lives on the fourth floor, but you probably know that already?"

"Oh, yes, I know that. Have you contacted him?"

"No, I was thinking that perhaps you would go there yourself. He's home at the moment."

"He's always at home. And he's still as active as ever?"

"To the highest degree. He is one of the three kingpins the national chief of police really wants to get. But it's been more than fifteen years since he last did time, so you can't say that the outcome matches the desire."

"Unfortunately not. Do you have anything specific in relation to the Swedish woman?"

"No, it's only a guess."

Simonsen considered the proposal, but in reality he had already made his decision.

"Okay, I'll go over there and talk to him."

Pedersen asked, "Obviously I've heard of Doctor Cold, but why do you call him Snotfather?"

His boss and Troulsen laughed. Simonsen said, "We called him that in the old days, but apparently it's gone out of style. Because of his nose, which is strikingly large, and because the nickname annoys him, which unfortunately is the only way he has been harassed by us for years. Would you like to go along and meet him?"

Both of his detectives shook their heads. Troulsen said, "I'd rather go home. Journalists keep calling me, and my wife is also getting questions. I need to be with my family."

He looked at his watch. Technically it was still too early for him to leave the office, even though he had started his working day while most others were asleep. Simonsen sensed his hesitation and said, "Yes, journalists are a meddlesome rabble. But go home then, if I have your word that you will show up for work tomorrow, regardless of this inconvenience?"

"Yes, I promise. If I'm not fired first."

"You won't be fired, and the press attention will stop at some point, it always does. Refer them to me if it helps you."

"I won't need to do that."

"Then stop whining, and say hello to your wife from me."

CHAPTER 35

The man who opened the door to Konrad Simonsen was well dressed, with good manners and cold, crafty fish eyes. His name was Marcus Kolding and he was a trained medic, thus the nickname Doctor Cold. It suited him well. Better than Snotfather, thought Konrad Simonsen, not without a trace of disappointment.

If the man was surprised to see his guest, he did not show it.

"The homicide chief himself, I see. To what do I owe this honour?"

Simonsen made no attempt at flattery. That would be a wasted effort.

"I need your help."

"Then speak up, but we'll stay right here. I don't want you inside my home. It's nothing personal, just a principle I have when dealing with the police."

"Completely all right with me. *Liz Suenson*, does that name mean anything to you?"

The man thought about it and then answered guardedly, "Maybe. Why?"

Simonsen showed him two photographs.

"Does she resemble these two women?"

He looked and considered again, this time more briefly.

"Maybe. Why?"

Simonsen showed him yet another photograph.

"Because perhaps she ended her days like this, and because you yourself have a grandchild the same age. That's why."

"What do you want to know?"

"Is Liz Suenson her real name?"

"No."

"Then I want to know what her real name was, and what she did for you."

Kolding thought about this with a distrustful expression on his face. Finally he said, "She was Finnish, and she travelled back and forth between Denmark and Sweden... not one of my important employees."

"Courier?"

The man nodded.

"What did she do here with you?"

He answered affably, "She was pretty."

"Yes, she was. Her real name?"

"I can't remember, Finns don't have names, they just have letters in random order. But I can get it, if it's important."

"It's important. What happened to her?"

"She disappeared suddenly, it was in 1992 or maybe 1993, but she didn't take anything with her that belonged to me, so we thought she had gone back to Finland."

"You didn't search for her?"

"No, not particularly. She was, as I said, not... trusted."

"How did she travel for you? I mean car, train, bus, airplane?"

"Train, and I will also give you the name of a town. It's so long ago that it lacks significance. I won't say anything more."

"And that town is?"

"Hässleholm."

"Where did she live when she was in Denmark?"

"No idea, maybe with a friend, maybe at one of my hotels. I'll find that out."

Simonsen gave the witness his card.

"That sounds good. Call me about the name, and whatever else you find. It's urgent."

"Within half an hour. Was it that psychopath you have in custody who took her?"

"That I don't know."

With small circular movements the man massaged his gigantic nose, a bad habit that had earned him one of his nicknames among the police. Then he said, "I don't like that he's taken one of mine, I really do not like that. He almost deserves a taste of his own medicine... maybe after a little fun with a blowtorch."

"He deserves to be in prison, and so do you."

"Then I hope you're more effective at containing him than you were with me. Is there anything else?"

"No, but thanks for the help."

The man closed the door without another word.

CHAPTER 36

Misfortunes were still piling up on Wednesday. Arne Pedersen and Pauline Berg informed Konrad Simonsen about the latest events when their boss returned to

271

Police Headquarters. Berg went through a short but unpleasant list.

"The gangster king you just visited called. You weren't here, of course, so he was transferred to me. Liz Suenson's real name is Elizabeth Juutilainen, and we've retrieved a mug shot from 1988, when she was arrested for drug smuggling in Tampere. She was twenty-five years old in 1992, when she disappeared. The Finns are sending more data as soon as possible, but unfortunately she fits Falkenborg's female preferences, so it is quite probable that she is his fourth victim."

Simonsen muttered, "Yes, that doesn't surprise me. What else do you have?"

"A message from Anna Mia, your daughter that is—"

"And?"

"You can't make connection with her until tomorrow. It had something to do with cell-phone coverage and atmospheric disturbances in the region."

The information annoyed Simonsen more than he cared to admit. He would have enjoyed talking with Anna Mia as a brief respite from what was turning into a lousy day. He tried only half-heartedly to conceal his disappointment as he asked grumpily, "How can she call and say that she can't call? That doesn't make sense."

Pauline Berg thought quickly.

"Maybe the ship was just about to sail into the atmospheric disturbances. I've never been in the Caribbean, so what do I know?"

Pedersen interjected drily, "Don't shoot the messenger, Simon."

"Yes, obviously. But did she say anything else?"

Berg looked briefly at Pedersen, who behind his chief's back rolled a finger around in front of his mouth as a sign that here a slightly creative interpretation was permissible. She took the hint.

"Well, she said she was doing well, but also that she missed you a lot and was looking forward to coming home. And she sends greetings."

Simonsen lapped up the words, and Pauline Berg could continue with her list.

"Yes, then there's one more thing. That is, maybe you, Arne, should…"

Pedersen took the opening.

"You have been given a public rebuke by the police commissioner. She was at a press conference ten minutes ago and denounced the department's methods concerning your instructions to Poul."

In glaring contrast to what his subordinates had expected, Simonsen's mood visibly brightened.

"Really! And what else happened? What about Poul?"

"Nothing. She made a point of saying that he can't be reproached. It was you and you alone who bore responsibility—you've been over-eager, she maintained—and she herself, of course, as your immediate superior. She will summon you for a serious talk, as soon as this investigation is over, and the leadership in general will not comment on the eavesdropping case. But she emphasised that if anyone was interested in hearing more detailed information on the matter, they could attend your press conference at five o'clock."

"Was that all? What about further questions from the press?"

Berg said, "No questions. After she read the statement she left, arrogant as an ice queen. If you ask me, I think it's really unfair of her to treat you like that."

"Sticks and stones. It doesn't bother me."

Pedersen stared at his boss in surprise.

"I didn't even know that you had called a press conference. Is that something Ms Ice & Cold ordered you to do?"

"Speak respectfully about her, she always speaks respectfully about you. And no—I decided on the press conference this morning, so it's not about the eavesdropping on Poul Troulsen, although that will come up of course. Actually I would really like the two of you to participate, if you have time? So the photographers have something to aim at, and I have someone to pass the unpleasant questions on to."

They agreed, although they were surprised. Everyone expected the boss to be rattled by the treatment he had been subjected to, but instead he seemed more satisfied than he had been in a long time.

"Anything else?"

Pedersen briefly informed him.

"We've obtained serial numbers on some of the notes Falkenborg has withdrawn, but obviously that has no major significance now."

Simonsen agreed and ignored the information.

"Anything else?"

Berg and Pedersen shook their heads. Neither of them had anything else. On the other hand Malte Borup did. He had just blundered into the office with the day's final blow for the Homicide Division. The student asked, out of breath, "Have you heard what he got? Andreas Falkenborg, that is."

They all shook their heads.

"I've seen it on the Internet. He got four days."

Pedersen corrected him tolerantly. "You mean, four weeks?"

"No, days. Four days. Until Sunday morning, I'm quite certain. He was not taken into protective custody. The judge was content to extend the arrest, whatever the hell the difference is."

They sat like statues, looking doubtfully at each other. The student lowered his head. With his unruly hair and sorrowful eyes he resembled a whipped dog. He had expected praise for bringing the information so fast. Simonsen was the first to pull himself together. He said in annoyance, "The difference is that we don't get the weekend off. Among other things."

CHAPTER 37

Questioning the witness Bertil Hampel-Koch turned out to be one of the more remarkable experiences of the Countess's career.

The conversation was arranged hurriedly and took place in Kastrup Airport, where the director could spare an hour before he had to board his flight to Brussels. The Countess would clearly have preferred to wait until Monday for the interview, but that was impossible. The meeting was Part One of Helmer Hammer's carefully outlined plan to deflect the searchlights of the Danish press from Hampel-Koch's visit to Greenland in 1983. Or perhaps it would be more accurate to say a very small part of the Danish press, as only two journalists had shown interest until now, but that was evidently enough for the under secretary. The second phase of the two-stage rocket would be fired according to plan at Simonsen's press conference at five o'clock.

In the car en route, on the Øresund highway, the Countess thought that she could not remember her boss ever before having voluntarily called a press conference, if you could characterise his participation in Helmer Hammer's project as voluntary. She also thought about what in the world she would question Bertil Hampel-Koch about, unless their chat became purely pro forma, which on the other hand she hoped it would not, for that would force her to fabricate for the journalists. So preferably an interview that had no purpose related to the investigation. And, if it were up to her, without too much openness between the two of them that could easily turn awkward. It would be more like half an hour of mutually agreed play-acting.

She turned off the highway and drove slowly into the parking area, curious to know whether the director had as much control of the logistics as his secretary maintained while instructing the Countess simply to park her car and then she would be contacted. The airport area was under greater than average surveillance, and hidden eyes presumably already followed her car on various monitors. An unpleasant thought. She rotated the rear-view mirror and quickly ran a brush through her hair.

Inattention made her brake a little too hard when a young woman suddenly materialised out of nowhere in her path. The woman looked like a spread from a teen magazine; with her whitened smile and designer clothes, she posed for a few seconds in front of the car, smiling from ear-ring to ear-ring to show her joy at nearly being run over. Then she got in on the passenger side and introduced herself fervently by her first name. Beate, she said. The Countess decided to kill her as soon as she got the chance.

On Beate's instruction they drove around the terminal buildings and through a gate where the guard waved them on, before they stopped by one of the pavilions in the domestic area. Beate strode ahead, clip-clopping with her boot heels the final stretch into the building and over to a door, which was indicated with a wide smile, after which Beate clip-clopped off. The Countess knocked and opened the door.

Inside it looked like an inexpensive but pleasant hotel room. It was small, with more furniture than its size justified. Along one wall was a bed and parallel to it an oblong table with a chair set at either end. An armoire, hand basin and TV were also squeezed in. The walls were painted pale blue and were bare apart from two framed pictures of almost identical sunsets, decorative and indifferent, one over the table, the other the bed. Bertil Hampel-Koch was sitting in the chair farthest away, facing her. He closed his laptop, stood up and edged around the furniture to receive her. The Countess had only met him once before, and then he had behaved repellently, but it quickly became clear to her that this was not an approach he intended to repeat. His welcome was friendly, his posture open and positive.

The Countess set her handbag down on the bed, while Hampel-Koch edged back to his chair. They sat down at the table and looked awkwardly at each other.

She had tried her best to prepare for the start of their meeting in particular, and he had obviously done the same. He said, "I hope we can get this over in an hour, otherwise I would very much like to know now so I can arrange a later departure. But I would prefer to avoid that if possible."

"An hour is fine."

She wanted to say more than enough, but thought better of it.

"Thanks, I'm happy about that. I ordered coffee, but I think they've forgotten me."

"That's no problem, I'll manage without."

He pushed his glasses up on his forehead, focused on her and then said with emphasis, "I am sincerely sorry about all this mess, which I can only blame on myself. The arrangement that your boss should regularly brief me about your investigation was my idea. My bad idea, unfortunately. I thought I could combine a personal interest in that way with a ... non-personal one. That was stupid, almost counter-productive. Someone in my ministry has wondered about my role and put a couple of journalists on my trail. At least, I suppose it must have happened that way. I don't know who tipped off the press, presumably personal enemies of mine, but that doesn't matter. In any event, I ought to have foreseen there'd be fall-out. Besides, I should have told the police long ago about my stay at the Søndre Strømfjord base in the summer of 1983, which to put it mildly I have had ample opportunity to do. But I didn't, which has made a lot of extra work for me now. You'll have to excuse that, and please pass on my apology."

The Countess took note of this and appreciated his honesty, which seemed genuine enough. On the other hand she immediately noticed his wildly fluctuating tone of voice and it struck her that he was just as uneasy about their meeting as she was, a fact that did not make the situation any less awkward. She started with a question based purely on curiosity.

"How do you know that one of your own employees tipped off the press, as you put it? Couldn't the source be the police? It would definitely not be the first time."

He nodded, as if to acknowledge her point, and then interjected, "The journalists in question have acquired a picture of me as a thirty year old, and it is a copy of a photograph in my personnel file that can be found on our intranet, if you have access. There are other things too that point to an inside source, though I can't be certain. Does that have any significance?"

"No, probably not. Let's get started, shall we? Unfortunately I forgot my Dictaphone, so I'm just going to take a few notes, if that's acceptable?"

She pointed to the pad in front of her, and he nodded.

"In June 1983 you travelled to Greenland in connection with your participation later that year with the Sirius sled patrol. Your trip was to Station North in Northeast Greenland, and en route you had a stopover at the American military base in Søndre Strømfjord. Is that correct?"

"Yes, that's right."

"You spent four days, more precisely from Thursday, July the seventh to Sunday, July the tenth, at Søndre Strømfjord, while you waited for good weather so you could continue."

"Yes, that's right too. The weather can be pretty rough that far north, even in the summer. Going home I flew by way of Mestervig on the east coast, and there were no problems."

That was the first hurdle. Now she had heard about the trip directly from the source and could pass that on later with a reasonably clear conscience. That Søndre Strømfjord was not the only stopover on his trip to Station North, and the actual reason for why they were sitting here, remained unsaid. She wrote meticulously on her pad. When she was finished, she said, "Did you make your trip under the name Steen Hansen?"

"Yes, I did."

"Why was that?"

He spoke about his uncle, who at that time was Danish defence chief, and about his fear of the negative impact the family relationship might have on his companions during the sled journey. The Countess thought that the explanation sounded convincing and was presumably true. Then she asked the only question to which she did not know the answer in advance.

"You also maintained that your position was that of geologist. Why is that?"

Bertil Hampel-Koch's cheeks took on a pink glow, and he did not answer immediately. Not until he had regained his normal colour did he say, "Yes, that's also a little embarrassing."

The Countess interjected soothingly, "Don't worry about that. Regardless of what you tell me, I've certainly heard it before. Besides, it's not my task to judge you. And definitely not on something that happened twenty-five years ago."

The words helped. He told her in a low voice, "At that time I was newly married, and we were expecting our first child. That was good news, of course, but also a little frightening. So I suddenly got the opportunity to be anonymous on that base, and I thought that if on top of that I lied about my job, no one could trace me when I left. Although... well, that proved not to be the case."

She didn't respond, letting him dig himself deeper.

"In that way I could be a bachelor for a couple of days, if you know what I mean."

"Yes, I think I've got the point."

"Good Lord, I was twenty-eight years old. I would never behave that way now."

He looked imploringly at her, and she discovered to her surprise that he was angling for sympathy. She said casually, "No? Married men's way of thinking usually grows a bit more relaxed over the years. You met a nurse, Maryann Nygaard."

He lowered his eyes.

"Yes, and I got her—"

The Countess interrupted him quickly.

"Now, now, you don't need to go into detail. This has no relevance to me. I'm only interested in the big picture."

She thought that she might just as well have said that from there on she was only interested in passing the time, until she could reasonably maintain that he had been questioned. He answered, relieved, "Well, then. I guess you are."

He was a miserable witness, which did not make the next twenty minutes any easier. To put it mildly, he could not remember much about his stay at the base, and not a thing that the Countess could use. She concluded by presenting him with a picture of Andreas Falkenborg from the year 1983.

Bertil Hampel-Koch looked at the picture for a long time. There was no doubt that he really wanted to help, but was unable to.

"No, unfortunately."

"His name is Andreas Falkenborg, but he went by the nickname Pronto."

He shook his head apologetically.

"Falkenborg was a trained engineer and employed at the base as an assistant electrician. He also flew helicopters."

280

Again a pause, and again a shake of the head.

"So you don't know about any connection between him and Maryann Nygaard either?"

"Unfortunately not. The only thing I know is that there was a kind of group around Maryann and her Greenlandic friend. I can't remember the name of the girl, but she was just as pretty as Maryann and… that is, Falkenborg was not part of that group."

Not part of… The Countess wrote down the information in block letters followed by four exclamation points. Then she thought that she should stop while the going was good. She closed her notebook.

"You have been a great help. Thanks very much for sparing me the time."

He frowned and scratched his neck thoroughly with one finger. Then he said seriously, "I truly hope you catch Maryann's murderer. When I heard that she had been killed, I was both shocked and relieved at the same time. It's a very strange feeling that I've never had before. For many years I believed that she… died because of me. That wasn't the case, but…"

He stopped short, and she waited politely until he continued.

"I can't find any words that are suitable, so I'd better not try. In any event I won't forget this, I can promise you that. I hope one day to be able to reciprocate."

The Countess didn't want his gratitude; she had her own problem. Simonsen's medium had insisted that she should cling firmly to Bertil Hampel-Koch, alias Steen Hansen. She had clung and clung for the past seven days. It was a matter of life or death, she had been told. Yet she had ended up in a dead-end and wasted a lot of time to no obvious benefit. Until the last she had hoped for a revelation that had not come. Now she was left empty-handed. And regardless of how much she twisted and turned even the most impossible scenarios, where the director perhaps played a role in the murder of Maryann Nygaard, none of them was even remotely probable. So what now? The answer was obvious—nothing, it was over. Nonetheless she tried to hold a door open.

"I hope to be able to come back to you another time, if I have further questions."

It was clear that the comment puzzled him, but she received his non-committal, polite confirmation. Then she gathered together her things, shook hands with him and deliberately stepped out of her role as she took her leave.

"Now you be sure to greet our common acquaintance the prime minister from me when you see him."

Bertil Hampel-Koch feigned a smile and agreed.

CHAPTER 38

So as not to arrive late at the press conference, the Countess rushed back from her conversation with Bertil Hampel-Koch. The result was that she was the first to take her place on the podium. She was followed shortly afterwards by Konrad Simonsen, Arne Pedersen and Pauline Berg. The Countess nodded curtly to her boss with a meaningful look on her face when he arrived; the questioning of Hampel-Koch had gone as expected. He reciprocated with a raised thumb. Then she had plenty of time to form an impression of the gathering.

The press conference was well attended; altogether about fifty journalists and photographers participated. With satisfaction the Countess noted that no TV cameras were present. The two channels that had announced their arrival had been promised a special interview with Simonsen and herself immediately afterwards. The reason given for this was that the police wanted to prevent certain sensitive circumstances related to the investigation from being broadcast directly. The explanation had been accepted.

At the scheduled time voices in the room lowered to a soft murmur. The Countess straightened up in her seat and became serious. The conference began, and Simonsen was immediately fired upon from all sides. The day's top story was twofold: partly the arrest and indictment of Andreas Falkenborg, partly the police's interrogation methods during and after the arrest. Words like "fiasco" and "blunder" were heard, and the head of the Homicide Division had to take many digs, as he was not exactly well liked by the country's crime reporters. Respected perhaps, but definitely not loved. Over the years he had withheld too many good headlines from them. For the most part however her boss managed fine, and on those few occasions where his temperament threatened to clear the next day's front pages, Pedersen was capable of taking over.

The Countess herself said nothing. Instead she systematically scanned the journalists present and soon found the two she was looking for. They were sitting at the back of the room looking frankly bored. The older one was a big man with a shaggy black beard, who reminded her of the Hollywood version of a Cossack. The younger was pale with small, round glasses and a permanently suspicious expression, as if he didn't really believe what he was hearing, no matter who was speaking, because that was his nature. She secretly observed them for a long time, while pretending to stare blankly into space whenever one of them turned their eyes towards her. It was their fault that the press conference was being held at all, and it was her task to fulfil the promise made in the Botanical Gardens to Helmer Hammer to get them interested in something other than Hampel-Koch's Greenland trip in the late summer of 1983.

Gradually the inquisition lost momentum, and Simonsen's responses began to be repetitive. She kept herself ready and finally came the question that she'd known was planted, just not with whom. She had guessed at a handful of suitable candidates, but completely missed the mark. Her cue was advanced by a veteran among the crime reporters, a man in his sixties from one of the smaller daily papers, the last person she would have thought would dabble in such things. His question was directed to Konrad Simonsen.

"You have questioned the Foreign Ministry director Bertil Hampel-Koch on several occasions in this case. Why is that?"

Simonsen seemed a trifle confused by the comment.

"Yes, well, we have. In relation to Maryann Nygaard, who was killed in Greenland. He is helping us produce information from the American… I mean, from other places. Besides, he personally visited the military base in Søndre Strømfjord in 1983, only a couple of months before the murder took place, so in that connection we have also shown… I mean, that part I haven't…"

He looked at Pedersen, who shook his head, and then at the Countess, who completed the answer.

"Bertil Hampel-Koch was at the base for four days in July, when he made a stopover en route to Station North, where he was going to participate in the activities of the Sirius patrol. At that time he was a clerk in the Defence Ministry, and the trip was a kind of bonus for good work. And it is correct that he has contributed information from his short time at the base, just as quite a few other people have done."

The follow-up question came from a younger man in the first row.

"Four days in July? That is several months before Maryann Nygaard was murdered."

"Yes, and as mentioned he is absolutely not the only one from the base we have spoken to. In addition, Hampel-Koch got to know Maryann Nygaard during his stopover."

"Can it be said that Hampel-Koch has been involved in gathering concrete evidence in relation to your indictment?"

"It is not the job of witnesses to gather evidence, but it can be said that he has helped us a great deal. As I said, along with a number of other people."

It was evident that the subject did not hold the gathering's interest. Some comments were murmured but no one seemed concerned. This changed markedly with the next question, which came from the Cossack. His loud, sonorous voice reached all the way around the room when he asked, "Why did director Bertil Hampel-Koch travel to Greenland under an assumed name?"

The words "assumed name" made everyone prick up their ears. Perhaps there was a story within the story that was about to unfold. Vigilant eyes were directed towards the Countess as she explained the connection. She concluded elegantly, as she almost apologetically noted to Simonsen, "But I don't know how relevant this is."

She didn't escape that easily, however. The Cossack followed up.

"It seems strange that at the same time he maintained he was a geologist. Can you also explain that to me?"

The Countess thought for a moment and began her response with the standard line that would attract the attention of any journalist. She said hesitantly, "I don't think you need to write that."

Then she told them about Hampel-Koch's sudden opportunity to act like a bachelor again for four days, without fear of a long-lasting relationship.

Most of her audience agreed with her. It was uninteresting as well as personal. An alert female reporter guessed the connection and asked the tactless question, "Was it Bertil Hampel-Koch who got Maryann Nygaard pregnant?"

The Countess swooped on her without mercy. She pointed at the journalist with an accusing finger.

"That's an incredible supposition that belongs in the gossip columns, I don't think—"

Simonsen cut in authoritatively, "Now stop this prying into other people's bedrooms! I have a murder case with at least two victims, and I don't care to waste my time on such nonsense."

The Fourth Estate pounced on Simonsen's feigned slip of the tongue. The Countess sensed the hunger in the gathering before the questions mounted in an ugly cacophony. *At least two women killed, what do you mean by at least two?*

The Countess was forgotten, Bertil Hampel-Koch was forgotten, everything was as it should be. She looked towards her two journalists again. The suspicious one threw out his arms in despair, and shortly after that they both left the room. She did not feel any particular triumph as her eyes followed them to the door. She thought that was what you deserved when you habitually used words for your own ends and lied without quite saying an untruth. The world was reduced to a game, a game without joy. Then she thought about Simonsen, who had borne the full brunt of it, and about what she would make him for dinner.

CHAPTER 39

"The criminal justice system is an overrated crock of shit."

Poul Troulsen said that at every opportunity the next couple of days, and everyone was tired of listening. It was irritating, even though they all knew he didn't mean it and that it served as an outlet for his frustration. Along with the rest of the Homicide Division he was slaving away at full steam to produce evidence that might connect Andreas Falkenborg to his crimes and thereby prolong his imprisonment. The returns so far were meagre. The key figure refused to be questioned, so it was not possible to continue that route. A large portion of the man's current and past circle of acquaintances had been tracked down and questioned, an extensive but fruitless process. No one could contribute any information the police did not already know.

What remained was technical evidence, and here recovering possible DNA traces from Maryann Nygaard's grave in the Greenland ice cap was their best chance. Theoretically such traces could be well preserved in frozen condition, even though almost twenty-five years had passed since the crime took place. Perhaps it was still possible to determine that a helicopter had once landed close by the grave. There was nothing wrong with optimism, but it had no basis in reality. On Friday afternoon Simonsen came back from a meeting with Kurt Melsing, head of the Forensics department. He went to the Countess's office, where Troulsen, Pauline Berg and the Countess were eagerly waiting for him. One look on their boss's face, however, told them that the meeting had not gone positively. Simonsen was clearly in a lousy mood, and their spirits plummeted before a word was spoken. The Countess commented, "It didn't go too well, I see."

Simonsen collapsed into a chair in despair.

"It went to hell. The technicians have nothing, and if they do come up with something, which is highly unlikely, it won't be for a while. So good ideas are more than welcome."

Berg tried half-heartedly.

"This morning I got the name of Catherine Thomsen's friend slash lover. Her name is Vibeke Behrns, but unfortunately at the moment she is hiking in Finnmark with her two brothers and can't be reached. They are coming home in less than a week. But I don't know whether she even knew Andreas Falkenborg."

Troulsen said despairingly, "We can't make use of that here and now."

Berg asked worriedly, as if the truth had still not occurred to her, "But what then? I mean, he's not going to be released, is he?"

No one answered her, and she repeated the question. This time almost shrilly. The Countess cut her off.

"It doesn't help to get worked up, and besides it's not our decision."

"But the judge can't release a mass murderer into the community."

"She quite certainly will, if we can't produce further evidence. Or more exactly, any evidence whatsoever."

She turned towards Simonsen.

"Isn't there anything positive at all?"

"No."

"What have you done with Arne? Wasn't he there with Melsing?"

"He went round to see the prosecutor, to convince her to try to get the arrest extended. But she'll never go along with that. We have nothing new, and she doesn't like to be made a fool of, for which you can't blame her."

Troulsen said, "There are still a couple of days. We've got to try and pick up the pieces and then hope for a miracle. Should we do a status report and divide up the tasks?"

Simonsen agreed, without enthusiasm.

"Yes, we'd better do that, but let's wait for Arne. Pauline, I have a special task for you. You will go to Hundested and speak with Jeanette Hvidt. I want her either out of the way or concealed. And go up there this evening. If you have other plans, then cancel them."

Pauline Berg nodded. Although it clashed with her personal plans, it was obvious that she had no choice. Instead she said carefully, "Can't we hold him for other things? Maybe tax evasion. What about the fact that his customers always pay in cash and without an invoice?"

"The Al Capone model."

It was Troulsen trying to be witty. The Countess shook her head despondently.

"The idea is actually not that bad. It's just way too late. We have no earthly chance of producing something sustainable before Sunday. But I have thought of a different possibility. We know that he bought half of a house and arranged a move, just to get Carl Henning Thomsen's fingerprints on a plastic bag. Isn't that correct?"

Simonsen confirmed that half-heartedly.

"*Know* is perhaps saying too much, but we strongly assume that. He spares no efforts once he has selected a victim. Where are you going with this?"

"He places the plastic bag he later murders Catherine Thomsen with over his Mozart bust, after which her father sets his fingerprints on it during the move."

"Yes, that's what we believe. And what he more or less confirmed during his interview. Why is that interesting now?"

"Because the Mozart bust is connected to Falkenborg, and the plastic bag is connected to the murder of Catherine Thomsen…"

She let the sentence remain open. Simonsen concluded hesitantly for her.

"And if we can connect the plastic bag to the Mozart bust, we have him. The idea is interesting, go on."

"There's not much more to say. I am thinking that the fingerprints are logically dependent on the surface on which they are placed, or in this case pressed against. Maybe the contours of the bust can be found on the impressions. Or maybe the technicians can find unambiguous traces of the bust on the inside of the bag. Because I assume that it still exists in some archive or warehouse."

The others nodded. It was the best suggestion they had so far been given on how they could move ahead. Although time was very short.

Troulsen asked the obvious question.

"Why didn't you say this before?"

The Countess answered him without hesitation.

"Because I just happened to think of it now."

The three others looked at Simonsen. He concluded, "In any event, it's worth asking Melsing about. Call him, Countess. Get hold of him no matter where he is. Poul, you find out where the bag is. And make sure someone can deliver it, if we're going to use it this evening."

Fifteen minutes later the Countess was back with good news from Melsing.

"There are some chances of linking the bust to the plastic bag. Melsing had a couple of ideas, which I did not completely understand. He and his department are ready to get started, as soon as they have both objects. The problem is time. Twenty-four hours is far from enough for the ongoing investigations. A week is more realistic, and then only if they work around the clock, but…"

She smiled. Simonsen and Berg were hanging eagerly on every word.

"If they can find traces of plaster inside the bag, and they can determine that tonight, Melsing is willing to talk up his findings to the judge. And that will guarantee us a week more to work with."

Simonsen struck a clenched fist against the tabletop and exclaimed, "Yes!" Then he added, "So we got our miracle after all."

It lasted for five minutes. Then Troulsen came back, almost exuding frustration.

"The plastic bag no longer exists, it was destroyed. I've spoken with the Næstved police, and Catherine Thomsen's murder was considered solved, so in 2002 when they got new space for the archives—"

Simonsen interrupted him.

"I don't care what happened. Is it certain that it's gone?"

"Yes, unfortunately."

CHAPTER 40

"Someone has to stop him."

Jeanette Hvidt's brown eyes flashed with anger, but the girl's outburst also contained a touch of anxiety. Pauline Berg did not answer; she did not know what to say. Jeanette repeated, this time almost shrilly: "Someone has to fucking stop that crazy psychopath."

The two women were sitting on a lawn with a view of the Isefjord. A fresh breeze from the water was blowing towards them, and Berg had its salty taste in her mouth. The shadows were long, the late-summer day waning. A short distance away, out of earshot, sat a handful of young people drinking beer. They were Jeanette's third-year classmates at the Frederiksborg High School in Hillerød, who were patiently waiting for her. The group was on their way to a party when Pauline Berg caught up with them and after a brief discussion isolated her witness. A young man turned his head and watched for a long time when he saw Jeanette waving her hands in the air, but it was doubtful he could hear what she had called out. The wind snatched away the words. Berg noted that despite his age he looked big and strong, and thought that was exactly the type of protector the girl could use. That is, may have use for—hopefully it would not be necessary.

"What about men... do you have a boyfriend?"

Berg indicated the girl's friends with a toss of her head.

"Do you call them men? What does that have to do with you anyway?"

"Wait a minute, Jeanette. I didn't come up here on a Friday evening just to annoy you, and you know that perfectly well.

If it makes you happy, I had to cancel a date this evening that I've been looking forward to for days, but some things in life are more important than others, and at the moment you're more important than my date. My boss thinks so, and I think so too."

The girl thought for a moment and then said, "Your boss is named Simonsen, but you call him Simon, isn't that right?"

"Yes, it is."

"Is he a good boss?"

"Now and then he can be tough, but all in all, sure, he's good."

"I've met him, did you know that?"

"I know."

"I liked him, he was really sweet with my grandma, in a nice, quiet way."

"Yes, that sounds like Simon. It doesn't surprise me."

"I didn't know she had been assaulted. No one ever told me that. It's strange, there are so many people I know who knew it, but they never told me a thing. It feels kind of false—you think you know people, and then you don't at all when it comes right down to it."

"I know just what you mean. Some secrets are known by a whole generation, but never talked about, as if everyone would prefer to forget. I'm sure we'll be that way ourselves when we get old."

The girl looked at Pauline Berg with surprise.

"Do you think so?"

"Definitely."

"I never looked at it that way. Would you like a beer?"

"No, thanks, I'm driving, and besides I'm on duty."

"Don't cops ever drink on the job?"

"Occasionally, it's like with everyone. Most rarely drink during work hours. Tell me, where are you going exactly?"

"Copenhagen, the train leaves in half an hour. We're going to a party."

"Why don't you go over and ask the others to leave without you, and I'll drive you to Copenhagen when we're finished?"

Jeanette thought for a moment about the proposal, after which she got up. Pauline Berg observed her body language while she explained to her friends. It was clear that she had a central place in the group. Shortly after that her friends left.

"Were they upset?"

"Really upset, really upset. No, they weren't, I'll see them later. The psychopath gets out Sunday at the earliest, isn't that right?"

"Yes, Sunday morning."

"So I can party the whole night without looking over my shoulder. This may be my last party."

Her smile was lovely, but Pauline Berg shuddered anyway.

"Let's not say things like that, this is not something to joke about."

"No, I know, it just seems so unbelievable. Suddenly, in less than a week, there may be a monster like that chasing after me. Tell me, is he big?"

"Bigger than you."

"If he tries to do anything to me, I'll kill him if I can."

Berg thought that sounded like a splendid idea, but was doubtful what she could allow herself to say, so instead she commented, "We were talking about boyfriends."

"I don't have one at the moment, but I can get one by Sunday if that's what you mean. Are you thinking as a kind of bodyguard?"

"Yes, I am, and don't say that you can manage by yourself. It's not only about having a man taking care of you, it's also about being two. That is, that you aren't alone."

Jeanette Hvidt had common sense.

"But that's impossible, you can't be together all the time. I mean, glued to each other day and night, who could stand that? And how long would it go on?"

293

Pauline Berg chose to be honest, apart from not directly saying that the investigation at the moment was at an impasse, and that the Homicide Division had produced no results worth mentioning in the past few days.

"Admittedly that's a problem, but as you can imagine we are working at full steam. I'm talking here about many people whose sole job is to render Andreas Falkenborg harmless. We are turning over every stone in his life, and at one point or another I am convinced we will find something we can nail him with. The problem is that I can't tell you when that will happen. Actually I want to hear whether it's possible for you to go somewhere else for a while. A place that only you and I know about."

The girl seriously considered the suggestion, while she finished her beer and reached for another from the plastic bag by her side. Pauline Berg considered suggesting a soft drink, but refrained. Jeanette did not seem intoxicated, nor even affected. She said, "It won't work."

"Because?"

"I'm sure you've noticed that I'm one year older than the others."

Berg nodded that of course she had. The truth was she hadn't noticed, but she could remember how, when she was nineteen, one year more or less had major significance.

"I really have to slave to finish school, almost all the others are more academic than me. That's just the truth. Where they only need to study for fifteen minutes, I need an hour, and even though I really worked at it, I had to do second year over. It won't do for me to be away from school for a long time, because then I won't be able to prepare for my exams. I'm not that smart."

"You seem very goal-oriented. Do you know what you want to be?"

"A doctor, and I'm going to be one some day."

"I believe that. But tell me one thing, have you considered cutting your hair short? It could be very attractive on you."

Jeanette looked at Pauline Berg's hair and answered soberly, "The same for you."

Berg said temptingly, "Okay, let's get our hair cut together, it's a deal! I'll find a fancy salon in Copenhagen, and you won't pay a thing."

The girl shook her head.

"It won't work."

"Why not?"

"Because."

She shook her hair away on the left side and exposed her ear. It was deformed, curled together to half size.

"I'm saving up for an operation, but it's expensive. I'll have to go abroad, England or Germany, so there will be accommodation and travel on top of that."

"Good Lord, it's not that bad."

"Well, *you* don't think so."

"You're not just for decoration."

Jeanette's reaction was surprisingly aggressive.

"Do you really think I want to show off an ear like this? Are you stupid?"

Pauline Berg ignored the insult, but dropped the haircut idea. She tried an alternative.

"If we disregard your education for a moment, do you have a place you could go?"

"Yes, I have. And you'll have to excuse me for snapping at you, I just had a few ugly experiences when I was younger. But that's not your fault."

Berg placed her hand on the girl's arm and said kindly, "That's all right. Where could you possibly go?"

"Helsingør, my uncle lives there, and he would be happy to have me stay with him for a while."

A quick calculation told Berg that based on security-related as well as economic considerations this solution would be preferable. If the girl refused to leave her home, the police would be forced to protect her, and that sort of thing was very expensive. She said, "They have high schools in Helsingør too, and we'll arrange all the practical aspects. I can also promise you competent tutoring to ease the transition, which we can suitably define as until you have earned your diploma, regardless of whether you move back or not. How does that sound?"

All things considered Pauline Berg did not know whether she had any authority to promise this, but surely the government would save a lot of money with such an arrangement and be better served besides. Jeanette Hvidt quietly shook her lovely head.

"It's so strange, all this, like a bad dream."

"Yes, I understand how you feel, but what do you say about Helsingør?"

"I say that I don't believe in it that much. What about my subject combination? And then I'll have new teachers too, not to mention new classmates."

Pauline Berg swore to herself; it would be so much easier if the girl voluntarily found an arrangement.

"We have found traces of your picture on Andreas Falkenborg's computer, and he has read your interview on the Internet."

Jeanette reacted as Berg had both hoped and feared.

"That's disgusting."

"Yes, disgusting. But the truth is that he has his eye on you."

"It was those retarded reporters. I didn't want to say anything at all, but they persisted and persisted. Obviously that's beside the point now. Is there more? I want to know."

"When we questioned him, he said that *they were breeding* and putting *new ugly cuttings* into the world. We think he was referring to your grandmother and you."

"I'm a new, ugly cutting. Is that how it is?"

"Yes, that's how it is."

Jeanette Hvidt started crying, and Pauline Berg held her quietly. Before she drove the girl home, they decided on Helsingør. She never made it to the party.

During the drive back to Copenhagen Pauline Berg daydreamed about the honour and prestige she would achieve if she could pressure Andreas Falkenborg into irrevocable confessions. Information he could not retract, and that would hold up in court. She had the means, if she dared. But it *had to* succeed, because if it did not… "Then the shit will hit the fan, Then the shit will really hit the fan," she chanted to herself.

It was an expression she had learned from her grandfather, and she liked saying it. It sat well on the tongue.

When she hit Lyngby, she called Simonsen. After some difficulty she got hold of him on the landline in his own apartment where he was picking up a few things. She informed him that Jeanette Hvidt would go to stay with her uncle in Helsingør, and about the funds needed for various academic support arrangements, which he immediately accepted with the comment that he too could count. After the call she decided to stop by Police Headquarters briefly, after which she intended to devote the rest of the evening to Ernesto Madsen, although she'd had to reduce her plans considerably after she was sent to Hundested.

At Police Headquarters she ran into Arne Pedersen, who was happy to see her. And surprised.

"What are you doing here?"

"I was going to use some data."

"Then you could have called. You knew I was here."

"Hmm, it's…Well, it's somewhat personal. It's for a girlfriend."

"You're well aware that it will cost you your job if you're caught doing that sort of thing? It's actually illegal, and logs are kept."

She shrugged, unconcerned.

"Malte showed me how to get around the log months ago."

"That doesn't make it legal, but of course that doesn't concern me."

"You're right, it doesn't concern you."

She smiled and had a desire to kiss him. Instead she tossed her hair back and laughed without really knowing why.

"Has anything happened?"

"No, unfortunately. I have people who are busy with Elizabeth Juutilainen alias Liz Suenson, but we won't find her right away, not to mention link her to Andreas Falkenborg. Yes, and I've talked with Simon, he told me about your work in Hundested, but you know that yourself. That was a good result, by the way."

"Thanks. Was that all?"

"Hello, you haven't been gone more than three hours. What did you really expect?"

"Nothing, but one can always hope."

"Oh, by the way, we have received a long official report from the Americans. It's a bang-up piece of work they've done, and it must have cost a bundle, but there's nothing sensational. We can now definitely connect Falkenborg to that helicopter trip. On the other hand it turns out that unfortunately DYE-5 was in posses- sion of two snowmobiles, which expands the inhabitants' action radius considerably."

"The helicopter and the distance between DYE-5 and Maryann Nygaard's body were otherwise the only thing that really damaged him."

"Yes, but that part is weakened by those snowmobiles, although it's hard to imagine that you can transport two people on such a machine."

"We don't have much."

"Almost nothing. The fact is, we need a miracle, if we're going to hold him."

"And the fact is also that we're not getting anywhere, isn't that right, Arne?"

"Yes, it is. Are you coming in tomorrow?"

"Unfortunately not until Monday, I have a hair appointment in the morning and a family gathering the rest of the weekend. Simon gave me time off, unless something earthshaking happens."

"We'll cross our fingers for that. How did Jeanette Hvidt take it?"

"Reasonably. She cried a little, but she's a strong girl. And then she said something that I keep thinking about: *Someone has to stop him*."

Pedersen sounded almost desperate when he answered.

"Well, that's what we're working on."

She gave him an affectionate farewell hug, thinking that life was full of compromises.

CHAPTER 41

In police circles Asger Graa was a frequent topic of conversation. There were many stories about him in circulation among his fellow officers, each more amazing and absurd than the other, most of which were pure invention. But it was an established fact that more than anything he wanted to be a detective in the Homicide Division and for that reason regularly made enquiries to Konrad Simonsen, who did not want to make use of his talents. It was likewise fair to say that Asger Graa was not always an easy person to associate with, primarily due to his know-it-all attitude and awkward manner, which among officers who didn't know him was wildly exaggerated. Before she came to the Homicide Division, Pauline Berg had worked with him sporadically on a vice case and found him to be a good deal more accommodating than his reputation. When she called him, he remembered her right away and agreed to her plan without many questions.

They met as agreed on Saturday evening at Polititorvet outside Police Headquarters. He was waiting for her, but looking in the wrong direction, so she had plenty of time to observe him. The man was in uniform and it suited him. He was big, which would be an advantage if Andreas Falkenborg ran amok as expected. He was almost a stereotype; he looked like a born police constable and virtually radiated authority. Berg, on the other hand, did not look like herself. Earlier that day she had had her hair cut to resemble a rough drawing she had done. It was dyed black too. From an optician she had purchased a pair of brown contact lenses that proved to be easy and straightforward to put in.

Pauline Berg responded to Asger Graa's formal handshake, and instructed her new partner on how the conversation with Andreas Falkenborg should proceed. She graciously allowed Graa to thank her profusely for his big chance. He did not comment on her changed appearance.

She asked, "Did you bring the Dictaphone?"

"Yes, and it's working, I've checked it several times."

"When you start it, I want you to skip the introductory format. You know, where you give the time, place and our names."

"Yes, ma'am, but that's highly irregular."

"I don't want him to know my name."

"Can I say my own and omit yours?"

"No, and now stop discussing this with me. In the Homicide Division we know what we're doing."

"Yes, of course. That's not what I meant."

"Good, so we're in agreement on that. Besides, you're not going to say anything at all. Only I will speak with him. He may get scared when he sees me, but just ignore that. You should do something if he attacks me, and in that case just hold him back so we can get out. Under no circumstances must he be harmed, do you understand that?"

"Yes, every word. So I'm mainly along to protect you?"

"You could put it like that, but bear in mind that I'm more than capable of protecting myself. Of course he's a man, but I'm half his age and in excellent shape. And I wouldn't say it's probable that he will attack me."

"I'll get between you in a flash. That is, without injuring him."

"Just what I had in mind. You're easy to work with. I'll tell Simon that."

"Simon? Do you mean Chief Inspector Konrad Simonsen?"

"Yes, but we call him Simon."

She said that to impress him and had not counted on his reaction.

"He doesn't know about this, does he?"

"What do you mean?"

"I mean, Chief Inspector Simonsen has no idea that in a little while we'll be questioning Andreas Falkenborg. Isn't that right?"

Pauline Berg realised she had underestimated the man. She answered carefully, "It's easier to get forgiveness than permission."

"And your new look, is that to pressurise the murderer? You resemble his victims."

This was something between a question and a statement.

"If the interview goes well, then you'll have something to tell your grandchildren, and if it doesn't, we'll leave. No harm done, as they say."

"What about the prisoner's lawyer, does he know we're coming?"

"It's a woman, and no, she doesn't. But she knows, and we know, and everyone knows, that he has killed four young women, and that early tomorrow morning he will be released, unless someone does something."

The argument made an impression, and she continued quickly along the same lines.

"It's not like we're going to beat him to a pulp or anything. We're just going to talk to him, and the whole thing will barely take more than ten minutes, but maybe we'll save a young girl's life, who knows?"

Asger Graa considered this.

"What do you want him to confess?"

"He is going to tell me where he buried one of his victims. Her name is Annie Lindberg Hansson, and he killed her in 1990."

"Okay, but if you don't get anywhere, I also want a chance to try. I often make an impression on perpetrators."

"That almost sounds like you mean to put the screws on me."

"It wasn't meant that way, but if this goes wrong and gets out, you're not the only one who'll get your knuckles rapped, so it's reasonable for me to have a chance too."

Pauline Berg pretended to consider this, and then said, "It's a deal. Come on."

The walk through Police Headquarters was more hair-raising than Berg had imagined. Although the jail was far from the Homicide Division offices, and Police Headquarters was a big building, she feared running into someone she knew. Worst of all of course would be Arne Pedersen or Konrad Simonsen, who presumably were somewhere in the building. For this reason she took a roundabout route, which proved to be a good idea as the only person they met was a police cadet they didn't know, who took no notice of them. Graa said, "I've never seen your jail. Is it big?"

"There is room for twenty-five, but it's almost never full."

"Who do you have in there? It's the worst of the worst, I hear."

"Then you've heard right."

"I can see why you're keeping him there."

"It's not like that. He's in there only because he will be released tomorrow, unless we succeed in a little while. It wouldn't pay to move him, or he would have been. He's not violent in that way. On the contrary he's been isolated from the other prisoners for his own safety."

"Okay, I see. Tell me, how do we actually get in?"

"We'll be let in, what did you think?"

"Well, I mean, how have you arranged it? That is, without your boss knowing?"

"There won't be any problems, if that's what you're afraid of."

"I'm not afraid, I was just thinking—"

"Stop that."

Pauline Berg was right that they would be let into the jail block without problems. An older guard, who looked like he was counting the hours to retirement, led them at a shuffling pace to Falkenborg's cell and unlocked it for them.

The room they entered was small, ten square metres sparsely furnished with a narrow bed, a desk with chair, wardrobe and small refrigerator, all fastened to the floor or walls. A window at the back allowed a pale light into the cell. Andreas Falkenborg got up from the bed as the two officers came into the room. He had been reading a book, a travel account from India, Pauline Berg noted. To begin with it was Asger Graa who with his uniform and size attracted the man's attention. She believed for a moment that Falkenborg would not react at all to her appearance, but when he saw her, he stiffened and stood stiffly to attention. His jaw dropped and a trickle of saliva dribbled out of one corner of his mouth.

Graa took the opportunity to rig up his Dictaphone, which he placed on the desk, and then asked formally, "Andreas Falkenborg, do you have anything against talking with us for a few minutes?"

The officer received no answer and asked again, but with the same negative result. He shrugged his shoulders and handed over to Berg, sitting down on the bed and waiting. Falkenborg reacted like a frightened animal when Asger Graa was no longer standing between him and Pauline Berg. He fled to the farthest corner of the cell, where he sank down into a crouch. She walked backwards and positioned herself by the door, aware that the situation could easily get out of control. From his crouching position the man guardedly followed every one of her movements, but the increased distance stabilised him. He closed his mouth. Anxiety was no longer the only emotion on his face—undisguised hatred almost steamed toward her.

"Andreas, you killed Annie, tell me how."

He did not answer, nor did she expect him to. The sound of intermittent aggressive breathing through his nostrils filled the cell.

"Do you want me to come over to you?"

The threat struck him like a blow. He threw back his head and looked imploringly up at Asger Graa, who said, "You had better answer her."

Falkenborg half stuttered, half snarled, "She must... must... must not be here."

"Then tell us what you've done, damn it, and she'll go away. How hard can it be?"

Berg added, "Yes, tell me about Annie. Then I'll leave."

For the first time he broke away from her gaze and looked down at the floor in front of him instead. It felt like an eternity, but shortly after that he turned towards Asger Graa.

"Annie was like her, she forced herself on me, what should I do?"

Berg answered him harshly: "I'm not interested in what you should do, but in what you actually did."

"Killed her, you know that. She deserved it. And you do too, you witch."

Graa warned him, "Watch what you're saying now."

"I hate her."

"Tell us about your murders, as she requests."

"I waited for Annie to come on her bike. It was dark. Then I caught her and put her in a bag."

Anxiety, hatred, defiance, it was hard to tell which emotion was uppermost in Andreas Falkenborg then. His abrupt confession, made without a proper caution, could not be used for anything. Neither of the two officers was in any doubt about that. Nor that his comments were meant as provocation.

"It was nice, and now she's gone for ever."

Quietly and calmly, as if she had all the time she needed, Pauline Berg found a hand mirror in her bag, and critically inspected herself without paying the slightest attention to the two men. Then she fished out a tube of bright red lipstick and slowly unscrewed it. She inspected it, holding it up towards the light. She heard Falkenborg gasp, but withstood the temptation of looking at him. Instead she started putting lipstick on.

"You know perfectly well what you should tell me. No need for any irrelevant talk. Well, what will it be?"

While she waited for his reaction, she continued working on her lips, and when no answer came, she added, "Well, get going, I don't have all day. Where did you kill Annie? And above all, where did you bury her? And be sure to include everything, little Andreas, or else I may come over there and give you a kiss."

"She mustn't do that, I can't stand her. She mustn't talk that way."

Pauline Berg was quicker this time.

"I'm waiting, Andreas—but not for long."

"Yes, I will, yes, I will. You stay where you are."

"Where did you kill Annie?"

"On the terrace in my summer house. I swear it was there."

"Her bicycle?"

"Næstved Station, I put it in the bike rack."

"And where did you bury her?"

"But it wasn't that way."

Berg looked at him for the first time since she had started with the lipstick, and saw how he was suffering. Casually, as before, she put her things back in the bag and took a step forward, more threateningly.

"Yes, Andreas, that's how it was. And I want to know where."

One step more.

"Where, Andreas? Tell me where."

It was Asger Graa who answered her.

"Uh, I don't think he can, look at him, he's almost… gone."

Andreas Falkenborg was trembling uncontrollably. His eyes spasmodically rolled up in his head. He was obviously in no condition to continue. You did not need medical knowledge to see that he was balancing on the edge of a mental breakdown. Pauline Berg was close to crying from disappointment as she left the cell.

Outside she heard Asger Graa make his own attempt to question the suspect.

"Detective Pauline Berg is leaving the room. Listen here, my good man, the game is up. Please tell me where you buried the deceased."

It took a few seconds before it occurred to her what had happened. A cold chill ran down her spine as, surprisingly calmly, she realised that her attempt had gone as badly as it possibly could.

CHAPTER 42

On Sunday morning at six o'clock Andreas Falkenborg was released from the jail at Police Headquarters. He was led out of a back entrance to avoid the waiting journalists and on Hambrosgade was released on his own recognisance, as the court and judge had decided. Konrad Simonsen showed up for the occasion, if you could call it that, feeling that it was wrong to stay home and sleep while a serial killer was set free. Afterwards he went to his office to mine away at the heaps of paperwork that always piled up in investigations like this.

At nine o'clock Arne Pedersen also arrived at work and shortly after him Poul Troulsen. The three men put their heads together in Simonsen's office. Pedersen asked Troulsen, "Why didn't you take the weekend off?"

The older man shrugged his shoulders.

"You were here, and I think I owe you a little extra effort. I wasn't too active on Wednesday, Thursday or Friday."

Pedersen teased him.

"Not too active? You're joking. You were far too active last Wednesday."

"You know what I mean…"

He looked at his boss.

"…and I still think it's unfair they put all the blame on you."

Simonsen stuck out his lower lip.

"Yes, it's cruel, the world is so mean… mean."

Troulsen shook his head.

"I'm starting to look forward to retirement."

"Hmm, we have to talk about that at some point, Poul. There are a number of different arrangements, that if you stick around a couple more years—"

"Forget that."

"Okay, well, no need to decide right now. How far are we with the Finnish girl, Arne?"

"We've got her data, but you know that, and otherwise not much has happened since Friday. The narrowest time frame we can establish in which she disappeared is between the seventeenth of April and the third of May, 1992, presumably from Hässleholm Central Station. Falkenborg's old farm was a few kilometres south-west by Finja Lake, but Elizabeth Juutilainen was never seen with him. The Swedes are working on the case."

"I'm hearing that you don't expect we'll get any further with her."

"It's hard. The witnesses we've managed to trace are not the sort to go talking to the police. What they have to say is extremely limited… basically nothing."

Troulsen commented, "Actually it's a paradox: one form of criminality shouldn't overshadow the other, if I may say so. I mean, narcotics circles have just as much interest in getting serial killers behind bars as ordinary law-abiding citizens."

Simonsen said, "In theory you're right, but they don't think that way. Or very rarely in any—"

Pedersen jumped up from his chair.

"Say what you said again, Poul. Right away, it's important."

"The thing about the narcotics smugglers?"

"Yes, damn it, what was it you said?"

"That they ought to be just as interested that we catch serial murderers as anyone else, and that it's a paradox they aren't."

"No, not that, the other thing you said."

Simonsen recited calmly, "Actually it is a paradox: one form of criminality shouldn't overshadow the other, if I may say so. I mean—"

He got no further.

"Yes, that was what she said! Exactly that."

"Who said, Arne?"

"The new teacher at the parents' evening. She said that she always spoke softly to the children, because she did not believe that too much noise should be drowned out with even more noise. Now it also has a logical sense, yes, obviously—what an idiot I've been! If we have the transcript of the questioning of Andreas Falkenborg you'll see it. Yes, and the conversation in the car between Poul and him, that's the same."

Both of his listeners gave up trying to make immediate sense of his outburst. Simonsen found the printouts. Pedersen browsed eagerly, almost feverishly, through them after which he read out loud to them.

"This is from the interview. Simon, you are asking him about Annie Lindberg Hansson.

K.S.: She resembled the other women to a T.
A.F.: So it must be me. Yes, I would think that.
K.S.: Where did you bury her?
A.F.: I didn't.

And this is from the car. Poul, you are also pressuring him in relation to Annie Lindberg Hansson.

P.T.: ...so it's Annie now—where did you bury her?"
A.F.: But I haven't done that.
P.T.: Why drag this out?
A.F.: But it's the truth, I haven't done that.

Stop right there, can't you see it?"

They could. It was Troulsen who answered.

"You mean the pig?"

"It was a gigantic sow that stank for months, while it rotted. That is, rotted outside on the tree. Now you haven't seen it, of course, but I have, it's an old poplar, and I would bet that at the same time the pig rotted, Annie Lindberg Hansson was sitting inside the tree. The poplar resembles an upturned, giant-sized shaving brush. The trunk must be a metre-and-a-half wide and no more than four metres up to the thin branches that stretch out in all directions. When I was a kid, there was a poplar like that on waste ground near us, and it was hollow, rotten from above and down inside, but outside the tree seemed healthy enough and put out leaves and branches every year. We kids climbed up and squeezed through the branches so we could lower ourselves down into the hollow trunk with a rope, almost all the way to the ground. I'm damned certain—she's in there."

Simonsen held his men back. Both of his subordinates were full of enthusiasm and wanted to go to Præstø immediately. It was extremely tempting, but the trip was postponed until the next day, and the chief was unyielding.

"No, I don't want any more surprises in court. This time it will go precisely by the book. We will arrange the legalities today and get permission to cut down that poplar tree, if we have the slightest suspicion. But in that case it will be the technicians who do the job. You'd better find a good corpse dog for early tomorrow morning!"

Troulsen tried one last time.

"But we could at least go down and look, we can easily do that."

"Tomorrow, Poul, tomorrow."

Both men should have known their boss better and realised that it was pointless to pressure him. They tried anyway. At last however they accepted the postponement. Pedersen asked searchingly, "Can't we take Pauline along? She and I have been there before."

"Fine by me, but she's sick, she called last night. Said we shouldn't count on seeing her until at least the middle of the week. A summer flu, she said."

"Oh, good Lord—yes, there's a lot of that in this heat. What about Falkenborg? How much surveillance do you have on him?"

"I have two teams that change three times every twenty-four hours."

Troulsen asked, "Isn't it a mistake not to keep as much control over him as we possibly can? It would be unbearable if he gives us the slip, just when we can nail him on Annie Lindberg Hansson. Keep in mind that Ernesto Madsen could not understand that episode with the pig, it fell outside the pattern, and suddenly it doesn't any more. I don't like the fact Falkenborg's withdrawn so much cash either. That sounds like he's planning to disappear."

Simonsen said regretfully, "In an ideal world without budgets, I'd throw all the resources we have at him. But now the situation is obviously different, I'll add two more teams."

They went their separate ways, feeling considerably more uplifted than when they'd arrived. Simonsen called the Countess and told her about Arne Pedersen's hypothesis. She too urged him to drive to South Zealand right away. For once she was flatly rejected.

That same evening Andreas Falkenborg slipped away from police surveillance. It happened in the heart of Copenhagen, where Frederiksborggade runs into Nørre Voldgade. Four unmarked police cars took part in the shadowing, so that two were responsible for staying ahead and two behind Andreas Falkenborg's easily recognisable blue Mercedes the whole time it was apparently driving aimlessly around in the city. The other two were held in reserve, ready to intervene when the lead car missed the route. The job was easy, on the verge of boring. The man they were following drove calmly and sensibly, more often too slowly than too fast, and the officers were thus not particularly attentive when their subject, in complete accordance with traffic regulations, stayed in the inside lane at a red light alongside Nørreport Station. It was the second time within five minutes that they'd found themselves at this exact spot, which ought to have sharpened the officers' attention. The last time however the light was green, so they'd followed the traffic and glided past the station. In contrast to now. One of the two officers in the following car said tiredly, "God, how long does he intend to drive around here?"

"We'll see," said his colleague in a bored voice. "At least this is more fun than sitting staring at the entry to his apartment. Here there's a little variety, and … what the hell!"

The officer reacted quickly. He opened the car door without looking and it banged into a bus that had pulled up alongside the police vehicle. He squeezed out, wriggled past the other motorists and ran the fifty metres to the station as fast as he could. When his colleague saw that the Mercedes was empty, he understood and followed. But Andreas Falkenborg's head start on them was too much, and both men arrived too late.

They conferred briefly, after which one ran down the stairs to the platforms while the second officer called the other surveillance teams. Soon eight officers were gathered at the scene, but to no avail. After a hectic fifteen minutes they gave up, and the leader of the surveillance operation reported the depressing news to the officer on duty at Glostrup Police, who promised to inform the Homicide Division immediately.

But the news arrived at the worst imaginable time.

While the desk sergeant was receiving the information about Falkenborg's disappearance, his commissioner showed up alongside him wearing a serious expression. Kindly but firmly, he took the desk sergeant's phone from him and interrupted the call. The explanation followed immediately.

"Your daughter just called."

Anxiety came in waves. The desk sergeant nodded, he was in no condition to do otherwise.

"It's your grandson. He's been admitted to Herlev Hospital with meningitis. It's serious, Mads. The boy is in a coma. She's asking for you to go there."

The commissioner drove him.

Almost twelve hours passed before Konrad Simonsen was notified that Andreas Falkenborg was beyond the supervision of the authorities and had been so for almost half a day.

CHAPTER 43

The evenings were getting darker, without anyone really noticing it. It was not all that long ago that the lilacs were blooming, the summer holidays lay ahead, and the light nights only got longer and longer. The woman in the S-train observed her reflected image in the window beside her. Without vanity, although she was quite pretty. She shrugged to herself. At the end of every summer she had a melancholy feeling of not having achieved what she wanted to, in the good part of the year. The time ahead of her always appeared longer than the time behind. Perhaps that would change when she grew old.

The S-train rolled into Nørreport Station, and many passengers got off and on, faces drawn and harassed. Endlessly trying to snatch back a second or two. She observed the new arrivals. It was an art she had mastered completely—looking at people without them realising it. And then drawing them, if the opportunity presented itself. But she was choosy about that. Not all faces were equally interesting, there had to be something particular about the ones she chose, and none of the newcomers found favour in her eyes. A young girl sat down beside her, not even noticing her, absorbed in a phone call. She moved her backpack slightly so the girl would have room. The doors whistled, and the S-train pulled out.

Shortly after that a man in his fifties came into the compartment. He seemed restless, constantly looking back and forth, as if someone were following him. He took a seat a little farther forward, still wearing a hunted expression. She studied him thoroughly, and her pulse raced.

It was his ordinariness that excited her. A face that could only be described by what it was not, by its very lack of distinguishing characteristics. As if he were created neutral. He could be a refuse collector, he could be a bank manager, in both cases he would pass unnoticed. At the same time there was something confidence-inspiring about him; this was a man you could feel safe with. What was ordinary was never dangerous. She took the sketch pad out of her backpack and decided to herself that when she was through drawing, he would be called the Middleman.

"Shut up! Those are beautiful. Can I take a look?"

The young girl had finished her phone call. The idiotic comment did not impress the artist, but nevertheless she handed over the pad. She did not like to reject people. Not even this evening, although basically she would rather go home. He wanted to pick her up at Grimstrup Station, a carefully chosen, deserted place where no one would see her getting into his car. Like a forbidden plaything.

"What is that?"

"A wall in England."

"That looks boring. It's nothing but stone. Why'd you draw it?"

It was hard to explain, she barely knew herself. Why had she saved for five months to go to London for just two days? Two days when for hours she had drawn a Roman wall in the middle of the world's biggest financial district. A peeling ruin, dominated on all sides by luxurious, blue-glass facades. Forms, contours, surfaces, angles—she had enjoyed every minute.

It was as if the girl guessed her thoughts. The date under the drawing combined with the stickers on her backpack probably betrayed her.

"Did you go to London just for that retarded wall?"

"I want to be an architect someday. But take a look at this."

She took back the sketch pad and leafed past the wall drawings.

"He was a guide on a horror tour. His name is Patrick."

The young man had walked past her, leading a small group of tourists. With a booming voice and exaggerated gestures, he told lurid stories. She was intrigued by his larger-than-life presence, the confidence with which he wore his over-sized tweed jacket. She followed on behind the group. In the beginning she stayed on the edges, she hadn't paid for the tour after all, then her confidence increased as she saw that she was welcome anyway.

"He was talking about Jack the Ripper, a serial killer in the 1880s, who terrified the East End of London. He murdered prostitutes, cutting them up horribly with a knife. He killed five women. At the time the Ripper roamed its streets Whitechapel was a slum. Today it's an ultra-modern neighbourhood."

She and Patrick had coffee together when the tour was over. They laughed together and acted silly. He told her he was going to drama school; recited Shakespeare just for her. It stayed at that.

The girl said, "I hope they hanged the murderer."

"He was never caught, and since then there have been lots of theories about who he was. Every conceivable type of fine, highly

315

educated gentleman, but I think he was more anonymous. The quiet type, someone no one would ever dream of suspecting."

At Hillerød Station she took leave of the girl and joined up with a handful of people waiting for the local train toward Frederiksværk. Suddenly the Middleman was standing behind her, without her having heard his approach. She turned and smiled casually at him. Maybe she would have another chance to draw him.

CHAPTER 44

In Præstø Arne Pedersen's theory that the poplar tree contained the earthly remains of Annie Lindberg Hansson was given reliable support in the form of a young, black female German Shepherd who answered to the name of Cathy, as long as it was the dog handler who said it. Cathy scratched at the tree and barked, while her owner meaningfully gave the detectives the thumbs up. Pedersen pointed to a rusty plate and said, "It sounds strange, but at one time there was a dead pig nailed up here until it rotted away. Could that have affected your dog's behaviour?"

The handler patted the animal and answered, "I really don't think so, but we can try from the other side, just to be sure."

He ordered his dog around the tree, shouted an unintelligible command, and the animal's reaction was repeated from the opposite side.

"And that means?" Poul Troulsen enquired.

"That there is a body inside the tree, unless Cathy is wrong."

"Is she often wrong?"

"She's never wrong."

Pedersen set up a ladder which he had borrowed from the teachers, who were following the course of events tensely from their kitchen window not far away. He climbed up and with difficulty swung through the many unpollarded branches, aiming his powerful flashlight down into the trunk. Troulsen asked from below, "Is there anything to see?"

"Nothing, only detritus and withered leaves, but it's hollow, like we thought. Should I try to go down? It won't be easy."

"No, let's leave the rest to the technicians. If anyone is going to destroy evidence, it should be them and not us."

A few hours later a chainsaw was powering into the old poplar. A technician dressed in what looked like a spacesuit operated the saw. The branches quickly disappeared, the trunk itself put up more resistance, but block by block the tree was cut down. The process was slow. Every time a piece of trunk was sliced off, two other technicians carefully removed twigs, leaves and humus from the hollow space. Only towards afternoon, when the tree was barely two metres tall, did anything finally happen. One technician said quietly, "Okay, now we have her. I can see a hand."

Gently, almost solemnly, he gathered a portion of composted leaves, which he let fall behind him, then said, "Yes, she's in a plastic bag, the poor girl."

Pedersen already had his cell phone out. It was the news he and Troulsen had been waiting for all day. He called Konrad Simonsen and was connected immediately. With triumph in his voice, which he made no effort to conceal, he said, "She's been found, and there is no doubt that it's him. Same murder method."

Then he listened for a long time. After a while Troulsen began to feel worried. Something was wrong, his colleague's facial expression had lost every trace of optimism. Pedersen ended the call, looking unhappy.

"What's happened, Arne? You're completely pale."

"Falkenborg is gone. He fooled his surveillance team yesterday evening, but we only found out this morning because some blockheads from Glostrup made a total mess of it. Since then everyone has been searching for him, but with no result."

"Shit."

"There's more. Jeanette Hvidt has disappeared, and several witnesses saw Falkenborg at her uncle's house in Helsingør."

Troulsen took hold of Pedersen's arm and turned him around, shouting, "What the hell are you saying?"

"He overpowered her in a bicycle shed in her uncle's garden. That was the only thing Simon told me. You'll have to wait to hear more until we get to Copenhagen."

"But how could that happen? We were going to watch her. Didn't she have anyone to protect her?"

Pedersen released himself from his colleague's grasp and repeated slowly, "That was all Simon told me. I don't know anything else."

Troulsen folded his hands behind his neck and bent his head. Then he cursed bitterly and impotently.

CHAPTER 45

While in Præstø Arne Pedersen's moment of triumph was transformed into defeat, Pauline Berg was lying on a reclining chair on her terrace, trying once again to figure out what she should do with herself. The initial shock of the fiasco on Saturday evening had subsided. With a little luck maybe the episode would remain undiscovered. She had talked with her boss yesterday and twice today with Pedersen, when she had asked for news while faking a heavy head cold. After all, Andreas Falkenborg was under intensive surveillance so she was in no danger, and with her police training she was in an excellent position to protect herself, especially considering that besides her course in hand-to-hand combat she was also in possession of a 9mm Heckler & Koch, the standard issue pistol.

"I'll have to get my hair dyed back again as soon as possible."

No one answered Pauline, who was talking to herself. She repeated the sentence in slightly varied form and concluded that unfortunately she would have to withdraw some of her savings to cover the outrageous eight hundred kroner the hair treatment cost. Pauline Berg yawned. She was comfortable here but really ought to think about starting on dinner. Last night she had slept poorly, and fatigue was gradually starting to get the better of her. Maybe it didn't matter. She could have a couple of sandwiches for once, and if Asger Graa simply kept his mouth shut and came to dinner and shared the sandwiches with her…

She heaved her head up with a start, aware that she was about to fall asleep. Then she set the alarm on her cell phone, which lay on the garden table beside her, and closed her eyes while a cuckoo called from the forest, as if it could not come to terms with the fact that it wasn't night-time either. She was soon out like a light. A quiet little snore escaped from her nostrils, barely audible unless you were close by.

When she woke up, she was immediately aware that she had slept much longer than planned. It was dusk already and she felt cold even though she had a blanket over her, which surprised her. She didn't remember bringing it. She picked up her phone. The battery was flat. She had been asleep for almost three hours. She cursed to herself, even though there was nothing wrong with taking an unplanned long nap other than that she might have to postpone her planned painting project until tomorrow. She got up, stretched to get the sleep out of her body, folded up the blanket and went inside. With the blanket over her arm, she locked her garden door and pulled on the handle a few times; the door seemed solid. She thought that she must get a curtain she could close so as to screen off the terrace. Sometime when she had the money.

In the house she briefly considered changing her routine around. She was hungry, but usually did her daily ballet exercises before dinner and not after. She went to her practice room, which was one of the first she had furnished. Here she changed into a leotard, placed herself at the barre and expertly went through her drill. Outside it had grown dark and she observed her own reflection in the window until a twinge of discomfort took hold of her. She was unused to seeing herself with black hair, and the sight reminded her of Saturday's fiasco with Andreas Falkenborg.

After her exercises she took a quick bath. She was in a strange mood, as if the day was somehow out of sync. She had put the blame on her black hair, but there was something else too. Something was wrong. Maybe it had been a bad idea to call in sick. She seldom took time off for no good reason, and usually had a bad conscience when she did. She was starving besides, which was her own fault, of course, but that didn't make her any less hungry. She tried to remember what she had in the refrigerator to put in her sandwiches while, feeling oddly ill at ease at being naked, she hurried out of the bath and into her bedroom to get dressed. At the same time she decided to call Ernesto Madsen and ask whether he felt like visiting her. That would be nice, really nice. Then she realised that for that she would need to find the charger for her phone, which was not in its usual place in the socket below the night stand by her bed. She tried in vain to remember where she had put it, and at the same time cursed her customer-unfriendly telecoms company for having a four-week waiting time for a landline connection.

The sandwiches did her good. Both Ernesto Madsen and the charger were forgotten in favour of a quiet evening alone in front of the TV. A rerun of *Pretty Woman* was exactly what she needed. She took her glass and empty plate and went out to the kitchen. After putting the dishes in the dishwasher she carefully wiped off the kitchen table, although it had barely been used. Then she found a can of cat food in the kitchen cabinet, opened it, took a spoon from a drawer and crouched down while she scooped half the contents into the cat's bowl. Then it was as if she stalled. A desire to keep sitting there on the floor came over her. As if she had found completely the right place to be, however irrational that might seem. She tried to laugh off her own behaviour but remained sitting for a while, gathering the strength to stand up. Once upright again she put a plastic lid on the cat food can and set it in the refrigerator, while she repressed the urge to sit down again.

Pauline Berg enjoyed the film. Although she had seen it many times, it was just as good every time. Then suddenly a text crawl broke in over Julia Roberts and announced an extra TV news broadcast in ten minutes. Pauline shuddered. News that was important enough to interrupt programming was seldom good. A brief channel surf to text-TV was uninformative, so there was nothing to do but wait. The film no longer captivated her. She used up the next few minutes calling for Gorm, around the house and out on the terrace, without the animal making an appearance. He usually showed up at mealtimes, but on the other hand he had become considerably more independent since they'd moved, now that he had a game preserve that had to be tended. Sometimes she heard vicious cat fights at night, and some mornings he came home scratched, tired, and proud as a peacock. No doubt he had benefited from the change of scene.

She sat back in her chair just in time for the extra broadcast, activated the sound, which she had put on mute before so she could listen for the cat better, and barely glimpsed an image of the TV studio with two serious announcers before the TV went off with a little pop. Not only the picture and sound disappeared, the standby lamp went out too. She tried to use the remote control to switch off and start again, but with no effect. The same procedure on the buttons of the TV was no use either. Her first thought was that with her immediate financial crisis this might mean several months without a television, but then she remembered that she had bought the set no more than five months ago, so it was still covered by the warranty.

Irritated, she went into her study and turned on the computer. Outside rain was striking the window, and the irregular percussion of the drops and the wind howling around the sides of the house made her feel exposed, so she drew the curtains. As soon as the computer was functional, she opened the web browser and connected to the *Dagbladet* news portal, but experienced disbelief when instead she was directed to a website for the Louvre museum in Paris, even though the address field quite correctly showed *dbnews.dk*, which she had also typed. She tried *dr.dk* and got the same result. The next three addresses ended up in a similar situation. She had experienced many strange things with her computer, but never anything this peculiar. She considered restarting, but first she activated her Windows Messenger, eager to get in contact with the outside world, which with the cell phone, TV and now the computer seemed to be withdrawing. For that reason she was very relieved when the program window popped up as usual, and she could put aside her paranoid thoughts. Three friends were on-line, and she chose an old schoolmate, whom she normally avoided because he almost worshipped her, but a little adoration was just what she needed on an evening like this, where everything was messed up.

Princess Pauline says:	Hi Mads, have you seen the news? My TV is dead.
Mads from Rødovre says:	Pauline, great to talk with you!!! News OK, what do you want to know?
Princess Pauline says:	Extra broadcast on TV about what?
Mads from Rødovre says:	You ought to know that, aren't you still a cop? :-)
Princess Pauline says:	Still a cop, home sick today, what news???
Mads from Rødovre says:	Why do you write that, I haven't bothered you :-(
Princess Pauline says:	What do you mean???
Mads from Rødovre says:	1/3 2/3 1/8 3/8 5/8 7/8 7/8 5/8 3/8 1/8 2/3 1/3
Princess Pauline says:	That was complete gibberish, try again.
Mads from Rødovre says:	Old witch with the coal-black hair, the clock is striking, the clock is striking
Pauline all alone says:	Don't you mean yellow-green?
Mads from Rødovre says:	No, it's coal-black, disgusting whore.
Mads from Rødovre says:	Send news, start news, enjoy news.

She looked nervously over her shoulder towards the door to the study, while the Windows Messenger screen disappeared and an hourglass told her that the computer was working on an unknown job she had not requested. Suddenly a face appeared, a weeping, horror-stricken face that she recognised immediately. The sound of Jeanette Hvidt's pleading voice, punctuated with sobs, streamed out of the speakers, while the girl on-screen threw her head back and forth in a vain attempt to avoid her fate.

"I don't want to, don't do it, won't you please stop?"
"He is angry at her, she is impolite, she must have another blow with the staff."

"No, no, I'll do anything you say, whatever you ask for."

"Everything that *he* says, everything that *he* asks me to. That's what she will say."

"I'll do anything he says, anything he asks me to."

"Then she will tell about the song."

"This song is for you, Pauline."

"She must not cry when she says it. Otherwise she'll get something to cry about."

"Excuse me, I will, don't do that. I will."

"Then she will say it again, with a smile on her ugly face."

Pauline watched, paralysed, how Jeanette Hvidt tried to smile while the tears rolled down her cheeks. The video continued:

"This song is for you, Pauline."

"Then she will sing the song."

"Can you guess where he is, can you guess where he is, because I put the mask on, misk mask mask on…"

"No, she is singing it wrong. Because *he* has put the mask on… that's what's fun. How stupid she is. Then she will sing again, the right way, or else she'll get the staff."

Jeanette Hvidt sang again, though scared out of her wits. It sounded awful, crazy and heart-rending, but that was not the reason Pauline Berg put her hands over her ears.

"Can you guess where he is, can you guess where he is…"

Suddenly the song stopped, the camera zoomed in a little, then the picture froze and immediately dissolved in ten thousand asynchronous washed-out pixels only to materialise again a moment later. This time Jeanette Hvidt was not crying. Instead she sat anxiously covering her ears while the Belphégor demon cautiously approached her from behind. Pauline clenched her fists, Jeanette Hvidt clenched her fists. The demon behind her grew bigger and bigger, until finally she could see the watchful eyes in the loathsome mask. Only then did she understand: the little camera that was attached to the upper edge of her screen no longer showed Jeanette Hvidt at all.

Pauline Berg whirled around on a wave of adrenaline that surprised them both. The man behind her took a step backwards. She grabbed the first thing she could lay her hands on, a solid ceramic mug that stood next to the keyboard, and at the same time heard herself scream while her brain vainly bombarded her with warnings that this was the dumbest thing she could do. His instinctive retreat when she turned around gave her just enough time to put herself in a defensive position with legs slightly spread, side turned and the coffee mug poised ready to strike. They stood like that, facing each other for what seemed like an eternity. Behind her a woman started howling like a tormented animal, but Pauline ignored that and concentrated on her opponent, aware that with every split second that passed her odds improved.

He had lost the advantage of surprise, and the more she looked at him, the less afraid she was. The mask was no advantage to him in a fight; on the contrary it limited his view. Slowly she inched towards him with her feet angled and her body slightly leaning forward, as she aimed a kick towards his testicles. As if he was reading her thoughts, he hitched up his sweater and took out her pistol.

"She will follow him to his car."

The pistol was pointed firmly at her abdomen, and at that distance he could not fail to hit. She did not answer him, Jeanette Hvidt's howling behind her stopped, and only the low-frequency hum of the computer broke the silence.

"She will follow him to his car, otherwise he will shoot her."

If it was courage or anxiety that drove her she never knew. Perhaps it was simply desperation, or possibly she had unconsciously registered how unprofessional it was to stick a pistol in the waistband of your pants, as if they were playing cops and robbers.

"Do you really know how to shoot a gun like that? Have you even released the two safeties? That's a police pistol you're holding, a kind you've never had in your hands before, I can see."

Her voice probably shook, she could hear it herself, but the words were said. He took another step backwards and turned the pistol while he observed it as best he could through the holes in his mask.

"She must not say such things to him."

"I'm not a stupid little goose you can scare with your childish devil facade."

"She does not say such things, she will get the staff."

"I can't see any staff, Andreas. You must have forgotten it."

He stamped on the floor.

"She is not saying that. I can't… he will…"

She was no longer afraid of the gun, which was now limply pointing at the ground. Her disdain about the safety had hit the bull's eye. Again she started to inch forward, while she mocked him venomously.

"You're messing up your performance. Think if your father saw you now, how he would laugh. See, he was a man who knew how to take a girl… did you get that, little Andreas?… take a girl, but you've seen that yourself, of course, so you're not unaware of it. You on the other hand are nothing more than a shell of a man, an overgrown boy who caused his mother to get beaten, because you…"

Falkenborg let the pistol drop and left the room. Immediately after that she heard the key being turned in the lock.

Without wasting a second she gathered up the pistol and discovered to her annoyance that there were no bullets in it. The next priority was the window. If she got out quickly he would not be able to catch her before she reached the forest. That idea wouldn't work, though; the window was blocked from outside. She shoved and pounded on the window frame with all her strength, to no end. Plan C was the computer. She turned it off by pulling out the plug, then turned it on again and restarted the machine, after which all the power in the house went out.

In the darkness she sat down on the floor, her limbs shaking and her heart galloping in a wild ride. She forced herself to think. Her reaction was normal, she knew, and the most important thing was not to feel like a victim. She had won the first round, but now the situation had again turned to his advantage. He had the initiative and the chance to get another weapon besides, this time one that was more effective.

For a while she considered trying to block the door, but ended up only setting a chair under the door handle. In the darkness it was difficult and would hardly hold him up for long. Then she pulled the curtain from the window without fearing that he was standing outside. The mask didn't scare her any more, only the man inside was dangerous. The rain had stopped, and a pale moon illuminated the night, but there was no trace of Falkenborg. Then she caught sight of her car out in the driveway and happened to think about the extra keys in the desk drawer. In the moonlight she found the drawer and felt her way to the keys, which she put in her pocket. Then she pulled one curtain down, tore a solid strip off and folded the fabric around her right hand, while she squeezed the ceramic mug. She smashed the pane with five hard, quick blows, which removed most of the glass from the frame, and without deliberating jumped outside on to the garden path.

When she hit the ground, she quickly unwrapped her hand, let go of the mug and seized a long shard of glass, around which she folded the strip of curtain. Then she got up, looked around and called with the full force of her lungs.

"Well, Andreas, are you coming to fight with me, you disgusting wretch. What about it?"

Determined, but without hurrying, she went over to her car, opened the door and got in. As soon as she was inside, she locked the doors, after which she set her weapon on the passenger seat and put the keys in the ignition. Her foot did not encounter the pedals however, but instead hit something unfamiliar and soft. She reached down, picked it up, and saw her dead cat staring at her through the plastic wrapped around its little head.

Pauline Berg was able to suppress her instinctive horror and force herself to look quickly out of the rear window. She turned the key, heard the engine start, thought that it smelled like a hospital in here without understanding why, looked back one last time and this time stared directly into his grotesque countenance. The rag over her mouth and nose struck her mercilessly a moment later. The last thought she had was that he was much too strong.

CHAPTER 46

There was a high level of activity in the Homicide Division starting in the early-morning hours. Large numbers of detectives were deployed in the hunt for Andreas Falkenborg. He and Jeanette Hvidt *would* be found before it was too late. If it wasn't already, which everyone feared but no one said out loud. Across the country the case had the highest priority in local police districts, and those close to Copenhagen had called in extra personnel upon instructions from police leadership. In many places officers who otherwise would be off duty also came in to work.

Konrad Simonsen sat at the top of the hierarchy among the myriad of men and women involved in the operation. As division head it was his job to use his resources as effectively as possible and above all to ensure that all enquiries from the general public were quickly and competently followed up. Yesterday the case received big headlines with extra news broadcasts and long TV reports. This morning the front pages of the newspapers also had Jeanette Hvidt's kidnapping as the lead story and the finding of Annie Lindberg Hansson's corpse in Præstø as a titillating aside. The result was predictable. Any Dane with eyes in their head now recognised Falkenborg's portrait and quite a few his white commercial van and its licence plate too, for which reason phones in police stations all over the country, and Police Headquarters in Copenhagen in particular, were abuzz with tip offs from well-intentioned citizens.

Arne Pedersen was in Simonsen's office, waiting while his boss finished a phone call. It was the third time within half an hour, which was irritating but unavoidable. Simonsen could not isolate himself for the callers who were transferred to him were carefully screened and deemed to have very important information, which unfortunately was not always the case. Like now, for example, when with eyes rolled up he slammed down the receiver.

"Anything interesting?"

"No, not really. You'll have to go down to the switchboard, Arne, and reorganise the system. This isn't working. I think they've deployed some inexperienced people in one of the chains. They're afraid to make decisions and are transferring calls to me just to be on the safe side."

"I'll do that as soon as we've finished speaking."

"We haven't even started, as far as I recall. What was it you had?"

"Two things. First look at this, I want to show you a video."

Pedersen had rigged his laptop. Simonsen stood behind him and muttered, "I hope it isn't long."

"It will take thirty-two seconds."

"Okay, what is it we're looking at now?"

"A safe deposit box in Roskilde Savings Bank in Lejre, at ten minutes past nine yesterday morning. Are you ready?"

The film started and for a couple of seconds showed a room that was empty apart from rows of bank boxes. Immediately afterwards a man came on to the premises, unlocked the door of one box and carried out a drawer. Only when he turned around could you see that it was Andreas Falkenborg. He set the drawer on a table in the middle of the room and took out an object. Simonsen asked, "What is that he has?"

"You can see it more clearly in a bit, but it's a Belphégor mask. Look there."

He froze the image, and the demon's gruesome face looked out at them from large, empty eyes.

"A technician has gone over it, the image quality is minimal, as you can see, but she improved it by putting several frames together, so that—"

"I don't care what she did, Arne. What is the result?"

"That he made the mask himself, presumably as a child. As far as we can see, it's constructed from cardboard and papier-mâché."

"The original mask that he wanted to scare Agnete Bahn with in her time?"

"Yes, I believe so. It must be his dearest possession. It's probable that he has used it every time he has committed a murder."

"We have to assume that. Make sure there's a man assigned to the bank. No, make that two, and plainclothes of course."

"It's done."

"Excellent, and then I want Falkenborg's picture distributed to all the financial institutions in Zealand and shown to every single employee, in case he rents or has rented another box. If he comes into a bank, they should react to it like a robbery attempt. But bear in mind, for heaven's sake, that he shouldn't be held, only shadowed. To start with, this is our best chance to find the girl."

"This will produce a series of false alarms all over the country."

"Not if the personnel know his appearance, but we'll deal with that. Find a reasonable man to put on the case, and make sure he gets help from the police commissioner. She's good at this sort of thing and will love giving us a hand in this situation, count on that."

"I'll go up and see if she's free, as soon as we're done."

"First the switchboard, then the commissioner, and if she's not around, get her out of the meeting she's probably in."

"Yes, boss."

"You'd better also get her to contact the Swedes and see whether they can be talked into a similar effort in the Malmö and Helsingborg region."

"It's noted."

"Good, more about that?"

"No, but I have something else."

"Which is?"

"The Countess and I were discussing that it's strange he would know where Jeanette Hvidt was. Almost nobody knew, and we have also spoken with his lawyer about how she could show up out of nowhere, and it turns out that he had recorded a message on her answering machine on Tuesday afternoon, which she only heard on Wednesday at just past noon."

"What did he say in that message?"

"That he would be arrested early Wednesday morning and brought to a place called *HS*."

The phone rang. Konrad Simonsen ignored it and almost shouted, "What in the world is that you're saying? Did he say *HS*?"

"Yes, like we say, and not *Police Headquarters*, like most people do. But he said 'a place that's called HS...' Clearly he doesn't know what that is. And, well, that information...that is, that he was going to be arrested...if possible that's even more confidential than Jeanette Hvidt's uncle's whereabouts in Helsingør. So I've been playing around with a chart, to see which one of us knew what and when. And, unfortunately, it was unambiguous."

Simonsen was well aware of where this was heading. He asked anyway.

"Who is he eavesdropping on?"

"You."

The homicide chief's reaction was subdued. From his briefcase he found his personal keys and set them in front of Pedersen.

"Make sure if you can that these are people who don't know me personally. If they find anything, then leave the shit there. Maybe we can use it to lure him out. Also have a check done with Poul, with yourself, with Pauline, and you might as well include Malte too. And the same applies as with me: let the equipment stay there, if there is any, and if those concerned consent."

"I'll do it right away."

"Stop that nonsense! You can't do everything right away. This has third priority, no one's at home right now. Anything else?"

Pedersen looked crestfallen. It was no time for praise but he hadn't expected criticism, even if perhaps it was justified.

"No, nothing else."

"Then you'll be busy."

There was no let up for them the rest of the morning, but unfortunately without a trace of the man the whole country was searching for. Simonsen showed no emotion when he was informed that Pedersen's suspicions held water, and that his own as well as Pedersen's and the Countess's homes had been broken into and bugged with tiny microphones plus associated central receivers, which transmitted all conversations over the cell-phone network to an English server on the Internet. Presumably they had been there ever since Simonsen's Greenland trip. Not even when the case took on a new, far more personal turn in the afternoon did he let himself be distracted by his personal reactions to this invasion of his privacy.

The same could not be said however about his two closest co-workers. Pedersen and Troulsen came rushing into his office with every sign of panic in their eyes. Simonsen interrupted his phone call by simply hanging up, while at the same time he prepared himself to hear that Jeanette Hvidt's corpse had now been found. Troulsen's words dragged Simonsen right out of his delusion.

"He's got Pauline."

For a moment time stood still, as if Simonsen did not really want to let the message sink in. Finally he said, "Tell me."

Pedersen started crying, so it was the older man who had to explain.

"We haven't been able to get hold of her, so the microphone technicians—they're from the intelligence service—drove to her house. Her car is still in the driveway with the door open, a window in her house is broken, she's nowhere to be found, and her cat was thrown alongside the car."

"Thrown alongside? Explain."

"It's dead, and it has plastic wrapped around its head."

"The cat has been smothered, did I understand right?"

"Yes... no, not completely."

"Then express yourself properly, man."

Troulsen had to make a violent effort. Simonsen's anger did not help him maintain his composure, more like the opposite.

"Its neck was broken, after which plastic was wrapped around its head. The plastic probably comes from a roll in her kitchen cupboard, they're in the process of taking fingerprints now, but everything suggests that he has been all over her house."

Simonsen's next question was the most difficult he had ever asked. Nevertheless he managed to keep his voice neutral.

"Do we have any idea whether she is dead?"

"No, more likely he's taken her with him, but we don't know that for sure. There are dogs en route."

Pedersen said suddenly, "Her cat's name was Gorm."

This absurd outburst was directed at himself. Simonsen took a look at him and then commanded, "Poul, you drive to Pauline's house and take command, and that applies whether there are intelligence service people there or not. Make sure the technicians don't delay you, not even if they howl about *contamination of the crime scene* and threaten you with Melsing's wrath. Speed is far more important than evidence for us. Do you follow me? I hardly need tell you that this is the most important job of your entire career. If decisions must be made, then make them, and make them quickly. I'll back you up regardless. Understood?"

"Yes."

"This morning Arne placed some experienced people as second chain on the switchboard, take all of them with you."

"Okay."

"If Pauline is alive, time is the most critical factor."

"If kidnapping victims aren't found within twenty-four hours, there is a high probability that—"

"Yes, yes, yes, so let's get going."

Troulsen hurried out of the office. Simonsen turned towards Pedersen.

"Arne, you're going home, but I'll find someone you can talk to first."

"A psychologist? I'm just upset about this, why should I—"

"A colleague and perhaps a nurse, but I don't have any more time to argue. Come along."

Pedersen stood up meekly and let himself be led to the door. Tears were rolling down his cheeks. He made no attempt to brush them away.

"Promise me you'll find her, Simon?"

"You can count on it. I'll find her for certain."

"Quite certain? Do you swear? Quite, quite certain?"

"Quite, quite certain. You can be sure of that."

Alone in the office Simonsen allowed himself five minutes in which as coolly as possible he prioritised his time. When Troulsen and Pedersen had told him of Pauline Berg's fate, he had briefly lost control of his bladder, and the underside of one trouser leg was wet. After his trance, where he sat like a sphinx behind his desk with only his brain working, he grabbed the phone and called the Countess, who was in Helsingør. Without beating around the bush he reported the situation and ordered her back to Police Headquarters.

As soon as he hung up, he had his worst sweating attack ever, this time combined with a galloping heart rate. He tried to ignore his body and concentrate on his work. It was not successful. Anxiety was weighing him down. He took off his shirt and with difficulty yanked his undershirt off over his head. It was soaked through, as if it had been in the washing machine. He counted to ten a couple of times slowly, recited the days of the week, then the months of the year, and counted again. Over the course of a few minutes he began to feel more like himself.

At the back of his desk drawer he found a bottle of cognac, took a substantial gulp and put the bottle back in place, after which he lit a cigarette. Not until he had finished that did he feel more or less on top of things again. Then he took out a spare set of clothes he always kept packed and ready, and changed everything he had on.

Shortly after his indisposition Anna Mia called. He faked a bad connection, hung up and ignored her next two calls as he counted himself lucky that at least a thousand kilometres separated her from Andreas Falkenborg. Then he thought about Jeanette Hvidt and Pauline Berg and promised himself not to die before he found them. The irony of this allowed him to ignore his physical discomfort, although for the first time ever it was crystal clear to him that his physical resources were failing—he was not in good shape.

Forty-five minutes later the Countess was back at Police Headquarters. She went directly to Konrad Simonsen's office. He had just concluded his instructions to a handful of officers who had each been given separate assignments. The Countess noticed that only a few of them greeted her on their way out, and several avoided meeting her eyes, as if she were taboo. Simonsen called after them, "And remember that he should only be shadowed, not arrested. Make sure that order reaches everyone. Everyone has to know: shadowed only!"

The men confirmed this wearily. The Countess thought that this was probably at least the third time they'd had that order repeated to them. When they were alone, she asked, "Anything new?"

"No, nothing. We're getting a lot of calls about his car. False alarms until now, but it's only a matter of time, I hope."

He looked deep into her eyes, like a racing cyclist sizing up a competitor on a mountain leg. She met his gaze without hesitation, well aware that she was being checked over. After what seemed to her like an eternity, he said, "You're ready, I can see."

She sensed a touch of reproof in his tone of voice, but decided to ignore it. He said, "Arne is losing his mind, but doesn't want to hear about being anywhere but here. I pissed in my pants like a child when I got the news, and you... you're just ready."

The Countess's voice was distant but informative. "I've been here before, Simon. The rest of you haven't. Many years ago I had a son. I don't any more. Nothing is worse than that. But I don't want to talk about it. Not with you, not with anyone, ever. So tell me what I should do now."

He registered her words, but could not make sense of them. That required time, time he didn't have. He gave her orders and thought that he should have done so to begin with.

"Arne is, as I mentioned, incapacitated, and I don't have the energy to deal with him. He's your responsibility now. Make sure someone keeps an eye on him, if you can't get him to go home, but keep him away from me. And above all, have his pistol confiscated. I don't care how, just see that it's removed. The last thing I need is a loose cannon on deck. He has highest priority, do you hear me?"

"Yes, where is he now?"

"I don't know, figure that out yourself."

"How is Ernesto doing? Is he incapacitated too?"

"No, strangely enough. I think he took some pills, but so long as it doesn't affect his thinking, I couldn't care less. We can use him now. Do you have the personal item from Jeanette Hvidt that I asked you to bring?"

The Countess produced a silk scarf from her bag. It was in shades of blue mixed with gold thread. Simonsen said, "That looks expensive."

"Louis Vuitton, about fifteen hundred kroner, if I remember correctly."

"Couldn't you have chosen something more everyday?"

The Countess explained quietly, "It was her uncle who chose it for me. She got it as a present for her eighteenth birthday and likes it very much."

"Okay, excellent. Then you'll find something correspondingly personal that belongs to Pauline. Try her office first, break open her hiding places if they're locked. If that doesn't work, drive to her house. Poul and a lot of others are up there, you can ignore

337

them. Then go to Høje Taastrup, she's waiting for you. On the way back you'll pick up some clothes for us both, or else get someone else to do it. We can't count on going home until this is over."

"Yes, sir."

"And you'll call at once, if she has anything to tell."

"*She* is your medium, I assume?"

"Yes."

"Why don't you ever say her name?"

"She doesn't like that. But Countess, there is one more thing, and this is perhaps the most important."

"Let's hear it."

"You will stay updated the whole time about what I'm doing. Half an hour ago I had a bad spell. Really bad, in fact. I couldn't function for a while, no matter how much I wanted to. You should be ready to take over if necessary."

For a moment she seemed shaken. "I don't think—"

"There's no one else. You can, and you will, if it's required of you. Otherwise it's not up for discussion, that's an order you must obey. Understood?"

She got up from her chair, went around the desk and wrapped her arms around his head.

"Yes, Simon, it's understood."

They allowed themselves a few seconds without words. Then she noticed that he was pressing a hard, angular object into her hand. She let him go and looked down with surprise. It was a small, carved figure of bone.

"A *tupilak*, a really fine one."

"It keeps evil spirits away."

"Yes, everyone knows that."

"I got it in Greenland from Trond Egede. It may sound crazy, but will you please carry it with you in your pocket?"

She kissed him on the forehead, happy about the present but also feeling a twinge of irritation. Again and again he protested that he was not superstitious. But when push came to shove … She pushed the thought aside. What choice did she have? Then she kissed him again, this time more fervently, without caring whether anyone came into his office.

Troulsen barged into the room. He was shooing an officer ahead of him whom he placed in the middle of the floor, as if he were a mannequin, after which he sharply commanded, "Tell them, and make it brief."

Asger Graa told them everything. Simonsen and the Countess listened in disbelief, and afterwards for a minute or so none of them said anything, not even when Graa started begging their forgiveness.

"I'm sorry about this, I am truly sorry about this, and I realise that it means my chances for—"

Troulsen interrupted him callously.

"Be quiet."

And then to Simonsen: "Do you have anything for him to do?"

Simonsen curtly shook his head. The Countess said to the contrite officer, "Go away."

Asger Graa shuffled out with bowed head. Before he had closed the door, Troulsen started itemising the information he had from Pauline Berg's home.

"The sequence of events is now established, but unfortunately there is not much to help us track them down."

Simonsen agreed. It was what he had expected and feared. He said, "The Countess has a few things to see to that are urgent. Start with your conclusions. Do we think that Pauline and Jeanette Hvidt are alive?"

"Yes, most likely."

Simonsen turned to the Countess. It was unnecessary, however. She was on her way out. Then he asked Troulsen, "Well, what happened?"

"Falkenborg's fingerprints were found all over the house. He had basically been in every room, probably while Pauline was out though we don't know where. Maybe in town to shop or something."

"When was this?"

"Yesterday morning or afternoon. A technician found his fingerprints on a carton of milk in her refrigerator, the date stamp confirms it. We're in the process of investigating where and when she used her debit card."

"A carton of milk? Why?"

"We don't know. It looks like he went around rooting in everything."

"What else?"

"He has manipulated her computer. It's now being investigated, but the nerds aren't done. Her TV is destroyed, apparently he short-circuited it."

"Okay."

"In the evening, about eleven o'clock, he chased her and locked her in a room. She managed to bring her pistol along but no ammunition."

"That sounds strange."

"That's our theory at the moment, but maybe it will change in the hours ahead. I concentrated more on where she could have been taken than on what happened in the house."

"Naturally, go on."

"At some point she broke out of the room where she was locked in. He had put screws in the window frame outside, so she couldn't open the window, but she smashed it."

"Not too many details, Poul."

"Sorry. Well, after she climbed out of the window, she made a kind of weapon out of a big shard of glass by folding some material around one end. We found it in her car, but unfortunately it wasn't used. He was waiting for her in the back seat and pressed a rag soaked in chloroform against her face. The car has been taken for technical investigation."

"What did he do with her then?"

"Carried her through the forest that is right by her house, and over to his car which was parked on the other side. The dogs could easily follow the whole way. Then we lose the trail."

"Was it the commercial vehicle?"

"We found tyre tracks, they are also being examined, but an initial assessment from the technicians confirms that. You'll be getting some complaints from them about me, I assume."

Simonsen's hand gesture clearly showed how much he cared about that kind of thing at the moment. He said, "What about the cat?"

"It was killed alongside her car, neck broken, then wrapped in plastic from Pauline's kitchen. Just the head that is. Maybe that was to scare her."

"While she watched?"

"We don't think so, but it's unclear. Maybe it was lying somewhere so she got a shock when she saw it."

"Her car keys?"

"In the ignition."

"And the extra keys?"

"Damn it, that was a mistake. I didn't look for them."

"Presumably that means nothing. Do we know positively that she was alive when she was carried through the forest?"

"No, but there's a high probability of it."

"Explain why."

"Because we found a roll of duct tape—that's his favourite tool—dropped by the side of her car."

"You don't tie up a corpse, and you don't sedate a woman to kill her immediately afterwards, when you could just as well do it right away. Is that what the arguments are?"

"Yes, and I don't think that's wishful thinking."

"Hardly. Do you have anything else?"

"I found a receipt for a pair of brown contact lenses corresponding to what the idiot from before told us about Pauline's eye colour."

"It doesn't sound very interesting."

"Yes, it is, because I couldn't find the lenses."

"You mean, she had them in?"

"No, the whole case was gone. It wasn't in the waste basket either. I think Falkenborg took them. I'm terribly sorry to say that but it's what I think."

Simonsen said heavily, "She's going to have them on when he kills her?"

"Yes, that's the way it is. That's what he's going to do, Simon—kill both of them."

CHAPTER 47

The anaesthetic had given her a headache, a condition that was seriously worsened by the infernal din that blasted at regular intervals and threatened to burst her eardrums. She could not see, and only gradually was she aware of her own situation. She noticed a rag in her mouth and a strip of tape around her neck holding the rag in place and pinching her cheeks when she moved her head, which was hard to avoid, every time another wave of noise hit her. Her face was covered with cloth that felt like the synthetic silk lining of a coat, but the covering was carelessly executed, because if she lowered her head and looked down she could see light below her and a small section of concrete floor. White, dry dust penetrated through the opening, several times causing coughing fits that threatened to choke her, because the rag in her mouth prevented normal breathing. The particles came in cascades in tempo with the noise, and she quickly learned to hold her breath when it was at its worst. The powerful stimuli from absent vision, maddening noise and intolerable white dust meant that she only belatedly showed an interest in her body. She was sitting on a chair whose legs did not move a millimetre when she tried to wriggle it. Her wrists were also linked to the armrests with cuffs on each side.

This torture lasted a long time, but gradually she could also distinguish other sounds: a tool that rattled when the noise stopped, occasionally the characteristic swish of a broom, and then the scraping of a shovel, besides footsteps on a hard floor. There were also occasional outbursts from a person who was working hard, and once a brief, angry sentence, the meaning of which she was unable to catch. Later the infernal noise was replaced with more digging sounds, but by that point she was well aware of what was going on. Andreas Falkenborg was preparing her final resting place, which apparently was to be below a concrete floor. Strangely enough she did not feel overwhelmingly afraid. Not even when she suddenly noticed that he had put her contact lenses in while she was anaesthetised.

Her sense of time had gone. She had difficulty determining how many hours passed before hands carefully removed the covering from her head and the gag from her mouth. The white, glaring light in the room blinded her. She blinked and little by little recovered her full vision. Her kidnapper had the mask on. Otherwise he was wearing shorts and a shirt with rolled-up sleeves. The combination was bizarre. He was sweating profusely. Immediately in front of her, only a couple of metres away, a hole in the floor had been excavated as expected, a good metre-and-a-half parallel with the wall. The room she was in was clearly a cellar with bare, greyish-white concrete walls. Opposite her a three-foot-tall wooden cross painted black was set up, and a single, bright bulb shone from the ceiling. To the left was a red-painted metal door and not much else, apart from herself and the chair she was sitting on. She looked down and saw that it was attached to the concrete floor with sturdy plates. Only then did she discover that there was another person present in the room. To her right, with her chair jammed against Pauline's, sat Jeanette Hvidt, also tied up.

Andreas Falkenborg stood watching them for a long time through his mask. Pauline Berg heard Jeanette struggle with tears in small, smothered sobs, and thought that regardless of their hopeless situation it was crucial not to show anxiety. Even so she could not think of anything reasonable to say. Suddenly Jeanette said, "Won't he just kill the cop? I'll do what he says. Always. I'll always do what he asks me to."

The words came out surprisingly clear, and Pauline realised that they made sense. She had not thought about it herself, but Jeanette was right, the grave was hardly meant for two, it was too small for that. She also registered the girl's form of address and naturally noticed her lack of solidarity, which under the circumstances Pauline shouldn't blame her for, but did anyway. She said neutrally, "May I have some water?"

Falkenborg was over her like a hawk.

"She says, Will he give her some water?"

"If I'm going to be the first to die, that's the way it is, but I'm thirsty. Can't you give me something to drink? I really need it. Why are you letting me suffer like this? It's just not your style."

She was careful not to provoke him. She was convinced that he intended a gruesome death for both of them, the question was when and in what order. On the other hand he was not a sadist. He would not cause her unnecessary pain for his own enjoyment.

He answered her angrily.

"She's talking wrong, she won't get any water."

A quick deliberation made her give in.

"Will he give me a drop of water? I'm very thirsty."

Falkenborg considered while he adjusted his mask. She thought that with the material along the sides and his limited air intake it must be hot and uncomfortable. Finally he said, "She will ask for it again."

"Will he give me some water to drink?"

"She can have water, but she has to wait."

He left the room. The heavy iron door echoed behind him, but Pauline was able to see a corridor outside the cellar room, whatever use that would be to her. When he was gone, Jeanette said in a whisper, "You mustn't antagonise him or we'll get the staff. It's terrible."

Pauline Berg remembered the so-called staff both from the video on her computer and Falkenborg's empty threats in her study.

"What kind of staff are you talking about?"

"He gives a shock with it, it hurts like crazy."

"An electrical prod? Like for cattle?"

"I don't know, I think so. It's horrible, you can't imagine how bad it is."

"I don't see any prod."

"He doesn't have it here, it—"

The door opened again, and Jeanette Hvidt fell silent. Falkenborg returned with a pitcher of water. He set it in front of Berg.

"She will open her ugly mouth."

She opened her mouth and tipped her head back. Carefully he poured the water, pausing at times so she could get air. She drank greedily without thinking of leaving any for Jeanette. Only when she couldn't drink any more, and the pitcher was almost empty, did she ask, "Will he give Jeanette the rest?"

Falkenborg poured the rest of the water into Jeanette's mouth, then he set the pitcher on the floor and said, "He will draw lots on who will go into the bag first. That is how he wants it to be."

She asked quickly, "Will he tell us when it will happen?"

"Tomorrow one will go into the bag. Tomorrow, when he has cement for her grave."

"And the other, what will he do with the other?"

"He will also get her into the bag. That's what he will do. Both of them will go into the bag, first one, then the other. Then the other will be afraid."

Again he adjusted his mask and then started reciting a nursery rhyme as he tentatively touched the two women's knees.

"*Ohn Dohn Dehn, Mamma Futta Fehn...*"

She interrupted him scornfully.

"Can you stop groping my thigh, you lecherous old pig? Tell me, have you no upbringing, Andreas?"

He leaped back. Pauline Berg was hoping for a miracle. The insult was an expression of desperation, she knew that, but she had to try something, and she could not think of anything else. Falkenborg was shaken for a moment.

"Sorry, I didn't want... I, he... He says ugh to her repulsive thighs. She will not say such things, and he says ugh. Ugh, ugh, ugh, he says."

He shouted as he left, this time leaving the door open. Jeanette Hvidt sobbed in terror.

"Now he's getting the staff. You have to beg for forgiveness, promise to behave. Oh, no, I'm afraid."

Falkenborg was soon back, and sure enough he was holding a cattle prod in his hands. Jeanette Hvidt pleaded.

"Not me. She was the one who was bad. She was misbehaving, she should have the staff for her impudent mouth, but not me. I'll do everything he says, everything he asks for."

Berg noticed how Falkenborg's formulations were encoded in Jeanette's language, then her body exploded in a quivering, white pain that tensed her like a spring and sent unbearable spasms through her from head to toe. She screamed with the full force of

346

her lungs, it was impossible not to. Jeanette Hvidt was right, the pain was indescribable.

Her tormentor took a step back while Jeanette shouted, "She deserves more, she was very bad, but not me. I'll do what he says, she should have my shock."

Falkenborg did not immediately follow Jeanette's suggestion. Instead he said, directed at Berg, "She can scream as much as she likes. Scream, like she does on her way to the witches' Sabbath, on her way to Blocksberg, and when she is burning for Saint John's."

Jeanette Hvidt pleaded.

"Yes, let her scream, she said bad things to him…"

"She will keep quiet."

Jeanette fell silent immediately. Then he aimed the prod again towards Pauline Berg, who tried in vain to avoid it, but the jolt never came. He only struck her lightly on the knee and again started his selection process, as he let the prod move from knee to knee with each new syllable.

"*Ohn Dohn Dehn, Mamma Futta Fehn, Futta Fehn, Futta Fehn, Ohn Dohn Dehn.*"

CHAPTER 48

In Høje Taastrup the Countess was at her first clairvoyant consultation ever. It took place on the fourth floor of an apartment complex not far from the station. She had expected a different setting, perhaps a gloomy villa with a tower room and ravens on the roof, but that was not the case. The nameplate on the door said *Stephan Stemme & wife*, and it was the husband who answered when she rang the bell. He was a skinny old man with a starved, bony face and deep-set eyes that drew things in but gave nothing back. They settled accounts in the entry, cash and no receipt. He carefully put the money in a worn black pouch he removed from a bureau drawer. Then he locked the drawer, took the key and knocked on a door immediately to one side.

"You may call her Madame."

His voice was dark bordering on rusty, and his French-sounding *Madame* grated gutturally, almost sternly, as he opened the door for the Countess.

The room she entered was light and pleasant, all philistine comfort as a shield against life's shocks and spills, from the peach-coloured curtains to the collection of well-scrubbed and combed grandchildren whose portraits decorated the light-green walls. There was however a glaring surplus of mahogany, which the Countess found unbecoming, yes, ugly actually, although it was intended to be pretty.

Madame received her from the Biedermeier chaise-longue where she was reclining when her guest arrived. She did not get up, but was content to extend a limp white hand in welcome and straighten herself up a little from her couch. She was a small, almost fragile woman in her late fifties, well-dressed in a modern grey tailor-made suit and with an artfully draped white shawl around her spindly shoulders. Her face looked tired, mouth hanging partway open; only her glass-clear, sparkling eyes made an impression. She did not use makeup or wear any jewellery it seemed. The Countess sat down in a chair opposite her. The woman said, "You are busy, you have a meeting later this evening."

Her voice was oddly flat and almost without intonation, as if she was reporting a series of numbers. The Countess asked scept-ically, "Is that something you see?"

"It is something I know. Konrad just called. Apparently you turned off your cell phone. You should be back at Police

Headquarters by seven-thirty and certainly no later than quarter to eight. I promised to give you the message."

"Thanks, that was good of you."

"This is the first time you've been here, and I sense in you a certain distrust of my abilities. That doesn't matter, it's how it usually is with newcomers. Basically it's healthy. A person must be uncommonly gullible not to doubt me to begin with."

The Countess did not really know what to say to that. She was content to shrug her shoulders and hold up her hands in mock surrender. She was privately sure that the woman always used this self-deprecating introductory speech. Anyway she had a little account to settle now that she was here. She asked, "A few days ago you insisted on the phone that I should *hold on tight to Steen Hansen*, as you put it. What good would that do?"

"How in the world should I know? But you have obviously encountered a person by that name, I see?"

"It's a very common name."

The other woman did not conceal her irritation. The Countess met her eyes with scepticism in her own. They sat that way for a few seconds, staring each other down, until Madame said, "Today you have told a secret to the one you love. You regret having done that. He loves you too, but you can't really work that out together. You're like the old joke about how porcupines mate. The punch line is: very, very carefully. Well, shall we get started? What do you have for me?"

The Countess felt anger rise inside her and restrained herself only with great difficulty. She felt exposed. Her mouth tightened, and her eyes narrowed. Only then did she discover that her doubt about this woman's supernatural talents had suddenly shrunk considerably. Silently she produced from her bag Jeanette Hvidt's scarf and a belt that belonged to Pauline Berg, and handed them over. She asked, "What should I do?"

"Listen."

"May I speak to you while you are in trance?"

"I am not in a trance, and of course you may. I can always ask you to be quiet if you are disturbing me."

The Countess nodded. How hard could it be? It was nothing more than a very ordinary chat with the dead. With each hand Madame rubbed the belt and the scarf in turn between her fingers, while she looked around the room. Shortly after that she said, "There is a woman who was killed in a bookshop."

She said the sentence declaratively and completely without reflection over its odd meaning.

"And another woman who has been a ballerina. Several women…all of them women. The two you are seeking are in a…"

She hesitated and rubbed again; shortly after that she continued.

"I am sensing a white chapel, but something is wrong. Jeanette and Pauline are in a white chapel. They are together, and they are alive. There is something about bombs…the chapel has been bombed I think, during the war. It's gone. *A Cockney knee trembler for fourpence*…back then the neighbourhood was poor, today it's affluent. I see expensive glass facades, but that makes no sense to me. I also perceive that there is a name coincidence, something or other, that gets mixed up, some roots…around the chapel and in relation to some girls' names…diabolical delusions. Yes, now a man is coming. Ugh, he is repulsive, definitely one of the worst I have encountered. He is both very well-known and completely unknown. The others disappear, they don't want to be with him. So now we might just as well stop."

Madame set down the objects. The Countess was deeply disappointed.

"Was that it?"

"Yes, you should look for a white chapel or a crypt. The two women are there."

"Why did you stop?"

"He did not want to help, it was quite obvious."

The Countess made a resigned gesture and then asked Madame a series of clarifying questions about the mysterious white chapel. With no further result. For want of anything better she returned to the man who had obviously scared the other spirits away.

"Why can't you use him?"

The woman stared out into space and let her eyes run appraisingly up and down, as if she was looking at her own reflection. Then she concluded firmly, "No, he is evil."

"Is he still there? Or whatever you say."

"Yes, and I'm sure I'll have a lot of trouble with him. He is not the type you can get rid of easily."

"Couldn't you try to speak… sense him anyway?"

"Yes, if you wish, but no good will come of it."

This time she was content to touch the objects fleetingly. For a while she said nothing, then she said, "He has rattled off a poem. A vulgar poem… what is it they're called? Oh, well, a hateful, mean satirical song, which he maintains is about him. It's hard to understand, old-fashioned and not Danish. There was a politician, who saved a prostitute, and then otherwise it's like the children's song with the ten little Indians who get fewer and fewer. I think anyway. He has killed someone, there is no doubt about that. Let's stop here."

"No, keep going."

The woman took a fountain pen and a pad from the coffee table and started writing. When she was finished, she said definitely, "Now we're done."

"What does it say?"

"A rhyme: it is the last four lines of his old poem, which is rewritten. Or perhaps translated, I couldn't work that out. He wants to be in the newspapers again."

"A rhyme to whom?"

351

"To you, but I don't think you should read it. It won't be of any help and will only do you harm."

The Countess ignored the warning and reached for the pad. Madame handed it over without further objection and Pauline read:

Two little girls tremble with fear,
Child laughs in the dust with his catch so dear.
First girl in the bag, and the other is alone,
The one without curls will die as skin and bone.

Loathing struck the Countess then, and for a few seconds she gasped for air. She quickly got hold of herself again, sufficiently in balance to receive Madame's toneless instructions.

"You are stubborn, the nobility often are. Now you will reap what you have sown. But sometimes stubbornness can be an advantage. You will experience that this evening."

The drive from Høje Taastrup to Søllerød did the Countess good. The metaphysical encounter had not been pleasant, and she was happy to escape from the strange couple. She had little to show for her visit in investigative terms. She called Simonsen and, when she did not get through, left a message about Madame's white chapel on his answering machine, happy that it was not up to her whether the information should be taken seriously or not. The rest of the way she tried to shake off the memory of the other things she had experienced by letting Bob Marley blow her head clear at full blast.

At home she emptied the mailbox and dumped the bundle of advertising directly into the rubbish bin before she went in. The rest, three letters and a package, she tossed on the kitchen table when she was inside, after which she put on coffee, watered her flowers and quickly packed clothing for herself and Simonsen.

After lugging the suitcase to the back of her car she returned to the kitchen. The coffeemaker was still gurgling, and she thought she would either have to buckle down and decalcify it or else buy a new one. While she was waiting she browsed indifferently in her mail.

The letter on top was a statement from one of her banks; she threw that out. The next was a parking ticket, and she remembered that her windscreen wipers had dispatched the first copy on to the street; she was indifferent to that as well. The last letter was a bill from her private detective for ten pictures she had already received by email. She did not bother to open that either. The package remained. In the mailbox it had been under a home-delivered Sunday paper and therefore might have come by courier on Saturday afternoon or Sunday morning. No sender or recipient address was given, and with a feeling of paranoid suspicion she balanced it in her hands a short while, after which she tore it open.

The book was new, as if it came straight from the printer. The dust jacket showed a bluish-grey Boeing B-52 bomber hovering over a desert of ice, elegant and at the same time powerful with its slender fuselage and the gigantic V-shaped wings, each carrying four potent jet engines. Title and author were printed in capital letters and hatched in the colours of the American flag. *On Guard in the North* by Clark Atkinson. She opened it to page one and noted that her present was a copy of the very rare first edition from 1983. The non-existent edition. To top it off, it came with a personal greeting from Helmer Hammer. Freehand and not without talent, the under secretary had sketched a pair of magnolias, heavy with flowers, as they appeared in early June. Behind these a few strokes suggested the geometry of the Palm House. The message was brief and personal: *Dear Countess, I certainly owe you a lot of G. Best, Helmer.* For good measure the G was embellished with a pair of eyes on its lower curve, so that it resembled a smiley face.

Under normal circumstances she would be happy, both with the book and this acknowledgment from the under secretary. But these circumstances were not normal, far from it. Her odyssey into recent Danish history seemed very far off and had no significance now. She squeezed Hammer's present in among her cookbooks, poured coffee into a vacuum jug, looked at her clock and left. To begin with, however, she travelled only a short way up the street, where she stopped parallel to a parked blue Renault and rolled down her window. The driver of the other car did the same while he put a finger to his lips and then indicated behind him towards his female partner, who was sleeping in the back seat. The Countess knew him in passing, but could not remember his name. She handed over the vacuum jug and two mugs to him. He took them, whispering, "You are an angel."

"How long are you on duty?"

"Don't know, the plan has not quite fallen into place, but a long time. We've only been here a couple of hours."

"Lousy job to be ordered out to."

"It's voluntary now, but it doesn't matter. Just be sure to catch that mass murderer, and find his hostages alive."

The Countess promised to do as he asked. Just!

CHAPTER 49

The drive from Søllerød to Police Headquarters was unpleasant. The Countess ran into rush-hour traffic and had far too much time to see how life in Copenhagen continued as it always had, despite the kidnappings of Pauline Berg and Jeanette Hvidt. Even though she knew she was being stupid, it made her angry and even more depressed than she was before. She tried to dismiss her anger before she went into Konrad Simonsen's office. It was difficult.

Her boss was sitting on a chair above an over-sized map of Zealand, which he had set down on the floor in front of him, and barely said hello when she came in. The map was divided with red ink into a series of quickly and carelessly marked-off areas, which she did not immediately recognise. She started by opening a window; he had been smoking.

Simonsen said, "Do you know how many churches there are in Zealand?"

"No idea. Quite a few, I presume."

"Exactly. There are an awful lot of churches with districts that don't follow municipal boundaries, or other worldly boundaries for that matter."

He rattled off facts about parishes, deaneries and dioceses. The Countess recognised his mood well. Pent-up irritation meant that he had a tendency to make lists, without realising it himself.

"The white chapel? Is that what you have in mind?"

He ignored her.

"And furthermore cemeteries, crematoria, parish halls and a wealth of private chapels in various castles and estates. Not to mention all the various Catholic monastic orders, which no Christian soul can tell apart—Capuchins, cappuccinos, whatever they call themselves. The whole mess combined in a perfect hodgepodge … but naturally each with their pestilential cloisters … at least one pestilential cloister that is, often several."

He was talking fast, frantically, and his normal caution not to lose himself in detail had obviously been cast aside. She was worried to see that his face was flushed, beads of sweat visible on his forehead. She commented quietly, "You're sweating."

He wiped his face with a handkerchief. Then he said, sounding more under control, "You shouldn't be nervous, I'm not about to submerge myself in details. I am just so confoundedly angry, which by the way I don't have time to be. At least I was able to let off a little steam."

"I'm not afraid of you losing yourself in the details, more about your health, Simon."

Simonsen allowed himself a little smile.

"You shouldn't worry about either. That sweating is only when I don't breathe deeply and regularly, and it passes quickly. This afternoon I had a definite attack, and then I was a little unsure, but now I've discovered that I can provoke it myself by…what the hell is that called, when you make yourself short of breath on purpose?"

"Hyperventilation."

"Exactly. As soon as I do that, I start sweating like a pig."

"That's not normal."

"No, I agree. But it's not something we have time to worry about now either. There are more important matters, don't you think?"

"I think that you should breathe properly, and then tell me what made you so angry."

"A meeting in forty-five minutes at the Ministry of Justice. And I'm sure you can guess who called it."

"Helmer Hammer?"

"Nice! And I naively believed that the whole menagerie of them could be ignored after our press conference last Friday, but no. I have to go to a meeting with the police commissioner and the national chief of police and director this and chief administrative officer that and general commander bleepity-bleep, not to mention the head of the intelligence service, however he comes into the picture. But they're *not* telling me what to do. I intend to shift responsibility for the meeting to you, and if you don't care to go—for which I would not blame you for a second—I'll send Poul. And if *he* doesn't care to go either, I'll send Pauline's dead cat. Then Grand Duke Hammer will maybe realise that we have more important work to do than playing press secretary for him and all his dignitaries."

The Countess asked carefully, "What is the meeting's agenda?"

"Something meaningless about information sharing, I think. It was the police commissioner who called it, and that could easily be a pretext she thought of on the spot when I asked. That would be just like her. When the mighty whistle, she's not exactly the type who asks impertinent questions, and certainly not about something as petty as an agenda."

"Do you mean that you're not coming?"

"I told her that I would do everything in my power to find a qualified co-worker with a gap in their calendar, but that it was especially hard, considering the circumstances."

"What did she say to that?"

"Nothing. I don't think she even got what I meant. But that's her problem."

The Countess looked at her watch and decided to let the matter rest a while. Instead she asked about the map on the floor.

"Are you thinking about putting the whole machinery in motion around that chapel? I mean, we don't have much to hang that information on. And there is nothing to indicate that Andreas Falkenborg has any particular religious affiliation, or am I wrong there?"

"No, that's correct. Actually I'm dropping our chapel line of inquiry to start with. Despite the fact I can't bear to think that maybe later that will turn out to be a mistake. But I simply don't have the resources at the moment."

"Resources? We have plenty of resources. Our colleagues are reporting for work voluntarily on a large scale. Ordinary people too incidentally."

"Yes, but that doesn't help much here and now. Tomorrow and the day after tomorrow our main priority is to get a super-effective covert surveillance of Andreas Falkenborg established, once he is recognised. There is hardly any doubt that he will be, if he so much as sets foot in a public area. We have a network of experienced people stationed in strategic places in the capital so that regardless of where he is discovered, we can shadow him on a large scale within fifteen minutes. That's crucial. Under no circumstances must he slip away from us again, and if he discovers that he is being followed, that's just as bad. For obvious reasons."

"You don't want to bring him in?"

"No, I don't. My guess is that there is a greater probability of finding the women if we shadow him. That's my assessment, and that's how it will be to start with."

The Countess supported the decision. Simonsen continued.

"If he isn't found by Wednesday at the latest, we have to assume … assume that it is more reasonable to initiate a search for where he has concealed Pauline and Jeanette Hvidt. But it has to be organised. A lot of well-intentioned people, running around aimlessly, does more harm than good. And there we have the core of the problem, because those who can organise are mainly the same people now keeping themselves ready for surveillance. I'm giving up the white chapel search because otherwise I risk being torn between two things, not because the tip is dubious. Crypts and chapels may well be an excellent place to start, because we don't have anything better at the moment."

The Countess let out a meditative sound and then said as casually as she could, "No, I can see that. We're stymied, even though maybe Madame is right about her chapel. It's so annoying that we can't borrow people from the intelligence service. They would be tailor-made for that surveillance task."

Simonsen muttered, "They'll never agree to it. Think of the risk to the security of the realm in the meantime."

"But maybe someone could convince them to help us out?"

About to get to his feet, he turned his head slowly and caught her eye. For a long time they looked at each other. Finally she said, "Madame called you a porcupine."

"Hmm, I'll have to bring that up with her. When I'm dead. Fetch Ernesto Madsen, I want him along, and let's see about getting out of here."

CHAPTER 50

The meeting was held in the Ministry of Justice on Slotsholmsgade in central Copenhagen, and its timing alone indicated the seriousness of the situation. All the participants could easily have found a more pleasant way to spend a mild September evening. But the kidnapping of two young women, presumed to be in mortal danger if not already dead, demanded the attention of even the highest-ranking members of the Danish bureaucracy. Or so Helmer Hammer said. The story was high-profile in both print and electronic media, and all the participants wished to be, or at least feel like they were being, updated about the police effort.

The police commissioner, national chief of police, head of the Danish Security and Intelligence Service and the public prosecutor for Copenhagen and Bornholm were present, in addition to a chief administrative officer from the Ministry of Justice and the Minister of Justice's personal secretary, as well as Bertil

Hampel-Koch from the Foreign Ministry and Helmer Hammer from the Prime Minister's office. The only participants in the meeting actively involved in the search were Konrad Simonsen, the Countess and Ernesto Madsen, whom Simonsen had insisted should take part, to which no one had objected.

The police commissioner smiled across the table at her homicide chief. She was dressed in a brown dress with grey-white flounces and resembled a muffin. She looked nervous to find herself in such company. Simonsen smiled back. Director Bertil Hampel-Koch suggested himself as keeper of the minutes and noted down his assignment before anyone could object, after which out of respect for the hierarchy he gave the national chief of police the floor.

The chief was a handsome man, well-proportioned with a classic profile and a mass of silver-grey hair, which always seemed to be freshly trimmed. He habitually wore a serious expression that meant few could relax in his company. Added to that were his expensive, gold-rimmed glasses, which he removed when he thought his viewpoints were especially important, basically every time he opened his mouth. In writing he was either a genius or an idiot. At Police Headquarters and all over the country his subordinates cursed his vague orders, which always left plenty of room for interpretation and correspondingly released him from any responsibility if something went wrong later.

This evening he surprised them however, not only by keeping his glasses on but also by giving the floor in turn to Konrad Simonsen without unnecessary preamble.

"I hope that this meeting will be as brief as possible," the homicide chief began. "I acknowledge your right to be informed of our progress, but I also believe you will understand that every minute I'm sitting here takes away from time spent on locating police detective Pauline Berg and the student Jeanette Hvidt, and time is the most critical factor at the moment. So if this meeting does not proceed both quickly and constructively, you will have to manage without me and my associates."

There was no ambiguity about this declaration, and given Simonsen's comparatively low rank it was also slightly provocative, but the majority of the participants nodded their acceptance. Only the Minister of Justice's secretary commented sourly, "I'm sure others can take over from you in the meantime."

She was a younger woman with short, light hair and a pair of large, red plastic earrings that, oddly enough, suited her. Simonsen sent her an angry look without quite knowing how else he should respond. Support came from an unexpected quarter. The head of DSIS, who was not known for his forbearance, growled curtly, "Nonsense. Simonsen is right. Let's get started."

The ball was once again in Simonsen's court. He made a brief status report of the police's immediate efforts. A detailed presentation was out of the question, but on the other hand he concealed nothing, not even Pauline Berg's unauthorised questioning of her kidnapper, or that Andreas Falkenborg had succeeded in breaking into Arne Pedersen's, the Countess's and even his own home and eavesdropping on them, with catastrophic consequences for Jeanette Hvidt. None of those present reproached him for that however. Instead the national chief of police removed his glasses and asked, "You say that you can use the microphones to set a trap for him, how is that?"

Again the head of DSIS broke in.

"There is no reason for us to know. The last time Falkenborg was pressurised a little, it became a hell of a problem for us with the media, but the truth is that perhaps it could have

361

prevented the mess we're in now if the police had been allowed to get on it when they had him."

The subject was dropped, which suited Simonsen fine, as neither he nor anyone else had yet succeeded in finding a plausible pretext that might lure Falkenborg out into the open. The chief administrative officer from the Ministry of Justice summarised.

"In other words, Falkenborg's white commercial vehicle, and the warehouse you assume he has some place or other, and where he possibly is now, are the best options with regard to tracking him down?"

Simonsen's reply was unambiguous.

"Yes, and not only the best, basically the only concrete ones. Furthermore we have initiated a series of general measures, such as heightened surveillance at financial institutions, petrol stations, ATMs, hotels, restaurants, swimming halls, community centres, camping grounds, traffic junctions, Internet cafés, libraries, and so forth—"

The Minister of Justice's secretary interrupted and asked, "You are also guarding his home, aren't you?"

Bertil Hampel-Koch, who was sitting next to her, whispered something that made her ears turn the same colour as her earrings. Simonsen continued without answering.

"However we perhaps have one clue that may lead us further. When we searched Andreas Falkenborg's apartment, we photographed a key which we believe may be to the warehouse he obviously keeps somewhere in the capital region. The key has a series of numbers prominently engraved on it. None of the lock specialists can identify it, so we've released it to the press and expect it to be shown widely in newspapers and on TV as of early tomorrow. This sort of thing almost always produces a result. Someone must know what the numbers mean, and perhaps even what the key is to."

The chief administrative officer from the Ministry of Justice asked sharply, "Why isn't this already being done in the news broadcasts this evening?"

"Because we didn't get to them in time."

"But you said yourself that time was of the essence."

For the third time the head of DSIS broke in.

"It's people who conduct investigations, not machines, and just because a matter is time-critical, it doesn't mean it doesn't take time to investigate. But perhaps you think that the Homicide Division has been sitting around HS playing cards? Is that what you're suggesting?"

"I don't need to put up with that from you."

"Then stop asking silly questions."

"I'll decide for myself what is silly and—"

Simonsen struck his hand on the table, so that the noise resounded.

"I don't have time for bickering, and I don't have time to explain why one thing hasn't happened before another either. You can set up a commission to find that out afterwards, if the two women are killed."

These words created quiet and a brief stand off until the public prosecutor coolly intervened. "Since no one else wants to say it, I will. The kidnapped detective works in your department, and you and your co-workers are presumably strongly personally affected. Would it be an advantage to transfer the ongoing investigation to DSIS?"

Simonsen had expected the question and decided that he would not comment on it if it arose. The proposal was not unreasonable, however unwelcome it was. It must be left to others to assess whether it should be put into effect. From the mood around the table, it seemed the prosecutor's words had not fallen on stony ground. However Helmer Hammer, who until now had not made a peep, said curtly, "No! Konrad

Simonsen is the operational leader, and *everyone* backs him up in his actions. Period."

As no one wished to challenge the authority of the Prime Minister's office, the matter was decided. Hampel-Koch departed from the topic and asked instead, "Have the two women already been killed?"

Helmer Hammer gave him a sideways glance. Hampel-Koch's timing was perfect, like a magician deflecting the audience's attention from his hat by conjuring a dove from his outstretched hand. Now it could be shown in the minutes that everyone was in agreement with Simonsen's continued leadership of the case, in that no one had openly expressed disagreement with the decision.

Simonsen let Hampel-Koch's question go to Ernesto Madsen, who said, a little nervously, "I don't know, but there is no doubt that if he has not already killed them, he will, and will do it very soon. He does not intend to hold them prisoner longer than absolutely necessary."

"And what would delay him? I mean, is there any cause for hope at all?"

"I don't know about that, but with respect to the first part of your question it may be that he has to prepare the ritual he conducts when he murders."

"Is that important to him?"

"Extremely important, he will not deviate from it a millimetre. Everything must be done exactly like his previous murders, all the way down to the slightest detail. For example, we know that he pretends to cut the nails of the women who don't have long—"

Simonsen interrupted him.

"Not so many details."

The Minister of Justice's secretary gave a counter-order.

"Yes, I would like to hear that."

Ernesto Madsen complied with Simonsen however and concluded, "Everything should be just like it always is."

The gathering needed a few seconds to absorb the message, then Hampel-Koch asked, "But what preparation is there that may take time?"

"Unfortunately almost nothing, but for example he must have a red lipstick, and if he doesn't have one, then he'll have to find a shop and buy one."

Everyone could see how quickly that could be done, but Simonsen pointed out, in a feeble attempt at optimism, "Bear in mind now that he's being searched for everywhere, so maybe it's not quite as straightforward for him as it sounds."

The psychologist added, "He will certainly also have dug their grave before he kills them. Maybe that is delaying him. He threw himself into these two kidnappings without his customary time for preparation. In all other cases where he has killed, he has been able to arrange the whole thing long before he seized his victims. That could hardly have been the case this time."

Doubtful looks were exchanged around the table. The odds were not in the women's favour.

There were several questions for Ernesto Madsen.

"Could it perhaps help to appeal to him, I mean via TV? Perhaps an appeal from someone he knows?"

It was the national chief of police, this time with his glasses on. The idea was both close at hand and constructive, but Madsen shot down the proposal.

"It wouldn't help in the least."

The head of DSIS wanted to know, "Will he kill them together or separately?"

Madsen misunderstood.

"Do you mean in the same plastic bag?"

The chief administrative officer from the Ministry of Justice grinned scornfully, but was quickly subdued by an angry look.

The head of DSIS did not let himself be shaken, he simply said, "That was poorly worded, I'm sorry. I mean, whether perhaps he will allow some time to pass between the two killings."

Simonsen said honestly, "That's a good question, I should have asked it myself."

Ernesto Madsen answered hesitantly, "I haven't really speculated about that, but now that you mention it…Everything must be as it always is, otherwise the whole thing is ruined for him. That is a good point…actually I would think he will not kill them at the same time. He will presumably be completely finished with one before he goes to work on the other. Yes, two at a time is not probable. He will perhaps let a day go by between the killings, to deal with the practicalities, although perhaps that is more my wishful thinking than anything psychology tells me."

The Minister of Justice's secretary asked crossly, "When you find him … that is, if you find him … I understand that the idea is he should be shadowed and not arrested. Is everyone in agreement with that decision?"

The question was aimed directly at Simonsen, who answered.

"No, certainly not, but that's how it will be done. My assessment is that our best chance of rescuing the women is if we follow him to his hiding place. But I admit that I'm in doubt. It also depends on when we find him, and he will not be allowed to move around for days. On the contrary we are convinced that he will refuse to talk to us when he is first captured, and then we are seriously up against the wall."

The head of DSIS picked up the thread and carefully addressed the gathering.

"If it becomes necessary, I wish that we could pressurise him into telling us where his victims are. Especially if one, or both of them, is still alive."

It was a feeler, everyone knew that, and everyone also knew that this subject was extremely controversial. Simonsen had long since worked out his own attitude. He would do everything in his power to get Jeanette Hvidt and Pauline Berg back alive. A situation where Andreas Falkenborg was in jail and steadfastly refused to speak, while his victims rotted in some secret place, was simply unacceptable. For that reason he was particularly interested in the others' opinion. Carte blanche from above to go beyond the boundaries of normal questioning would affect to a great degree his decision about letting the man be shadowed in favour of arresting him immediately. Overall this meeting had developed far more productively than he had foreseen.

The prosecutor asked the head of DSIS carefully, "Do you mean physical pressure?"

The man confirmed, "Yes, that's what I'm talking about."

The national chief of police reached to remove his glasses, had second thoughts apparently and let them stay where they were, while he tried to avoid answering the question. "We can take a position on that problem if it becomes relevant."

The police commissioner and the chief administrative officer from the Ministry of Justice were in agreement, Hampel-Koch frowned, after which Helmer Hammer, in crystal-clear turns of phrase, shot the tacit proposal to the ground. He spoke slowly and ominously.

"You can use all lawful means, including those that go to the edge, such as the episode that was reported in the press last week, but torture in any form whatsoever is completely ruled out regardless of the situation. If it does happen, the perpetrators will be prosecuted and their superiors held accountable, under their professional sanctions and the Penal Code."

He looked directly first at the police commissioner and then at the national chief of police, and added slowly, "And that responsibility goes all the way up, don't be in the slightest doubt about that."

A short pause allowed his words to sink in, after which he clarified, "Denmark does not use torture, period. And torture is torture regardless of various linguistic circumlocutions of the word. No one should imagine that there are limitless opportunities for interpretation. This is a direct signal from my boss, and I can assure everyone present that it is deeply felt, both politically and personally."

He was looking straight at Konrad Simonsen now.

"As long as Andreas Falkenborg is in the custody of the state, he will not be physically harassed."

Then he turned to Bertil Hampel-Koch, in his capacity as minutes-keeper.

"What I just said should be stated unambiguously in the minutes, including that responsibility does not stop at operational level in the case of any incidence of torture. Please read back what you've noted."

Hampel-Koch read, and Helmer Hammer confirmed it. Again he looked at the police commissioner and the national chief of police, who both nodded acknowledgment. Only then did Hammer let the meeting continue.

Hampel-Koch immediately took the floor and in his high-pitched voice directed an extremely surprising question to Helmer Hammer.

"If this concerns the two women's lives, and the serial murderer is *not* in the custody of the state, will you then admit that it may be necessary to use questioning of a particular type?"

The head of DSIS added, "That is, as a very last resort."

Helmer Hammer shook his head with irritation and answered, "You are not specifying what form of questioning, so I do not think that your comments give reason for any comments on my part."

Simonsen noticed sweat break out at the bottom of his back and feverishly loosened a few buttons on his shirt. Suddenly it was crystal clear to him why he was sitting here; why indeed the meeting had been called at all. Helmer Hammer's comment was word for word synonymous with the sentence he had praised in such glowing terms in the Botanical Gardens less than a week ago—a sentence that now gave Simonsen permission to do the impermissible. The Countess also understood what had happened. They had just been given the green light to do whatever they wanted with Falkenborg when he was captured, so long as no one found out about it. Her jaw dropped open, a little trickle of saliva escaping from one corner of her mouth. The head of DSIS handed her a napkin without looking at her. Instead he turned to Ernesto Madsen and asked, "What do you think, based on your professional insight, the probability is that Falkenborg will let himself be questioned by the police if he is captured?"

"It is slight."

"How slight?"

Simonsen could feel the heat rising in his cheeks. Ernesto Madsen answered, sounding mystified, "That I couldn't say, just slight."

The time had come for Simonsen to take the lead. He wanted DSIS people added to his surveillance effort, and thought that perhaps he had gained an unexpected ally in the form of the head of DSIS himself. The man was evidently quite clear about the under secretary's underlying message. Presumably the only listener here besides the Countess, Simonsen and Bertil Hampel-Koch who was. Simonsen turned to him.

"I could use a large number of your people to help with our surveillance effort. They are better trained for that sort of thing than mine are."

A miracle happened, the head of DSIS gave a positive response.

"Excellent, but under my command."

"Yes, but you'll report to me. An investigation doesn't have two leaders. That's a recipe for disaster."

The police commissioner backed up Simonsen and plunged into a long rigmarole about unclear paths of command, which in her view was a disaster on a par with the plague and marginal tax pressure. She was interrupted by the head of DSIS, who growled, "I can live with Simon… that is, Konrad Simonsen… as chief for a couple of days."

The matter was now settled. The final decision however lay with the national chief of police. He said hesitantly, "Yes, well, it could be that way, we should consider—"

He got no farther. The chief administrative officer from the Ministry of Justice made things awkward.

"This is a bad idea, which my boss opposes. The security of the realm must not be weakened by this diversion of resources."

The Minister of Justice's secretary added cynically, "This concerns only two human beings, after all."

Her earrings bobbed in time as she nodded her head to underscore her argument. Simonsen said in an ice-cold voice, "If you make that sort of comment again, I'll slap you. And don't think that's an empty threat, because you'd be wrong."

Flustered, the chief administrative officer got up and moved away from the table, the national chief of police tried nervously to pour oil on troubled waters by postponing the matter to the next day, Ernesto Madsen, the head of DSIS and the prosecutor laughed openly, while the Minister of Justice's secretary feverishly rooted through her handbag until she found an inhaler.

Finally Helmer Hammer cut through the confusion. Turning to the chief administrative officer, he said, "I think this is a good idea. If your boss has any objections, she knows where she can reach me."

Then he directed his gaze at the national chief of police, who hesitantly stated, "Then let's minute this then. Yes, we'd better do that."

The Countess thought that a huge distance separated the courteous barefoot stroller she had spent time with in the Botanical Garden from the consummate powermonger she had just seen in action.

Hampel-Koch made a note, and the matter was concluded. Only two minor issues remained, of which one took an unreasonably long time to settle. The national chief of police spoke uninterrupted for ten minutes about overtime hours and his strained budgets, even though hundreds of officers all over the country had voluntarily reported for unpaid duty to help find a colleague in extreme distress. Simonsen found this grandstanding sickening, but said nothing. He was delighted when Helmer Hammer at last could bear to hear no more and stopped the lament.

"I assume that you've sent a memo to your minister?"

"I haven't done that yet."

"Then we'll wait until you do, the matter is not urgent."

Simonsen got in the last word at the meeting, as he said without beating around the bush, "If police detective Pauline Berg gets through this, she will not be punished for her questioning of Falkenborg, and unfortunately that must also apply to the idiot she persuaded to go with her. She has suffered enough. No doubt he has too, although the two can't be compared."

It was a surprisingly unified gathering that broke up shortly afterwards.

CHAPTER 51

On his way out of the Ministry of Justice the head of DSIS approached Konrad Simonsen. He said in a quiet voice, "We need to talk. Now!"

Simonsen agreed; it was what he had expected. And hoped for.

"We can walk over to HS, and talk on the way."

The head of DSIS considered this and then shook his head.

"Bad idea. Do you know Agnete and the merman?"

"If you mean the underwater sculpture in Slotsholmen Canal, then yes."

"We'll meet there in ten minutes, I have a place in the vicinity where we can talk undisturbed."

Out of habit Simonsen glanced at his watch, but his objection about lack of time remained stuck in his throat. The head of DSIS turned and left.

Fifteen minutes later Simonsen and the Countess were waiting at Højbro Plads. The Countess studied Suste Bonnén's sculpture below them. Simonsen was watching with irritation for the head of DSIS, stressed about the time they were wasting. When he arrived shortly afterwards, he did not comment on the Countess's presence. Instead he led them across the street at a forced march. Simonsen noted how he struck his heels hard against the asphalt as he walked, and thought that this must be a military habit. He tried to keep up and hoped that the walk would not be long.

A short distance down Højbro Plads, right across from Vilhelm Bissen's statue of Bishop Absalon, the head of DSIS guided them to the right and through a gate. Here he cut across a small courtyard flanked by old warehouses, now reno- vated and converted to luxury apartments, and over to a main door where he quickly acquired access with a card and PIN code. He turned on the light and asked them to sit down. There were paintings and lithographs all over the place: lean- ing up against the walls, on the central table that dominated the room, and in piles on the floor. The Countess guessed this was a storeroom for a gallery.

Still out of breath, Simonsen said, "Although I'm sure this is important, I *must* be back at HS very soon. And by the way, thanks for your support at the meeting."

The head of DSIS smiled. That was seldom seen. The man was not socially inclined, and stories about his reserve were legion.

"It was nothing. I assume you are clear about what we got permission to do in there? If it becomes possible and necessary."

"Yes, thanks. It had occurred to us both."

The head of DSIS looked at the Countess as he spoke. She slowly put the unpleasantness into well-considered words.

"Helmer Hammer just gave us carte blanche to cut Andreas Falkenborg into little pieces to get him to tell us where he has concealed his two victims. So long as no one knows about it. A week ago he told us in great detail about Nils Svenningsen's atomic letter, and how the top official at the time controversially gave permission without expressing himself directly. Well—from that we are meant to infer that if it is kept secret, we can in a literal sense put the thumb- screws on Falkenborg."

"Exactly. And presumably you are also aware that that message was the only reason the meeting was held at all? The other idiots were just props to cover Helmer Hammer and his ministry if something goes wrong. Apart from Bertil

Hampel-Koch, naturally. You might almost think that Helmer Hammer is somehow dependent on you, but that doesn't concern me of course. The next question is obvious. Do we intend to make use of our... shall we call it, new tool... if it comes to that?"

Simonsen had expected the question and answered without reservation.

"If it's the only way out, then clearly yes."

Both men looked at the Countess. She asked the head of DSIS, "Tell me first how you come into the picture. Were you informed of this in advance?"

"Of course not. I'm in the picture because I was invited to the meeting. I'm simply reacting as was expected of me. Tell us then what your attitude is. Are you also prepared to bring out the rack if there are no other options?"

She held his gaze.

"If it can save Pauline's and Jeanette Hvidt's lives, then without the slightest hesitation. But under no circumstances as revenge or punishment."

The head of DSIS clapped his hands.

"Then let's consider the matter settled. Now we only lack *how* and *when*. Let's take the latter first. I can have my people ready within the next two hours, and they will put an iron ring around him so he will soon be tracked down. I just don't understand why this didn't happen long ago. You know his appearance, you know his car, he is being searched for everywhere, and still he's been roaming free for over twenty-four hours and apparently moving around the Copenhagen area at will. What in the world is happening here?"

The question was directed at Simonsen, who winced. Nevertheless he answered frankly.

"I don't know, but we wonder too. Unfortunately his appearance is very ordinary, as they say, but he ought to be located today. We are beginning to think that perhaps he has acquired another vehicle or possibly uses public transport. Despite the fact that the psychologist is convinced of the opposite."

"If you don't find him soon, it won't matter. If that's not already the case."

The Countess asked angrily, "Don't you think we're aware of that?"

"Yes, sorry, of course you are. So let's presume you find him tomorrow, and I get him in the net..."

He looked at Simonsen.

"...because I assume that this is still the agenda. You're not going to bring him in, are you?"

"No, absolutely not. He would almost certainly refuse to talk, and then we're checkmate. Especially after this evening, when my bosses had the legal principles of the realm emphasised to that degree."

"Okay, I was counting on that too. But here comes the hard part: *how*? Do you have any ideas?"

The Countess shook her head despondently. Simonsen said, "Yes."

They looked at him with equal parts surprise and interest.

"You both know Marcus Kolding, commonly known as Doctor Cold..."

He told them about his visit to the bagman last Wednesday, and how one of Falkenborg's victims was the Finnish woman Elizabeth Juutilainen, who as Liz Suenson had served as Kolding's courier.

When he was done, the head of DSIS considered the unstated proposal and concluded hesitantly, "It's not enough, Simon. Kolding is not a man who does political favours, and he can easily curb his thirst for vengeance if it pays him. He'll want something else, but I'm sure you know that."

Simonsen turned towards the Countess.

"Go out into the courtyard. There is no reason for you to have joint responsibility in this."

"No!"

He accepted this without putting up a fight and asked the head of DSIS, "Do you have easy access to the archives of Special Economic Crimes?"

"I have ready access to all archives, but you do too."

"Not without attracting attention."

"Hmm, what do you want?"

"We have a relatively high-standing informant in Marcus Kolding's organisation."

The Countess was not able to hold back a gasp. The head of DSIS nodded.

"You want to tip off Kolding about his mole as payment for his help with Falkenborg?"

"Yes."

"And you know what that means?"

"Yes."

"You will make contact with the Doctor yourself, when Falkenborg is found?"

"Yes."

"Fine, but we are still missing two things. I will be forced to pull my people away once the Doctor has his hands on Falkenborg, and that order we must not formally take responsibility for. The blame game, you know. I'll try and think of a way around that for both of us. But my last point is the most important—Simon, it will take at least a full day *after* Falkenborg is found before this can be put into effect, which means that you will be under enormous pressure from all sides to arrest him. I know full well that you have just had your absolute operative status served to you on a silver platter, but can you hold out against external interference that long?"

"I have no other choice."

The Countess was less vague.

"You take care of your part, we'll take care of ours. Are we almost done here?"

They were. Outside the gate on Højbro Plads they went their separate ways. The head of DSIS shook hands with them, which felt strange, but they both reciprocated. Before he left, he said in a mixture of seriousness and irony, "Life for one, death for the other. I didn't think you had it in you, Simon."

"Then you were wrong, although I could have done without your cynical comment."

"You mean my cynical, true comment, don't you?"

Simonson did not answer and he and the Countess quickly left.

CHAPTER 52

In the dark Jeanette Hvidt was sobbing desperately, while Pauline Berg tried to think. It was difficult, her situation seemed to be hopeless, and there was apparently nothing she could do to change it. Her two handcuffs as well as the back of the chair they were attached to were solid restraints from which she could not possibly free herself. All that remained was help from outside, but Andreas Falkenborg's words that they could scream as much as they wanted did not bode well for that solution either. To start with she could not think of anything to do other than using her five senses, as far as possible, at least to identify the situation she was in. And then with all the mental strength that remained to her, try to control the panic that was constantly threatening to take over. She turned her head and said harshly to Jeanette Hvidt, "Stop that snivelling."

The girl did not obey but cried even louder. Berg shouted, "Shut up! Or do you really want to die down there in that hole?"

The crying stopped partially. Jeanette sobbed, "I don't want to die. I'm not the one who's going to die."

"Then be quiet. Do you think it helps to cry?"

After a while her sobbing stopped, and she said, "You're the one who lost. You're going to die when he comes back."

"Yes, I know."

"You're going into the bag, not me."

"Yes, damn it; me, not you. Do you need to spell it out?"

Jeanette did not listen, but continued speaking.

"I'll do everything he says, he won't kill me."

Berg was in two minds how best to approach the girl; tell her the truth and risk her going into a complete panic, or pretend to believe in her foolish hope. For now she chose the latter.

"It might work out that way, but listen to me now—"

But Jeanette was not listening. Instead she persisted in her delusion.

"I can be his slave for the rest of my life, never talk back, always be obedient."

"Yes, that's fine. Would you care to listen to something different?"

"There is only one grave, it's for you. He's keeping me."

"Sure, sure—but then you'll be alone, Jeanette."

"I have him."

The answer came hesitantly. It was clear that the girl was balancing on the brink of a breakdown, but Pauline Berg still detected some grasp of reality in her words. She refrained from commenting and waited. Shortly after that Jeanette said quietly, "I know he's going to kill me too."

"Yes, he will."

"He measured two graves. I saw that before you came. He drew lines on the floor, but they're covered in dust now."

"Did he have the mask on when he was measuring?"

"That other grave is for me. He just hasn't dug it."

Pauline Berg then said as firmly as possible, "Jeanette, you have to listen to what I'm saying."

"Excuse me, what was it you were asking about?"

"If he had the mask on when he measured the…when he measured."

"My grave."

"Yes, your grave, damn it. Did he have the mask on?"

"He always has the mask on."

"No, he doesn't, I've seen him without the mask. He's just a very sick man."

"Do you think they're searching for us?"

"You can count on that. They're searching everywhere."

"You're a cop, so they're searching twice as hard. They'll really want to find you."

"They really want to find both of us, and we're going to help them if we can."

"How can we do that?"

"I have an idea. To start with we'll use our five senses, one by one, to see whether we can determine anything based on that. Do you follow me?"

"Not quite, what good would that do?"

"We don't know yet."

"So when will we know?"

"Just do as I say, okay?"

"Okay…but there is one thing."

"What?"

"I'm sorry for what I said when he was here. That wasn't nice of me."

"It doesn't matter now."

"I'm so afraid to get the prod, it hurts terribly. I can't bear the thought of it."

"Then don't think about it. Tell me instead whether you can remember the five senses."

"Of course I can: smell, hear, feel, see and taste."

"Let's try vision first. Now we'll be quiet, open our eyes wide and then look around as much as we can. Do you follow me?"

"Yes."

Pauline Berg slowly turned her head from side to side with eyes wide open, ready to capture the slightest visual impression. There was none, the darkness was total. After a while she interrupted the activity.

"What did you see?"

"Nothing. It's completely black."

"The same here, but I think I can smell paint."

"The paint is from the cross. I didn't think we'd reached smell yet."

"No, that wasn't the idea. Tell me about the cross."

"He set it up yesterday, and then it was freshly painted, I think. He was giggling the whole time he was doing it. As if he was proud. The point was for me to be afraid, but I was more scared of the prod. I was also supposed to say when it was hanging straight."

"He's sick. Now let's try to feel. Put your cheek and ear against the wall, and try to feel as much as you can. I'll do the same."

The wall was granulated and felt cold. Pauline Berg also thought it felt damp and concluded for both of them, "It's an outside wall."

"Yes, it is."

"Fine, and now listen, this is the most important sense. Are you ready to concentrate?"

"I'm ready."

The two women listened in the darkness. For a long time Pauline Berg did not hear anything other than her own and Jeanette Hvidt's suppressed breathing, but then suddenly she picked up a faint, deep rumble vibrating through the cellar.

"Did you hear that, Jeanette?"

"Yes, it's the S-train."

Berg kept her voice down as best she could.

"How do you know that?"

"The bunker isn't very far from the tracks."

"We're in a bunker?"

"Yes, it's buried in the ground."

"Why didn't you say that before? I mean, that you knew where we are?"

"You didn't ask me, and I thought you knew that too."

Pauline admitted her mistake.

"No, I didn't, but tell me what you've seen. Where are we?"

"Hareskoven, I think it's called, you know, the forest. Our bunker is buried in the ground."

"What is there around us?"

"Trees."

"Nothing else?"

"A path."

"It ends here?"

"Yes, I think so, but I'm not sure."

"How do you know that we're close to the S-train ?"

"I could see it from the car when we turned into the forest, and when he dragged me in here, I could clearly hear the train. The tracks are not far away."

"Where did you sit in the car?"

"Beside him, but I didn't dare do anything except look. He had his prod and … well, you know."

"How many times has he given you shocks?"

"Once when he caught me, it was in my uncle's garden, and then twice down here one after the other, because I was crying and using ugly … shouted at him, called him names and such. No, three times down here. He made me scream after I sang for you."

"Tell me, were there people on the path?"

"No, but it was raining."

"Do you think that was why?"

"I don't know … no, I just don't think very many people go this way."

"So it won't help to cry out for help?"

"No, I think no one can hear us."

"Can you tell me anything else about our bunker?"

"It's called an air raid shelter, and you can rent them for thirteen hundred kroner a month plus electricity."

"How in the world do you know that?"

"He told me. I don't know if it's true."

"Why did he say that?"

"To humiliate me, I think. When I came there were bags in here, he carried them into another room. He said the price, when he said that he had paid three years in advance, and that no one except him ever came here. But that's not correct."

A little light bulb came on for Berg.

"What do you mean? Has anyone else come while you've been here?"

"Yes, you."

"Well, yes, but besides me?"

"No, only you."

Berg thought for a moment and said, "If he's rented this bunker, it's only a matter of time before they find us. They are trawling through his entire life at the moment. Every single day he's been alive."

"He didn't rent it in his own name, he bragged about that. He also said what he called himself, but I can't remember."

"Did you see anything else on your way in?"

"Yes, there was a red square in the grass. I don't know what it was."

"What do you mean?"

"The grass was red there. I don't know why."

"How big a square? What colour red? Tell me."

Jeanette Hvidt told her. When she was done, Pauline Berg asked, "Tell me, what colour was his car, can you remember that?"

"Red too. The same colour, now that you mention it. Do you think he painted it?"

Berg made light of it. Her fellow prisoner was afraid enough already, there was no reason to worry her further. But this was not good. Her colleagues were searching for a white car, not a red one, a detail that could be decisive. She tried to sound optimistic.

"Okay, let me think over what we'll do."

"Don't we need to smell and taste?"

"No, we've done enough for now."

Pauline thought intently for a long time, trying with all her might to think of something that might prevent the death that Falkenborg had threatened her with when he came back. Then suddenly she had an idea, and the more she thought about it, the better it seemed. She pushed as far to the left and up on one side as she could because of her handcuffs, while at the same time she curled up and pressed her head down toward Jeanette Hvidt's manacled hand. Her many hours of ballet exercises had made Pauline limber and paid off now; she sensed that the process had almost succeeded. Jeanette Hvidt asked, "What are you doing?"

"Jeanette, see whether you can stretch your fingers and feel my hair…in a moment, when I say to."

She twisted and curled up again toward the girl's hand. When she was in place, she said with difficulty, "Now, Jeanette."

383

"I can, but why should I touch your hair?"

Pauline sat back in place. It was impossible to hold the position very long at one time.

"In a moment, when I'm down again, you will twist a tuft of my hair around your finger and hold as tight as you possibly can. And you should only take a little bit of hair. When that has happened, say so, do you follow me?"

"Yes, if that's what you want."

They both performed the exercise. Jeanette said, "Now I have a tuft."

Pauline jerked her head upward with all her might. An awful pain in her scalp told her the result. Even though she was prepared, she groaned out loud.

"What happened there, did I pull your hair out? Yes, I did, I can feel it!"

"Yes, you did. That was the idea. Now you will try the same, bend over towards my hand as much as you can."

"No, why should I do that?"

Berg explained about the girl's grandmother and Andreas Falkenborg's psychological profile and a few other things she made up. She concluded, "It's our only chance. If we've pulled out our hair or maybe only part of it, he'll let us be. Then we're not interesting to him any more."

"Do you want to pull all your hair out?"

"As much as I can."

"Did it hurt?"

"Only a little, it was nothing."

"I don't believe that, you screamed."

"That was the first time. Besides we can take it in tiny little bites, there's enough time before he comes back."

"But then he'll be furious when he sees it. We'll get the prod, both of us. We'll get the prod lots of times. I don't want to."

"Would you rather be in the bag?"

Jeanette started sniffling again, but shortly after she said, "I'll try as you say."

Pauline heard the girl groan as she bowed forward. She herself extended her fingers upward, as far as her handcuffs allowed, but their exertions were of no use. Jeanette tried as best she could, each time in a different position according to Pauline's instructions and encouragement, but nothing helped. At last they gave up. Jeanette was simply not limber enough.

"Jeanette, you should pull my hair out, then we'll think of something else for you later."

"No."

"I'm not asking you, I'm ordering you. You have no choice."

"I won't do it. Do you think I'm stupid, or what? Then he'll take me instead of you. I don't want to die so that you can live."

"I said that we'll think of something else for you."

"What is that? I want to know first."

Pauline leaned over and bit the girl hard on the upper arm. She screamed with pain.

"Ow, that really hurt, why are you doing that? I haven't done anything to you."

"Just get started, and now. Without discussion."

"I don't want to, you crazy bitch. I hope he roasts you with his prod."

This time Pauline bit twice, the first time as hard as she could. Jeanette howled in fear and pain.

"Do it, or should I bite a chunk out of you until you realise that this is serious?"

Jeanette was bitten four times before she gave in and obeyed orders. Tuft after tuft disappeared from Pauline Berg's head; soon she noticed blood flowing down her cheek and then her neck. The pain was unbearable for a long time, until at last she did not think it really concerned her any longer. Jeanette cried unhappily, but obediently held tight, when she was asked to. After a long time, half crying, half sniffling she said, "I can't get hold of any more now, will you please stop biting me?"

Pauline did not answer her. On her left side she could still feel hair against her cheek. She straightened up in the chair, after which she turned her head and alternately began to pound and grind it against the coarse bunker wall behind her. It hurt even more than before if possible, and she was soon moaning with pain. In spite of that she kept on and on and on.

CHAPTER 53

In the small hours between Tuesday and Wednesday Konrad Simonsen snatched a restless sleep in his desk chair. He had taken off his shoes, put his legs on the desk and—mostly for peace of mind and out of habit—used his jacket as a kind of duvet. At five o'clock in the morning he was wakened by the phone. An officer told him that he had a witness he ought to interview personally. The man sounded tired, but Simonsen recognised his name and knew that he was experienced. Not the type to disturb you for no reason, and definitely not at that time of day, so he agreed to the questioning without objection, after which he fell asleep again. Shortly after the officer was in the room escorting a woman in her twenties.

Simonsen collected himself. After five minutes in the bathroom, where some cold water on his head chased away the worst of his fatigue, he felt reasonably functional. When he returned the officer introduced the woman.

"This is Juli Denissen from Frederiksværk, and she encountered Andreas Falkenborg on Monday evening. She also has important information about his car."

The officer placed a thin report on the desk and stood to attention expectantly. Simonsen skimmed it and noted that the witness had been questioned twice before. Both times during the night. He turned to the woman.

"Would you mind waiting outside for a moment?"

He had to repeat the request before she understood, after which she left the office without argument. She left her lovely multicoloured bag behind. He noted that her gait was unusual, as if her upper body was not quite synchronised with her legs. He closed the door behind her.

As soon as she was outside, the officer asked, "Do you want a summary? I can see that you're really tired."

"No, but I want to know whether she is reliable. Or rather, I assume that you've checked her thoroughly."

"As thoroughly as we could during the night, and nothing indicates that she is… mental."

"What's your own assessment?"

The answer came with conviction.

"She's as normal as you and me. Otherwise I wouldn't involve you."

Simonsen mumbled inaudibly, sent the officer away and showed the woman in again. They sat opposite each other at his desk. He browsed through her papers again and said matter-of-factly, "You are twenty-four years old, divorced, attend the Technical School in Frederiksværk, live alone with your two-year-old child."

The woman confirmed this and suppressed a yawn, which she excused with a lovely smile. Involuntarily Simonsen smiled back. It was hard not to.

"Can you tell me a little about your daughter?"

If she was surprised by the question she did not show it. Without hesitation she complied with the request, as if it was the most natural thing in the world to talk about her child at five-thirty in the morning to the head of the country's most-discussed investigation. While she spoke, he observed her thoroughly, which did not seem to embarrass her. She was slender, below average height, with long dark hair and high, soft cheekbones; definitely pretty in her particular way. She had a surplus of charisma, but her eyes made the greatest impression. They were brown, happy and trustful when they met his, without submission but also without arrogance. He discovered to his surprise as she was speaking that he liked hearing her voice, and he let her continue a bit beyond the point where he felt convinced she was not concealing any pathological defects. At last however he interrupted her.

"You think you encountered Andreas Falkenborg on Monday evening, on the local train to Frederiksværk?"

"Yes, I think so. And I also saw him on the S-train to Hillerød. He got on at Nørreport Station."

"Tell me about it."

"Where should I start?"

"You were in Copenhagen. What were you doing there?"

"I had been in London for two days and came from the airport..."

Her explanation was thorough and precise; the times fitted with Falkenborg's disappearance from his attendants, and she could also describe his clothing. At Hillerød Station they both changed trains, and by chance they were sitting so that she could see his reflected image in the window. In Grimstrup, four stations from Hillerød, she and Falkenborg were the only passengers who got off, and he had walked to a small parking lot next to the station where his car was parked. She had watched as he drove away.

"Can you describe the car?"

"Yes, it was a red Volkswagen Multivan."

"You are quite certain. Do you know about cars?"

"My father is a car mechanic. I grew up with cars."

"Do you know why you're sitting here?"

She nodded, almost apologetically.

"Because his car was red."

He nodded too. Then he found a photocopy of a drawing in her papers and placed it before her.

"You made this portrait of Andreas Falkenborg, as you sat on the train to Frederiksværk. Why did you do that?"

"I always draw people on the train. It's a habit. I draw them if I think they look interesting, or simply to pass the time."

"Why were you in London?"

"To draw an ancient wall."

"That sounds strange."

"I want to be an architect."

"Where was your daughter while you were in England?"

"With her father."

"What shade of red was Falkenborg's car?"

"It was dusk at the time, and then colours are hard to determine. But it was like the Danish flag, I think."

"Did you draw other people on your train ride?"

He switched between topics, back and forth, to confuse her; she managed every single question with honest, simple answers. Except for the last.

"You live in Frederiksværk. Why did you get off in Grimstrup?"

"That's not important, and I've promised not to talk about it."

She emphasised the word *promised*, as if now they didn't need to talk any more about it.

"Who did you promise?"

"Someone I know."

"Did anyone else see the car besides you?"

"Not quite so well."

"Who?"

"Someone I know."

Simonsen sighed and quietly explained.

"You called us four times yesterday evening. Then you came on your own initiative here to Police Headquarters at night, where you insisted on making a statement. This is the third time you're being questioned, which means that we take your testimony seriously, which I'm sure you're well aware of. But I don't have room for mistakes. At the moment two women are in extreme danger at best, so there is no room here for keeping secrets, regardless of what you've promised whom. Furthermore, I don't understand why you didn't call until almost a full day after your train ride. I would also like an explanation for that."

Juli Denissen thought deeply and came up with the wrong answer.

"I guarantee that the car was red. You have to believe me. The rest has no significance."

Simonsen swore to himself and considered whether he should take the time to talk sense into her. He decided it was not worth wasting the energy. He tried the silent treatment for a short time, until he firmly shook his head. Then he called for Poul Troulsen and felt miserable about it. She deserved better.

After Juli was picked up, he had a hard time getting her out of his mind, and he was very relieved when a good hour later Troulsen returned and hustled her back to her former place, while he explained.

"She was picked up by her lover at Grimstrup Station, and together they drove to his summer house in Asserbo. He has a wife and children and according to Juli keeps his affairs as far away from the rest of his life as possible. For example, he didn't want to meet her in Hillerød for fear that someone would recognise him. Both of them saw Falkenborg's car, he however only fleetingly, but he hasn't contacted us, although he maintains the opposite with respect to his…with respect to Juli."

He referred to the woman, who sat with bowed head looking sad.

"When the announcements in the media kept referring to a *white* commercial vehicle, she stepped in herself, and… well, the rest you know. Her acquaintance, by the way, is one of us. That is, still according to Juli."

Simonsen felt anger bubbling up and made no attempt to subdue it. His voice resounded in the office.

"I hope for his sake that he's not. Who are we talking about?"

Troulsen said the man's name. Simonsen knew who he meant; a middle-aged, competent man he had worked with numerous times. He asked, perplexed, "The police constable?"

"Yes, if we're to believe Juli. He denies any acquaintance with her whatsoever. I just spoke to him, and he was quite definite about it. He says he has never met her, she has never been in his summer house, he has never picked her up at any station, and so on and so forth. *Never* to everything I said. I've ordered phone information on them both. Unauthorised, but we don't have time for anything else. It will take about an hour before we have them, and—"

Juli Denissen interrupted him then.

"Did he say that he doesn't know me?"

The question was directed at Simonsen.

"Yes, and now I really am having doubts about your story. You are going to remain here a while longer, until I find out which of you is lying."

A film of moisture passed over her eyes, which she quickly blinked away before it formed tears. She tightened her jaw for a couple of seconds and regained control. Then she fished her cell phone out of her bag and started working the keys while she said,

"I have some pictures. Just a moment… my phone isn't working, it has a mind of its own, but I can't afford to buy a new one."

The two men waited until her phone worked properly. It took time, but she was successful at last. She explained, "The first ones are from the summer house, the others were taken at my place."

Neither of the officers said anything for a while. Then Simonsen whistled.

"Bring that creep in here, Poul. Tell him on the way that the Ministry of Justice must have his resignation by the end of the day. And if he makes the slightest bit of trouble… Well, I hardly need to tell you. But first of all get him to confirm the colour of Falkenborg's car, and if he does, call and change the search description. Make sure that our own cars and all taxis get the message right away."

Troulsen answered tiredly, "It actually tallies with the five calls we've already received from witnesses who have seen Falkenborg in a red car. But it has been yellow too of course, and…"

The woman said sadly, "Do you have to punish him? He's having a hard time. And yesterday I told him that I didn't want to see him any more."

She sounded as if the break-up was punishment enough. A few tears rolled down alongside her nose. Troulsen ignored her and left. Simonsen felt sorry for her. She was obviously under the illusion that the world was good, and would probably have to pay dearly on a regular basis for her positive view of life. He placed his hand on her shoulder, and she seized it quickly.

"There are hundreds of police officers who will be ready to break every bone in his body when they hear this, so his continued employment with us is impossible."

"You don't need to tell anyone."

She let out a little sniffle, which he did not respond to, and then another.

"Now I'll make sure you get a ride home."

He stroked her hair gently a couple of times and thought that some people you meet too late. Then he sent her away.

CHAPTER 54

The sharp light came on without warning and totally blinded the two women, so that the first they knew of Andreas Falkenborg's presence was the cry of lament he let out as soon as he entered the room. As little by little they regained their sight, they saw him jumping around on the floor in front of them, waving his arms and legs like a child out of control. Occasionally he shouted furious reproaches at Pauline Berg for the calamity she had inflicted on herself.

"You shouldn't have done that, you don't understand anything, you stupid goose!"

His mask hung crookedly, and he made no attempt to straighten it. Pauline said nothing to start with. She had been jolted from a troubled sleep, and the pain in her scalp struck her again full force. She had bitten her lips bloody besides.

"You're going to get a shock that will make you lose the rest of your hair, that's what you deserve!"

Jeanette Hvidt twitched nervously when he heard him mention the electric prod, and stammered, "She did it herself. I told her not to, but she begged me, and I couldn't do anything about it. But I'll do what he says."

Falkenborg straightened his mask and stood quietly for a moment while he observed Jeanette, who continued to protest her innocence. He commanded curtly, "She will be quiet."

Jeanette fell silent immediately. Pauline said in a controlled voice, "You can torture me as much as you want, with your cowardly electric stick, but that won't make my hair grow, Andreas. Maybe it would be a good idea to think about getting as far away as possible while you have the chance. Here in the Copenhagen area thousands of people are searching for you, and it's only a matter of time before they find you. And in that connection there is a little unwritten rule within the police force that you probably aren't aware of, but you soon will be in a very unpleasant way."

To start with he ignored her bait. Soon however he asked, "What rule is that?"

"That anyone who tortures a police officer gets the exact same medicine from their colleagues when he is caught. And, believe me, you're going to be caught."

"You're lying."

"All right then. By all means keep on living in your dream world, I don't care. Go and get your silly prod, if you want. I'm not half as scared of it as you will be when they use it on you. By the way, that couldn't possibly be a substitute for your dick, little Andreas, could it? You know, I think it is. You're impotent, aren't you? Even there you can't live up to your father, you miserable little creep."

"Shut your damn mouth."

"Certainly not. Aren't you going out to get the prod? Just admit you can't manage without it."

"You can't allow yourself to talk that way. As a police officer you have a duty to talk properly."

"Andreas, there is no end to your childish idiocy. Go out then and get your prod, and let's get it over with. I'm just going to

394

say to you that whether or not you give me a shock, I'm going to say you did when we're found. I'll say the same thing too if you bother Jeanette, and it will be a real pleasure to see you writhing in pain while three of my colleagues hold you, and another one empties the whole battery into your forehead."

Falkenborg pleaded.

"You mustn't do that, that's wrong."

"Then see about getting away while you have a head start. Here in Hareskoven you don't have a chance. They already started going through the bunkers yesterday, it's standard procedure with kidnappings so I'm sure they'll be here soon. Tick, tock, tick, tock, Andreas—can you feel time running out?"

Jeanette also sensed the new division of power and added, "Then you'll get a taste of your own medicine, you pig. And if you kill me, I guarantee that sooner or later my boyfriend will find you and poke your eyes out."

"She will keep quiet."

"You keep quiet yourself, you psychopath."

He turned on his heel and left the room without closing the door behind him.

As soon as he was gone, Jeanette's fear got the upper hand again.

"Oh, no. If he gets the prod, I can't bear that."

Berg shushed her, and both of them listened for a long time. Finally Jeanette said, "Do you think he's gone?"

"Yes, I think so, but I couldn't hear a car."

They waited a while without anything happening, and again it was Jeanette who broke the silence.

"And then someone will come and find us?"

"Yes, they will."

"You said they were already starting to go through the bunkers. That it's standard."

"Yes, I'm sure they are."

"How many are there?"

"I don't know."

"You're lying. It was a lie, right?"

"You were very brave, Jeanette. Your courage saved your life."

This evasive manoeuvre of Pauline's did not succeed. Jeanette insisted on the truth.

"Wasn't it a lie?"

Pauline Berg answered harshly and angrily.

"Yes, it was a lie. A lie that means you are sitting here alive and not down in that hole while he shovels dirt and chunks of cement over you. Are you satisfied now?"

Falkenborg's triumphant howl filled the room; he was standing in the open door. The mask was missing.

"I knew it, I knew you were trying to cheat, you cheater!"

He was gone again, only to return to the room soon afterwards, this time with his mask on and a pair of sturdy hearing protectors on his ears besides. In one hand he held the prod, in the other two pieces of fabric. The sight was ridiculous, but neither of the women laughed. He placed himself in front of Jeanette Hvidt and shouted, "She will open her mouth."

The girl obeyed immediately, and he stuffed one piece of fabric in her mouth. Then it was Pauline Berg's turn. She clenched her teeth, he raised the prod and held it a few centimetres from her neck without saying anything. Pauline opened her mouth, and the result was the same.

Falkenborg removed his hearing protectors and his mask. He set both down on the floor, and for the next hour Pauline had impotently to watch while he worked. Occasionally he left the room to get materials, tools, and whatever else he needed. A large plastic tub, two buckets of water, two sacks of concrete mix, masonry tools and a long concrete finishing trowel. From time to time he made small talk with her to mock her. Everyday things, indifferent comments, mixed with swear words and dark threats.

"In the old days you had to mix the concrete yourself. It was easy to remember anyway: one, two, three—one part cement, two parts sand, and three parts gravel or small stones—but no one bothers to do that any more. Today you buy it pre-mixed ready for use."

Then he retrieved a small table and unfolded it by the side of the grave. Carefully he picked up his mask and set it on the table. He left and returned immediately with scissors, lipstick, a roll of duct tape and a plastic bag.

"First the concrete will have to set, then we can get started. Meanwhile you can rot in that chair, and we'll see whether anyone is looking for you. Yes, go ahead and cry... cry as much as you want. You made the bed you're lying in. You should have stayed away from me, hussy."

CHAPTER 55

A high-pressure system, which the weather reports predicted would last for the next few days, had announced its arrival, and the sun was now fierce against the windows of the Homicide Division after the morning's grey drizzle. Inside Konrad Simonsen, the Countess, Poul Troulsen and Ernesto Madsen were holding a meeting in Simonsen's office. All four of them were sweating, and the three men looked tired. Only the Countess appeared relatively healthy, primarily due to a good layer of makeup. Troulsen yawned and asked Simonsen, "What are we waiting for?"

"Nothing, I'm just trying to collect my thoughts."

The older officer looked at his boss and thought that he seemed even more pent-up than the day before. He noted at the same time the sternness beneath the Countess's careful facade. Not that this was surprising in any way, for with every minute that passed without finding the women—or at least Andreas Falkenborg—the chances of a happy outcome grew smaller, and that sort of strain told. He yawned again, this time without bothering to cover his mouth.

The Countess yawned too. The morning and most of the night before had been spent organising and carrying out the search for the two women, with crypts and chapels being given first priority. It was a slow process that required concentration and methodology. Now, with the planning over, they could not do much except wait; wait and hope. A quiver around her eyes revealed her state of mind, and she massaged her temples lightly while trying to convince herself that there was still a chance for the two women. She glanced at her boss, sitting with eyes squeezed shut, lost to the world. He had been working for three days straight and pushing everyone to give their all. He swept personal concerns tyrannically and consistently off the table with the result that the whole division was about to drop from exhaustion. The same must apply to him too, although he did not talk about it. Since the meeting last night he had withdrawn into himself and was hard to reach, even for her.

Finally he said, "We have only one item on the agenda, namely Falkenborg's residence and warehouse, which in practice means news about his keys, his car and his computer, and the search for him in crypts and chapels which I initiated this morning. The car is your inquiry, Poul. What's the status?"

Troulsen took out his notebook, browsed a little back and forth, and said, "Maybe I should start by saying that Pauline actually produced some solid pieces of evidence against Falkenborg before she…I have just spoken with a Vibeke Behrens, who was apparently Catherine Thomsen's girlfriend back in 1996 and '97, and it turns out that she knew Andreas—"

Simonsen said quietly, "His car, Poul. The rest doesn't matter now."

Troulsen seemed confused for a moment. Then he accepted the direction and said, "Yes, of course. Sorry, but I'm so damn tired. So, his car has been seen in over fifty places in the capital region since the hunt was announced, including fifteen times within the past two hours alone. That is, after we sent out the information that it's now red. The most interesting observation happened at a parking lot not far from Skovlunde Station, about ten kilometres north—"

"We're aware of where Skovlunde Station is. Do you know what he was doing there?"

"Yes, eating at a hot dog stand. A woman saw her chance to take a picture of both him and his car with her cell phone, and then she called us, but when we got there he was gone. But now at least we know that his car really is red."

The Countess asked, "How long did it take before we were on the scene? That is, I mean in the form of a water-tight surveillance, not just the first officer."

"Less than half an hour. It was the DSIS people, they're very effective."

"Half an hour? I'm not particularly impressed."

"That's due to ignorance, because you should be. If we had conducted that action ourselves, it would have been at least—"

Simonsen said, "Okay, okay. Go on, where else has he been seen?"

"At 8.35 a.m. at the hot dog truck and later at Buddinge lumberyard, it's next to Buddinge Station. Here he bought two sacks of pre-mixed concrete and paid cash. This happened at 9.16 a.m."

Madsen asked, "What would he do with that?"

It was Simonsen who answered. The information was not new to him, so he'd had had time to think it through.

"A realistic suggestion unfortunately is that he is going to repair a cellar floor. You can figure out for yourself why."

The psychologist said, "Yes, I can easily figure that out, but perhaps this is good news."

"What do you mean?"

"I don't think he will kill either of them before everything is ready, and that means that the time for his first killing at a minimum is pushed ahead to this morning. That's something anyway. Then perhaps his other murder will not happen until tomorrow."

Troulsen expressed what they were all thinking.

"If it makes any difference since we have to find him first. But however that may be, we have another indicator of where he has been today, and this is quite fresh. I discussed it with Malte, and it's just a matter of calling his audio server, or whatever it's called."

The Countess said, "*Audio server*? I don't follow."

"Yes, it's something technical, and I can't really explain it, but it's where he stores the audio files from the surveillance of your and Simon's home. His microphones and transmitters are connected with some networks, and you'll have to talk with Malte about the other details. However that may be, he logged in on his server from a PC in Lyngby at 12.41 p.m., a good half an hour ago, but unfortunately this was done via an unprotected wireless network, and also..."

Troulsen leafed through his notes.

"The IP address is unknown but being worked on, whatever that means. But we can say with certainty that he was at Ulrikkenborg Plads in Lyngby at twenty minutes to one."

Simonsen asked, "Do we know if he has been on his server earlier today, and how often he goes in and checks?"

"That data is being generated. It hasn't been easy to trace him. It only became effective when Interpol started monitoring directly in England, where the server is physically. He has circumvented the barriers here by going across the US. I admit I'm just echoing here what others have tried to explain. I apologise."

"It doesn't matter, so long as you can tell us what the result will be."

"That we can see where his laptop computer has been, and as he presumably has it in his car, then where he and his car have been, under the assumption however that he has regular contact with the server."

"When?"

"They promised it within an hour, and it's been almost that long, but it doesn't help to pressure them. They're working as fast as they can."

"Pressure them anyway."

Troulsen obeyed. He took out his cell phone and went outside. Shortly after that he was back.

"Five minutes, then we'll have a map and a list, they're sending it up."

Simonsen ordered, "Tech has a woman who is expert in geographic information systems, I think it's called. She can extract relevant conclusions—"

Troulsen interrupted. "She is already waiting in my office along with two mathematicians from the University of Copenhagen."

"Brilliant. Then I have something to say about the key, but unfortunately it can't be done quickly. The number on the key's rivet goes with a corresponding padlock, and the set was sold by a hardware chain about ten years ago. The product was obviously intended for people who have a lot of padlocks in one place, but sadly it doesn't help us find that place."

There was a knock on the door; the Countess opened and received an envelope from an officer. She pulled out the contents, unfolded a map of the capital region on the table, and quickly read through the accompanying list while the others studied the map. Troulsen said, "It's unbelievable that he can drive around like this when everyone is searching for his car. I mean, it's not just us. There are taxi drivers, postal workers, bicycle couriers... anyone with eyes in their head."

Simonsen said, "It's just a matter of time. Maybe he's been lucky so far. Some of the calls we've received certainly tally with our map here. How many points are there?"

The Countess checked her list and answered, "There are sixteen, five of which are from today."

"Ernesto, what is he doing basically? He drives around, as if he thinks he's invisible, apparently aimlessly. Can you explain that?"

The psychologist attempted.

"So long as he has not killed the women, he presumably is not thinking about anything else, including his own safety. What he will do afterwards is hard to predict. I don't think he knows that himself, but presumably there will be a phase where he is more or less confused, and as long as that lasts, he is not likely to move far from the places he knows."

"And when he is no longer confused?"

"He will probably flee. My guess is to Sweden, which he apparently has visited before. But how long—"

Simonsen's cell phone rang. He said, "Be quiet, they're only calling if it's top priority."

They were silent while he listened and shortly afterwards said thank you. Then he said, quietly and without discernible joy, "We have him, and DSIS has set up an iron ring he won't slip out of."

"Where?"

"The bank in Lejre. He has returned his mask. There is a team of technicians en route, but this is bad… on the inside he puts marks, red marks with lipstick. Four of the marks are old, but one mark is quite fresh. It was put there very recently."

Troulsen asked quietly, "You mean that one of the women is dead?"

The police officers looked at Madsen, who stammered, "Yes, one of the women has been killed in his usual manner. I thought that he would totally distance himself from—"

He was interrupted.

"And the other?"

"I have no idea. But he put the mask back in the safe deposit box, so something has not gone as planned."

The Countess, on the verge of tears, asked Simonsen, "How long will it be before we have an answer?"

"Not until tonight, they'll call me."

Madsen asked, "Answer to what?"

"DNA test, to see which of them the lipstick was used on."

The Countess was now crying openly, but at the same time was sufficiently composed to think about others too.

"We won't tell Arne or their families either. Not until we have an answer."

The psychologist asked, sniffling, "How long can you survive without food and water, if we assume that one woman is still alive?"

The Countess answered him, her eyes blinded by tears.

"Food is no problem, it's the lack of fluid that is deadly. She's young, that's good; the weather is warm, that's bad. Five to six days, then it starts to get critical. Less if you are sick or in poor condition. A lot also depends on will."

Suddenly she felt as if her own words were alien and irrelevant. She happened to think then of the clairvoyant's four loathsome lines of verse, which now filled her mind and blocked out any normal thought process.

Simonsen noticed her expression.

"Pull yourself together, Countess. You have work to do."

She nodded while she fought back her tears. Simonsen observed her expressionlessly. Troulsen's eyes were shiny too, and his hands were shaking. He said in a cracked voice, "I think I know what may have happened. Pauline has probably taken her contact lenses off and swallowed them, as soon as she got the chance. But now you can just as well bring him in, Simon, because he will never—"

Simonsen shouted so that it echoed.

"No, he's not coming in! And you, Ernesto, tell everyone who asks that you are certain he will return to his hiding place. I don't care what psycho-babble you package it in, just do as I ask. I do *not* want him arrested now. Is that understood?"

They understood him.

At that moment Pedersen slipped in the door and placed himself without a word at the back of the room. The Countess asked him a question, but received only monosyllabic words in response. Troulsen tried too. He did not answer at all. They let him be, he was doing no harm. Shortly after that they got more news about Falkenborg. He was staying at the Hotel Grand in Herlev, a small hotel not far from the centre, where he had checked in three days ago.

Simonsen instructed the Countess.

"The head of DSIS is on his way, and you will be the one who liaises with him. I assume that he has some electronic gadgetry so we can follow Falkenborg's movements on a screen. Get the big meeting room set up as a control room. I will be back in a couple of hours at most, but I'm turning off my cell phone so you can't get in touch with me meanwhile."

"What do you mean by control room?"

"I don't know, it's just an expression. But we should be able to follow his movements on the big screen. And get the staff restaurant to provide water and sandwiches... Damn it, do I have to arrange every single detail myself?"

"No, I understand. Control room is an excellent designation. Just get going."

Troulsen asked in amazement, "Where in the world are you off to? What is more important than this?"

The Countess had herself fully under control. She cut him off brutally.

"Mind your own business, Poul. And trust that Simon is capable of minding his."

Troulsen backed out. He had never heard the Countess talk that way before.

CHAPTER 56

Marcus Kolding and Konrad Simonsen met in Hareskoven, by coincidence less than three kilometres from where Pauline Berg sat alone in the bunker, fighting for her life. They left their cars and walked side by side through the forest in the pleasant sunny weather. Simonsen started by thanking the man for his assistance in identifying the Finnish girl, Elizabeth Juutilainen, and received an indifferent shrug in response. Their subsequent conversation was barbaric, primitive, but also rewarding for both of them. *Life for one, death for the other*—the comment by the head of DSIS to Simonsen after the meeting at the Ministry of Justice was about to become bloody reality. Marcus Kolding considered the homicide chief's proposal for a long time before he summarised in a neutral tone.

"I kidnap and torture your mass murderer, until he comes out with where he has hidden the women. In return you tell me the name of the informer you say I have in my organisation."

"Yes, that's the deal."

"What about the psychopath... What's his name again, I've forgotten it?"

"Andreas Falkenborg."

"Do you want him back alive?"

They walked a dozen steps before it occurred to Kolding that he would not get an answer. Then he said in a business-like way, "Okay, I understand."

The only controversy between the two men was about when Kolding would get his information. Simonsen held firmly to his proposal.

"When you get him to talk—not before."

"How do I know that you won't cheat me? Although that would be very stupid of you, obviously."

"You can't know that, and stop threatening me. You have to trust that you'll get what I've promised you."

"Or that these aren't false accusations against one of my employees that you have fabricated to suit your agenda?"

"They will be in a form which you can judge for yourself."

"An audio recording?"

"You'll have to see."

Doctor Cold confirmed the horse trade by standing still and extending his hand. Simonsen took it with displeasure. They agreed on the practical details and soon they were back at the cars, where neither of them felt compelled to shake hands again. Simonsen left first; his interlocutor sat in his car and waited a few minutes, while in the meantime he rubbed his large snout with characteristic rotary movements.

CHAPTER 57

Pauline Berg was alone in the bunker. Andreas Falkenborg had killed Jeanette Hvidt before her eyes and buried the body in the concrete floor of the bunker. But her brain refused to process what she had seen. Gradually as she slipped into a state of exhaustion and dehydration, she felt certain that Jeanette was still sitting by her side. She patiently instructed her fellow prisoner.

"Try chewing on your gag. Many times but carefully, without hurrying. Then finally you can force it out with your tongue. You mustn't give up, do you understand?"

She had a hard time making out the reply.

"Remember, you're going to be a doctor. You will be a good doctor."

Finally she sensed how Jeanette's mouth slowly worked the gag, just as she herself had done it. The sound calmed her until another sound blended in—an extended scraping sound that made tears leak from her eyes without her knowing why. She concentrated on not remembering, resumed the encouragement to Jeanette Hvidt, again and again, then recited the days of the week, the months, the planets—all to divert her thoughts. Then suddenly the darkness was broken and again she saw Falkenborg, with a finishing trowel, smoothing the wet concrete over Jeanette

Hvidt's grave, so that it was level with the floor of the bunker. Other gruesome sounds and horrible images forced their way in, and she heard her screams die against the walls in a dull distortion, which better than anything else jolted her into awareness. Desperately she shook and tore at her chains, until fatigue forced her to give up and sit sobbing impotently for her parents to come and rescue her. Then the darkness once again became her friend. For a brief, clear moment she realised that time was running out, but that basically did not concern her. Then she excused herself to the woman no longer sitting by her side for her panic, and fell into a troubled sleep.

CHAPTER 58

The investigation had proceeded without help from Arne Pedersen for the last couple of days. He wandered around Police Headquarters as he wished, attended the meetings he wanted to, but no one counted on him or involved him in any decisions. Reports of his incapacity had quickly spread, with the result that wherever he was, he was treated kindly and considerately, but also as if he was not really present. The first twenty-four hours after the news of Pauline Berg's kidnapping had obviously been terrible for him and he was of no use at all in an investigative capacity. Many of his colleagues encouraged him to go home, which he steadfastly refused. He wanted to be with the others until the whole thing was over;

anything else would be unbearable. As no one really had time to get involved, they left him alone and got used to him. Like a daddy-long-legs, he thought with bitter irony. Like a daddy-long-legs.

To his own great surprise he had no problem sleeping. The nightmare about the witch, his mother and finally Pauline Berg, who perished in a plastic bag, was absent. Possibly because the reality was more horrific. He did not know the reason and did not care. He could sleep, for whatever reason, and that was the most important thing. All he needed to do was lie down on the floor in his office, and a few minutes later he was snoozing like a child, so it was hardly surprising that he was the most well-rested police officer in the whole complex and certainly in the Homicide Division. The thought pleased him, but he kept it to himself. He said nothing to anyone, about that or anything else. But maybe it was just by sleeping that little by little he got hold of himself.

Konrad Simonsen noticed he was getting better. They had breakfast together. That is, at the same table in the cafeteria, not while working, not at all.

"You look like you're doing better, Arne."

The Countess added, "It's good to see. I'm happy about that."

He sat and concentrated on his food. What should he say? That Simonsen himself looked like shit? That they both did? Like a pair of fools, just waiting for something terrible to happen.

Someone had taken his car keys, and he knew why. He also knew they were keeping an eye on him. It was easy to figure out: slightly too long a look here, a glance there, and his office regularly visited by colleagues who didn't really want anything except to see how things were going. Even when he slept, he had monitored their comings and goings. The old trick with a paper clip in the door, before he closed it completely, had exposed them. How stupid did they really think he was? He was forty-two years old and had been a police officer for almost twenty years, almost half his life. Still they treated him like a boy scout, a pure amateur. His pistol was gone, but he had no need of it, it was just a nuisance. A small penknife from his desk drawer and a police truncheon were all he needed. Idiots!

On Thursday afternoon his wife had brought him clothes. They chatted together for fifteen minutes about the twins and, when that subject was exhausted, about the good weather. And how he was to be sure and eat properly. She kissed him, both when she arrived and when she left, a routine that was always observed, just like automatically looking to the left before you turn on to a street. When she was gone it struck him more clearly than ever how far they had drifted from each other. As if they lived in two different worlds. But he was happy about the clothes. When he was arrested, he wanted to be presentable. Well dressed, showered and shaved. He had never liked shabby prisoners; had learned to live with them, sure—because they were by far the majority—but deep down he despised them, and he did not want to be that way himself.

The alarm from his cell phone woke him at two o'clock, and he took ten minutes to ease the soreness out of his body with small, improvised gymnastic exercises. The Japanese slept on the floor on rush mats, he had read. Hardy people, and it was undeniably practical to be able to put your bed away in a corner. Japan, Australia, China, Brazil—he had always dreamed about taking a long journey, but his life had gone in a different direction. There was always something that was more important. Through the window he stared out into the night and thought that his journey would have to wait a few more years. Then on stockinged feet he slipped out into the corridor and sneaked past Simonsen's office. Light was seeping out from under the door. The heart of the

410

Homicide Division the room had once been named, by whom he could not remember. Filled with contempt he mimed spitting against the closed door, after which he found the nearest bathroom and got ready.

Months could pass without the Countess swearing, so when it finally happened, she commanded everyone's attention at once. In this case everyone meant Simonsen and the head of DSIS. They were in Simonsen's office, wide awake, almost speeding, reviewing tomorrow's theatre piece, which simply *must* not go wrong. The head of DSIS underscored that regularly. *There is no plan B, it's this or nothing.* A few times in varied form: *If it doesn't happen tomorrow, it never will*—or whatever he could think of. It was almost as if he liked saying it, but it didn't become any less true as a result. The Countess's cell phone hummed; she looked at it and burst out in a panic, "Damn it! Arne has taken off."

Simonsen leaped up from his chair, which tipped over.

"No! Where is he? How do you even know?"

"His cell phone. I automatically get an SMS when it is more than a hundred metres away from HS. Don't ask how."

The head of DSIS was calmer.

"He's more than a hundred metres away?"

"Two hundred or so."

"Then relax. There's plenty of time."

Simonsen complied. He picked up his chair and sat down, a little embarrassed by his own reaction. He said to the Countess, "Maybe he's just getting a little fresh air. Do we even know where he's going?"

"Don't be stupid."

"Is he armed?"

"Hardly, I have his pistol."

Simonsen looked at the head of DSIS.

"I assume that your people will stop him, before it goes haywire."

The head of DSIS confirmed that, but did not do anything. He scratched his temple with one knuckle and said quietly, "There is also another possibility."

The following two seconds felt very long. The Countess looked down at the floor and kept quiet. Simonsen stared at her, appalled.

"Tell me, have you gone crazy? No, under no circumstances. Absolutely not!"

The head of DSIS got up and left the office. Shortly after, Simonsen followed his example. The Countess watched him, her mouth set in a hard line, and thought that sometimes her boyfriend was a fool. It would have been so easy for her to have let Pedersen continue. All she'd needed to do was ignore the SMS. But the decision must be Simonsen's and no one else's. That's why she had looked away. She tried to convince herself. For that reason only.

The night porter at the hotel was a little too quick to open the door when Arne Pedersen showed him his police badge through the glass. That should have warned him. And if not that, then in any event when with virtually no explanation needed, he was given a universal access card and shown Andreas Falkenborg's room number. The young man behind the counter pointed.

"Number twelve, that way, third room on the left."

Pedersen took a deep breath before he carefully opened the door and entered the room. While his eyes grew accustomed to the darkness, he got his truncheon out and took the few steps through the little entryway. Carefully he felt on the wall for a switch, after which the light came on. His surprise was complete. On the bed sat two men of his own age. There was a third standing not far from him.

"Good evening, Arne."

He turned towards the door by which he had just entered. The man at his side said quietly, "Spare yourself the trouble. There are two more officers outside."

Pedersen let go of the truncheon, which fell to the floor with a dull thud. He asked despairingly, "So what now?"

"Nothing, except that we're driving you back to Simon. Don't worry, we completely understand how you feel."

CHAPTER 59

The next twenty-four hours told on the employees of the Homicide Division and made them old before their time. Even the head of DSIS, who, according to rumours in Police Headquarters, had been involved in a bit of everything in his career, adopted the same shuffling gait and anguished look as Konrad Simonsen, Poul Troulsen and Ernesto Madsen. Only the Countess got through the crisis without making a display of her desperation, which was surprising. She was the one most closely linked to Pauline Berg, if you didn't count Arne Pedersen, who was now spending most of his time in his office, staring unproductively into space along with a young officer who had been designated to keep an eye on him. Malte Borup also felt weighed down, but was functioning more normally, especially on Friday morning when he caught the Countess at a table in the cafeteria, where she was sitting by herself having breakfast.

"May I sit here?"

"Of course you may. Tell me, aren't you having anything besides Coke? You can't live on that. What do you eat, by the way?"

"Not much, I'm afraid."

"Are you short of money?"

"No, it's not that. I'm just not hungry."

The Countess buttered a roll from her own plate and pushed it over to him.

"Eat that."

The student politely obeyed, eating without great appetite. Between bites he asked, "What good is a DNA test like that really? I mean, are we completely sure she's dead?"

"A DNA test is one hundred per cent valid, but the only thing we are somewhat sure of is that Jeanette Hvidt is dead. Her DNA was found in the lipstick he used to put a mark on his mask. We don't know whether Pauline is alive. I thought you knew that."

"That's what I understood. Do you think she is dead too?"

"It's impossible to guess, I don't think anything."

"I think she's alive. I firmly believe that."

"That's good."

"I wish we could bring the murderer in and beat him until he tells us where he's hidden her. I know we can't, but that's what I wish. Or maybe inject something into him to make him tell the truth."

"It doesn't work that way."

"No, unfortunately. It's crazy, Pauline may have to die because we will protect a psychopath who has murdered five women. If I was the one to decide, then... well, obviously it's not fun to think about, but better that than Pauline dying."

"It won't happen."

"That she dies?"

"That's not what I meant, but let's talk about something else."

414

"What would that be? That Falkenborg guy is just driving around and around, when he's not snoring in his hotel room. I don't understand why we're going to keep on sitting and staring at that. I can't stand being down in the control room or whatever you're calling it, it's like being at a funeral. And I just don't understand why we're letting him be."

The Countess thought that the vast majority at Police Headquarters would agree with him. Simonsen was having a harder and harder time maintaining that surveillance of Andreas Falkenborg was the right strategy, even though she and the head of DSIS were doing everything in their power to support him. But he needed time to get his under-the-table agreement with Marcus Kolding completely in place.

"Maybe something will happen today."

"What would that be? Do you know something?"

"Wait and see, Malte."

"They say it's going to be just as hot as yesterday, and that's not good either, right?"

"No, that's not very good."

"It's hard to drink anything yourself, when you think about her. But actually I came over to ask you if I could slip home for a couple of hours during the day. It's Anita's birthday, and I haven't even bought her a present."

"No, Malte, you have to stay here. We may need you at short notice. In return you can do what you want while you're waiting, so long as you keep your cell phone on."

Half an hour later frustration at Police Headquarters over Simonsen's delay hit a high point in the form of a dozen officers who forced their way into the homicide chief's office, some in uniform, most in civilian clothes, all with serious expressions on their faces. Simonsen was sitting behind his desk, fighting off sleep, when the group arrived and quickly filled the office.

An older officer, known for his controlled manner and with broad support in all camps, was the spokesman for the group. He stood quietly by the door and waited until everyone was inside. Then he said, coolly but clearly, "This can't go on any longer, Simon. It will soon be twenty-four hours since we have known where Falkenborg is, and it is obvious to everyone besides you that he does not intend to return to the place where he has hidden the two women. So either you arrest him, or we will—with or without orders."

Simonsen stared at him and the other man held his gaze without wavering. The chief inspector picked up the phone, got hold of the Countess and ordered in a clear voice, "Arrange for the national chief of police to come down to my office as quickly as possible."

Then he took a report at random from his desk and started reading it. The waiting men became more and more restless. One left the office, another attempted an explanation but was stopped by Simonsen's raised hand.

Less than a minute later the national chief of police arrived, and Simonsen asked, "From what I understood at the meeting yesterday, I have operational responsibility for the Falkenborg investigation. Or perhaps I've misunderstood?"

For once the national chief of police spoke clearly.

"No, you have definitely not misunderstood. It is your responsibility, and yours alone."

He looked around at the gathered police officers, slowly removed his glasses and added angrily, "What's the problem? Is there anyone here who hasn't understood that? Or perhaps still can't accept it?"

"That I don't really know. But if it is the case, do I have your support to suspend them until this is over?"

Again the national chief of police observed the men, this time with an expression like thunder. Then he hissed, "You have my permission to fire them without pension if they put any obstacles whatsoever in your way."

Simonsen looked up at him and said quietly, "Thanks. I'll manage the rest myself."

The national chief of police put his glasses back on and left, the homicide chief concentrated on his report again, and soon he was alone in the office.

A short time later Simonsen, the Countess, the head of DSIS, Madsen and the police commissioner met. The head of DSIS had also brought a secretary along, an impeccably dressed young man who said nothing but efficiently tapped on his noise-reduction keyboard, even before the meeting had started. Everyone was tired of the wait, which seemed to lead nowhere but to a steadily increasing state of frustration. Only the police commissioner seemed fresh. She was in a gaudy tailor-made suit that made you think of a street juggler or a parrot. She looked at the secretary and asked the head of DSIS, "I thought this was an informal conversation, why have you brought someone to take minutes?"

"You and Simon are using a lot of my resources at the moment. It's bad enough that my budget is shot to pieces without me having the slightest thing in writing later on."

"But this meeting is not about finances at all."

"Everything is about finances."

"What a lot of nonsense."

"It's about how my resources are being used, I have to be able to document that at the end of the year."

Anyone who knew the police commissioner could see that she was angry, but she was able to maintain her composure. She said flatly, "I want the minutes for review before they are distributed."

The head of DSIS agreed, and the meeting could begin. Simonsen was first to speak.

"I know that we're all tired and frustrated. The last few days have been hard, and none of us thinks it has been fun to sit and watch that screen without being able to do anything, while knowing that Pauline's situation is perhaps getting more and more—"

He stopped mid-sentence and thought to himself that this was the most miserable introduction he had ever given a meeting, and that basically he didn't care. Then he continued.

"Sorry, I'm tired, and I got tongue-tied, but I'm sure you understand what I mean."

They did, and Simonsen went on.

"It's clear that if nothing happens soon, we will be forced to do something. The question is what, and we will clarify that at this meeting. There are various possibilities, but to begin with we need a brief status report."

He looked at the head of DSIS, who took over.

"There is not much beyond what you already know. At the moment he's having breakfast at his hotel in Herlev. Yesterday he drove around more or less aimlessly. Occasionally he connected his laptop and looked for anything new from his eavesdropping, and other times he surfed around on the Internet and read news, mainly about himself. To top it off he wrote an entry to a blog, in his own name besides, but it was vague and harmless."

"How closely is he being covered?"

It was the police commissioner who wanted to know.

"Very close. As closely as possible. We have people around him all the time, and a transmitter has been placed on his car besides, so we can constantly follow where he is. That is what you see on the screen as a blue circle."

He pointed towards the big screen on the wall, which showed a map of Herlev with a stationary blue circle in the middle of the image.

The Countess asked, "The transmitter won't fall off?"

"Of course it won't, it's specially designed for the purpose, located on the inside of the fender over the right rear wheel and attached with powerful magnets. You can get it loose if you pull on it firmly, but ordinary movements from the car don't affect it."

"What about his cell phone and hotel room? Are they being bugged?"

The head of DSIS sent Ernesto Madsen an irritated look, as if he wanted to tell him that he was there as a psychologist and should keep his mouth shut when police-related subjects were discussed. Nevertheless he answered curtly, "Falkenborg has three SIM cards, but does not use his cell phone. And yes, his room is bugged."

The psychologist did not let himself be cowed.

"But don't we risk him playing hide-and-seek with all that bugging? He is an expert in the field."

The head of DSIS snorted.

"He's no expert! Our instruments are at least two generations on from the trash he peddles, and the technicians we have are light years ahead in both knowledge and experience. He's an amateur, we're professionals, don't forget that."

This torrent of words closed the mouth of Ernesto Madsen and at the same time concluded the review by the head of DSIS. Now it was Simonsen's turn again.

"Which brings us to the serious part. That is, what do we do now? There are only two options: go on like yesterday or else bring him in. Neither of these is enticing, and I will not go along with the first one. We are about to reach the length of time a person can go without water, and we have to allow ourselves time to work on him. For that reason I will arrest him today, no later than noon, unless he breaks the pattern from yesterday. This is not up for discussion."

Madsen said darkly, "You shouldn't count on him letting himself be questioned. I'm almost certain he won't."

The police commissioner added, "And we have no way of forcing him to speak, but you're aware of that, Simon."

"I'm quite aware of that."

"I should tell you that when he is in our custody, I'll be assigning some people to assure me that no irregularities occur. I know that Pauline Berg is our colleague, and I know how you feel, so I intend to ensure that everything is done correctly."

The Countess asked sarcastically, "Don't you trust us?"

"No."

Madsen threw up his arms in despair and exclaimed, "This is a load of shit."

The head of DSIS was straight on him.

"Your personal opinions are of no interest."

Then the police commissioner got involved.

"The man is right."

"The man should contribute something constructive for his nine hundred kroner an hour."

Madsen blushed, and Simonsen said quietly, "There is perhaps a third possibility that could be tried?"

The Countess gave him the pre-arranged cue.

"What possibility is that, Simon? All of us would like to hear it."

"I am thinking that perhaps a person can get close to Falkenborg and gain his trust. He is in many ways very naive and gullible. It's worth a try, if we compare it to the alternatives."

The head of DSIS thought quickest.

"It doesn't sound like a bad idea, I'd like to hear more about it. Is this something we should brainstorm or do you have it wrapped and ready for us?"

"Brainstorm."

The Countess was also quick on the trigger, and the police commissioner smiled proudly; what capable people she had.

"If it were me, I know what I would do."

Simonsen said, "Do tell."

"That notorious key that we believe is to the padlock to his warehouse... somehow we've acquired the original, right?"

It was the head of DSIS who answered her.

"We took it from his bunch of keys in the hotel room yesterday and replaced it with a copy we had made. The original has been sent for technical investigation; we can't definitively conclude whether it has been used recently, but the thumbprint was made within the last two days, so we will proceed from that. You got the report a long time ago."

"Yes, I've seen it, but I haven't read it closely yet. Simon, we are responsible for the surveying of cellar rooms, how intensive is that investigation?"

"As intensive as we can possibly make it. The Home Guard and others are helping us. They are going from cellar to cellar everywhere, and attics too naturally, to see whether they can find the matching lock. There are also photographs of a similar lock in the newspapers, with a call for private citizens to help. But so far without result, apart from the fact that we have found twenty-three padlocks from the same manufacturer, which doesn't help at all."

"No, but it's the story I could start with if I met Falkenborg. Some officer who had behaved rudely because the police wanted to look through my cellar. Maybe talk about the key, and definitely about all the people who are working on the case, and see how he reacts."

Ernesto Madsen's assessment was not encouraging.

"He will not react, because he won't even talk about it."

The head of DSIS said, "That is to say, that you recommend it."

"What do you mean?"

"I mean, you say nothing about the fact that it may do harm, and if it doesn't succeed, there's no downside, so we're right where we already are."

Ernest Madsen said, a little confused, "That's right, of course, but in any event it should not be—"

The head of DSIS interrupted him.

"You should know, Ernesto Madsen, that my own profilers have great respect for your work, and they are quite impressed by your report about Falkenborg's relationship with his parents. Personally I too think you hit the nail on the head, although I do not have the professional background for an informed critique. I got a lot out of your revelations about his mother in particular. If you could please give us an outline of that, so it's fresh in my mind, I'd be grateful."

Simonsen noticed that the head of DSIS was well prepared. He added, "That's a good idea, but make it brief, Ernesto."

Madsen spoke, and the Countess in particular listened intently. At one point she interrupted politely, "Please explain that again. So you're saying that if I behave submissively and arrogantly at the same time, I have the greatest chance of making friendly contact with him? But how will I do that in practice? Let's say, for example, that I just sat down at the table where he is eating, then to whom am I being arrogant and how should I be submissive?"

"Well, for example, you could be arrogant to the waiting staff, especially if they're young."

The head of DSIS exclaimed enthusiastically.

"Well thought out, Ernesto. Perhaps we can arrange for a young waitress, that can be done, if we know the place in advance."

"But you're not going to do that, are you?"

"Well, no. Good point. What would you recommend other-wise? Don't hold back."

The Countess was on the same track.

"Yes, who would you advise me to be submissive to?"

Simonsen added, "This is brilliant! Weaving the Countess's role into your survey of his psychological relationship to his mother... that makes it relevant while also saving time."

The police commissioner herself joined in the chorus of praise, and Madsen did all the weaving he could manage. The keeper of the minutes did his job, and neither the police commissioner nor the psychologist realised that they had been drawn into the head of DSIS's carefully thought out agenda.

CHAPTER 60

Andreas Falkenborg decided to have lunch at the highway cafeteria in Solrød south of Copenhagen. The Countess managed to slip into the line at the till two places ahead of him. The microphone, placed like a beautiful brooch in the lapel of her tailor-made suit, was connected to a transmitter in her handbag, and the sound came through clearly on the speakers in the control room at Police Headquarters, Copenhagen. Everyone present listened tensely. The police commissioner gestured sympathetically when she heard the way the Countess belittled the woman at the till in a bad-tempered onslaught about the quality of the food versus its price. And waiting to go into the cafeteria with her tray until shortly after Falkenborg had taken a seat was obviously successful too, for a little later they heard the Countess ask:

"May I sit down here?"

"Yes, if you like. But there are plenty of vacant tables."

"I like company. Tell me, did you hear that stupid goose?"

"I heard her."

"Wasn't she rude? You'd have to go a long way to find a girl as stupid as that."

"Yes, maybe she was."

"Don't you ever get mad at that sort of girl? I almost can't control myself when I'm treated that way. But maybe it's just me?"

"No, I know what you mean, they are irritating."

"You can say that again. Well, I'm glad I'm not the only one who thinks she shouldn't be employed at a place like this."

"No, I can see your point."

"Excuse me, could you please keep an eye on my food while I visit the bathroom?"

"Yes, sure. I'll do that."

"Thanks. My name's Nathalie by the way, what's your name?"

"Pronto is what people call me."

"Such a nice name. Pronto—I like that."

The head of DSIS said, "What in the world is happening? Where is she going with this?"

Simonsen, who by now was starting to admire the acting abilities of the head of DSIS, kept strategically quiet, so Poul Troulsen, who to begin with did not like the man and had already had two minor encounters with him, answered acidly, "Maybe she's going to pee."

"Nonsense, she would have taken care of that in advance."

Shortly afterwards the Countess's voice was heard again:

"I've gone out to the parking lot, actually I'm squatting behind his car, but that's because it's parked closest. This has failed completely, I think he knows he's being watched. He keeps looking around furtively all the time, and he seems to have suspicions about two of the agents. As you can hear, I'm in the process of making contact, but the close surveillance has fallen through."

The head of DSIS stood up, slightly red in the face. Without raising his voice but in an ominous tone he asked Troulsen, "You're not sleeping with her, so now I'm asking you—is she capable? That is—does she know what she's talking about, or is she just one of those paranoid female cops who let themselves get carried away and see ghosts when things heat up?"

Troulsen answered him confrontationally.

"She's capable, and you're disagreeable."

"This is no time to argue. Okay, Simon, it's your ass, but I assume that we break off?"

Simonsen was no great actor, and even though he had practised his line, it sounded affected. He said, "I don't know… yes, that is standard procedure. I mean, I can't really decide what I want or don't want, and poor Pauline, she—"

The head of DSIS pounced on him, cold and confrontational.

"Make your decision, man, tell me! Don't you realise it's urgent?"

The harsh words did not help; almost the contrary. Simonsen shook his head heavily and breathed rapidly in short, brief bursts. Suddenly sweat was running out of every pore. The attack made him resemble a boiled crab and was far more convincing than his previous dilly-dallying.

The head of DSIS threw out his arms in despair and turned instead to appeal to the police commissioner, who after a few long seconds authoritatively cut through.

"Cancel the surveillance immediately."

The secretary made a note.

Like the Countess, the head of DSIS also had a microphone on his lapel, on the inside. He quickly turned the lapel, made connection via a small switch that was hanging down on a cord, and slowly and clearly gave the command.

"All units withdraw out of range of vision immediately. I repeat—all units withdraw out of range of vision immediately. Without exception. Safety distance of at least five hundred metres."

Simonsen had pulled himself together. The police commissioner stared at him, worried, and he apologised.

"I'm sorry, that won't happen again."

The head of DSIS supported him to his boss.

"That kind of thing is an occupational hazard. It's good that you were here and could give the order, that was the right thing to do."

He looked at Simonsen, who seemed to have regained control of himself.

"Brief stress attacks are normal under severe pressure. It even happens to me, that's just how it is, but I'm sure you know about that."

The police commissioner felt reassured and said, "Yes, of course I do. I know very well that it doesn't mean anything."

The Countess's voice returned, and those present listened tensely.

"Thanks for your help."

"With what?"

"Keeping an eye on my food."

"It was nothing."

"Do you come here often?"

"No."

"The food is very good, don't you think?"

"No, not really."

"Are you picky? Well, I actually eat everything, within limits that is, but there is one thing that is certain, and do you know what that is? It was Ponto, wasn't it?"

"Pronto."

"Pronto, yes. Well, that was what you said. Do you know what is certain?"

"No, I don't."

"That I'm going to have a cognac with my coffee, and I would like to treat you to one too."

"No, thanks."

"And that is because I am simply so upset. I tell you, I am shaken."

"No, why is that?"

"Because this morning two police officers wanted to search my cellar, and they were so shameless that you don't know the half of it."

"No."

"Just think, they ordered me around, as if—well, they were searching for two girls, who...Hey, where are you going? You're not even finished... damn it anyway. I'll go after him, that will have to be plan B, so I hope he reacts better than this."

Simonsen said quietly, "It was worth a try."

Troulsen tried to be optimistic.

"Let's just see what his next response is. I really think this is our best chance."

The head of DSIS snapped, "It's a little late to say now."

No one answered him. Shortly after that the Countess whimpered through the speakers:

"Excuse me, Andreas Falkenborg, yes, I know your name, I'm not who I said I was. But you know where my daughter is, and you know that she will die if you don't help me. And I believe deep inside that you know what you have done is wrong. You mustn't take her away from me. Think about your own mother, how much she suffered, but all that you did to her, you can make good again by giving me my child back. Her name is

427

Pauline ... yes, yes, I'll be going now, but for God's sake, think it over. For your mother's sake and the peace of your own soul."

Troulsen commented, "He didn't even answer, is that good or bad?"

The head of DSIS asked, "Didn't he say something in the background? Very faintly?"

Simonsen thought that the man was laying it on too thick, and did not support the assertion. No one else commented either. Shortly afterwards the Countess's voice filled the room:

"I'm standing out in the parking lot, and what just happened made a big impression on Falkenborg, although he waved me away. But now there's no need for this microphone. I'll call you in a little while, Simon."

Twenty seconds later Simonsen's cell phone rang. He took the call and relayed the conversation as he listened, talking in turn to the others and to the Countess. It worked well, everyone could follow what was happening.

The Countess said, "The timing is going to be close, Simon. He's still sitting in his car, but if he leaves, and the DSIS people spot him, the whole thing is messed up. And where are Doctor Cold's gorillas? I don't see any sign of them ... Wait a moment, here they are now."

Simonsen relayed to his listeners:

"She says that he felt touched, he seemed almost contrite and depressed. His attitude was completely resigned. He waved her away because he was starting to cry. Now he's circling his car, apparently at a loss about what to do."

The police commissioner wrung her hands and let out a short, "Yes."

Simonsen instructed the Countess.

"No, you must not approach him again, leave him alone for a while."

She said, "Now Doctor Cold's people have caught up with him. It went fast, and no one noticed anything, but the timing is bad… No, now the driver is going to the truck where I put the transmitter. So you might as well continue."

Simonsen informed the gathering.

"He is walking around the parking lot, now she can't see him because of a bus… Then he comes out again, he goes back to his car and gets in… And now she says that he's driving away."

The head of DSIS pointed up at the big screen and said, "We can see that for ourselves, Simon."

Simonsen shook his head slightly then said to the Countess, "No, you shouldn't follow him, come back to HS. We have him tracked."

The Countess answered Simonsen, "Keep your fingers crossed that the surveillance team doesn't notice his car when it leaves the parking lot. See you in a bit."

The optimism lasted for almost an hour; Falkenborg was on the move, driving on the South Freeway that led to Rødby on Lolland, and everyone was anxious when he turned off it; some more than others, however. Troulsen said, "Soon he'll be at the Farø Bridge, where do you suppose he's hidden her?"

The police commissioner was somewhat more subdued than before.

"Maybe he's in flight, that's also a possibility."

The Countess, who had joined them, answered, "I don't think so, he seemed very, very affected."

"But when will he exit the freeway? This is almost unbearable to watch."

Suddenly the head of DSIS said, "Something is wrong, he is driving too slowly. My people are a kilometre behind him, I'll ask a team to drive up."

It took a long time before he came back. Not until Falkenborg was stopped at Falster just before Guldborgsund did the security chief come into the room again, trembling with excitement.

"We lost him, that's not even his car. He tricked us at the parking lot in Solrød and put the transmitter on a German truck that's going to Rødby."

Everyone was shouting at each other. Except for the police commissioner, whose face turned ash-grey and who dabbed her cheeks with her mineral water. No one had seen that happen before. There was confusion for a while until Simonsen became the focal point of everyone's gaze. He said calmly, "Go and put out a search for him again, Poul, there's nothing else to do. And this time we'll bring him in when we find him."

Troulsen left, and the head of DSIS consoled the police commissioner.

"Your order to cancel the close surveillance was correct. I am almost certain that it will be backed up everywhere, even though you have no operational experience. Unless there is a major investigation…but it shouldn't concern outsiders who orders who to do what. I will personally take responsibility, so long as I don't have to lie to an official inquiry. What do you say, Simon?"

"Naturally we're in agreement on that, and I would have done exactly the same. Can't we just avoid putting the command in the minutes? It's not reasonable that only one of us takes full responsibility."

The police commissioner livened up a little.

"Thanks, I won't forget that."

Neither of the two men believed there'd ever be an official inquiry, however; these things would obviously be taken care of internally. Or perhaps simply forgotten.

The story of the fiasco spread like wildfire through Police Headquarters. Gradually people began to gather in the control room. Individually or in small groups, the officers came in silently and took empty chairs or lined the walls. No one spoke, and the spontaneous gathering had no purpose. It felt simply as if everyone was used up; four days and nights of unbroken high-pressure effort had finally culminated in this. No one imagined Pauline Berg had any chance left now. Her rescue was beyond the scope of the police and could only be achieved by an even higher power. An older detective understood that better than anyone; he knelt and said a prayer, while others in his vicinity lowered their heads and, according to conviction, supported him as best they could. Arne Pedersen left the room, his caretaker followed. Both of them were crying openly. In the midst of the confusion sat Simonsen and the Countess, holding each other's hand and waiting in anticipation. And then all at once the prayer was answered. The big screen suddenly changed its image, and a green circle appeared on a map of Denmark. One voice shouted excitedly above the rest.

"That's the damned forest road to Avnsø, I know that place. It's deserted out there, what do you suppose he's doing?"

And another interpreted the green, blinking figure.

"He's talking on his cell phone."

The ring tone from Simonsen's inside pocket was timed so that no one needed a closer interpretation. The homicide chief took the call, while everyone in the room held their breath. Simonsen listened; Doctor Cold's voice was business-like, as usual. Simonsen, who by now was used to misleading anyone observing him, said aloud, "It's him."

He listened then added, "Between Källna and Össjö, right on the highway in a little birch grove, yes, I got that… And that's where you buried Liz Suenson?"

The Countess was ready with pen and paper and wrote that down.

"Bunker in Hareskov between Skovbrynet Station and Hareskov Station, I follow you... No, you mustn't... Yes, you're sick, and we can help you. Stay where you—"

Simonsen dropped his cell phone and shouted, even though everyone was hanging on every word from his lips in advance.

"Malte, are you here?"

The student answered and instantly received his orders.

"Air-raid shelter from 1955, rented from Værløse Municipality, it must be Furesø Municipality today, at the end of a forest path near the S-train. Find the address, as quickly as you can. Poul, you get hold of an ambulance, use the emergency number, say that they should dispatch it from Herlev Hospital, that's the quickest, and make sure there is a doctor along with it. Tell them they should drive toward Hareskoven and that the driver will be given the exact destination en route."

Troulsen ran out, and Simonsen gave further commands.

"We should also have some patrol cars... that must be Gladsaxe Police District, someone take care of that... and also cars for Falkenborg. He is at... well, you can see that on the map, but it had better be quick, he's about to do harm to himself."

Several officers hurried out of the room.

The first report back came verbally and a good deal faster than anyone had expected. An officer called in.

"Andreas Falkenborg is dead. He poured gasoline over himself and the inside of his van, a lot it sounds like. He is burned beyond recognition, but there is no doubt that it's his car. The fire department and several patrol cars are on their way, but that will take some time. The officers that are there now just happened to be in the vicinity."

The head of DSIS commented, "I'll take care of that aspect personally, if it's all right with you, Simon?"

"Yes, do that."

No one reacted with particular dismay to the information about Falkenborg's death. They seemed almost indifferent. Jeanette Hvidt's fate was also pushed to the background. Only news about Pauline Berg was important. Simonsen thought however about Doctor Cold's *fun with a blowtorch*, and shuddered. Then he shook the thought away and concentrated on the present. Redemption arrived ten minutes later with a call to his cell phone. He relayed the message quietly to his audience in the control room.

"They have Pauline now. She's alive."

CHAPTER 61

Although the rest of the evening was nothing but aftershock, it was exhausting for Konrad Simonsen and the Countess. First they were at the hospital, where they waited a long time before the doctors and Pauline Berg's family granted them a minute with the patient. She smiled weakly when she recognised them; they could barely manage to return it. Then Simonsen insisted—even though he could barely stand up—on driving to Hundested, where he felt that he owed Rikke Barbara Hvidt a visit. Fate had been pitiless to the blind woman, and in the midst of all the joy that Pauline Berg had been rescued, Simonsen could not forget the woman who had paid such a high price for Andreas Falkenborg's madness. But they arrived too late. Despite supervision, Rikke Barbara Hvidt had succeeded in biting an artery in two, while the staff at the nursing home thought she was sleeping. When her suicide attempt was discovered, she had already lost a lot of blood, and she passed away in the ambulance.

On their way home they passed Frederiksværk, and Simonsen had an impulse.

"Do you have any desire to give your cell phone away?"

"Sure, if you like. To whom?"

"To a young woman whose cell phone doesn't work."

The Countess abstained from further questions. They made a detour so that he could accomplish his errand. It did not take long. The rest of the way home the mood was flat, and neither of them said much. The Countess drove, Simonsen stared out into the night. Suddenly he said, "I guess Rikke was his sixth victim, poor woman."

"You could say that."

Conversation stopped there. A little later he commented, "The ones who are high up, types like Helmer Hammer and Bertil Hampel-Koch... They never get dirt on their hands. They make certain of that."

She did not answer him; what was there to say?

"Do you think what we did was wrong?"

"No, Simon, I don't. It's disgusting and grim to think about, and I will do everything I can to repress the memory of it, but when I saw Pauline, I loved you more than anything on earth. You did the right thing, the only thing you could do."

"It doesn't feel that way."

"But that's how it is, and remember, you were not alone in it. I also bear my share of responsibility, or blame, if you will."

"And I'm happy about that. Do you think we can put this behind us?"

"Yes, we can. We have each other, and we also have Pauline back among us, if we should ever be in any doubt that we did the right thing."

Simonsen nodded into the darkness.

***

The same night Andreas Falkenborg's unhappy childhood claimed its seventh and final victim. The man who left the bar and went into the alley to pee, himself had a number of murders on his conscience. Overdosing addicts to get them out of the way was one of his specialities; threatening and beating up bar owners, so they would buy even more of his boss's illegal products, was another. Many considered him a stupid swine, but few dared tell him that. A hard-boiled criminal was not someone you chose to have a falling out with.

What only a few people knew was that the man kept a leg in each camp. He worked for Marcus Kolding's organisation, which for years the police had kept under so-called Level One surveillance, reserved for the most influential, extended federations in the criminal underworld, while at the same time he was the highest-ranking informant the authorities had in the same organisation. Although he was not exactly part of Doctor Cold's inner circle of dubious personnel, his tips from time to time produced excellent results. To some degree a blind eye was turned to his personal rap sheet, which he found advantageous. Now his life had been exchanged for that of a young officer.

In the alley the man held his beer glass in one hand and prepared to relieve himself with the other. After that there was a warm dampness around him, while a slight, almost inaudible sigh of relief escaped him.

The knife was thrust from behind into his neck and severed his windpipe before he could scream; there was only a faint rattle. The glass shattered when he fell; beer, urine and blood mixed into an ugly fluid that slowly seeped out over the pavement and made its way into the gutter.

There is a price to be paid for everything.

A NOTE ON THE TYPE

The text of this book is set in Adobe Caslon, named after the English punch-cutter and type-founder William Caslon I (1692–1766). Caslon's rather old-fashioned types were modelled on seventeenth-century Dutch designs, but found wide acceptance throughout the English-speaking world for much of the eighteenth century until replaced by newer types towards the end of the century. Used in 1776 to print the Declaration of Independence, they were revived in the nineteenth century and have been popular ever since, particularly amongst fine printers. There are several digital versions, of which Carol Twombly's Adobe Caslon is one.

ALSO AVAILABLE BY
LOTTE AND SØREN HAMMER

THE HANGING

The electrifying first instalment of the Konrad Simonsen series

On a cold Monday morning before school begins, two children make a gruesome discovery. Hanging from the roof of the school gymnasium are the bodies of five naked and heavily disfigured men. Detective Superintendent Konrad Simonsen and his team are called in to investigate this horrific case. When the identities of the victims and the disturbing link between them is leaked to the press, the sinister motivation behind the killings quickly becomes apparent. Up against a building internet campaign and even members of his own team, Simonsen finds that he must battle public opinion and vigilante groups in his mission to catch the killers.

'Delicately crafted and supremely atmospheric'
DAILY MAIL